CLOSER THAN SHE THINKS

I'm not afraid, Victoria tells herself.

But she's never been able to lie to herself. She knows the truth. Out here alone in the dark on this windswept stretch of beach, she *is* afraid.

Because she knows someone—*something*—is following her. She hears nothing, sees nothing, but *feels* it nonetheless.

I'm stronger, stronger than whatever it is.

For a second she considers hurrying back to Nate's. But she won't do that. No, that is *not* something she will do. She will continue to walk forward, back to town, just picking up her pace a little bit—

That's when the white hand thrusts itself from the dark and grabs her wrist . . .

Books by Robert Ross

WHERE DARKNESS LIVES

DON'T CLOSE YOUR EYES

Published by Pinnacle Books

DON'T CLOSE YOUR EYES

Robert Ross

PINNACLE BOOKS

Kensington Publishing Corp.

http://www.kensingtonbooks.com

PINNACLE BOOKS are published by

Kensington Publishing Corp.
850 Third Avenue
New York, NY 10022

All Kensington Titles, Imprints, and Distributed Lines are available at special quantity discounts for bulk purchases for sales
promotions, premiums, fund-raising, and educational or institu-
tional use. Special book excerpts or customized printings can
also be created to fit specific needs. For details, write or phone
the office of the Kensington special sales manager: Kensington
Publishing Corp., 850 Third Avenue, New York, NY 10022,
attn: Special Sales Department, Phone: 1-800-221-2647.

First Pinnacle Books Printing: July 2003

10 9 8 7 6 5 4 3 2 1

Printed in the United States of America

Wednesday, May 15, 3:15 A.M.

"Mommy!"

Josh McKenzie's sheets are damp, and his little heart is racing like the Road Runner.

"Mommy!!!!!"

He bolts upright. The moonlight paints a white stripe across his bed, illuminating the one-eyed face of the little rabbit who sleeps beside him.

"Mom—eeeeeeeeee!!!!"

Suddenly there's light overhead, orange and stark. In the doorway his mother blinks her eyes. "I'm right here, baby," she's saying. "I'm right here."

Her yellow hair sticks up crazily from yesterday's mousse. Her flannel nightgown clings to her right breast in static electricity.

"Mommy, Mommy," Josh chirps, his voice funny, as if it's not his own. "I had a nightmare."

"It's okay, babe," his mother assures him. "I'm here now."

She sits down on the side of his bed the way she's done before. She pulls him into her warmth, his face pushing into her flannel. But his mother's embrace does little good. Josh remains afraid, his little body still hiccuping in terror. He doesn't understand. Usually this is the end of his nightmares: in his mother's arms they recede into the dim memory of sleep. The smell of his mother's powder, her hair gel, her cigarettes, usually counteracts his terror, dissolving it like bathtub suds when you drop in a bar of soap.

But not this time.

"He's *here,* Mommy," Josh tells her, one eye peering over the crook of her elbow. "He's *here.*"

"Who's here, Josh? There's no one here."

"He *is*, Mommy. He's here." He pulls from her embrace, glancing around his room.

Everything looks just the same as it did when he went to sleep. The Pokémon balls on his desk, the GameBoy on the floor, the Power Rangers poster on the wall, the picture of him and Mommy and Grandpa hanging opposite his bed.

"Baby, no one's here." His mother stands up and walks across the room. "See, baby? Just you and me." She slides open the closet door. Josh shrinks back in his bed. "Nothing. See?"

He pulls his stuffed rabbit closer. "But I got to tell you, Mommy," Josh says. "I gotta tell you the dream."

She smiles wearily. "Why don't you just try to forget it, babe? It wasn't real. There's nobody—"

"If I tell you, it'll go away," he says. How he knows that, he isn't sure, but he feels absolutely certain it's so. His body still shakes. Sweat still beads his brow.

His mother frowns in concern, placing her hand on his forehead. "Baby, you're burning up. Let me get you some asp—"

"No, Mommy, please! Please just let me tell you my dream!"

She looks down at him. "Okay, Josh. Go ahead. Tell me the dream."

She sits down beside him again and takes him into her arms. The words come rushing out of his small frame against her bosom.

"There was this man," he says, "in a tall hat. I was sitting on the sidewalk in front of our house and he was walking toward me. He was far, far away at first, but he just kept on walking, closer and closer, and I just kept watching him. You know how you tell me all the time that I shouldn't talk to strangers? How if any man ever comes up to me and asks me to go with him, I should run far away as fast as I can? Well, I was thinking that in my dream, but I couldn't run. I saw him coming, but I couldn't move. He just kept getting closer and closer, and I knew he was coming to get me. He finally got right up next to me and . . . and then . . . he smiled!''

His mother grins a little herself. "That's not so scary, baby."

"But, Mommy—he had worms in his mouth!"

She manages a little laugh and pulls him closer. "Well, yuck."

"They were like—coming through his teeth, and—" He pauses and looks up at her. The terror is gone. He feels a sudden relief, like the kind after he's finally gone pee after holding it all the way home from Grandpa's. The relief settles across him like a warm, comforting blanket. "And I guess that's it," he says. "I knew I'd feel better if I told you."

His mother places her hand on his head. "And you've gotten cool again. Still, I'm going to get you some children's aspirin and a cold cloth." She moves to stand. "Is it okay if I go now, just to get you the aspirin?"

"Yeah, it's okay now, Mommy. I'm not scared anymore."

She smiles. When she returns with the two chewable tablets in her hand and a wet facecloth draped over her arm, Josh has already fallen back to sleep.

Kathy McKenzie has had a long day. She'd just drifted off to sleep when Josh's cries awakened her. She hadn't gotten into bed until nearly one o'clock, finally finishing the laundry that had been piling up all week. She'd had no clean underwear left in her drawer, and Josh had used the last towel in the bathroom while getting washed up before bed. She did four loads, the whites carefully sorted from the colors, lugging the plastic basket up the wooden steps from the basement each time. She'd folded Josh's T-shirts and underpants and placed them outside his door, not wanting to wake him. When she was finally finished, Kathy desperately craved a cigarette but successfully fought off the urge. She just flopped down exhausted onto her bed.

Sleep hasn't come easily. Each time she began to nod off, she'd wake up, the burning in her chest stronger. *I won't give in,* Kathy scolded herself silently, forcing herself to shut her eyes and not look over at her purse on the table, where inside was concealed one last pack of smokes, in case of emergency.

It's not that bad. I can fight it off. If I give in now, everything's lost.

Of course, Josh had cried out then, and any hope of getting some real sleep this night was shattered. Josh wasn't the kind to have nightmares very often, but when he did, they were usually doozies. He was a resilient boy, for which Kathy was thankful. It wasn't easy growing up in a small town where everyone knew your whole life story. Josh had already heard the whispers about his father, and Kathy had tried to be as honest as possible with him. "What matters," she's said to him, time and again, "is not what other people say, but what you *know*. And you know that you are very loved. By me, and by your grandpa, and by all your true friends."

How much did Josh remember of his father?

He wasn't quite two when Kathy had finally called the cops that last time, crawling on her hands and knees up those very same wooden basement steps. She had pulled herself up, step by step, dragging one useless arm beside her, dripping blood between the spaces of the steps—plop, plop, plop onto the concrete floor below. Sly had pushed her down the stairs; she'd later learn her left arm and two ribs were broken, and her right knee was splintered. How long she lay there, crumpled like a burlap sack of potatoes at the foot of the stairs, she didn't know. She woke up hearing Josh crying upstairs. Her first thought was that Sly had hit him, too. She had no clue as to her own injuries; the pain was a general thing, from head to feet. She had no choice but to crawl, dragging herself step by step. Her baby needed her; he might be hurt, worse than she.

He wasn't: Josh was just hungry, standing in his crib, his face red and bloated from tears and frustration. She couldn't stand, couldn't take him in her arms to console him, and that was far worse than anything else. She could only try to reassure him from the floor, but it did no good, just made him scream harder. Sly had ripped the phone out of the wall, but—stupid crackhead that he was—he'd forgotten the cell phone in the bedroom. Kathy pulled herself with her right arm across the linoleum kitchen floor, making a horrible squeaking sound, and then down the hardwood of the hallway. She was in luck: the cell phone was under the bed, where Kathy often stashed it. She pressed 911.

Her knee aches her suddenly. *Stop dwelling on the past,* she scolds herself. She sits down on her stool in front of her vanity and rubs her knee. *He's gone. Secure behind iron bars and concrete walls for at least another three years. Josh doesn't remember him. Never speaks of him. Grandpa is enough Dad for him, even if he lives an hour away.*

Still, Kathy worries—worries that Sly will get out, that he'll come for Josh. She had indeed told her son many times that if any man ever approached him and tried to take him away, he was to run with all his might as far as possible in the opposite direction. Maybe she'd frightened him. But better that he be frightened than fall into Sly's hands.

Looking into her mirror, she sees the circles under her eyes. She'd worked a double shift today; Berniece had called in sick, and so Kathy had stuck around for supper hour as well. Old Mr. Lamphere had been particularly ornery tonight, sending his cheese rarebit back to the kitchen. Kathy made him a peanut-butter-and-jelly sandwich as a replacement. She'd been annoyed at having to give up her break to do it, but she really didn't blame Mr. Lamphere. She's not sure she could eat that processed orange cheese goop over toast and bacon, either.

Worst thing was missing dinner with Josh. Usually her job at Barnstable Convalescent allowed her to be here and waiting when Josh got home from school at three. Her shift was normally six-thirty A.M. to two-thirty P.M. She'd get Josh up at five forty-five A.M., make him a quick breakfast of oatmeal and toast, then drop him by Pat Crawford's on her way to work. He'd wait with Pat's son, Kyle, until seven-thirty when the bus picked them up. It was a routine that worked—so long as no crisis erupted to knock it off course. If Josh got sick, she'd have to call in sick; Berniece had filled in for her a number of times. So Kathy felt duty-bound to stick in there for the supper shift, calling Pat and asking her to keep Josh until she got home at seven P.M.

"And could he eat with you all, too? I hate to ask. If it's too much trouble, I can pick up a pizza from Gerry's on my way—"

"No, no, Kathy. Don't worry about it. Of course, Josh can eat with us. I'm sure a good meal of meat, potatoes and vegetables would do him some good."

10   *Robert Ross*

Kathy slides back into bed now and turns off the light, trying once again to ignore her craving. She quit smoking a week ago, and so far is very proud of her accomplishment. But remembering Pat Crawford's superior tone pisses her off. Like she doesn't feed her son balanced meals! Okay, so they eat pizza a lot, and sometimes they drive over to Wendy's in Orleans—hey, where else can they get those damned Pokémon balls? *Pat Crawford's just a privileged bitch who can afford to sit around on her butt all day because her husband is a fucking real estate agent who's selling off this town bit by bit and making himself rich from it. . . .*

Kathy feels her eyes closing against her thoughts. *Don't put out such negative energy,* she can hear Berniece telling her. *What you put out comes back to you, sweetie.*

Off in the distance the foghorn calls, low and sorrowful. It usually soothes her, as it has all her life. But tonight, in that moment just before sleep, she feels it's a warning that comes too late.

She opens her eyes suddenly. It's daylight. She looks up. There's a man standing over her. A man in a tall black top hat.

She's sitting on the sidewalk in front of their house. She can still hear the foghorn.

Dear God, she thinks, looking at the man, *don't let him open his mouth.*

She knows what's behind his thin red lips, and she can't bear to see it. He keeps his mouth closed, in a tight, straight line. He beckons with his hand to follow him.

She does, although she'd prefer not to. She keeps trying to stop, or at least slow down, but he always turns back and looks at her. She's terrified that he'll open his mouth; she figures if she just follows him, she won't have to see what's inside.

They go out to the beach. "No, please," she says, but it's like talking underwater. Her voice sounds strange to her ears. She hears the motorcycle on the boardwalk. She turns and sees Sly, with a bundle tied to the back of his bike. Something's kicking from inside the bundle. She knows it's Josh.

"Let him go!" she screams, but it's no use. Her voice is still muffled, and since when did Sly listen to her, anyway?

The Harley roars off down the boardwalk, the way it used to when she was sixteen, gripping Sly from behind, the wind in her hair.

"No! No! No!" she screams.

"Yes, yes, yes," comes the voice of the man in the tall hat behind her. She spins around and looks at him. She can see the worms now, slipping and slithering around on his tongue, between the gaps in his rotting teeth, over his thin, dry lips. He comes closer. She can smell him. She has a weird, intrusive thought: *I've never smelled anything before in a dream.* But this is fierce and unavoidable: a wet, musty, wormy smell, like the streets after a heavy rain. The man leans in and kisses her hard. The worms wiggle inside her mouth. She tries to scream, but only manages to swallow the worms, one after one after slimy one.

"Well, good morning, Josh," calls Mr. Silva, the postman. "No school today?"

Josh looks up at him with tired eyes. "My mother's not feelin' so good."

"Sorry to hear that." Mr. Silva reaches around in his bag and pulls out a bill from ComElectric. "Sorry all I got for her today is this. Afraid it won't do much cheering."

Josh takes the letter. His eyes look different to Mr. Silva, as if he'd gotten no sleep in weeks.

"You feelin' okay yourself, son? You don't look so good, neither."

Josh shrugs. He's sitting on the front step, moving a toy race car back and forth on his leg.

"Looks like it's gonna rain again," Mr. Silva observes. "Feels like spring won't ever get here. Still so cold and damp. But it'll come around. Spring always does, and then summer. You lookin' forward to summer vacation, Josh?"

The boy just shrugs again.

"Well, tell your mom I hope she feels better," he says.

"Mr. Silva."

The postman looks up. Behind the screen door stands Kathy McKenzie. Her face looks weird, distorted through the screen.

"Well, howdy, Kathy. Josh here tells me you're not up to snuff today."

"Mr. Silva, could I possibly . . . just for a minute . . . possibly talk to you?"

Her voice is trembling. Hiram Silva steps forward to look up at her. He knows all about the tough breaks Kathy McKenzie has had. He and his wife, Betty, have often remarked that they feel real sorry for Kathy, having to raise that boy all alone in the little cottage on Cranberry Terrace. She was from such a good old local family, too: Betty and Hiram had known Eddie and Delores McKenzie for years. They thanked God that Kathy's miserable ex-husband, Sly Sankner, was locked away in state prison and that Kathy could finally rest easily. She's a hardy one, that Kathy McKenzie, a real survivor. Everyone says so.

"What's wrong, Kathy?" Hiram asks her. "Are you okay?"

"Please, Mr. Silva . . . please. . . ." She sounds so pathetic. She disappears back inside the house.

The postman looks down at Josh sitting on the step. "I better go in and see if she's okay," he says awkwardly, stepping past him and opening the screen door. Josh doesn't respond, just keeps running his race car down his leg and over his knee.

Inside the McKenzie house Mr. Silva notices a strange smell. *Almost like . . . a locker room,* he thinks. Sweat. Steam. The couple times he's been inside the house before it had always been so fresh and clean-smelling. Now he walks down a hallway strewn with cigarette butts. "Kathy?" he calls. "You okay? Where are—?"

He spots her sitting at the kitchen table, leaning on her elbows, looking down, her hands in her hair. On the table are dozens of cigarette butts, overflowing from a small tin ashtray. "Kathy," he says, approaching her.

On the wall the cuckoo clock suddenly chirps ten times. It startles him. Kathy doesn't look up.

"I had a dream," she says.

"A dream?" he asks.

She shifts a little in her seat. Her hair, dyed blond, nearly white, sticks up in stiff clumps. The back is matted to her head. "I've got to tell it to you. . . . Please . . . just let me tell you the dream and it'll be okay."

He rests his hand on her shoulder. She's burning up. He can feel her shaking.

"Maybe I should call a doctor," he offers weakly.

"No," she says. "Please. Just let me tell you my dream."

Hiram Silva is not a young man. Next year he's set to retire after forty years with the post office. He's a good man, well-liked. Everyone in town knows his story, too. He and Betty had a daughter, Rose, who would have been about Kathy McKenzie's age if she had lived. But Rose died of leukemia when she was eight. Everyone came to her funeral, including Kathy McKenzie's parents. Nearly everyone had come back to the Silvas' little house on Pearl Street afterward, bringing their casseroles, fruitcakes and *linguiça,* the Portuguese sausage. Hiram had eaten *linguiça* for weeks after Rose's funeral. He can't bring himself to touch the stuff anymore.

Funny how he thinks of Rose as he bends down now beside Kathy McKenzie, stroking her hair.

"All right, Kathy," he says. "Go ahead. Tell me the dream."

"There was a man," she says breathily. "A man in a tall hat . . ."

And so she tells him . . . about following him to the beach, about Sly on his Harley, about Josh in the sack, about how the man kissed her, about the worms. . . .

Hiram Silva feels terribly uncomfortable listening to it all, especially about the kissing and the worms down the throat. He's sure Betty would say it was a sexual thing; she reads a lot of books and says all dreams are sexual. Hiram's not sure, but as much as he wants to help poor Kathy McKenzie, all he wants to do right now is get out of there, back to his route.

Kathy does seem to brighten. "Oh, dear God," Kathy says. "I do feel better." She looks up at Mr. Silva. "Thank you. You must think me crazy."

"I'd still call a doctor if I were you," he advises, but already, even though he's no longer touching her, he can feel the temperature in the room dropping. The sweaty smell seems to be dissipating, too.

For the rest of the day, Hiram Silva delivers the mail with his usual promptness and efficiency, even when the rains come again, heavy and drenching. He pulls on his old blue post-office-issued slicker and runs from his truck up each and every walk, belying his sixty-three years.

Yet many of the citizens of Falls Church comment that day how distracted Mr. Silva seems, how distant. There's little of the usual chitchat with the women on their front porches, no exchange of town news when he stops in at Clem's Diner. That night, Betty Silva notices her husband eats very little of her pot roast and boiled potatoes, and she questions why he's still awake at eleven-thirty P.M., defiant in his plaid La-Z-Boy recliner, forcing his bleary eyes to stay open for Jay Leno.

"You don't even like him, Hiram. Come to bed."

"I'm just not very tired," he lies to her—the first lie he's told her in forty-two years of marriage.

He couldn't have told her why he was procrastinating. He wasn't even fully aware of it himself. There was just a sense of being on the edge, cautious, careful.

Yet after about ten minutes he gives in, catching his chin thudding against his chest, and climbs into bed beside his wife. He looks once at the photograph of Rose they keep beside their bed, running his finger along the outline of her face, then turns off the light and pulls the sheets tightly up to his chin. He falls asleep a few minutes after he hears the clock in the living room softly chime twelve.

That's when he sees the man in the tall black hat with the worms living in his teeth.

Thursday, May 16, 8:35 A.M.

Nate Tuck peers through his blinds and grimaces. "Aw, shit," he grumbles.

He should be used to it by now, the rain. It's been raining straight for three whole days. He's lived here on the Cape for the last seven months. All through the winter he'd been pelted by icy rain and lashed by nasty windstorms. What's a little more now that spring is finally here?

Except it wasn't. April showers were supposed to bring May flowers, but Nate hasn't seen a single blossom in Falls Church yet. Winter just seems determined to hang on. And these rains the past few days—fierce and torrential, like a biblical plague. Cold too. It's barely 35 degrees this morning, and the icy tempest smacks Nate straight in the face as he opens the door and makes a headlong dash for his car. He can hear the wind spinning the weather vane on the roof of his cottage like a mad dervish. From across the dunes the Falls Church lighthouse wails.

"Jesus," Nate says, slamming the door to his car closed and catching his breath behind the wheel. The windows are fogged up. He starts the ignition and flips on the defroster. The wipers swing madly against the glass.

"Jesus," he says again, and thinks of Oakland. Sure, it rains in northern California—sometimes *a lot*—and the Bay Area has more than its share of wind and fog. But it was never so damn wet and raw—so goddamn *bitter*. Especially not in May.

"Hey, it was your choice to move out here, Tucky," the chief had laughed the morning after Nate's first major ice storm last December. "I told you the winters weren't gonna be easy."

A small circle of clarity is growing on the windshield. Nate fights off the temptation to help it along by rubbing his sleeve against the glass. This is a police car, after all, even if it isn't marked. Nate grins to himself. It wouldn't do to streak up the windshield and make identification of suspected felons more difficult.

"You must be very brave," the only woman he'd dated since moving to Cape Cod had said, batting her eyelashes coquettishly at him. "I admire police officers tremendously. The way you put your lives on the line all the time."

What was her name? Betty Silva had fixed them up, right after Nate had taken the job as the chief's assistant. Some silly niece of hers from Brewster. Or Harwich. One of those towns. Georgeanne. That was it. Georgeanne Medeiros, with the big black hair—on her head and on her arms.

Nate laughs remembering it. Georgeanne Medeiros could imagine whatever scenarios she wanted, but, in truth, cops on the outer Cape didn't often put their lives on the line. Especially not in Falls Church, that little claw of sand jutting out into Nantucket Bay. More than one person has referred to Falls Church as an island. This past winter, when ice storms closed the one road into town, Nate understood the island mentality. If the whole Cape sometimes felt disconnected from the "mainland" of Massachusetts—linked by just two bridges and a ferry that shuts down in September—the residents of Falls Church endured isolation as an everyday fact of life. Sure, some folks played on bowling leagues up in Orleans, and most everybody made the trip to the Cape Cod Mall in Hyannis every few weeks, but more often than not, folks in Falls Church stayed put. And if a big nor'easter blew in and the causeway that linked the town to the rest of the Cape iced over, they had no choice but to make do with what they already had.

Until the past couple of years, Falls Church had been a sleepy little fishing village mostly bypassed by the hordes of tourists heading up Route 6 to fancier destinations, like Chatham and

Provincetown. But town officials were trying to change that. A couple of trendy restaurants and a bunch of chichi shops had opened up along Main Street. Sargent Crawford, the local real estate agent, was marketing the town as an unspoiled, pristine summer getaway, and home prices were skyrocketing. New construction dotted the cliffs north of the village, and several old families had converted their homesteads into condos, making a mint and moving off-Cape. The year-round population had dwindled to just under one thousand, with many of the homes in town sitting dark from November to May.

Nate peers through the windshield. He can see the lighthouse at the end of the dune. To the north the land washes away in a spray of sea salt and foam. Behind him the gnarled limbs of beach plum trees bravely stand against the wind, dotted with defiant little green buds, promising as yet an unimaginable spring.

He puts the car in drive and eases down to the road. In his rearview mirror, his little two-room cottage looks beaten down by sand and wind. It was an artist's cottage in the 1960s, built out of driftwood and stone in the space where the dunes met the woods, with a small kitchen/living area and a bedroom the size of a large closet. But that was all Nate wanted. He hadn't moved to the Cape for luxury living.

Turning left onto Lighthouse Road, he drives along the beach, passing the rows of summer cottages, even smaller than his, boarded up still. Some have been there for decades; some are new, built by developer Richie Rostocki to cash in on the town's fledgling tourist appeal. In a few weeks the owners of the cottages will arrive and take down the plywood, sweep out the sand, hang the curtains and turn the water back on. Each cottage is named for a flower: Daisy. Aster. Hollyhock. Begonia. They're rented by the week or the month, sometimes for the whole season. In summer the town's population swells to over a thousand, and with the new construction it's estimated to go even higher. Chief Hutchins has been thinking of hiring a temporary cop for the summer to supplement the three full-time officers. Still, even with the increased population, Nate can't imagine any additional help will be needed. The worst that ever happens is a fight at Dicky's, the one bar in town.

Nate's broken up his share of altercations there, as often between girls as between guys.

"Hey, you're kind of cute," one girl said to him on New Year's Eve, after he'd pulled her by the back of her blouse off another girl. She was probably nineteen, twenty. Too young to be drinking.

"Can I see your ID?" Nate asked.

She complied, after some grumbling, and the name on her license made him freeze. *Siobhan Moore.* What kind of crazy joke was that? How many Siobhan Moores were there in this fucking world? He looked at her. Pretty, blond—but nothing else was the same. Still, he let her off with just a warning. He couldn't have handled writing a report with the name Siobhan Moore.

Nate had just turned thirty this past February. He told no one. When his mother called from Oakland, he let the machine take the call. He preferred to be alone, a fire in his small fireplace, a pizza from Gerry's on his TV tray, ferocious winds rattling his windows.

He passes someone in a yellow VW van heading back toward the lighthouse on the point. With his policeman's eye he notes that it's not a familiar vehicle; he's come to recognize most every car in town, and certainly knows which cars regularly head out this way, which isn't many before Memorial Day. He imagines it's an early tourist.

He reaches town and hangs a left onto Main Street, pulling into a parking space in front of Clem's Diner. He jumps from the car across the puddles on the cracked sidewalk and yanks open the door to Clem's. The warm, dry heat smacks him as surely as the rain had earlier. Not to mention the smells: coffee, cinnamon rolls, bacon spitting on the grill. The place is filled with locals, as usual. Dave Carlson, the local mechanic, is huddled in a booth with Sandy Hooker, the red-cheeked, white-whiskered harbormaster. Max Winn, the snarly old tax assessor and collector, talking to no one as usual, is hunched over a plate of greasy scrambled eggs. Catherine Santos, the fiery librarian, butters her bran muffin.

"Well, good morning, Detective Tuck," chirps Marge, snapping her gum from behind the counter, her dyed orange hair held back in a bun under a fraying hair net. Nate sidles onto a stool as she fills a cup of coffee for him. "Miserable enough this morning for ya?"

"Just the way I like it," he teases, winking at her. "Marge, fill me one to go, too. I got to get over to the station and relieve Rusty."

"How's my nephew doing over there?" the waitress asks.

Nate smiles. The junior member of the force was Dean Sousa, Marge's skinny, stuttering twenty-two-year-old nephew. He was the clumsiest cop Nate had ever seen, but also the most earnest. Dean Sousa was nothing if not dedicated: he reminded Nate of Barney Fife. "He's coming along fine, Marge," he assures her with a secret grin. "Just fine."

The swinging doors to the kitchen push forward and out waddles Clem Flagg. He's a fat man, topping three hundred pounds, with a bald head and octagonal spectacles perpetually perched at the end of a pointy nose. He makes the best Belgian waffles on the Cape; the plaques and citations attesting to the fact hang on his diner's walls. There are photographs of him with a couple of governors and one with John F. Kennedy Jr., only a month or so before he died. Everybody stops for breakfast at Clem's.

"Nate," Clem says, a pudgy pink finger in front of the detective's face, "you tell our esteemed chief that if he doesn't catch those kids who are vandalizing the old church soon, we're gonna form a vigilante crew and go after 'em ourselves." He leans across the counter toward Nate. "They keep me up most every night."

Nate shrugs. "Tonight at Town Meeting they're discussing what to do with that old building, Clem."

Clem straightens up, rolling his eyes. "They should've burned it down years ago. No good ever came of that hellhole. I've got a right mind to do it myself."

Nate smirks. "Well, I don't want any vigilantes in this here town, especially not with *you* leading the pack, Clem."

He sniffs, hooking his fingers into his belt and drawing up his barrel chest. "You shoulda seen me in Vietnam, Nate. I was in *fightin'* form."

Marge laughs, placing a lidded Styrofoam cup of coffee on the counter for Nate. "You were a *cook* in Vietnam, Clem. The only action you saw was slopping beans on plates."

"I'll have you know I once led a reconnaissance mission into the north. We went in by dark of night and scouted out the positions of the enemy." He arches his eyebrows at Nate and Marge. "It was *terribly* dangerous, probably the biggest thing I ever got into."

Marge snorts. "The biggest thing you ever got into was your *pants*."

Nate laughs, feeling the coffee invigorating him already. He stands, fishing out a couple of dollars from his pocket, setting them down on the counter. "You know, I'd swear the two of you were an old married couple."

"I'm still waitin' for Mr. Right," Marge confides with a wink as Nate zips up his jacket and makes for the door. "I might be fifty-four, but if you're ever looking to settle down, Detective, you give me a call."

Nate's still smiling as he walks into the station. He likes Marge Duarte. She's one of his favorite people in this little town. He likes her almost as much as—

"Betty?"

The first thing he notices upon stepping into the outer office is Betty's not there. Her desk looks untouched, and there's no smell of coffee perking. First thing Betty did every morning when she got to the station at eight o'clock was set the coffeepot going. Nate usually stopped for a cup at Clem's, but he'd drink four or five by afternoon, especially if it was Betty's coffee.

"Good thing I got this one to go," he murmurs to himself, setting his briefcase down at his desk.

"Yo, Tucky," comes Rusty's voice from the back office. He had night duty this week. His blue uniform makes an odd complement to his ruddy features, his red hair, his freckles. Rusty's a decade older than Nate, a father of two. Rusty had been up for Nate's job—number two on the force—and most in town figured he'd get it, too, having been with the Falls Church police for almost ten years. But the chief had his eye on retirement, and apparently he just couldn't see Rusty McDaniel taking over for him. So, after convincing the union, he had the town manager open up the search. Nate was brought in from the outside, a move that caused some resentment in town. But

Nate had just kept on smiling, doing his job, and the fact that he made it through the winter endeared him to most everybody. He was low-key, likable. Even Rusty likes him now.

Still, Nate always feels a little guilty walking in at nine when Rusty's been there all night. The guy's got a family, after all. *Guess that's what a college education does for you,* Nate thinks. *That, and meritorious service on the Oakland police force.*

Part of Nate believes Rusty *should* have gotten his job. When the chief hired him, he praised Nate as a "hero" to the community. Nate frowns remembering it. *What I did in Oakland was not heroic,* he thinks, as he thinks so often. *Not heroic at all.*

"You look a wreck" is Rusty's judgment. "No sleep last night?"

Nate scratches his head. "Actually, I slept great. Lately I've been crashing as soon as I hit the pillow. I sleep like a rock." He nods over at Betty's desk. "Betty not coming in today?"

Rusty yawns. "Search me. No call. Nothing. She just hasn't shown up."

"Not like her," Nate says.

"Not at all. I called, but there was no answer. I thought maybe I'd swing by on my way home just to check on her once you got here."

"Yeah. Do that." Nate doesn't like this. Betty Silva is one of the most conscientious people he knows. She'd been the secretary at the police station for more than thirty-five years. She ran the place as much as Chief Hutchins. On the rare occasion she was sick, she called bright and early, or sent Hiram by with a note. Nate recalls Betty being out just twice in the time he's been there, and both times she let them know.

"Not much in the blotter," Rusty's telling him. "But I did go over to the old church. Clem Flagg called at three-fifteen this morning to say he heard kids carrying on in there. But they were gone when I got there. As always."

Nate nods. "I already got it from Clem this morning. What do these kids *do* in there, anyway? We never find any bottles or cigarette stubs."

Rusty shrugs. "You know what Clem says he heard last night? Singing. Like *hymns.*"

"They're breaking in at three A.M. to sing *hymns?*"

"You try to figure out kids."

The door opens. A thrust of frantic energy causes them to turn their heads. Betty arrives, haggard-looking, her hair sogged down from the rain.

"Betty," Nate says. "You all right? We were starting to worry."

She drops her purse and some folders down onto her desk. She turns to them. "I am *so* sorry, fellas. Gosh, I really dropped the ball on this one. Look at the time. I feel terrible."

"It's not a problem, Betty. We were just worried."

She sighs. "It's Hiram. I don't know what came over him. He was burning up with a fever. I thought maybe he was coming down with the flu. But it was all because of a *dream*!"

"A dream?" Nate asks.

"I've been married to that man for forty-two years and I've never known him to have nightmares. But he did, last night. And he was awake at the crack of dawn this morning, impossible to console."

"Whatever could have upset him that much?" Nate asks.

"Who knows?" Betty shrugs her shoulders. "Oh, it was just—oh, I'm too embarrassed to go into it. Such *things* he said. Disgusting, loathsome things. But once he told it to me, he seemed to feel better. What *could* have filled his head with such nonsense?"

"Who can explain why we dream the things we do?" Rusty offers.

"Oh, I've read *lots* about dreams." Betty's animated now. She considers herself well read, devouring each new self-help and pop psychology book that appears on the rack at Woodward's Pharmacy. Her bright blue eyes sparkle as she talks; her surprisingly unlined face glows with enthusiasm. "All dreams mean something. But for the life of me, I can't imagine *what* Hiram's dream was about."

Nate and Rusty just exchange bemused glances.

"All I know is once he told me the whole sordid thing, he felt better. Even went to the post office to do his route. His temperature had gone down, so I couldn't argue with him."

"Well," Rusty says, "all's well that ends well, they say."

"I suppose," Betty admits.

"I'm glad you're okay," Rusty says. He yawns. "Well, people, I'm off. I'm beat."

"Have a good sleep," Nate tells him.

Betty moves across the room to fill the coffeepot with water. Rusty heads out; Nate settles down at his desk. Things revert to normal. In another hour Job Emerson would report for duty; by the afternoon Dean Sousa would clock in; then Rusty would be back again. Falls Church's finest, around the clock.

"But I'll tell you," Betty says, breaking the silence once they're alone, "it really shook me up. Look. My hands are still shaking."

She walks over to Nate's desk and holds them out. Her old spotted hands with their chipped pink nail polish do indeed tremble in front of Nate.

Nate takes them in his own. They're cold. He grips them tightly, warming them. Betty smiles, closes her eyes. "You're a good friend, Nate," she says.

The aroma of coffee fills the station.

The reporter from the *Cape Cod Times* arrives as scheduled at ten-thirty A.M.

"Detective Tuck?" she asks.

He looks up from his desk. She's a pretty woman, blond, in a brown rain slicker, her eyes heavy with mascara.

"I'm Monica Paul," she says. "From the *Cape Cod Times*."

"Oh, yes," he says, rising to greet her and shake her hand. "I'm sorry, but the chief isn't back yet. He's taking his wife to a doctor's appointment in Hyannis."

"Well, then, we must have passed each other." Monica Paul smiles. "But it was really *you* I wanted to talk with anyway."

"Me?" Nate feels his cheeks flush, as they do whenever the spotlight is turned on him. When Marge flirts with him at the diner, he goes red, and she teases him for it. He hopes it's not as noticeable to this reporter. "I thought the article was on the department."

She smiles. "Yes, but you're the hook. Being new to town, and a West Coast hero and all that."

"Oh, I'm no—"

"And I was told quite photogenic, too," she adds, appraising him up and down. "My sources were certainly right on *that* score."

His face burns.

"Uh, Betty," he says as the secretary returns from the ladies' room, "this is, uh, your name again was—"

"Monica Paul," she reminds him smoothly.

"Yeah. Monica Paul. From the *Cape Cod Times*."

Betty smiles. "Nice to meet you. Would you like a cup of coffee?"

"Thank you. I'd love one. What a miserable morning out there."

Nate gestures for Monica to take a seat in the chair beside his desk. She smiles, unwrapping herself from her raincoat to reveal she's wearing a tight brown pin-stripe suit, with matching jacket and short skirt. She sits, crossing shapely legs encased in black silk stockings. She withdraws her reporter's notebook from her jacket pocket and flips to an empty page.

"So," Nate begins uncomfortably, "I'm not sure what you want to know—"

Suddenly there's a crash. Glass shattering. He looks up. Betty's dropped the coffeepot on the marble floor. The coffee spreads out in a widening puddle.

"I am so—so—sorry," Betty says, near tears. "My hands— Nate, I'm sorry, my hands are still so shaky—"

He jumps up and moves quickly to her side. He puts his arm around her shoulder. "Betty, it's okay. It's okay. I can clean it up. Are you all right?"

"I'm still a little shaken up, I guess. I'll be okay."

"You want to go home?" he whispers to her.

"No!" she says sharply. "I want to stay here, do my job."

"Okay. But maybe you should just lie down a moment in the chief's office. Take a chill."

She smiles. "All right. Just to get my bearings."

He turns to Monica Paul. She's not in her chair anymore; she's mopping up the coffee with paper towels. "Hey, I'll do that," he says.

"No problem," she tells him.

He smiles. He walks with Betty toward the chief's office. PHILIP HUTCHINS, CHIEF OF POLICE is etched in gold leaf on the frosted glass of the door. Nate opens the door and eases Betty down onto the leather couch on the office's far wall.

"Just take a minute," he tells her. "Do that deep breathing you're always telling me about. You know, what you read about in that book. What's it called?"

She smiles up at him. "Diaphragmatic breathing," she says.

"Yeah, that," he says. "Do it."

Betty smiles again, closing her eyes.

He closes the door gently. The coffee's all wiped up and Monica is carrying the last shards of glass to the wastebasket.

"Hey, thanks," Nate says.

"I'd just be careful walking barefoot through here for a while," she tells him.

"Betty—well, she had a hard morning. She's usually not like that. She's really a tough lady." He pauses. "Usually."

"Oh, believe me, I've broken my share of coffeepots in the morning," says Monica.

He grins. He likes her. He hadn't expected to. He's never liked reporters much. Too pushy, too cynical. But this one . . . Not only is she a babe, but she's got a good heart. *You see?* he hears that old voice inside him insist. *There are other women out there. Siobhan wasn't the only—*

"So," he says abruptly, shutting off any dangerous thoughts. "Shall we get back to your story?"

"Of course," Monica says. He can feel her blue eyes searching for his, but he manages to avoid them as they retake their seats.

"Like I said," Nate tells her, "I really think Chief should be here."

"Oh, I'll talk with him. In fact, I had a brief conversation with him the day I set this appointment up. He told me all about your time on the Oakland police force and how thrilled the department was to hire an officer of your caliber."

He blushes again. "Well, that was kind of him."

She looks down at her notes. "You were given a merit award for saving a fellow officer's life. You helped break up a cocaine-smuggling ring in Oakland. You were a *star*." She smiles. "So what brings you to Falls Church of all places?"

He shrugs. "I came out here on—on a kind of vacation, I guess. One of the guys on the force had in-laws who had a summer place up in Truro. I came out, just for a couple weeks last spring, and, well, I saw the job posting and—I went for it."

"Were you looking to get away from Oakland?"

He shifts in his chair. "Not exactly. I liked the guys on the force. I had no beef with them."

"Then—something else?"

He smiles. "How about another question?"

She sighs. "All right, Detective. Let's see. Where did you go to school?"

"I majored in criminal justice at UC Berkeley and then went to the police academy in San Francisco."

"How long were you on the force in Oakland?"

"Six years."

"Tell me about the cocaine ring you busted."

His face flushes. "It wasn't just me. It was a whole team. I was just one guy."

"A guy who saved another officer."

His face burns hotter. "We made a raid on a crackhouse, and I saw a guy with a gun pointing it at my partner. I shot him before he had a chance to pull the trigger."

"Wow. Very *NYPD Blue*."

"Look. It was a yearlong investigation, and three officers got killed. *They're* the heroes, not me. Don't paint me as a hero."

"I admire your humility," she tells him.

He brushes her words away.

Monica curls her hair behind her right ear. "I imagine life here hasn't been quite so—*busy.*"

Nate gives her a little laugh. "Falls Church ain't Oakland."

"Maybe that's what you wanted."

"Maybe it was."

She makes a little sound, as if she thinks she's figured out something about him. He hates it when reporters do that. She scribbles something down in her pad.

"You're single?" she asks, not looking up.

"Um, yes."

"Anyone you're dating?"

He doesn't answer. She looks up at him, projecting innocence.

"I only ask because I suspect dating a policeman might be stressful. If there were someone you were dating, maybe they'd like to give a quote for the article."

He manages a tight grin. "No," he tells her. "I'm not dating anyone."

She smiles back, scribbling something else. "And you don't get bored here?"

"I wouldn't call what I do boring. We might not have crack-houses in Falls Church, but there's always something going on."

"Cats up trees and things like that?"

He smirks. "You're not going to get me to say anything unflattering about this town. I love it here. For the first time in a long while, I feel at home."

She softens. "I *do* know what you mean, Detective. I feel the same way about the Cape. Living in Barnstable has really given me a sense of—oh, I don't know—safety? Security?" She thinks of something. "But if Falls Church is like every-where else on the Cape, during the summer things can get a little prickly. So many tourists, so much potential for trouble. And there's always tension between the year-rounders and the summer people."

He nods. "There's some of that here, though Falls Church isn't as popular as Provincetown or Chatham or places like that, so we don't have the same hassles."

She's writing, and talks without looking up. "That's chang-ing, isn't it? New construction up on Cliff Heights is changing the character of the town—at least from what I understand."

"Yeah." Nate picks up an elastic band from his desk, begins playing with it between his fingers. "Well, you know being a newcomer myself, I always tell people not to be so afraid of change. I mean, the fishing industry is what kept this little town alive for a century and a half, but that's not so strong anymore. The fish are depleted and the state's got new regulations on where and how our fishermen can cast their nets—so the town needs some new revenue."

She's nodding, writing furiously. "But the place *is* becoming something much different from what it used to be. More tourists, but also more rich out-of-towners buying places—people like Carolyn Prentiss, I understand."

Nate sighs. Only a couple of times has he caught a glimpse of Carolyn Prentiss, the famous, reclusive Hollywood star, sitting in her limousine with that snaky manager of hers, Edmond Tyler, waiting for Noah Burt to finish pumping their gas at Dave's Sunoco. Carolyn Prentiss is beautiful all right, but hardly part of the town Nate's come to love so much.

Monica's looking up from her pad. "What's the most interesting part of your job?"

"Interesting?" He thinks a minute. "Well, being the chief's assistant means I get to know most everybody in town. And that's been great. I'd always read about small-town life, and always thought I'd like it. You know, walking down Main Street and saying hello to everyone and everyone saying hello back. You know them; you know their husbands and wives; you know their kids. You're not going to find that in a big city."

"Your family still in Oakland?"

"My mother." He swallows. "My dad died when I was ten. He was a cop, too."

"Ah." She looks at him, eyebrows raised. "Is that what inspired your career?"

"Oh, yeah. Most definitely. I had it in my head I was going to grow up and find the bad guys that shot my father." He grins. "Kind of like Batman, you know?"

She nibbles gently on the eraser of her pencil. "So your father was killed in the line of duty?"

"Yes, ma'am. That he was."

"Care to share any details?"

He sighs. "Well, just that he'd gone to break up a fight. Domestic violence. Routine call. His partner went inside, calmed things down. That should've been it." Nate looks past her, toward the front door of the station. "But then some idiot drives by. Pulls out a semiautomatic and blows my father away. He was just standing there. He never knew what hit him. Some gang member who didn't like cops."

"Was the killer ever caught?"

He shakes his head. "No. Oh, they rounded up a bunch of guys who could've done it. But they never fingered the exact one. Most of that gang got put away eventually, so I imagine the guy's probably behind bars, or was, at some point. Just not for my father's murder."

She's quiet a minute. "I'm beginning to understand the appeal of Falls Church."

Nate suddenly leans across his desk toward her. "I'll tell you what part of this job really fires me up," he says. "There are two unsolved murders here in Falls Church. Old cases that I've been going through. I'd like to find those killers and close the cases. Finally give some closure to the families."

"Two unsolved murders? In *Falls Church?*"

He nods. "You ought to include them in your article. If anyone has leads, they should contact me. Write that Chief Hutchins and I haven't given up on them, even if they're thirty-five and fifteen years old, respectively."

"Give me the details." She flips to a blank page in her notebook.

Nate slides an old manila folder across his desk. It's thick with papers and bound with an elastic band. Way back in 1967 Betty had typed GOOGINS, PRISCILLA on the tab. He stretches off the band and flips the folder open. "She was just nineteen." he says. "Here's her picture. You want to run it?"

"I think my editor might want to," she says, taking the faded senior-class photo from Nate and staring at it. Priscilla was a plain girl, with large dark eyes and dark hair pulled back in a ponytail. Around her neck, resting on a cashmere sweater, was a little gold cross.

"Her name was Priscilla Googins," Nate's telling her. "Her immediate family is dead, though she's still got some cousins around. Her mother was a Duarte, and they're related to the Sousas—and that name's all *through* this town."

"How was the girl killed?"

"Stabbed to death." He pauses. "On the altar of the old church."

Monica looks up from the photo. Their eyes meet. "On the *altar of a church?*"

"Twisted, huh? It was a nightmare for this town. I've talked with Marge, with Betty—with all the folks who remember. There were all sorts of theories, all kinds of weird speculations. People accusing this one, that one. For a while they blamed Priscilla's boyfriend, who was kind of a hippie. Lived in his van. Tommy Keegan was his name."

"But he was never charged?"

"No. I've done some asking around. People today say the only reason he was a suspect was because he looked and acted different. Long hair, burned incense, protested the war in Vietnam. Stuff like that."

"But why on the altar?"

"Don't know. It was an active church back then, one of those radical love-in sects that sprung up in the sixties. Priscilla had become a member."

Monica's clearly intrigued. "Perhaps it was someone in the congregation, then? Psychedelic drugs and all that?"

Nate scratches his head. "Possibly. I've been trying to find out more about them, but there aren't many left. Those who were members of the sect dropped out pretty fast after the murder. A few weeks afterward the church was shut down and has remained closed ever since. It's been boarded up since Priscilla died. The local kids think the place is haunted. They're always breaking in, throwing stones, smashing the stained-glass windows."

"With all respect, Detective, I think this unsolved church killing might just be a better angle for the story than even your heroic past."

"Well, I'd be glad of that." He thinks of an idea. "You know, you should stick around for Town Meeting tonight. The town owns the building. They're trying to decide what to do with it. It's become a real eyesore down near the pier, especially as the area is trying to go more upscale to attract more tourists. Catherine Santos, the librarian and head of the town's Heritage Museum, wants to restore the church, maybe move the heritage collection over there. See, the church is built on the site of the very first church in town, dating back to the seventeeth century—the church Falls Church was actually named for."

Monica nods. "Aha. I was wondering where the name came from."

"I'm not sure of the exact history, but back in the colonial days some folks broke off from one of the churches in Chatham and started up their own little village down here. Well, that church eventually evolved into the old church, and so there you have it. You know, you really ought to come to Town Meeting tonight if you want to get a flavor of the town."

"Maybe I will," she says. "If you'll have dinner with me."

Their eyes meet. It's an accident, and Nate darts his eyes

away from hers as fast as possible. "Uh," he stammers. "W-well, I've got a lot of paperwork...."

She's not easily deterred. "I noticed a pizza joint on my way in. I could get a pizza and bring it here to the station. We could eat together while we both work. After all, I'll need to go through this file some more if I'm going to write up a story on the girl's murder."

"Yeah. Well, okay. Whatever." He swallows. "I'll go through it and let you photocopy some materials. Some stuff is still confidential, so I can't give you that, you understand."

"Sure." She smiles at him. "So how's the pizza here? I haven't had good pizza on the Cape since moving from Boston."

Nate brightens. "Well, then, you'll just have to try Gerry's. Gerry grew up in Little Italy in New York. He and his wife came out here for the summer twenty years ago and stayed. Trust me on this."

"All right, Detective, I will."

They share a smile. Monica's eyes seem to be trying to get a reaction from him. Nate feels himself blush again.

"So what about the other unsolved murder?" she asks. "You said there were two."

"Yeah." Nate's happy to change the topic to something less flirtatious. He pulls over another file. This one is thinner. On the tab there's a label: MCKAY, PETER, OCTOBER 31, 1988. Nate opens the folder and finds another photograph to hand to Monica.

"This one is actually officially classified as a missing person, since no body was ever found, but we consider it a homicide. Poor little kid was out trick-or-treating with a friend, who claims she saw him go off with someone. Had the whole town in terror for weeks, thinking a childnapper was on the loose."

Monica looks at the photograph of the blond boy in a baseball cap. "How old was he?"

"Twelve."

"Poor little guy."

"Is that Petey McKay you're telling her about?" Betty has emerged from the chief's office. She looks better, almost like her old self. "What a tragedy that was. Halloween night. I'll never forget it. It was a terrible time. Just terrible. Remember there was that arson case at the same time. Oh, poor Petey.

His mother's never fully recovered. I saw her at mass last Sunday. She looks like a ghost, and has for the past fourteen years."

"It must be unbearable, the loss of a child," Monica observes, "especially when you don't ever truly know what happened."

Nate nods. Little Petey's face haunts him even more than Priscilla's. Such a little guy. Never had a chance in life.

"What's this arson case?" Monica asks. "Was it connected?"

Betty shivers. "Well, everybody has their own theory—"

Nate closes the file. "There's no evidence. But there was a family who had just moved to town. They had twin boys, hemophiliacs who had AIDS. There were some in town who felt that they should be sent away. There was a lot of ignorance at the time."

"The girl who was with Petey," Betty says, interrupting, "little Victoria Kennelly, was the only one to speak up against it at a special Town Meeting. Can you imagine—a twelve-year-old child shaming the adults! Well, from the mouth of babes comes a great deal of wisdom sometimes, though there were a lot of folks who held considerable animosity against the girl and her family." Betty folds her arms across her chest. "The next night, when little Victoria was out trick-or-treating, her house burned down and her family was killed, and the little friend she was with—Petey McKay—disappeared."

"But what makes you think the two things are connected?" Monica asks.

"There's no evidence of it," Nate insists, although in his heart, he's come to believe there must be a link. He sighs. "Look, I'll give you more details on both these cases. If you can write them up, I'd be very grateful."

"Oh," Betty says, "if Nate can solve little Petey's disappearance, he'll be hailed as a hero in this town."

"I think he's already a hero, even if he's too humble to admit it," Monica says, grinning slyly at him. "A genuine hero—way out here in our midst on the blustery Cape."

Nate can feel the warm blood surging up his neck and into his cheeks again. Damn, how he hates that.

Thursday, May 16, 12:00 P.M.

Right before she sees the face of the dead boy in the mirror, she's thinking about lunch, how there won't be any more green peppers in her tuna fish.

Victoria Kennelly pauses, knife in hand, as she prepares to spread the fish salad along the slice of cracked wheat bread. Looking across the room, she can see the hallway mirror, and for a moment she sees Petey McKay's face there, white and decomposing. She suppresses a little gasp.

"Go away, Petey," she whispers. "Go away."

Of course he does. He always does. She concentrates instead on her sandwich, happy that the tuna salad contains only mayonnaise and no peppers. Why anyone would want to put chopped-up green peppers in tuna salad is beyond her comprehension. But Jonathan did, and whenever Jonathan had made her lunch, she'd always have to pick the peppers out, one by one, or swallow them whole with her diet Coke.

She laughs. "Why am I thinking of Jonathan and his *tuna fish*?"

Maybe for the same reason you see Petey's face in the mirror. Maybe because you're lonely. Maybe because you're tired of relationships not working out, even relationships with great guys like Jonathan. Maybe because you're twenty-six years old, and you've never had any relationship last longer than three and a half months.

All because of Petey McKay.

Victoria sighs. At least that's what her therapist tells her. She walks over to the hallway mirror and looks at her reflection. She's still in her sweats, just back from a great workout at the gym. Her calves burn from the treadmill, a delicious sensation. She has an hour before she has to teach her first class, just enough time for a quick lunch. She makes all her own lunches now. Jonathan used to make her a lunch every day, wrapping it neatly in waxed paper and packing it carefully in a brown paper bag for her to take to campus. Jonathan had wanted to marry her, take care of her, make her lunches and dinners every day for the rest of her life.

He'd lasted longer than any of them. But three and a half months was hardly a record to be proud of.

Her thoughts are distracted by taxicabs honking their horns at each other on the street below. She peers out the window. Boston drivers can be insane. She can see Com Ave, traffic snarled, the rain still coming down. She can't imagine having a car in the city. How much easier it is to just jump on the T and head over to campus, bypassing all the craziness. And that isn't even considering how impossible it is to find parking spaces at night in the Back Bay.

She notes the time and wolfs down her sandwich. "Got to get a move on, girl," she says to herself. By subway it takes exactly nineteen minutes from her front door to her classroom. But she needs a quick shower first; she'd worked up a sweat at the gym.

She pulls off her sweatshirt as she hurries down the hardwood floors of the hallway. She drops it on the threshold into the bathroom, reaching around to unsnap her sports bra, letting that fall as well. It felt good to do that: now that Jonathan had moved out, she could leave her clothes lying around. Jonathan had always been scurrying around behind her, scooping up her discards, depositing them neatly in the hamper. It used to make her nutty.

The bathroom is old. One-inch-square black-and-white tiles make up the floor. The cracked ceramic sink stands over a rusty drainpipe. The tub is the classic claw-foot style. There was no shower, so Victoria rigged up a hose from the tub faucet and hung a portable shower curtain she'd bought at Home Depot. She couldn't bear to live without a shower.

She looks at herself in the full-length mirror standing beside the sink. Her nakedness surprises her. Almost as if she'd forgotten she'd removed all her clothes. She looks good. She gives herself that. She pats her flat belly, kept taut by all her crunches at the gym. Jonathan had adored her body. All of her boyfriends had. Her green eyes, her auburn hair falling past her shoulders, her full breasts, her trim hips. She works out four times a week. She wonders what she might look like at thirty, or at forty. Will she put on weight? Her mother had died at thirty-five. But try as she might, no matter how hard she works with her therapist, Victoria cannot remember what her mother looked like. Her father as well. Or her sister, Wendy. She has no photographs, either: they, too, were destroyed by the fire that claimed her family.

"Oh, Mama," she says, very softly, resting her head against the medicine cabinet, her eyes still shut.

Suddenly the room goes cold. Have the radiators cut off?

She opens her eyes. In the mirror she sees someone standing behind her.

It's not Petey. Petey she's gotten used to.

It's somebody else. Somebody far worse.

The Halloween ghost.

The kid with the sheet over his head.

The one who killed her family and took Petey to hell.

Victoria screams.

It's only for a moment, but she blacks out, losing her footing. She falls against the tub. She comes to when she whacks her left elbow against the rim, sending shooting, vibrating pain up her arm.

"Jesus," Victoria says, suddenly shaking all over. Her body convulses. She cups her elbow in her right hand. The pain still throbs.

She scrambles quickly back to her feet. Of course there's nothing in the mirror but her own reflection. She hurries out into the hallway. The apartment is quiet except for the clanking of the agitated radiators.

She wraps her arms around her body, still shaking uncontrollably. She looks back into the bathroom.

It's been years since she saw the ghost. A decade of therapy had pretty much wiped him out. Now she was left only with Petey, and she could usually send him away with a simple command. But the ghost—why had it returned? Why was she seeing it again?

"Dear God," she whispers.

Is she praying? She used to pray. After the fire, after Petey disappeared—the twin terrors of her last days in Falls Church—she used to pray every night for a miracle. She'd implore God to send her back in time so she could do it over again. This time she wouldn't go out with Petey trick-or-treating. She wouldn't leave her parents and Wendy alone in their house. She'd take them all far, far away from Falls Church—here to Boston, maybe, where there were thousands of people all around, where the nights were never quiet, where fear could be pushed far, far back into a little corner of her mind.

She steps into the bathroom again. She can't stop shaking. She steadies herself against the sink. "It was an illusion," she says out loud, but the sound of her voice rattles her. She hugs herself again, trying to stop her trembling.

In the years after the tragedies, she would see the ghost often: in crowds of children on the playground or in the rearview mirror, seated behind her on her schoolbus. He was always there in the corner of her eye, in her peripheral vision, in the dreams that came far into the night, in the deathly quiet hours just before dawn. She learned to stop screaming when she saw him. She just bit back her terror, held it deep inside her. *He can't touch me,* she convinced herself. *Otherwise, he would have by now.*

Eventually the ghost appeared less and less. It has been six, seven years since she's seen him last. All through Gregory, and Raoul, and Jonathan. Her boyfriends came and went in quick succession—her choice—and there were no appearances of the ghost.

"Why now?" she whispers. "Why has he shown up again?"

She reluctantly lifts her eyes to the medicine chest mirror again. No, nothing there behind her but the shower curtain.

She feels a surge of anger. "Just because I'm alone now,

just because I broke up with Jonathan, don't get any ideas," she says loudly. "I don't need a man to protect me. I've taken care of myself since I was twelve years old, and I'm *stronger than you!*"

That's what her therapist had told her—*convinced* her—when she was sixteen, when the ghost was still making regular appearances in her bathroom mirror. "Show it how strong you are," instructed the therapist, a heavyset black woman who seemed the wisest, strongest person Victoria had ever met. "It doesn't know who it's messing with."

Victoria stands up straighter. She's still rattled, but the trembling has lessened. "You hear me?" she shouts. "*I'm stronger than you.*"

She laughs suddenly, imagining her students witnessing their naked teacher yelling at an invisible foe. "Victoria, get a grip," she orders herself, still looking into the mirror. "You thought of Mom and Dad and Wendy. That's why you thought you saw the ghost again. That's why."

She lets out a long sigh. She's suddenly conscious of her heartbeat, how fiercely it's been beating. "Long, deep breaths," she instructs herself. One. Two. In. Out.

It must be getting late, she thinks. *I'm going to be late for class, and I'm giving them back their finals today.*

She reaches into the shower, turns on the hot faucet. The pipes shudder against the sudden released pressure. The water spills forth into the tub. It runs a few minutes before it warms up.

She takes another deep breath, looks around once more. "Stop playing Janet Leigh," she scolds herself aloud. "You're a grown woman. You spent *years* getting past this terror. It's *old,* Victoria. Old and tired. You are *over* it. You are *not* afraid of taking a shower in your own home."

She reaches in and turns on the cold. She adjusts the hot faucet, tests the water. It's perfect. She presses in on the shower knob, and the spray bursts into life.

Without looking back into the mirror, she steps inside.

"Come on, Vicki, let's go."

"Petey McKay, will you just wait one minute!"

Victoria presses her face against the screen door. Petey stands on the front steps of her home on Beach Road, impatiently shifting his weight from foot to foot. He's dressed like a vampire, with his hair slicked down and his mother's talcum powder patted thickly all over his face. Plastic fangs cup his front teeth, and red food dye is drawn in lines from the corners of his mouth to his chin.

"I'll be there in a minute," Victoria tells him. "I'm having a little trouble with my costume."

"Well, hurry up. We don't got all night."

"Victoria, try this," says her mother, coming into the living room with a tube of Krazy Glue. "But don't get it on your fingers."

Victoria's dressed in black Danskin tights and a heavy black wool sweater. From her hair protrudes two red rubber horns, affixed with tape. But the Devil's tail she bought down at the True Value won't stick to her tights.

She squeezes some glue onto the end of the tail and sticks it above her butt at the base of her spine. "How long do you have to hold it?" she asks her mother.

"A couple minutes. Just be careful. You don't want your fingers getting stuck."

Beyond them, in the living room, her father's watching the nightly news with Dan Rather. He's griping about the latest outrageous comment by President Reagan. "The man is a charlatan," he tells his wife. "He's against everything we ever believed in. He's still defending his decision to cut school lunches."

"Why do you watch the news, Bill? It just gets you riled up."

"What kind of a world are our daughters growing up in? What's happened to this country?"

"President Reagan has brought back patriotism," his wife argues. "He's made us proud again. And prosperous, too."

"Ahh," Bill Kennelly snarls. He's an old liberal from way back. There are pictures of him with long hair and peace signs, protesting the war in Vietnam. He used to belong to a group of radicals that met at the old church, but he doesn't talk much about that time. "All I know, Sylvia," he says, pointing a finger at the television set, "is everything I once believed in seems to be going down the drain."

Victoria pays her father no mind. He often goes into one of his political tirades when he watches the news. But she can't deny some of his influence has rubbed off on her. He'd been very proud of her last night when she spoke up against all the people trying to get the Denny twins kicked out of school — even if old Grace West had looked like she might put a curse on the whole family.

She releases the pressure on the Devil tail and it stays in place. "All *right*," Victoria exults.

Her sister, Wendy, one year older, leans against the door frame and crosses her arms over her chest. "I can't believe you and your little boyfriend are going *trick-or-treating*," Wendy says. "How *immature*. I stopped when I was *ten*."

Victoria sticks out her tongue at her. "Sorry I'm just not as mature as you were, dumbface."

Wendy sticks out her tongue in return. Their mother frets at them both. "Girls."

"Are you *ready*?" Petey calls impatiently through the door.

"Just about. Chill already."

"Now, Victoria," her mother says, "I want you home by nine o'clock. It's a school night, after all."

"Fine, fine." She walks over to her father's chair, kisses him on the forehead. "Don't let ol' Ronnie Ray-Gun get you too worked up, Daddy. It's almost Election Day." He just grumbles.

Her mother comes up behind her. "Just stay around here, Victoria. Don't go farther than Lighthouse Road."

Victoria steps outside. The night is brisk, but still not as cold as some Halloweens she remembers. She stoops down to tie her left black sneaker. Beside her on the step is the jack-o'-lantern her father had carved earlier in the day. They'd bought it at the Falls Church General Store, cut a hole in the top and scooped out its pulpy, stringy insides. "Gross," Vicki had said. "Like it's brains or something."

"And Victoria," her mother calls after her from the screen door, "don't eat any of the candy until we've had a chance to test it."

"Oh, Mom. Like I'm sure there's some maniac in Falls

Church who's slipping razor blades into Three Musketeers bars.''

Petey grins. ''After what you did at Town Meeting last night, I bet there's a lot of people who are gunning for you.''

Victoria shoots him a mean look. Her mother just shudders in the doorway and turns away.

They begin walking along Beach Road. A few other kids are wandering out onto the sidewalk now, mostly little ones with their daddies or mommies holding them by the hand. For a moment Victoria feels a bit silly in her Devil's horn and tail, as if she's much too old, as if Wendy was right.

''My sister said we're too old to go out on Halloween,'' she tells Petey.

''Your sister's a dumb-ass,'' he responds.

''You're right. She's like a *total* dumb-ass. She was so embarrassed when I got up at Town Meeting.''

''Hey, maybe we should go to Grace West's house!'' Petey suggests.

Victoria laughs. ''She'd *really* give us razor blades!''

They walk up to their first house, Victoria's neighbors across the street, the Druckers. Mr. Drucker runs the general store, and everybody always kids him because he has the same name as the guy who ran the general store on *Green Acres*. He has a couple of missing fingers, sliced off on the meat-cutter over the years, and Victoria always felt he was a little creepy. But his wife was even worse, as mean as they come. And of course, it's Mrs. Drucker who opens the door when they ring the bell.

''Trick or treat,'' they chirp.

Alice Drucker just glares at them. ''So if it isn't Miss Community Service,'' she says. ''Aren't you a little too grown-up to be trick-or-treating?''

''You're as young as you feel,'' Petey responds for her, flashing a big, impudent grin and holding out his bag.

Mrs. Drucker pulls back a little. ''Well, I'd think anyone who can get up in front of the whole town and act so high and mighty ought to think twice before she comes around begging house to house.'' And she closes the door without giving them candy.

''She hates me,'' Victoria says. ''Everybody in town does.''

''Not everybody,'' Petey says. ''My parents thought what

you did was right. They say everybody will realize that, sooner or later. Forget about old lady Drucker. She's a bitch anyway.''

They walk back through the grass as a couple of ballerinas and their father step up to ring the bell. Mrs. Drucker opens the door and gushes about how lovely they are, dropping treats into their outstretched bags.

Victoria and Petey turn up Center Street. "So what I said at Town Meeting—was it really so bad?''

"No way. You just pissed a lot of people off. They thought they were gonna win till you spoke up.''

Victoria shakes her head. "You can't just keep kids out of school because they have a disease. They didn't do anything wrong.''

"People thought they might give all the rest of us AIDS.''

Victoria sighs. "They were just being prejudiced. My dad said it was the same people who meet every week at Grace West's house. The Concerned Citizens of Cape Cod.''

"They don't like queers," Petey says, "and they think AIDS is a queer disease.''

"*Queer* is a nasty word, Petey.'' Victoria shakes her head. "I just couldn't believe all those supposedly grown-up people were standing and blathering on about keeping Bobby and Brendan Denny out of school. Like what did those two kids ever do to *them*?''

The townsfolk seemed to have gone a little mental last week. Everybody was talking about the new family, the Dennys, who had moved into one of those new lower-income places up on Cranberry Terrace, off Main Street. Victoria had heard the scuttlebutt around town. The Dennys were *trash,* Mary Silva whispered to Clem Flagg at the diner. They were *dirty,* Max Winn had insisted at the bank to teller Joanna Longstaff. "And the *boys,*'' Pat Crawford had told Victoria's mother at Edie's Cut and Curl, "that's the *worst* of it. They're *hemophiliacs.* With *AIDS.*''

At the special Town Meeting called to meet this sudden "crisis,'' Grace West had stood to insist that, "We can't let AIDS into our schools.''

Victoria's father, sitting about five rows behind her, shifted in his seat. "Aren't you going to *say* anything?'' Victoria whispered.

People had turned out in droves. A couple of AIDS advocates from Provincetown had spoken about the disease not being communicable through touch or shared utensils or toilet seats, but most of the citizens of Falls Church weren't convinced.

The Dennys sat a few rows away from Victoria. The boys, eight years old, were dressed in coats and ties, their hair slicked down despite stubborn cowlicks. They looked so uncomfortable sitting there, listening to the vile things being said about them. Their parents looked even worse than their sons.

"I think it's not even worth considering further," growled old Mr. Winn, the tax assessor. Victoria had always thought he looked like a skeleton, and this night he looked especially ghoulish. Eyes set in deep black sockets, sunken cheeks, worn black gums exposing long yellow teeth. He was part of Grace West's group, too. "I move we vote on it *now,*" he rasped. "Expel the children from the school system!"

"Dad, *say* something," Victoria urged.

He raised his hand with some hesitation. Victoria's mother gave him a supportive look.

But then Fred Pyle, the town barber, leaned in toward him. "Be careful about speaking up, Bill," he whispered. "This crowd wants blood."

Victoria's father lowered his hand.

"So what that I jumped up?" Victoria says, ending her recollections of last night.

"Nobody heard of a kid speaking at Town Meeting before," Petey told her.

"But I had to say something. Everybody else was too scared. Even my dad."

Petey laughs. "Well, you were pretty mad. Everybody could see that."

Victoria had been surprised to find her voice so clear and strong. "I can't believe what I'm hearing," she said. "I might be just a kid, but I know when people are acting crazy."

Suddenly she'd been surrounded by reporters, some from as far away as Boston. A *Cape Cod Times* photographer snapped her picture.

"Bobby and Brendan are good kids," Victoria had told the room. "They never caused any trouble. They're no danger to anybody. It's not like we're going to get any blood transfusions from them."

Reporters were scribbling down her words.

"They've already been through enough," Victoria said. "Imagine if they were your kids. I can't believe all you people—all you adults I've been taught to respect—would want to make things any worse for them. They've got it tough enough already."

The hall was silent. Grace West remained turned around in her seat, glaring at Victoria. But then a few people started applauding, and then more, and then more. Pretty soon most of the folks were on their feet. The vote was taken, and the Dennys were allowed to stay in school.

This morning the headline in the Falls Church section of the *Cape Cod Times* had read:

FROM THE MOUTH OF BABES: GIRL SPEAKS OUT FOR AIDS BOY

An editorial had commended her for her courage, calling those who shouted for the boys' expulsion "rabid reactionary rednecks without an ounce of compassion." How Grace West and her followers must have fumed reading that.

"Miss Santos at the library told me I was her hero," Victoria says. "So I guess not everyone hates me."

"See? I told you."

They walk up the old concrete steps toward the gray weather-bitten Cape house of old Mrs. Stoddard, a retired lady who lives here with her daughter, Francine. The dead brown leaves of late autumn collect on her doorstep. Petey rings the bell. Mrs. Stoddard's smiling when she opens the door but becomes somber when she spots Victoria. She doesn't respond to their "Trick or treat!" She just drops a couple of Pixie Sticks into each of their bags and closes the door.

"This sucks," Victoria says as they continue up Center Street, where the woods get thicker. "I shouldn't have come out."

"You can't hide away, Vicki. What you did was *right*. My mom and dad said so. They were leaning toward kicking Bobby and Brendan out, but after you spoke, they changed their minds."

"*Really?*"

"Yeah." He looks at her with an idea. "You know, maybe

we ought to go back out along Lighthouse Road. Those people don't get involved so much in town stuff. They probably weren't even at Town Meeting. We can really haul in the loot up there, and nobody will give you any attitude.''

"I don't know, Petey. I told my mother I'd be back by nine o'clock.''

Petey sighs. "I told mine the same thing. If we cut through the woods, we can make it.''

Victoria looks around at the little hobgoblins laughing as they toddle down the sidewalk. The moon is low, big and shiny and gold in a deep purple sky.

"Oh, all right,'' Victoria agrees.

In the shower, fifteen years later, she presses her face into the warm spray. *Why did I go?* she thinks. *Why didn't I tell Petey we should just go home?*

She finds herself praying, like she did when she was a little girl. *Let me go back in time, God. Let me make it right.*

The shower pressure burps, pulling back, then gushing out again. She opens her eyes. She stares down at the soap suds running down between her breasts.

Why am I reliving this? Why did I see the ghost again, after all this time? What's happening?

They make their way past the two little ballerinas. Victoria and Petey head through the Stoddards' backyard to walk up the hill into the woods. It's dark suddenly, with no streetlights and front porches to guide them, just the gold moon overhead. Long shadows stretch across the moonlight from a rusted old swing set. A dog suddenly starts barking from somewhere in the neighborhood—*yap yap yap yap yap*—as the sound of giggling trick-or-treaters echoes from several houses down the street.

"Petey,'' Victoria asks. "Do you think we're going to get married when we grow up?''

"To each other?''

"Yeah, you idiot.''

"I don't know,'' he says. "Why? Do you want to?''

"I don't know," she says. The hill behind the Stoddards' house is steep. The grass is damp and slippery. Vicki is behind Petey. Their black clothes cause them to almost disappear into the night. Victoria's mother had wanted her to wear one of those reflector jackets, but she'd refused. "Devils don't wear geeky reflector jackets," she'd protested.

"I was just thinking about it because Wendy called you my boyfriend. Are you?"

He snorts. "Don't go getting weird on me now, Vicki."

"How am I getting weird?"

"Marriage is a weird topic," he says.

"Well, I'm *sorry*." She considers for a moment stopping and turning back. She and Petey have been friends since kindergarten. They've lived across the street from each other all their lives. She knows twelve is way too young to be thinking about marriage, but she's suddenly very angry at Petey, as if because of him she's going to end up spending the rest of her life alone.

They've reached the top of the hill. The woods stretch off in front of them. Beyond the trees lies the road leading to the Falls Church lighthouse. The woods are dark, but slivers of moonlight dance within the gnarled branches, misshapen by the wind that sweeps in from the beach. If they stop and listen, Victoria and Petey can hear the surf. Every few minutes there's the low wail of the foghorn, coming from the lighthouse.

"Mrs. O'Keefe saw a coyote in her yard last week, you know," Victoria remarks.

Petey doesn't stop walking. He forges ahead into the woods. "If you want to go back, go," he says. Dead leaves crackle under his feet.

Why is she suddenly so ill at ease? It's not as if she's unfamiliar with the path. They've taken it many times out to the lighthouse. It's faster than walking down Beach Road and then all the way along the coast. As young as eight, Victoria would often skip along here alone, her flip-flops snapping in time with her eager steps. But in the sunbaked days of August, it was different. Now, with the path obscured by fallen leaves, in the darkness alleviated only by the pale moonlight, Victoria can't deny a tinge of fear.

"Petey," she says after they've crunched through the leaves for several minutes, "I think we're off the path—"

He stops. He looks around. They can hear the surf, still as far away as when they entered the woods. She's right. The trees are different.

"I think the path's over there," Petey suggests, pointing.

"Let's go back," Victoria says.

"I told you, if you want to go back, go."

They hear the snap of a twig, the soft crunch of leaves.

"Who's there?" Petey calls out.

Victoria peers into the darkness.

"I don't see anybody," she says softly.

Another snap, more leaves crunched.

"What if it's a coyote?" she asks.

"Anybody there?" Petey calls.

Silence. They begin walking again, slower now, back in the direction Petey thought they might find the path. Victoria stays close behind him, holding on to his vampire cape for support.

"Hold on," Petey says.

"What?" Victoria asks.

"Over there," he whispers. She can feel Petey tense up, go cold. "Do you see something?"

"Don't try to scare me, Petey."

"I'm not." She can tell he's just as frightened. "I think somebody's over there."

It's too dark to make anything out. "Where?" she asks.

"Look," Petey says quietly, pointing off amid the bare trees. "I think it's—it's a *kid*."

He breathes a small sigh of relief. In the distance Vicki can barely make out another trick-or-treater: some kid dressed as a ghost. Over his head he's got a white sheet that hangs down almost to the ground. He's just standing there, a white statue in the moonlight. He seems to be waiting for them.

"He looks our age," Petey says, noting his height. "I think Johnny O'Keefe said he was going as a ghost."

"Yeah," Victoria says, desperate to believe it. "It's probably Johnny O'Keefe."

"Yo!" Petey calls. "Is that you, O'Keefe? You heading out to Lighthouse Road, too?"

The kid in the white sheet just stands there.

"Come on," Petey says, gesturing for Vicki to follow him as he makes his way closer to the ghost.

Years later, each time Victoria would wake in cold, pounding sweats remembering that night, she'd hear again the snap of the twigs and the crunch of the leaves as Petey walked forward. She'd feel again the sudden heaviness in the air, the thick, dry warmth. She'd remember how from the moment they spotted the ghost among the trees, everything changed. The way they walked, the way they talked. Their movements seemed heavier, as if the force of gravity had all at once become stronger. Their voices became thick and muffled, as if Victoria's ear canals had suddenly filled up with water. Through the dead leaves they trudged, past the twisted trees deformed by the wind, past long, writhing shadows forever etched in her mind, under the obscure orange light of an autumn moon.

Ahead, the figure under the sheet waited.

"Oh, dear God," she murmurs as she puts her head back under the shower spray to wash out any last residue of the shampoo. "Oh, dear God, why am I remembering all this again?"

She couldn't bear to relive any more of it, but she does. How the gnarled hands reached out from under the sheet and gripped Petey around the neck. How she turned and ran, screaming, lost in the woods, until the sounds of fire engines led her back to her street, only to see the red glow against the night sky and smell the thick, acrid smoke that billowed up from her house. How she saw old Grace West standing in the crowd, watching the Kennelly house burn to the ground. How she collapsed and didn't really wake up for weeks to come, long after her mother and father and Wendy had all been buried, and little Petey gone without a trace.

"Get a *grip*, Victoria," she says, "you've processed all that. You've moved on." But there's no conviction in her voice. No command.

The faucet groans as she shuts it off. She hesitates a moment before pulling back the shower curtain. "Get a *grip*," she repeats, but her voice is frail and tiny.

She looks in both directions before stepping out of the tub into the steamy bathroom. She pulls a thin frayed towel from the rack to her body. Bending over, she swings her hair down in front of her, rubbing the towel briskly against it.

When she straightens up, her eye catches the medicine cabinet. There, where not a half hour before she'd seen the ghost, something's written in fingertip on the fogged-up mirror. She makes a little sound as she steps forward.

PLEASE FIND ME VICTORIA PLEASE
PETEY

"Dear God," she whispers, covering her mouth with her hands, before collapsing onto the floor in a paroxysm of shaking and tears.

The terror had come back. It's likely it had never left.

Thursday, May 16, 6:17 P.M.

Just as the sun begins to set, Teddy McDaniel and Jamal Emerson take aim at the old church's window, stones in hands.

"I can smash it before you do," Teddy challenges.

"No way, man," Jamal counters. "You're way too weak to throw that high."

They pull back their arms.

Both are sons of policemen: both know better than to vandalize town property. But the older boys at Veterans Elementary School had dared them to do it. Teddy is nine; Jamal is eight. Jamal, despite being younger, is taller and stronger, a fact that irks Teddy to no end. Teddy's dad, Rusty McDaniel, is best friends with Jamal's dad, Job Emerson, and so they expect their kids to be friends as well. They are, mostly, but like most boys their age, they're also rivals: forever challenging each other to little duels like this.

The windows of the old church are pocked with holes after years of assault. Some have been boarded up by the town; others, like the round one they're aiming at, have apparently been too high, out of the reach of vandals. It's made of blue-and-green stained glass. There's a dove right in the center. The setting sun reflects pink and orange against it. Long shadows stretch across the churchyard, still soggy from all the rain, and through the cemetery beside it, the broken brownstone slabs worn smooth by centuries of wind whipping in off Churchport Harbor.

"Ready?" Teddy barks.

"Ready!" Jamal answers.

They throw. Both rocks miss by several feet, not even coming close. They richochet off the side of the church. The boys duck so as not to get conked in the head.

"You missed by farther than me," Jamal charges.

"No way. You were *so* more off than me."

Jamal walks over to the side of the church through the tall, wet grass. He tries the door. It's locked with a rusty old padlock.

"Watch out," Teddy warns with a smirk, "or Prissy Goo will get you."

"I'm not scared of any ol' dead white girl," Jamal snarls.

Teddy picks up another stone. He throws it up at the window, missing again. He keeps up a steady barrage of stones against the church as Jamal tries to shake the door free of its lock.

Ping, ping.

"*Tell me tall or tell me true*," Teddy sings out—the rhyme Falls Church boys have sung ever since Priscilla Googins's bloody body was found draped over the altar of the church more than thirty years before. "*Tell me what happened to Prissy Goo.*"

It's a mantra the older boys have taught him, as older boys had once taught *them*—the password into their ranks. "Stand in front of the church and face it down," Steven Silva told him. "Dare bloody, gooey Priscilla to show her hideous face at the window."

Teddy throws another stone. And another.

Ping. Ping.

He'd begun hitting the glass, but the stones still don't break it. They keep flying backward, landing among the overgrown weeds of the churchyard. Teddy looks down at his hands, cursing how puny they are, how little strength is in them.

"Weakling," Jamal taunts, still rattling the door.

"Like you could do any better," Teddy shouts.

He lifts his eyes to the rafters of the old stone structure, its twin steeples rising coldly into the sky, one higher than the other. Lightning had struck the north steeple years before, and it remained charred and stunted now, like old Mr. Drucker's hand down at the general store. Teddy didn't know why his hand looked that way. He didn't dare ask.

A couple of languid old crows break Teddy's line of vision, throwing themselves from a ledge high above, their great ripped black wings fanning across the darkening sky. They make no sound. The boys, too, grow still. A chill wind from the harbor sweeps down across the cemetery and through the churchyard, swaying the long blades of grass. It rattles the chain-link fence that seals off the church from the marine-supply store behind it. Jamal stops shaking the door, looks up and shivers. He comes back to stand next to Teddy and look up at the window.

They see her at the same time.

Priscilla.

"Hello, boys."

They gasp. There's a man walking toward them. The shadows of dusk obscure his face. He approaches slowly, his hand outstretched.

"What's the matter?" he's asking. "Looks as if you've seen a ghost."

"*We did! We did!*" Teddy blurts. He looks at Jamal. "Didn't we?"

"Yeah," Jamal answers. "We saw her! *Up there!*"

The man has reached them. He's young, early twenties, not someone they've seen before. He's dressed in jeans and a sweatshirt that has UNIVERSITY OF MASSACHUSETTS lettered across his chest. He's wearing cool Nike sneakers.

"Who'd you see?" he asks, puzzled.

"*Priscilla,*" Teddy says, barely able to speak. "We saw her. I said the chant, and she came."

The man smiles. "Is she like the resident ghost or something?"

"She was *murdered* in there," Jamal tells him, impatient. He looks back up at the window, but he sees nothing.

"Oh. I see." The man follows Jamal's line of vision and looks up at the window himself. "You said you saw her in that window? The round one? With the dove on it?"

Jamal nods. Teddy says, "Yeah. That's the one."

"But, *guys,*" the man says, "it's stained glass. You can't really see through that, can you? Besides, there's the dove right in the middle—"

Jamal seems to consider this. "But I saw something."

"Me too," insists Teddy.

The man has stooped down so he's at eye level with the boys. "Guys, this is a house of God. No matter what bad things have happened inside, it's still a holy place." He smiles. "My name's Mark, and I want to buy this place. I want to make good things happen here again."

They look at him funny. "Are you a priest?" Teddy asks.

Mark smiles. "No. I'm a minister. And I think once I've had a chance to fix this place up, you might want to come back here. We're going to have games and contests and church fairs and lots of fun things."

The boys look unsure.

The man stands up again. "I'm heading over to Town Meeting tonight to officially make my offer to the town. I bet your parents will be there, right? What are your names?"

The boys tell him. They tell him their dads are cops, and Mark promises not to squeal about how he discovered them throwing stones. "I'm thinking about putting in a basketball court in the churchyard," he tells the boys, escorting them out through the fence. "The town needs one, don't you think?"

Jamal and Teddy enthusiastically agree. *Boy, Mark sure is cool,* Teddy thinks. Nothing like that cranky Father Roche at St. Peter's, where Teddy attends with his parents, or Reverend Shanker, the dotty old minister at United Methodist, where Jamal's family worships. Mark is the kind of guy who could make going to church seem cool—even if he didn't believe them about seeing Priscilla at the window.

And maybe they didn't, really. Maybe it was just the setting sun playing tricks with them. That's what Mark suggests, anyway, as they walk up Church Street, talking about Michael Jordan and Sugar Ray and who's hotter, Brandy or Britney Spears—and by the time they reach Town Hall, Teddy and Jamal believe everything that Mark has to say.

Thursday, May 16, 6:30 P.M.

Cooper Pierce didn't want the commotion. He *hates* commotion. If he had his way, he would have just hushed the girl as best he could and sent her out of his shop. He didn't want trouble. After all, he had to be over at Town Hall in half an hour for Town Meeting. He couldn't be late: he was a selectman, for crying out loud. He hadn't gotten to where he was by causing commotion. He'd risen up out of the ghetto of downtown Bridgeport, Connecticut, by following his father's example: slow and steady ambition, never marred by complaining or bitching. "You get more flies with honey than you do with vinegar," his father always told him, and Cooper had always followed his advice.

But tonight, when the girl came in and started shouting, his wife, Miranda, had done just the opposite of Cooper's instincts: she cried out at the top of her lungs; she screamed her head off, making even more of a ruckus than the girl, who was obviously on some kind of drug. Miranda screamed so loud that Darla Bennett had rushed over from Precious Moments and Gerry Garafolo barged in with some of his customers from the pizza joint. All of them gathered now to watch poor Kathy McKenzie go stark raving mad in front of them.

"Get out of here!" Miranda kept screaming, her hands in her hair.

"You rich bitch!" Kathy McKenzie shouted, getting up in

Miranda's face. "You and your husband think you own the town, living up there on Cliff Heights and looking down at all of us! But you're just no-good trash!"

"Get out of here!" Miranda screams again.

"You're destroying this town! You elitist snobs! You're tearing down everything my parents and my grandparents built! You're evil! *Evil!*"

Cooper just hangs in the background, aghast at the whole thing. He has no other choice now. He lifts the receiver of his phone to call the police.

"Kathy, Kathy, come on now," Gerry Garafolo is saying, trying to get her to back off. "It's me, Gerry, from the pizza joint. You know me. You and Josh come in all the time."

Kathy's foaming at the mouth. Literally. Cooper has always considered her such a nice young woman, eyes usually cast downward as she makes her way on the street. Most folks know about the rough time she'd had with that ex-husband of hers a few years back. But Kathy had seemed to get through all that fine. She worked hard, making a good home for her son, even if it was out in the low-income housing on Cranberry Terrace.

"Kathy, come on with me," Gerry's cajoling her. "Come on over to the pizza shop. I'll get you a cup of coffee—"

"You goddamn *wop!*" Kathy turns and spits at Gerry, who pulls back, startled. A couple of his customers rush her and tell her she's crazy.

Cooper can see Gerry Garafolo backing away now, stunned, shaking his head. "Nobody's ever called me that in my whole twenty years here in Falls Church," he's saying, wiping his face, hurt more by her hateful words than anything else. Cooper can relate. He presses 911.

He gets Dean Sousa at the police station and tells him to get over to the shop right away.

"It's Kathy McKenzie," Cooper tells him. "I think she's—on something."

"All of you!" Kathy's shouting. "All of you are going to *burn in hell!*"

"She looked all glassy-eyed when Dean arrived to take her away in the cruiser," says Darla Bennett to the crowd that's gathered, most on their way to Town Meeting. "I thought she was going to *hit* Miranda."

Miranda Pierce shudders, shaking her head. Her long conch-shell earrings—of her own design, like all those sold in her shop, a fabulous little place called Hornet that's attracted lots of wealthy out-of-towners—jingle a little as they move. "It looked like crack to me," she says.

Her husband is impatient, looking at his watch. "Dear, we need to get to Town Hall."

"Hmph." Yvette Duvalier, who runs the fanciest restaurant in town—indeed the fanciest restaurant Falls Church has ever had—raises an eyebrow. "Well, they say that husband of hers was a crackhead."

"He's in jail, which is where Kathy McKenzie should be," Miranda says.

"I always thought she was a straight-ahead kind of girl," muses Laura Millay, standing with her husband, Roger, the president of the bank. "But I guess we were all wrong about her." Laura shakes her head. She's a cool, icy blonde, with pearls to match: Grace Kelly or Tippi Hedren in a Hitchcock film.

"Look, we all need to get over to Town Hall," Cooper Pierce insists. "Enough of this. We have our civic responsibility to think about."

The whole incident has shaken him up. He's a man who doesn't like confrontation. That's not his way. Accommodation, cooperation. He might be black, but he's voted Republican in every election since he was eighteen. On the Board of Selectmen, he plays the peacemaker, trying to bring together the board's two extemist members, Mary Silva and Marcella Stein. It's a thankless job. It was his wife's idea that he run for selectman. She said they needed someone on the board who was friendly to the *business* interests of town, instead of surrendering the board completely to obstructionists like Silva and Stein.

"Cooper's right," Roger Millay agrees, urging his wife away from the scene. "Town Meeting will be starting, and there's a lot on the agenda."

They lift their hands in little waves. Cooper and Miranda Pierce watch them all walk off toward Town Hall.

"Really, Cooper, I'm much too upset to go in right away," Miranda says. "That *trash*—barging in here and calling us such horrible names!"

"Dear, she's a troubled girl. Let the police handle her. No lasting damage was done."

"No lasting damage? Cooper, everyone heard her charge that we were destroying the town! When, in fact, few have done as much as we have to build it up! I think we ought to press charges against her for slander—"

"Please, Miranda, you don't know what you're saying."

Miranda Pierce narrows her eyes. "Well, I know there's a lot of resentment brewing under the surface of this town. So much hatred stirring beneath those phony smiles."

Cooper sighs. "*Please*, Miranda. Come along."

She sighs, giving in. They cross Main Street toward Town Hall.

Thursday, May 16, 6:58 P.M.

Nate's surprised to see Kathy McKenzie in such a state, but he agrees Dean had little choice but to make an arrest for disturbing the peace. He hates having to lock her up in one of the holding cells downstairs—after all, she's always seemed like such a nice girl before—but what else can they do? "Fucking pigs," Kathy had hissed at Nate, who told Rusty, just in for night duty, to arrange for a drug test. The only explanation Nate can think of is that Kathy McKenzie, like that ex-husband of hers, is on crack.

He comes back to the conference room, where Monica Paul is eating pizza. "You were so right, Detective," she says. "Gerry knows pizza. So much better than the cardboard and Ragú sauce I've gotten accustomed to out here."

Nate smiles. He looks outside at the folks walking up Pearl Street toward Main. He knows they're heading to Town Meeting. The dutiful citizens of Falls Church participating in the oldest form of American democracy. The sun has set, and the rain, thankfully, has ended. There's even a hint of spring in the air, Nate thinks, a twist of forsythia. Warm air has drifted up the coast, turning the evening downright balmy with all the puddles of rainwater still on the street.

"I'm sorry I was called away," Nate says, turning to Monica. "But the girl who was just brought in—well, she was in quite a state."

"Oh, don't worry, Detective. I had these files to keep me occupied. Pretty gruesome stuff for such a small town."

"I appreciate you doing the article. I want nothing more than to solve those crimes."

She winks at him. "Count me in as an ally, Detective."

He looks at her. He can't deny he finds her very attractive. Monica had revealed she was divorced, her former husband convincing her to move from Washington to Boston. He was a big-time corporate lobbyist, and Monica despised the world he thrust her into. So she left him, heading out to the Cape to put her head back on straight. Here she fell in love with the quiet, simpler pace of life and decided to stay. A year younger than Nate, she is bright, witty and persistent. And she has the sexiest goddamn legs he's seen in a very long time.

"We should be heading over to Town Meeting," he tells her.

She nods, closing the files on the table in front of her. She stands, slipping her notebook into her briefcase. "Lead the way," she says.

He switches off the light as they head out of the conference room and outside into the damp evening. Nate takes Monica's arm, leading her through the parking lot toward Town Hall. He can see the lights blazing in the old structure.

Outside, leaning against a police cruiser, his skinny arms crossed against his chest, is Officer Dean Sousa. He's watching all the folks heading into Town Meering, nodding pleasantly as they pass.

"Isn't he the one who brought in that girl?" Monica asks. "He hardly seems strong enough to lift a baby."

Nate smiles. "Dean's my buddy. He's only been on the force a year. What he lacks in size he makes up for in—how shall I put it?—dedication."

They watch as Officer Sousa, spotting a couple of pretty teenage girls heading into Town Hall, rests his elbow against the roof of the cruiser and strikes a pose. Almost immediately, as if on cue, his elbow slides out from under him and he loses his footing. The girls giggle, looking over their shoulders at him as they head inside.

"The shakiest gun in the East, huh?" Monica laughs.

Nate grins as they cross the street. "That's why the chief

only lets him carry one bullet." He looks down at her. "In his *pocket*."

"I suppose that's off the record, huh?" she asks.

He winks at her. They approach Dean. "Evening, Officer," Nate calls out in greeting.

Dean brightens. "Yo, Nate." He looks at Monica and stiffens his back, pushing out his small shoulders. "Ma'am."

"Dean Sousa, this is Monica Paul, ace reporter from the *Cape Cod Times*."

Dean smiles. He's just twenty-two, with hardly any beard. He can't weigh more than 110 pounds. His uniform looks slightly baggy, but his badge and boots are polished to a high sheen. "Good to meet you," he says officiously.

"And you, too, Officer," she says, sparkling.

"So, Dean, I got your sister's invitation. I'll try to make it."

"Oh, I hope you do," Dean tells him. "It's my mom's sixtieth birthday."

"I'm not sure she'd want you announcing that on the street," Monica says.

Dean blushes.

Nate can't resist another grin. "What are you getting her, Dean?" he asks.

"A septic tank."

Nate laughs. "A septic tank? You're getting your mother a septic tank for her sixtieth birthday."

"She's awful hard to buy for," Dean tells him very seriously. "It's a first-class model. Two tons of concrete, all reinforced steel."

"You're a fine son, Dean," Nate tells him.

"I try."

Postmistress Bessie Bowe passes them with Noah Burt. "Evenin', Nate. Evenin', Dean."

"Evenin', ma'am," Dean replies, tipping his hat.

"Evening, Bessie, Noah," Nate says. He likes them, likes their story. Two lonely people who found each other in middle age, not letting social circumstances stop them from getting together. Noah pumps gas at Dave's Sunoco and he's black— Bessie's white. It's a sign of the times that they can walk into Town Hall hand in hand, not needing to hide their relationship.

Nate's glad that society has changed since he was a kid—for the better, he thinks.

"We should get inside," he tells Monica. "We'll want to get good seats."

She slips her arm through Nate's. "It was delightful meeting you, Officer Sousa," she says to Dean.

He starts to say, "You, too," but gets a little tongue-tied, so it comes out, "To you." Popping his eyes and blushing, Dean just settles back against the cruiser.

Inside, the hall is abuzz with people and noise. Nate and Monica are first greeted by Danny Correia, the town janitor. Danny's a little slow, but he's just the sweetest guy in Falls Church. Usually spotted pushing his broom up and down the halls, his hair sticking up in a dozen different directions, tonight Danny's all spiffed up in bow tie and tweed jacket. Somebody must have helped him get ready for the occasion; his hair is slicked down and for once he's closely shaven. Danny's always got a bright word for everybody. For Nate and Monica it's *"May the sun shine warm upon your face, if it ever shines again."*

Nate smiles, clapping Danny on his back. "It does seem that winter just won't let go, doesn't it, Dan?"

"Red sky in morning, sailors take warning," Danny says, somewhat of a non-sequitur. *"Red sky at night, sailors' delight."*

They pass into the lobby, Nate pointing out the architecture of the old building to Monica. Built in 1884, the Town Hall has two floors. The first floor houses the municipal offices and the lobby, which is filled with citizenry sampling the traditional baked goods brought by locals and spread out on five tables. Connie Sousa, Dean's mom, runs the local bakery, and she's brought all sorts of pies and cream puffs and Portuguese rolls. Marge Duarte brought a plate of corn bread, Ermengilde Moore brought some of her famous peanut-butter snickerdoodles, and Sarah Lipnicki whipped up some Rice Krispies treats. Of course, Yvette Duvalier of the exclusive Duvalier's Restaurant rolls in trays of fancy French crullers and chocolate-covered strawberries, but most of the old natives pass them by. Nate grabs a brownie; Monica pats her stomach and protests that after all that cheese pizza, she'd better forego any dessert.

On either side of the lobby, wooden staircases ascend to the second floor. There, at the top of the stairs, Isabella Sousa Cook, the venerable town clerk, is checking voters against a sheet of names taped to the table in front of her. Behind her, double doors open into an enormous white-paneled room, seating capacity four hundred, with a mezzanine around its perimeter.

"Isabella, this is Monica Paul, a reporter covering Town Meering for the *Cape Cod Times*," Nate explains.

The clerk looks up at him with small eyes behind thick black cat-eye glasses. She's got a painted beauty mark on her cheek in the form of a star and she's chewing gum. "Now, Tucky," she says, "you know I can't let any nonvoters inside the hall. She'll have to sit up in the mezzanine."

Nate smiles. "Aw, Izzy. She wants to see democracy in action, up close and personal."

She smirks. She moves her eyes over to Monica and lifts an eyebrow. "You married or single?"

Monica seems to bristle. "What does that have to do with anything?"

Isabella Sousa Cook grins. " 'Cuz I've been trying to fix ol' Tucky here up with a pretty girl ever since he moved here. You available?"

Monica returns her grin as Nate blushes. "Yes," she says. "I'm available."

"All right," Isabella says, "then I'll make an exception." She shakes her finger at Monica. "But you've got to assure me you won't raise your hand and try to influence any vote."

"She'll be good," Nate swears.

"I promise," Monica tells her as they pass the table and head into the hall. "On my honor."

Everyone's here, just as Nate had predicted. People are talking in little clusters while others are filing into the seats. Raincoats are draped over several chairs to mark them claimed. Up on the stage, at the far end of the hall, moderator Cliff Claussen, local attorney, dodders about, tapping on microphones and ruffling papers. He's tall and gaunt, with a thick mane of snow white hair and intense Siberian husky blue eyes. He's wearing a red-and-blue-plaid flannel shirt and khakis.

"He's been doing this for years, according to the chief," Nate whispers as he and Monica choose a couple of chairs halfway up the middle section. "But he's about eighty or something, so he sometimes forgets what we're voting on."

She winks at him. "Can I print that?"

"Yikes," Nate says, grinning. "I keep forgetting who I'm talking to."

A few of the selectmen are walking up the steps to the stage now. There's Mary Silva, sister to Hiram, her face set in a perpetual scowl; Cooper Pierce, natty as ever in blue blazer and gold tie; Marcella Stein, a bright red bow in her hair, her three-foot-wide ass showcased in jeans so tight coins can be discerned in her back pocket; and Richard Longstaff, a sad-faced guy who gives a little wave to his daughter, Kimberly, in the audience. Richard dotes on Kim since his wife died; she and these meetings are really all he lives for now, Nate observes.

"What's up with the mean-looking one?" Monica asks.

"That's Mary Silva. She's an old-timer. Still hasn't gotten over selling the old family property to Richie Rostocki back in the '80s. He got it from her for a song. Prime real estate on the cliffs north of town."

"Cliff Heights," she says.

"Bingo. So the developer made a fortune and all these summer people live there now, and a couple of uppity year-rounders, like Roger Millay from the bank and Cooper Pierce, the guy in the gold tie next to her. It just sticks in old Mary's craw."

Monica laughs. "Here not even a full year, and already you know all the secrets, don't you, Detective?"

He shrugs. "Everybody knows this town's secrets."

"H'lo, Nate," says Clem Flagg, lowering his enormous body into a seat behind him. "All set to do your civic duty?"

"As ready as you are, Clem. Hey, this is Monica Paul. From the *Cape Cod Times*."

Clem looks through his little octagonal glasses at her. "Well. Nice to meet you. Glad to see the *Times* hasn't forgotten that little Falls Church exists. We might not be as headline-grabbing as Hyannis or Provincetown, but we're here."

Monica smiles. "I'm profiling Detective Tuck. Care to comment?"

Clem squints one eye over at Nate. "If he doesn't arrest the hooligans who keep me up all night, I'll care to comment."

Nate just smirks as he watches the citizenry file in. It certainly is a quaint old tradition. Forget the ballot box: everything's decided right here, out in the open. If you're for something, you've got to be willing to take a stand for it. Everyone sees how everyone else votes. You raise your hand and that's that. Camps are formed; lines are drawn; venom is sometimes spewed—but by the next Town Meeting, all the cards are shuffled again and new alliances are formed.

Folks plan for the annual Town Meeting as if it were a cotillion. The ladies of Falls Church all buy themselves new outfits, and the men lay bets as to how certain votes will go. The kids look at it like some big fair, with all the home-baked goods in the lobby and the antics of their elders in the hall. The more serious ones sit wide-eyed beside their parents, watching the machinations of local government. The wilder ones are consigned to the basement to play with computer games or watch TV.

At least, that's how the chief has painted it. Nate looks around for him now. He hasn't seen him all day. Phil was taking his wife, Ellen, down to Hyannis this morning to see her doctor. Three years ago, Ellen had had a breast removed, and they thought the cancer was licked, but still she has regular checkups. Nate hopes there isn't a problem.

Job Emerson and his wife, Berniece, slide into the chairs beside him. "Hey, buddy," Nate says. The men clap each other on the back.

"I thought we were voting on our raises tonight," Job says, flipping through the program.

Nate reaches over to point the item out. "Eleventh on the list, but it's there."

"*Eleventh?* Means we'll get to it in June sometime. If we're lucky."

Monica clears her throat. "Eh-ahem."

Nate jumps a little. "Hey, I'm sorry. Job, Bernie, this is Monica Paul, from the *Cape Cod Times*. And this is Job Emerson, a fellow officer of the law, and his dearly beloved spouse, Berniece.''

Job nods hello, then nudges Nate with his elbow. "Not bad, not bad at all," he whispers.

"Easy, man," Nate says, and he can feel that damn blush spreading again.

The place is nearly filled up by now. Nate watches as Fred and Lucille Pyle take their seats, he of the barbershop and she of the cash register at the True Value. Behind them come Sargent and Pat Crawford, looking like each just stepped out of *Vogue*, Pat standing on tippy-toes to wave at someone at the far end of the hall. With them is Pidge Hitchcock, wife of the town manager. Ice queen of all ice queens, Pidge wears a perpetual expression of supreme boredom with everyone and everything in this small backwater town. She was from the Gold Coast of Connecticut, after all, just a hop and a jump from "the City," where (as she was glad to tell anyone within earshot) life was *much different* than it is in Falls Church.

Her husband, Alan, has just taken his seat onstage along with the remaining selectmen. He nods to Cliff Claussen, who stands from his folding chair with some difficulty and hobbles over to the podium. He bangs the gavel.

"Town Meeting," he rasps, just as a horrible high-pitched squeak emanates from the microphone, sending most folks' hands over their ears. Monica recoils next to Nate, her shoulder pressing into his. Cliff taps the microphone, ending the noise. "Town Meeting will now come to order."

He rambles on with the opening formalities. Nate senses some commotion off to his left. He turns to see Betty and Hiram Silva taking their seats in the row in front of him. Betty looks over at him with a small, weary smile. Hiram stares straight ahead, his jaw pushed out, locked in an expression of—could it be?—defiance and anger. *Hiram? Angry?*

Could they have had an argument? Nate wonders. It certainly looks that way. He's never known Betty and Hiram to argue.

Claussen clears his throat. "We have a couple big-ticket items on the agenda tonight, but we also have a number of other issues to vote on, so we ask for your patience and endurance. We hope to be out of here by eleven, and if you all cooperate, we will be." Claussen beams a smug little smile. Nate thinks if anyone ever told the old coot he couldn't moderate Town Meeting anymore, he'd fold up and die. Cliff clearly relishes being up there.

"Remember the rules," he admonishes the crowd, actually shaking a long thin lawyerly finger at them. "No addressing each other. You address *me* if you wish to respond to a previous statement. After suitable discussion of a matter, it will be moved for a vote, which needs to be seconded."

Job leans over to Nate. "Have you heard from the chief?" he whispers.

"No, and he's not here."

"Hope everything's all right with Ellen."

The first vote is on the repair of the pier. It goes fast: everyone agrees that some posts are rotting through and that the time has simply come. One of the fishermen left in town, Manny Duarte, brother of Marge over at the diner and uncle to Dean Sousa, stands to tell how he almost killed himself last month hauling in his catch of cod. "Damn pier started giving way under me," he says. Nate likes Manny as much as he likes his sister. He's one of the last of a dying breed: the self-sufficient fisherman, out on his boat before dawn, hauling in his catch as the sun sets, spilling all those flapping, glistening fish onto the pier. Manny stands there now, unshaven, in a dirty T-shirt, with his anchor tattoo rippling on his forearm. Nate notes how Monica seems to be writing everything down, absorbing all the color.

Next up is the school board budget. Martha Sturm, the elementary-school principal, stands in front of the room to make a pitch. She's a heavyset woman, late thirties, with short blond hair and wide brown eyes. Her voice has the well-modulated cadence of a prestigious college; Nate thinks she went to Smith. "You'll hear talk of how enrollment is down," Martha's saying. "You'll hear about how many of our old families have sold their homes and moved away. How fewer new families live here year-round, or have school-age children. You'll hear talk that suggests we might phase out our school, go regional, as we did with the high school some years ago. Well, I say, if we're to be a *smaller* school system, we can be a *better* school system. We need to upgrade . . ."

Nate begins nodding off. Martha's voice has a kind of hypnotic quality, lulling him to sleep. He feels his eyelids grow heavy. He catches every other word. . . . *Computers . . . Internet . . . proactive . . . competitive . . . children . . . future . . .*

But what jogs him suddenly awake is a very different word: *"Dyke!"*

He opens his eyes with a start. Hiram Silva is standing, shaking his fist. Martha Sturm has fallen silent, her face drained of all color.

"What the—" Nate says.

"Holy Jesus—" Job echoes.

"She's a goddamn *dyke!*" Hiram is shouting, waving his fist over the heads of those seated in front of him. "She's corrupting our kids! She's a lesbian! A lesbian! A goddamn *lesbian!*"

Poor Betty is frantic, near tears, trying to make her husband sit down, trying desperately to get him to stop ranting. Both Nate and Job push out of their row and rush up to them. Betty begins to sob as Nate takes her arm.

Hiram keeps shouting. *"She's a lesbian, and everyone knows she's sleeping with Kim Longstaff, young enough to be her daughter!"*

On the stage, Kim's father, poor Selectman Longstaff, nearly has a heart attack.

The whole room is in an uproar. Selectwoman Mary Silva, usually so prim, seems humiliated that it's her brother causing the disturbance. Cliff Claussen is banging his gavel. "Out of order!" he's rasping. "Out of order!"

"I'm sorry, Martha," Betty cries out, standing up. "Cliff, please, he doesn't know what he's saying. He's—he's been ill."

Hiram sits down in his seat and covers his face. Nate stoops down next to him. "Hiram? What's come over you? Hiram?"

The old mailman won't look at him.

Betty leans in beside her husband. "He hasn't been the same since this morning, since that dream."

Several townsfolk are standing to state for the record their support for Principal Sturm. Selectman Longstaff has excused himself, and his daughter has disappeared. Town Manager Alan Hitchcock has come down from the stage, his shiny bald head glowing as pink as his cheeks. "Detective," he whispers urgently to Nate, "get Hiram out of here before anything else happens. Or are you going to charge him with hate speech?"

Nate sighs. "Alan, come on. He's clearly upset. If Martha want to press charges—"

The manager is insistent. "I just want him out of here before anything else happens."

"Maybe I can help," comes a voice from behind Nate.

He turns around. It's a young guy, early twenties, good-looking, blue eyes, collegiate. He's wearing a University of Massachusetts sweatshirt.

"My name's Mark Miller," the young man says. "I'm a minister."

Alan Hitchcock blinks a couple of times. "Oh, so you're Mark Miller."

"Yes, sir," he says, and the men shake hands. "I was looking forward to meeting you. But I'd hoped under more pleasant circumstances." The young minister looks over at Hiram. "May I speak with him?"

"Go ahead," Hitchcock says.

Mark Miller steps in front of Nate and leans in to whisper a few words to Betty and Hiram. The townsfolk are now applauding the final speaker—Nate didn't see who it was, but he imagines it was somebody leading a rousing defense of Martha Sturm—and now Cliff is banging away again with his damn gavel. Nate looks over at the back of Hiram's head. He's responding to the young man. He's nodding.

"Who is he?" Nate asks Hitchcock.

But before the manager can answer, Hiram stands, Mark Miller resting a hand on his shoulder as he turns him to walk down the aisle.

Job and Nate slide back into their seats and Alan Hitchock returns to the stage. "Who *was* that guy?" Job asks.

"Damned if I know," Nate murmurs.

Cliff Claussen has called for a vote on the school budget. Everyone raises their hands. Volunteers walk up and down the aisles, counting hands. Nate hears Betty whisper, "Count us as two. Please. Tell Martha we both voted. *Both* of us."

Then she and her husband and Mark Miller—whoever he is—are out the back door.

* * *

Nate has a hard time paying attention to whatever is discussed next. He becomes aware of Monica's hand on his shoulder. "You okay?" she asks.

"That was not the Hiram I know," he tells her.

"I feel terrible for his wife," Monica says.

Nate cannot understand it. He's never known Hiram to have a prejudiced bone in his body. The Hiram he knew would never stand up like that and spit vitriol at a person. Hiram was a nice old man, everybody's favorite mailman. With a tip of his hat and a cheery "Good mornin'," Hiram greeted everybody in town. Everyone knew Martha Sturm was gay; she's never hidden it. And if she's carrying on with Kim Longstaff, that's her business. Kim's nineteen years old—a little young, maybe, but legal age. None of it would ever have mattered to Hiram before.

Just like the Kathy McKenzie he knew would never have acted the way she did. . . .

"What's his name?" Monica's asking, and Nate sees she's writing in her notebook. "Their last name is Silva, yes?"

"You can't write about that. You *can't.*"

"Nate, I'm sorry, but it's news. There are other reporters here. I'll *have* to mention it."

"*Really,* he's not himself," he pleads with her.

She makes a face as if to say it's beyond negotiation. Nate sighs. He looks over at Job, who just shrugs.

"All right, everyone," Cliff Claussen is saying into the microphone, his voice cracking a little. "We need to keep moving. Next item is the old church."

A ruffle of programs. Nate hears Clem clear his throat behind him. "Mr. Moderator," Clem calls.

"I recognize Mr. Clement Flagg," Claussen says.

"I'd like to go on record as saying something needs to be done and done soon," Clem says. "For nearly forty years that old place has sat vacant. It's got a bad history. And that history has caused every generation of Falls Church hooligans to vandalize it and cause commotion in the neighborhood. I represent a group of sixteen tenants who occupy the two Harborside Apartment buildings across the street from the church, and we are fed up with being awakened at night by vandals smashing windows and carrying on. For those of us who live there, the situation has become desperate. It has gotten *one hundred percent worse* in the last two weeks.''

Nate turns around, trying to see where Betty is, when Clem catches his eye. They exchange a small smile. Right now, he could give a shit about Clem and his complaints. He's worried that Hiram may have had a stroke. That's the only thing that could explain his behavior. He's read where strokes can sometimes go unnoticed at first, until the victim begins acting in unpredictable and uncharacteristic manners. Maybe he should suggest they drive Hiram up to the Outer Cape Health Clinic in Orleans. . . .

Selectwoman Mary Silva is speaking. She seems to have recovered her equilibrium. "Thank you, Mr. Moderator," she's saying, "and to respond to Mr. Flagg's complaint, I would agree that we are all tired of seeing a former house of God vandalized and desecrated. Perhaps our law enforcement officials might want to comment on the situation."

"Hey." Job nudges Nate. "That'd be you."

He sighs and raises his hand.

"I recognize Assistant Chief Nathaniel Tuck," Cliff says.

Nate stands. God, he hates public speaking. It's the worst part of the job. He feels his face flush and his throat goes dry. "Well, uh, Cliff," he begins, "I mean, Mr. Moderator, seeing as the chief isn't here, I guess it's left to me to comment." He shifts his weight, trying to get comfortable. "I can tell you that we are certainly aware of the problem. I've been over to check out the situation a number of times. Last January I did apprehend two youths and they were charged and referred to juvenile court for possession of marijuana and for trespassing. I know Officers Emerson, McDaniel and Sousa have also investigated numerous complaints there. In response to Clem's charge that the situation has become worse in recent weeks, I can only say we have investigated each complaint, but each time we have found no one on the property."

Nate clears his throat, tries to think if there's anything else he should say, figures there's not, so he sits down.

"Thank you, Detective Tuck. Mr. Flagg, you have more to add?"

Clem's back on his feet. "Yes, I do. I want to acknowledge

Nate and Job and Rusty and Dean for all their fine work. But I find it bizarre, to say the very least, that all of those vandals can get out of there so quickly. How is it that they're never caught? Last night—and I have half a dozen witnesses—it sounded as if a whole *congregation* was inside there—*singing*—at three o'clock in the morning!''

A dozen other hands fly up. Cliff Claussen sighs. ''I recognize Marge Duarte,'' he says.

Marge, a few rows behind her boss, stands to affirm Clem's story. So does her brother, the fisherman Manny Duarte. ''Those kids are blaspheming the Lord's songs,'' he says.

Recognized next is Yvette Duvalier. She's tanned and smiling, just back in town from winter in Fort Lauderdale, where she and husband, Chef Paul, own another eatery. They're reopening this week for the season, expecting another run of fabulous reviews and stellar clientele. The occasional Kennedy has frequently been spotted there, up from Hyannisport, as well as lots of folks with heavy Boston and New York accents.

Yvette still has a twinge of her native Montreal in her voice. She sports long red nails and short black hair, and Nate doesn't think he's ever seen her not smiling. Nate thinks it's a permanent condition of her facial muscles.

''As you all know,'' Yvette is saying, walking into the aisle to address the crowd as if she were Elizabeth Dole at a political convention, ''I'm a newcomer to this town. But for the past three years I have watched *such* an exciting transformation of its central commercial area. I have been *privileged* to be a part of that. I mean that. Truly *privileged*. I *adore* this town. Even though Paul and I don't live here in the winter, in our hearts we are year-rounders.''

She smiles, tilting her head, acknowledging Pidge Hitchcock and Pat Crawford with taps on the shoulder as she passes.

''Might I suggest that whatever we do with the old church, we look to the future of this town and consider our best hope for prosperity? I'm a dreamer. I admit that. But dreams can come true.'' She hiccups a little laugh. ''Let me try something here. Indulge me. A little exercise. Close your eyes and *go* with me on this.''

She closes her eyes and puts her red-tipped hands out in front of her, as if she were leading a class in transcendental meditiation. "A potpourri of shops in a renovated old church," she's saying, as if conjuring spirits in a seance. "Boutiques. Maybe a café on the first floor. We could call it the Old Church Mall. Oh, just think of it. All of the business opportunities we could have." She opens her eyes and glares into the crowd, suddenly galvanized. "Do you realize we do not have a *pottery shop* in this town? We don't have a crystal shop! And we have only *one* fine clothing boutique, our lovely Hornet, run by our own Selectman Pierce and his talented wife, Miranda."

Nate looks up at the stage as Cooper Pierce gives a little wave with his hand. The Pierces were, along with Job and Berniece, one of the few African American families in town. For Nate, they only went to show that blacks, given the opportunity, could be every bit as snobby as whites.

"But we need *so* much more," Yvette concludes. "Just think of what Falls Church could *become.*"

Nate grins to himself. Ah, yes, that's the rub, right there. The crux of all the tensions seething under the surface in this little town. Yvette Duvalier has one vision. Others, like those with their hands suddenly in the air, have quite another.

Yvette sits back down. Nate cranes his neck again, trying to see if Betty is gone for good. No sign of her. *There's got to be a break soon,* he figures. *I'll call her then.*

"I recognize Manny Duarte," Cliff intones.

"Mister Moderator, I need to respond to Mrs. Duvalier," Manny says. He pronounces "Duvalier" with the *r* at the end. "She asks us to imagine what Falls Church might become. Well, I can imagine it, because it's already become a different place from where I grew up. All these shops along Main Street, these fancy little boutiques she talks about—I remember when it was just the diner and a couple bait shops and the True Value. Now we got all these strange people coming in here every summer, changing the character of this here town. If anything, that old church should be turned into a youth center for our kids. Everybody's so concerned about tourists and summer folk, what about our kids? Mrs. Duvalier, you and your kind aren't helping—you're *ruining* this town!"

He sits down amid a chorus of cheers and applause.

Cliff Claussen is banging his gavel. "Mr. Duarte, *please* no addressing speakers directly! And I think we have had enough personal attacks tonight. That is not what Town Meeting is about.''

Nate feels Clem lean forward and tap his shoulder behind him. ''Then he doesn't remember the poor little Denny boys, the kids with AIDS, and little Victoria Kennelly,'' Clem whispers. ''Nobody seems to anymore. I'll tell you, Nate, that was far worse than tonight.''

There's scattered applause for Cliff's admonition. But something feels different. Nate's not sure, but he thinks that the applause is for show only. At least for some of the folks. He looks around at them. *How many of you feel exactly like Manny Duarte?* he thinks, looking at them. *In fact, how many of you feel like Hiram Silva?*

He watches them politely applauding. He likes most of these people. He likes their small-town ways, their eccentricities. But he's overcome suddenly with a sense of charade, as if the public faces they present to him and to each other are merely masks hiding a simmering brew of hatred, resentment and hostility. What's in their hearts?

Town Manager Hitchcock is speaking. ''We've heard some interesting suggestions for the old church here tonight. Let me add one more to the fire. The town has received a very generous offer to purchase the church, from a Reverend Mark Miller of Boston, with the intent of restoring it and preserving it as a house of worship. Earlier tonight I met Reverend Miller, but I don't know if he's still here. . . .''

''I am, sir,'' comes a voice. Nate turns. It's the guy in the university sweatshirt, the one who took Hiram away. Nate looks around to see if Hiram and Betty are with him, but they aren't. Mark Miller walks alone down the center aisle to the microphone.

''Nice butt,'' Monica observes.

Nate feels immediately and absurdly jealous.

Miller turns to face the crowd. He smiles. ''I'm glad for this opportunity to speak to you all tonight,'' he says warmly.

His eyes are bright blue; Nate can make them out even from where he sits. He seems far too young to be offering to buy the old church.

''A few weeks ago, I had the opportunity to come to town and look at the fine old structure of your First Church. I know some of its history, how Father John Fall brought a congregation down from Orleans to set up a community here in 1692. My heart broke seeing its disrepair. I was filled with God's spirit to somehow restore it as a place of worship, so I pooled my resources and made the offer to the town.'' He looks around the room, seeming to make eye contact with each and every one of them. When Nate feels his eyes, he pulls back a little, so intense is the supposed encounter.

Mark Miller is smiling. "Then tonight I've sat here listening to all of your suggestions, and I have been moved. It is clear to me that this community needs its old church more than ever. I want to do what you want—I want to create a place that serves you.'' He turns to face Yvette Duvalier. "I want to offer space to local artisans to offer their wares.'' He looks off toward Manny Duarte. "I want to create a place where our youth can come and find nurturance and support and a host of fun activities.'' He looks up at the Board of Selectmen. "And I want to showcase the history of this town and its people, and celebrate the lives of this community."

"My,'' Monica remarks, leaning over to Nate, "a savior in our midst."

Miller beams. "I want to do all those things that have been suggested here tonight—and more. I want to bring the church back as a gathering place for those of faith, a nondenominational house of worship, where all are welcome, where together we create a wellspring of goodwill for this community.'' He pauses. "Where we all can find the light of truth and wisdom."

He closes his eyes and clasps his hands together in front of him. "I will submit the details of my plan to the Development Board, should you vote to consider my offer. Thank you very much for listening to me. Thank you for embracing me into your wonderful community."

He walks down the center aisle, his eyes downcast. People watch him, turning their heads, some craning their necks as he passes. He sits in the very last row.

A few hands have gone up. Cliff Claussen peers into the crowd. "I recognize Catherine Santos, head librarian and curator of the Falls Church heritage museum,'' he says.

Catherine stands, a woman in her sixties, with a long gray braid down her back. "I just want to say I think Reverend

Miller has a wonderful idea," she says. "I, for one, would love to see the details of his plan."

"Hear, hear," comes several voices.

Nate looks behind him to see Miller's reaction. He sits there calmly, not smiling, not showing much of anything. Just sitting straight-backed in his chair, his hands clasped in his lap.

"I move that we vote to send his plan to the Development Committee," says Sam Drucker of the general store, waving his withered right hand that's missing two fingers. He's echoed by a chorus of seconds.

So they vote. It's nearly unanimous. Most, Nate figures, are voting to consider Miller's plan just to head Yvette Duvalier off at the pass, to squelch any ideas she might have for turning the old church into a mall. But Miller seems to have won the crowd's favor on his own, too; Nate can feel the buzz for the young minister in the folks around him.

"Aren't you voting?" Monica asks, noticing Nate hasn't raised his hand.

"Ah, it's clearly going to pass," he tells her. "Look at all the hands."

And it does. Just why he doesn't raise his hand, Nate's not sure; it just seems such a foregone conclusion. There's no need even to ask to see the hands of those opposed. Mark Miller beams his thanks and makes a great show of presenting a large manila envelope to the selectmen.

The rest of the evening drags on without incident. No more disruptions, no more outbursts, no more great flourishes of oratory. The police budget passes. People are yawning. As the night proceeds, more and more people slip out the back, more and more seats are left empty. Nate feels obliged to wait it out till the end. By midnight Monica tells him she has to leave so she can write up the story and file it for tomorrow's edition.

"But before I go," she whispers, "I want one promise from you, Detective."

"What's that?" he asks.

"That you agree to have dinner with me. And this time not just pizza."

He blushes. "Y-yeah," he stammers. "Yeah, okay." He manages a smile. "I'd like that."

She winks at him.

Friday, May 17, 12:01 A.M.

"Hello."

"Betty? Sorry to call so late, but I was concerned about Hiram."

"Oh, Nate. He's asleep, finally." She's whispering. She glances across the room toward the bed, where her husband snores deeply, his chest rising and falling.

"You know, Betty, I wonder if he should see a doctor."

She sighs. How tired she is. But for some reason she feels reluctant to crawl into bed beside Hiram. "You may be right, Nate," she says. "I think I'll suggest it in the morning. He was still too rattled tonight when we got back here to talk any sense to him."

"I'm thinking maybe he's had a small stroke. How else can you explain what happened? That wasn't him, Betty."

"No, it wasn't." She feels drained. "He hasn't been himself all day."

"Well, you get some rest, Betty. Come in late tomorrow if you want."

"Oh, no, no. I'll be there on time." She pauses. "But I'll tell you, Nate. That Reverend Miller sure helped calm Hiram down."

"Oh, yeah? You liked him?"

She hesitates. "Well, Hiram did. He listened to him very intently."

"But you, Betty? What did *you* think of him?"

She looks over again at the rise and fall of the sheet over her husband's sleeping form. "Oh, he was a very pleasant young man," she says. "But I just can't figure why Hiram listened to *him* and not to me. I can usually get Hiram to do anything, but he just wouldn't calm down for me. But Reverend Miller—well, he just talked to Hiram for a while, telling him to put his cares and worries aside, and Hiram did."

"Well, at least he's calm now, Betty. You can get some sleep."

She smiles uneasily. "Thanks for calling, Nate. You're a dear."

"Good night, Betty."

"Good night."

She hangs up the phone. She thinks for a moment she might watch television. *It's after midnight,* she scolds silently. *Get to sleep. Slip in beside your husband. He's not going to bite you.*

Betty drapes her robe over the back of a chair and sits down on the bed. Hiram wheezes and snorts. *This isn't his usual sleep,* she thinks. Hiram's always snored, but never like this.

She lies back against her pillows and pulls the sheet up to her chin. Maybe Nate's right. Maybe it was a stroke. A stroke would explain this. Maybe even explain that dream of his last night—that horrible, filthy nightmare Betty couldn't bring herself to describe to Nate and Rusty. It was Hiram's worst fear come to life.

"Everyone knows! Everyone knows!" poor Hiram had blathered to her this morning, his eyes wide and bloodshot, his body still trembling from his dream.

"Knows what, Hiram?"

That he's been impotent for twenty-five years. That's what the dream was about. Hiram was in a cottage on the beach, being forced to have sex with a roomful of stunningly attractive women, but he couldn't perform. When he looked around, the whole town was watching and laughing. And the man who had brought the women to Hiram had had worms in his mouth.

Betty shivers. What would the dream analysts she reads have to say about *that*? She turns her head on the pillow to look at her husband, her heart breaking. She listens to his deep, guttural snoring. Poor Hiram. Long ago she'd stopped feeling any need for sexual satisfaction, but for Hiram, his lack of sexual function has nevertheless been a shameful thing. He feels incomplete, and his shame has even kept him from asking his doctor for that new prescription Bob Dole's been selling on TV. In fact, whenever commercials come on hawking it, Hiram gets up and leaves the room.

She wants to reach over and stroke his hair, but he turns suddenly in his sleep, sounding even more like a buzz saw. "I love you, Hiram," Betty whispers in the dark.

It's a quiet night. She thanks God that the rain has finally stopped. The sky is clear, and moonlight fills her room. She hears the clock ticking, the hum of electricity in the house. She lays there with her eyes open, not thinking much of anything now, just watching and listening to the night.

I must be asleep, she thinks. *I must have fallen asleep.*

She's read about people who have conscious dreams—people who are aware when they're dreaming and can even affect the outcome of their nocturnal narratives—but this is the first time she's ever experienced it herself. She's standing out on Lighthouse Road, near the beach, near the cottage that Hiram had described from his dream. It's bright daylight, and the wind is strong.

I want to wake up, she thinks. She's read of people who can do that, too. If they don't like the way a dream is going, they can wake themselves up.

She's not sure why she wants to wake herself up. She just does. The dream feels foreboding, even if all she's doing is walking along the road and the wind is howling around her. It's a warm day. She can actually feel the sun's warmth. What a strange dream this is.

"Mama."

She's startled. She looks down. She hadn't realized she was walking with Rose. She's holding her daughter's hand.

"Sweetie," Betty says. "Oh, sweetie." She bends down to hug her daughter.

"But, Mama," Rose says, shrinking back from her embrace, "you let me die."

Betty freezes. *I want to wake up*, she thinks again. *Wake up. Wake up.*

"You let me die, Mama. You let them put my body in the ground, where it's cold."

Betty lets go of her daughter's hand. "You're in heaven, baby. With God."

"Not anymore, Mama." The little girl starts to cry. "Now I'm with *him*."

She points. A man approaches them on the road. A man dressed in dark clothes and a tall black top hat. "Rose, no, honey. You're not with him. I won't let him get you. I promise, baby."

"You promised me I'd get better," Rose snarls, *"but you let me die, Mama!"*

Her little girl's face is twisted in rage. Her pigtails fly out from her head. She begins clawing at her blue gingham dress. *"You let me die!"*

"Rose! Oh, baby!" Yes, Betty had promised Rose that she wouldn't die. When she was first diagnosed with leukemia, Rose had been terrified. She was only seven, but she was old enough to know that leukemia killed little children. She'd cried in Betty's arms, and Betty had promised to protect her, rocking her back and forth. But she hadn't, of course, and eleven months later, Rose was dead, dressed up pretty and placed in a little white coffin. Betty had lived with the guilt ever since.

The man has reached them. Betty's sobbing now as he drops one long skeletal arm around Rose's shoulders.

"Oh, go ahead, you devil!" Betty shrieks. "Open your mouth! I know what's there!"

He laughs. Worms slither from his lips. He bends down to kiss Rose.

"No!!!!!"

She wakes herself up.

Shaking uncontrollably, Betty manages to slide her legs off the side of the bed. Hiram is not disturbed. He goes on snoring that horrible rattle. Betty looks over at the clock but cannot read it, her body trembles so badly.

"Dear God," she whimpers, and forces herself to stand. Her

vision has changed: she sees her room almost as a negative image, a pulsating, flickering contrast of blacks and whites. She stumbles out into the hallway and steadies herself against the wall.

"You let me die!"

Rose's voice, still as crystal clear and as real as in the dream. Betty swears her daughter is in the house. In her old room . . .

"You let me die, Mama!"

Her voice *is* coming from her room. Betty looks down the hallway to Rose's door. It's ajar. There's a small golden light emanating from the room: the night-light Betty used to switch on every night in Rose's final weeks at home, just in case she woke up in the night and was frightened.

"Baby?"

"You let me die!"

Betty begins inching down the hallway, her back to the wall, her hands against it for support. She can barely walk, barely see, but she's drawn by the light. She moves agonizingly, her body still racked with convulsions.

She reaches her daughter's door.

"Mama!"

She peers inside. Rose is in the bed, just as she looked the day she died, drawn and shriveled.

Except worms are covering her entire body—slimy, slippery, glistening worms.

Betty screams.

She sits up in bed. *Dear God, I hadn't woken myself up at all*, she thinks.

Hiram's still snoring beside her. She's gasping for breath. She's terrified to move, not fully convinced she's awake. *If I step out of this bed, who knows what's waiting underneath to grab me?*

She knows what she needs to do.

The only thing she can do.

The only thing to stop the terror that surges through her mind and body.

She takes a deep breath, flings off the sheet and places her feet against the cold hardwood floor. She begins to shake again.

"The phone," she whispers.

I need to tell someone.

She runs from the bedroom, terrified something is following her. In the hallway she looks down at Rose's room. The door is closed. Is that how it was? Is that how they'd left it last? Or was she inside?

You let me die, Mama.

"No, baby," she murmurs, pushing herself into the kitchen.

The moonlight reveals the clock: it's nearly two A.M. Who can she call? Who would be awake?

The station. Rusty and Dean. They've got night duty this week.

She lifts the receiver with trembling hands. She hesitates for just a second, then punches in the numbers hard.

"Police," comes Rusty's voice.

She tries to speak but cannot.

"Police," Rusty says again.

"Rusty," she croaks.

"Betty! Is that you?"

"Yes. Rusty . . . listen to me."

"Are you all right? Is it Hiram?"

Her throat is dry and cracking. "I need to tell you . . . please. . . ."

"Tell me what, Betty? You want me to send Dean?"

"I had a dream," she rasps.

"A what?"

"A dream."

He pauses a moment. "Betty, are you okay?"

"Rusty, please. Please let me tell you the dream."

"Is this like Hiram's dream, Betty? What's going on?"

"I had a dream."

She's crying now. Something deep inside her knows that what she's about to do is wrong, but she's not sure why, and the need to tell Rusty is so overpowering, obliterating nearly everything else. She knows somehow that by telling him she'll feel better—but not for long. Not for long, and then it will get worse.

Still, relief would be so sweet right now. . . .

"Betty, you still there?"

"I had a dream," she says. "A dream about Rose . . ."

And so she tells him. He's quiet, listening, and when she's through, she tells him how silly she feels, then thanks him for being so patient. He asks again if he wants her to send Dean out, but she says no, that all she wants to do now is go back to sleep. He tells her that's what she needs, a good night's rest.

She hangs up the phone and sits down at the kitchen table. No, she doesn't want to go back to sleep, even though she's more tired than she has been in months. *Years.* As tired as she was when she was taking care of Rose, toward the end.

At least Rose's voice is gone from her head.

Betty Silva puts her face in her hands and begins to cry.

Friday, May 17, 9:18 A.M.

Her classroom was safe. Here Victoria never experienced any visions, saw no ghosts or dead little boys. Here she never felt any fear—not when she stood in front of her students talking about the French and Indian Wars, the Lewis and Clark expeditions or the Louisiana Purchase. She's sitting now at her desk, having foregone the gym this morning, just sitting here, smelling the chalk dust, the wood polish, the printer's ink of the textbooks. Tall windows fill the room with sun, turning the classroom into a kind of greenhouse. It's so warm in here that one wouldn't know that, outside, the third week of May still feels like the first week of March.

"Victoria, you're here early."

She looks up. Edna Danvers, one of her colleagues in the history department, is poking her head through the doorway.

Victoria smiles. "I'm just grading a few quizzes I never handed back."

Edna nods, crossing her arms and leaning against the door frame. "I have a few of those myself. So I've been wanting to ask you. How are you spending Memorial Day weekend? Fred and I have a cottage up in Maine. Not much, but big enough for us and the kids." She smiles. "And you, if you'd like to come."

Victoria smiles. Ever since Jonathan left, Edna's been very solicitous of Victoria's welfare, making sure she isn't alone on

Saturday night, inviting her to dinner or out to the movies. There's no question Victoria would enjoy a weekend away with Edna and her family, but she has other plans for Memorial Day. Indeed, for the whole summer.

"Thanks," she says, "but I'm going home."

Edna blinks. "Home? You mean, to Cape Cod?"

Victoria nods. "Falls Church."

Edna comes farther into the classroom. "I didn't think you had any family left there."

"I don't." She laughs. "Maybe I'm crazy. I just feel I have to go home this summer."

Home. She hasn't thought of Falls Church that way in years. What's *home* about it? Her family's gone; the house is gone.

"Well, we've got an extra cot for you at the cottage, if you change your mind." Edna looks at her kindly. "You just take care of yourself, okay?"

"I will, Edna. Thanks."

She watches as her friend disappears back into the hallway. *Take care of myself. That's exactly what I'm trying to do.*

Maybe, in fact, going back to Falls Church is the only way to take care of myself, once and for all.

After seeing the ghost yesterday and finding Petey's message on her bathroom mirror, Victoria had, at first, completely decompensated, once again becoming the terrified little girl she'd been fifteen years ago. Unable to teach class, she phoned in sick and called Caroline Jenks, her therapist, begging for an emergency appointment. Victoria could see the distress in Caroline's eyes, thinking that her patient had regressed, that years of therapeutic progress had gone down the tubes. *Now she's receiving messages written in ghostly fingerprints on her fogged-up mirror,* Caroline must have been thinking. *What next?*

But then something changed for Victoria. While sitting there in her therapist's office, it was as if a voice had spoken to her, clear as a bell.

You have to go home.

She had to go back to Falls Church. Things were happening there again. Bad things. How she knew this, she wasn't sure. But know it she did. She needed to go back to Falls Church and understand what was happening. That was the only way she'd ever understand her own ghosts.

And to start, she had to accept that those ghosts were not merely figments of her imagination.

"Look, Caroline," she said, feeling herself growing ever stronger as she gave words to her thoughts, "we're not going to get anywhere if you think it's not real."

"I didn't say it wasn't real, Victoria," Caroline said softly.

She laughed. "You believe that *I* believe it's real, isn't that right?"

Caroline shook her head in loving impatience. "How long have we been seeing each other, Victoria, and still you don't trust me?"

Victoria looked at her. Caroline's a dark-skinned woman with just a hint of a childhood Jamaican accent. She's soft-spoken, confident and never judgmental. In Caroline's office Victoria has always felt safe: like in her classroom, no ghosts intrude the sanctity of the space. It is a refuge: the bubbling of the fish aquarium, the soft pink light, the fragrance of burning sage in the air. When Victoria first moved to Boston, Caroline had given her the strength to believe she was stronger than her tormentors. She had made the ghost go away.

Until yesterday.

"He's real," Victoria whispered, desperate for Caroline to really, truly believe her.

"Who is he, Victoria?"

"I don't know."

"But whoever he is, you believe he killed Petey—and set fire to your house."

Victoria nodded.

Caroline hadn't responded. She just laced her fingers together in front of her, seeming to go deep within herself. As if she were fully realizing for the first time that Victoria's ghosts couldn't be made to go away through suggestion alone.

"I have to go back," Victoria told her quietly.

"Back where?"

"To Falls Church. I have to go back because it's happening again. I can feel it."

"What's happening again, Victoria?"

"The evil. The same evil that killed my family fourteen years ago."

Caroline eyed her carefully. "What would you do if you went back there?"

"I don't know." Victoria sighed. "I have no idea. I just know I have to go back."

"How long has it been since you were there? Not since shortly after the fire, right?"

Victoria nodded. "I was twelve."

"Do you have any friends, any family left there?"

"No. I haven't kept in touch with anyone. But there's a priest there, Father Roche. He was good to me after my parents died. I'd like to see him." She paused. "If he's still alive."

Caroline looked uncomfortable. "Victoria, I'm not trying to dissuade you. If you feel you need to go, then you should go. I'm just concerned that you need to think through all the feelings going back might bring up. Here you have friends. You have me."

Victoria was silent.

Caroline leaned forward in her chair, touching Victoria's knees. "How long would you stay in Falls Church?"

"I'm not sure. The summer, or part of it."

"And what would you do?"

She considered the question. "Walk around the town, I suppose. Visit my parents' grave . . ."

"And what else?"

Victoria steeled herself. "I'd go into the woods. I'd look for Petey."

"Because he told you to find him?"

"Yes."

Victoria had expected Caroline to try to talk her out of it. But instead the therapist stood and walked over to her desk, flipping through her Rolodex. "I want to give you the name of someone," she said. "I met him at a conference a few weeks ago. We had a long conversation about—well, about some interesting things. He seems like a good guy. He's in Falls Church, and he's someone you might want to talk to while you're there." She found the card and copied the name and number onto the back of one of her own cards.

Victoria looked down at the name: KIP HOBART. TRANSPERSONAL PSYCHOLOGY.

"Victoria," Caroline said, "you have become a very powerful woman. I've seen it happen, right here. I've watched as you blossomed. You became strong, independent, forthright. You have become a successful teacher, with the respect of your peers and your students. Whatever you find in Falls Church, whatever feelings it brings back—*you are stronger.* Remember that. You are stronger than what haunts you.''

Now Victoria feels, instead of terror, determination. *I am stronger than what haunts me*, she reminds herself, and believes it. *Something doesn't want me to go back to Falls Church. The same something that wanted me to leave, fourteen years ago. But it can't keep me away. The only way I can finally face what has haunted me for so long is to go back to Falls Church.*

"Ms. Kennelly?"

Victoria looks up from her desk. It's Michael Pilarski, one of her students.

"Michael," she says.

"Can I talk to you a minute?"

"Sure," she says, gesturing to the chair next to her desk. "Sit down."

Michael's a gangly kid. Like most of her students, he's a freshman—still a kid, really, away from home for the first time. Michael's blond, with a few acne scars across his cheeks, wearing his usual faded baggy blue jeans and a Smash Mouth T-shirt. On his feet he sports green Converse sneakers; slung over his shoulder is a ratty backpack seemingly made from an old American flag. His arms and legs are too long for his body, as if his torso hasn't yet grown enough to catch up with them. Michael's always been a little awkward in class, his voice cracking when Victoria calls on him, knocking over his books when he sits back down at his desk.

But she likes him. Michael's probably her favorite student.

At the beginning of the school year, he was vague and distracted. In one of their first teacher-student conferences, he'd admitted never being very good in history.

All those names and dates and battles—"I can't keep them straight," he lamented. "I'm no good at memorization." He was good in math, however, because there things followed logically, one after the other. One plus two equals three, and so on. Unlike history, there were no conditions, no exceptions that could change such basic facts.

Victoria had grinned at him. "That's precisely why I've never cared much for mathematics. It doesn't leave any room for imagination."

"And history does?" he asked.

"Yes, it does. Imagination is the only way to understand history There are *facts* of history, to be sure, but those facts mean one thing to one person and something else to another. Women experienced history differently from men. African Americans experienced it differently from whites. Poor people and children and Catholics and Jews—everybody relates to the so-called 'facts' of history differently. And facts don't mean anything if you can't visualize them—if you can't relate to them, make them relevant to your own life today."

He'd understood. He sat there across from her beaming. He had gotten her point.

From then on, Michael has excelled. Victoria's teaching of American History 101 is unconventionial; she barely uses the text and pays very little attention to routine dates and battles. Rather, she instructs her students to find original artifacts: probate records, land deeds, household inventories, diaries. Boston is the perfect site for such exploration, with records dating back to the colonial era. For Victoria, the study of history only matters if the *people* of history could be reborn as living, breathing individuals.

That is what makes Victoria's class so different from the other 101s. Victoria's class isn't about memorization: it is about learning what families ate for breakfast during the Revolutionary War period, how teeth were pulled, how privacy in the toilet was in many ways a twentieth-century invention. Students learn how crops were grown, how children were treated, how the holidays were celebrated. For their final papers, Victoria allows her students to choose topics without preapproval from her. Of course, there are parameters: the project has to be 100 percent original research, drawn from the kinds of sources they'd been using all year. No encyclopedias, no Web searches. Most of the kids have come to her after class, needing help in nailing down a precise topic, so she has a pretty good idea of what they'll be turning in to her. But alone among them, Michael hasn't come for any assistance. He's seemed very assured, even a bit cocky, about whatever it was he has chosen.

She looks at him and smiles. "Finally need some help on that final paper?"

"Actually, no." He grins, reaching down into his bag. "It's done."

"Well, I'm impressed. You still have a couple more days."

He holds his report in his hands, twenty or so pages stapled together in the upper left corner. "You really taught an awesome class, Ms. Kennelly."

She smiles. "Thank you, Michael. That means a lot. Is that what you came in early to tell me?"

He blushes a little. "Well, kind of."

"Thank you, Michael."

He blushes. "I'm from the Cape, too," he tells her. "Dennisport. That's what gave me the idea for my paper." He pushes it forward on her desk.

She glances down at the title. Centered neatly on the page, it reads:

Fire and Brimstone:
The Story of Father John Fall
and the Founding of Falls Church, Massachusetts

"Michael," Victoria says, lifting the report. Suddenly her hands feel a little shaky and she sets the report back down on her desk. "Wow. This is—"

"He left a journal," Michael says. "I found it in the state archives. Did you know there was a witchcraft trial in Falls Church?"

She blinks a few times. "No," she says. "No, I didn't."

"Yeah, like back in 1690. I don't remember the exact date. Dates aren't what matter so much, right? It was the action, what was going on. Just like in Salem. Man, it was pretty awesome reading that stuff. This Father Fall guy—he was like breathing fire all the time, casting people to hell. That's why he left Orleans. He considered them all sinners. So he set up his own congregation—Falls Church—hence the town name."

She places her hands on top of the report. It feels warm.

Uncommonly warm. *Must be from being in the boy's backpack,* Victoria assures herself.

"Well," she says, not understanding why her throat has suddenly gone so dry, "thank you, Michael. I—I can't wait to read it."

He smiles. "This class has meant a lot to me. It's been the best class I've ever had. And you . . ." He chokes up a little. "You're just the best," he tells her.

She melts. "Oh, Michael," she says. "That's so nice to hear."

But suddenly it's not Michael—not an appreciative, fawning student—sitting beside her. Rather—it's a corpse—a rotting *thing*—a demon in black—

Dear God!

With worms—*maggots*—moving through its skeletal teeth! Victoria screams.

The thing stands from its chair, reaching out for her.

She screams again.

"Ms. Kennelly?"

Victoria blinks.

Michael is looking oddly at her.

"You seemed to zone out there on me," he says.

"I'm sorry. I—I just—"

"No problem," he says, standing. "I do it all the time." He grins. "Though not in this class."

She tries to smile, but her heart is still racing in her ears.

He stands, slinging his backpack over his shoulder. "Well, have a good summer, Ms. Kennelly."

"Yes," she manages to say. "You too, Michael."

When he's gone, she looks down again at his report. She places her hands once more upon it. Still warm. Hot, even.

"I do not like thee, Father Fall," she whispers.

An old childhood rhyme suddenly and inexplicably remembered.

"The reason why I can't recall."

As she speaks, cold terror creeps from her head down to her fingertips.

"But this I know, for one and all—"

Her voice catches in her throat.

"I do not like thee, Father Fall."

Friday, May 17, 11:45 A.M.

Catherine Santos, town librarian and curator of the Falls Church Heritage Museum, is a lefty from way back. When she was sixteen, she wrote a letter to President Eisenhower asking him to end Senator Joseph McCarthy's investigations. Her father, a fisherman from Portugal who could speak hardly any English at all, was appalled at her hubris, but Catherine just found the whole McCarthy proceedings onerous. Un-American, in fact. Two weeks later, she received a form letter back from the president, promising her that every American had the right to believe what they chose, but offering no word against McCarthy. It was enough to galvanize the pretty young teenager into a lifetime of activism for social causes.

Now Catherine Santos is in her midsixties. She's never married; her life partner has been Falls Church itself. In the 1960s she rallied the antiwar protests, in the '70s she organized the support for the Equal Rights Amendment, and in the '80s she became passionate in the nuclear-freeze movement. The citizens of the little town have long since become used to seeing Catherine on the Town Green, in her checkered poncho and long gray braid, holding up signs condemning the sale of arms to the Contras or the bombing of Iraq. "That's just Catherine," they say to each other, honking and waving if they disagree with her politics.

For the past decade, however, Catherine's slowed down

somewhat, devoting her energies to the library and museum. But that doesn't mean her commitment to causes has waned. Right now, she's assembling the Gay History Month exhibit at the library. She makes sure she acknowledges all the various theme months: Black History in February, Women's History in March, and now Gay History for June. She think it's especially important this year, after the way Hiram Silva attacked poor Martha Sturm at Town Meeting. Catherine still can't get over that. Hiram was the sweetest man, without any hint of prejudice. Well, who knows what lurks in the hearts of humankind?

Who had said that? Suddenly she remembers a young man—from long ago—a man who had spoken words of love but, in reality, had been training them to hate—

She can see his face but forces it away. Instead, her mind suddenly recalls another Town Meeting. The one where everyone ganged up on those poor little boys with AIDS. Everyone had been acting so *crazy* then, Catherine thinks, until the Kennelly girl stood up and put them all in their place. Catherine Santos shivers.

"I still cannot get over Hiram Silva the other night," she says to her assistant, Helen Twelvetrees, another unmarried lady of middle years. "That was *just* not like him."

Helen shrugs. Catherine knows Helen is not nearly so liberal as she is: maybe Helen had thought the same thing as Hiram, deep down. And, come to think of it, hadn't Helen and her mother been part of that group that wanted to expel the little boys with AIDS some fourteen years ago? What was the name of that group? Why is it so hard to remember some things?

Concerned Citizens something. And the woman who ran it? Grace West—yes, that's it. Catherine pauses, scrunching up her face as she peers out of her office into the reading room of the library. Why does it take such effort to remember? Is her memory failing her? Or has she just pushed all of it so far from her thoughts, so troubling had it all been, that she now has trouble retrieving it?

But Catherine Santos is known for her encyclopedic memory. That's why she's made such a terrific librarian and town historian. She can practically recite the names of every family who's lived on every street in Falls Church over the past half century.

So why is it that particular episodes of the town's history feel as if she's *sleepwalked* her way through them?

She opens up a poster sent to her from the Human Rights Campaign. It's Harvey Milk, slain San Francisco supervisor and one of the first openly gay politicians in American history. She sees Helen exhale uncomfortably.

"Whatever happened to Grace West?" Catherine asks suddenly. "The woman who ran that group in the '80s? I remember you were a member."

Helen bristles. "Only because my mother insisted I join. I don't know what happened to Grace West. She moved out of town soon after . . ."

Helen's voice trails off.

"Soon after what?" Catherine asks. "Why is it so hard to remember?"

Helen sighs. "Soon after the fire."

"Yes," Catherine says. "The fire at the Kennelly house. That poor family. All killed except—" The memory floods back at her. "Except the younger daughter. The one who spoke out at Town Meeting."

Helen looks up at her with pained eyes. "Why are you bringing all this up, Catherine?"

Catherine sits down. "I'm not sure. I've just been trying to remember all of it." She looks at Helen. "And the Kennelly girl—she was with Petey McKay when he disappeared in the woods, wasn't she?"

Helen nods. "I don't like thinking about all that. It was a bad time."

"Do you sometimes have trouble remembering it even happened?"

"I dare say I'd never have thought of it if you hadn't brought it up."

So it isn't just me who struggles with the memories. Why are their minds so clouded? Other painful moments in town history aren't nearly so blocked: the shark attack in 1974, the resignation of Town Manager Hinkle in a corruption scandal in 1984. Why is it just certain episodes?

Suddenly Catherine's thinking of Dexter. Whenever she thinks of Dexter, she feels both a terrible sadness and a horrible guilt. Sadness because she had loved him and had wanted to marry him, and Dexter was dead. But guilt, too, because she so rarely remembered him, so infrequently mourned his passing. The man she loved. The only man she had ever loved.

I can't remember that time, either, Catherine realizes. The bad months in 1967, when she and Dexter had joined that group—what was it called again?—the antiwar group that met at the old church. Catherine was older than most of the group's hippie members; indeed, Dexter had been nearly ten years younger than she was, but they had fallen in love. The memory hits Catherine like a brick wall crumbling down on top of her. Why was Dexter so hard to remember?

Because that girl was killed—"Prissy Goo," the kids call her. The police suspected Dexter. Suspected all of them in that group of hippies and counterculture lovers in the old church. They chased Dexter down, didn't they? Catherine tries to remember. *Yes, they chased him down and shot him—right between the eyes.*

"Oh, dear God," Catherine mutters, covering her face with her hands.

"Catherine," Helen says. "Are you all right?"

"Yes, I'm fine." She stands, letting the memories slip back into oblivion, where they belong. She carries the Gay History Month materials over to a table in the reading room and begins setting them up. By the time she's finished, she's no longer thinking about Dexter or Prissy Goo or the little boys with AIDS. She doesn't even remember she had been thinking of them.

That's when a young man walks into the library. Catherine watches as he speaks quietly with Helen. It's that young minister, the one who wants to buy the old church.

"Hello," he says as Catherine approaches. "I'm Mark Miller. I'm going around town introducing myself."

"Yes," Catherine says, shaking his hand. "I remember you from Town Meeting."

He smiles. A handsome young man. *Not unlike Dexter,* Catherine thinks, stung by the sudden reemergence of her lover in her thoughts. Mark Miller is a little older than Dexter had been, but not by much. Midtwenties, most likely. A thick crop of wavy brown hair. Gentle blue eyes. A cleft in his chin. Really quite the handsome man.

"I remember you, too, Miss Santos," he says. "How you very admirably stood up and affirmed the school principal. I was very impressed by that."

"Well, I had to say something after what Hiram—" She recalls that Hiram was escorted out by this young man. "I saw you counseling him. Is he all right? You know, that was not at all like him."

Mark Miller sighs. "Yes, I know. The poor man. I've been stopping by every day to see him. I think he's doing much better now."

"Poor man. But poor Martha, too."

"Of course."

Catherine tries to smile. "Have you gotten any sense whether the selectmen will accept your offer on the old church?"

He smiles. "I'm on my way to meet with Marcella Stein now. I gather she has some questions. I think most of the others are excited by my plan."

"The church will need a lot of fixing up and repair," she tells him.

"I'm up for it," he responds.

Catherine considers him. Yes, she believes he is. She can see the fire of youth in his eyes. So much like Dexter. So very much like Dexter. And looking into Mark Miller's eyes, remembering Dexter is no longer difficult or painful for Catherine Santos. No, not difficult or painful at all. In fact, it's the easiest, most pleasurable thing in the world.

12:15 P.M.

In a small cottage named Petunia on the sandy bluff of Lighthouse Beach, two people are making very passionate love. Scattered haphazardly on the old sun-dried wooden floor are the remnants of their discarded clothing: a brassiere, a string of pearls, a pair of Gucci low-heeled shoes, dirty dungarees and work boots covered in mud and smelling of fish.

"Oh, *yes*," moans Laura Millay. "Give it to me."

Claudio Sousa thrusts harder, deeper. "Baby," he breathes, getting close.

Her nails spike his shoulder blades. "Drive it home, fucker. Drive it *home!*"

"Ahhhh—*yes!*" he exclaims, triumphant. "Yes! *Fuck, yes!*"

"*Yes!*" she echoes. "Oh, baby, you are the fucking *king!*"

He becomes aware of how loud they've been. He laughs a little, rolls off her, panting.

Behind them the waves crash against the shore. Sunlight fills the little room.

"Oh, Claudio," Laura moans, coming down from her orgasm. She turns her head to face him on the pillow. They kiss.

In her mind she's seeing the faces of the ladies in town: Yvette Duvalier and Pat Crawford and Miranda Pierce, and all the others. *They think it's Roger in here with me. They think it's my husband I meet here for a little afternoon delight. Right now, they're driving by, I'm sure, seeing my car parked out in front of the cottage, and they steam with jealousy. None of them have such erotic afternoon escapades with their husbands.*

Laura doesn't, either, of course, but she likes that people *think* she does. They'll never know that Roger is—as always—cloistered in his office on the second floor of the bank, not taking calls, not seeing anyone, hunched over spreadsheets and stock market reports. Laura *has* to tell people it's Roger in here with her, or else the gossip will start when her car is spotted out in front of the cottage nearly every afternoon. It's one of the cottages for which she secures rentals in her job as an agent for Seaside Realty. *If people think I'm in here with Roger, no one will knock, no one will bother. They might see Claudio's boat down the beach, but so what: he's a fisherman, isn't he?*

That part delights Laura more than anything else. Claudio Sousa is a *fisherman:* dirty, smelly, rough-skinned. Falls Church native Portuguese. His hands are liked old cracked baseball mitts, his face the color and texture of his work boots. But he's a stud: in twenty minutes he'll be ready to go again.

Just twenty-eight, too, another aspect of the whole affair that turns Laura on. Twenty-eight to her thirty-six—and Roger's fifty. Claudio certainly doesn't mix with their crowd; he doesn't live in one of the elegant new homes along Cliff Heights, where Laura and Roger—and Yvette and Paul Duvalier, and Pat and Sargent Crawford, and Cooper and Miranda Pierce—make their comfortable abodes. No, Claudio lives in a two-room apartment

on Grand Avenue, down near the pier. He spends his evenings
drinking at Dicky's Bar. There is grime beneath his fingernails;
Laura has never seen him freshly shaven.

Roger, of course, is *always* shaven, clean and close, smelling
of a sweet aftershave. His hands are soft, his neckties always
perfectly knotted, thrust forward cockily with a collar bar. He
wears starched shirts and drinks martinis. He despises the fishing
community, saying they stand in the way of progress. Too many
old families refuse to sell their properties—which means Roger
won't get the mortgages of condo conversions.

Claudio isn't a homeowner, but he does come from an old
Falls Church family that was. The Sousa family practically
owns the whole Wharf Block, prime real estate at the tip of
the town on the beach of Nantucket Sound. Claudio's grandparents still live in the old family homestead, a fabulous Victo-
rian begging for renovation. Claudio's father runs the marine-
supply store in town, his brother is town accountant, and cousins
include the Sousas and Duartes who run the bakery and the
fish market and the famous Clam Shack seasonal restaurant,
not to mention every citizen's favorite deputy, the hapless Dean
Sousa.

Stretched out now beside Claudio in the noonday sun, Laura
smiles as she plays with his hair, loving the fact that Roger
would be horrified by her consorting with such folk. She thrills
to the idea that anyone could come walking up the beach, look
through the windows and see them here. She revels in the
thought, actually: who might it be? Pidge Hitchcock? Pat Crawford? She giggles, writhing on the bed.

"You ought to put some clothes on," Claudio tells her,
swinging his legs off the side of the bed and snatching his
boxers off the floor.

"Why? It's glorious to lie naked in the sun."

He snorts. "Somebody might see," he says, pulling on his
underwear.

Laura smirks. "You didn't care about that a moment ago
when you had your rod stuck up my hole."

He grimaces at her. "You have a mouth worse than any
fisherman I know."

She laughs. "All my life I've had to be such a good girl.
I'm tired of being a good girl."

Claudio struggles into his tight, soiled T-shirt. His hairy biceps strain against the sleeves. "So then give Roger the heave-ho and move in with me."

She laughs. A tinkly, giddy kind of sound. "Oh, Claudio, you nincompoop. I have *children*. I have to think of them."

She did have children: three to be exact. David, Amy and Nora—thirteen, ten and six. All towheads like their mother. Laura thanks God every day they didn't take after their father, with his pinched little eyes and gray complexion.

"Think of *me* once in a while," Claudio snaps. He leans over toward her suddenly, his big brown eyes wide. "Maybe I want more than just an afternoon fuck."

"Oh, poor baby," she says, reaching up and encircling his neck with her arms.

He pushes her away and stands up. "Don't make fun of me. You can't do that. I love you, Laura. I've told you. I want to marry you."

Laura sighs. She supposes she'd better get dressed now. Claudio seems on the edge of one of his scenes. She reaches for her bra, but suddenly Claudio's bare foot stamps down upon it. She looks up at him slowly.

He's glaring down at her. "What if I said I wouldn't meet you anymore?" he asks.

She makes a sound in exasperation. "Give me my bra, Claudio," she tells him.

He kicks it, storming off to the other side of the room.

She gets dressed. She slithers on her stockings, rehooks her pearls around her neck. "Don't be mad, sweetheart," she purrs, sidling up next to her lover. He's still just in his boxers and T-shirt. "You know I love you, too."

"Oh, Laura," he says, breaking. He kisses her hard. Puts his hands under her armpits and pulls her up to him. She can taste herself on his lips.

"Claudio, Claudio," she says, catching her breath, gently extricating herself from him. "Don't get me going all over again, as much as I'd like it. I do have a job, you know. I have to show a couple of houses before the kids get home from school."

His eyes won't let go of her. "What happens when they're

out for summer vacation, huh? When am I going to see you then?''

She smiles. "We'll find a way, sweetie. Don't worry."

She reaches up and gives him a quick kiss on the lips. He opens his mouth as if wanting more, but she's quick to slip out the door.

"Toodles," she chirps, giving him a little wave. He stands in the screen door watching her.

Maybe it's time to find someone else, Laura's thinking as she slides into the seat of her Saab and starts the ignition. *Claudio's getting too attached. I can't have that.*

Hands suddenly grip her car door and she gasps. Someone's standing there. A man.

She looks up through her car window.

"Mrs. Millay?"

She doesn't respond.

"I'm Mark Miller."

Laura Millay looks up into the bluest eyes of any man she's ever seen. She feels her face redden, the warmth spreading from her cheeks down to her neck. She remembers his face: he's the minister from Town Meeting, the one who wants to buy the old church. What had he seen? How long had he been out here?

"Mrs. Millay," he says, "I was just walking by and recognized you. Someone pointed you out to me at Town Hall the other night. I'm looking for a realtor."

"Oh?" She relaxes, just a little. "Well, Reverend Miller, if it's about the old church, I represent the seller, not the buyer."

"No, no, not the church." He grins. "I'm looking for a place to live. I can't stay in a guesthouse forever. Perhaps you know of some year-round rentals?"

"Some." She looks up into his eyes. *What a handsome man. Young, but I like them young.* "Most units rent seasonally in this town," she says, "but there may be a few."

"Then I'll stop by your office," he tells her.

"Please." Laura Millay graces him with a dazzling smile. "Come by. I'd *love* to talk with you further."

2:00 P.M.

"Where the fuck is that flighty Laura Millay?" groans her boss over at Seaside Realty.

Sargent Crawford is a having a bad day. He's told his secretary to hold all calls for a half an hour. He's tired, he has a headache, and he hasn't eaten lunch. All morning he's been showing summer rentals to folks who are on a crazy last-minute rush to find something before Memorial Day. He's tried calling Laura several times on her cell phone to get over here to the office and give him a hand—but he keeps getting her voice mail.

"Damn woman," he grouses. Probably off on one of those afternoon rendezvous with her husband.

As if Sargent had the time—or the inclination—to fool around with Pat like that. Sargent has half a mind to drop Laura; she's probably the most unreliable agent he's ever hired. But with Laura comes Roger, and Roger knows how to give Sargent's clients a mortgage deal that looks sweet on paper but, in reality, kicks back a hefty sum to both banker and realtor. No, Sargent doesn't want to lose that link. So he has to put up with Laura for now.

And besides, he should complain? Sure, he's worked his ass off all morning, but he's got an awful lot of checks to deposit at the bank. He pats them with his hand, grinning. Sitting at his desk behind his closed door, Sargent Crawford rubs his temples. *Yes, Dad would be pleased to see how successful I've made our little real estate business.*

Which reminds him—he hasn't yet had a chance to read that newspaper account in the *Cape Cod Times* about the town. He has a stack of papers on his desk that he keeps meaning to read but never seems to find the time. All he can manage each day is to check to see that his ads appear correctly. But it was rare for the *Times* to do a piece on Falls Church. Sometimes Sargent feels the rest of the Cape forgets that they're here.

Still rubbing his temples, he pulls open his drawer and unwraps the egg salad sandwich Pat made for him this morning. It's loaded with paprika, the way he likes it. Good old Pat. She knows all his tastes. He might not want to mount her in the middle of the day the way Roger Millay seems to want to do with Laura, but he appreciates his wife nonetheless. Good old Pat.

He takes a bite and there's a soft rap on his door.

"What is it?" he barks.

"I'm sorry, Sargent," his secretary, Cassie, says, peeking around the door. "But it's your wife on the phone."

He picks up his extension. "Pat, sweetheart," he says.

"Sargent, dear, I know how busy you are, but I've just got my hands full here."

"Is the McKenzie brat still misbehaving?" After Kathy's arrest, the boy was brought to their house.

"Oh, darling, you don't even *know*. He's smashed several pieces of china. He took a red crayon and wrote *all* over the wall. He even wrote—a *curse* word, Sargent. A filthy word I can't even bring myself to tell you. I just can't . . ." Her voice trails off, and Sargent can tell she's begun to cry.

"Sweetheart, take it easy," he soothes.

"Josh has always been a very good boy before. I don't know what's come over him. I just called down to the police station and Nate told me they're keeping Kathy for observation. They may even send her down to Cape Cod Hospital in Hyannis."

"No luck finding the grandfather?"

Pat composes herself. "He must have a nonpublished number. I can't find any Edward McKenzie in Orleans."

Sargent sighs. "Then we've got to call Family Services. We can't keep the kid forever. He's clearly acting out because his mother's abandoned him."

"I've called the school social worker—"

Sargent growls. "That fat-ass Marcella Stein."

"Yes, and she said she'd contact Family Services. But I can't take any more of this, Sargent! I want him out of here, *and I don't care if he hears me say it!*"

Sargent has a vision of the boy standing beside Pat, looking up at her with those big soulful eyes of his. Brat or not, Josh is still just a little boy, and a deeply troubled one at that. "Easy, Pat, easy," he tells her. "Don't get him more upset."

Her voice trembles. "Will you pick the kids up from school today? I can't bear it."

"Yes," he agrees, although he has a full schedule for the

afternoon. He'll just have to find a way. "Okay, Pat. Just find a place to chill out."

"With this monster lurking around? I doubt it. Come home as soon as you can, Sargent."

She hangs up.

Sargent makes a face, then replaces the receiver. "Sheesh," he says. His headache throbs even more fiercely than before.

Poor Pat. *I guess this is what happens when you try to be good neighbors,* he thinks. He takes another bite of his egg salad sandwich, picking up the newspaper again. The headline reads:

FALLS CHURCH STRUGGLES WITH GROWING PAINS

That's for damn sure, he thinks. He pops the top of a can of diet Coke and takes a swig. It burns down his throat, the way he likes it.

"Monica Paul," he reads aloud, noting the byline. Why hadn't she called *him* for a quote?

> *The town of Falls Church numbers just under a thousand souls from October to April. Perched along the rim of a sandy offshoot of the Cape, it was once a sleepy little fishing village, populated by hardy Yanks and Portuguese. In days gone by, tourists would prefer the trendier destinations of Dennisport or Chatham or Provincetown, bypassing Falls Church completely. The village was too isolated, almost an island to itself. Indeed, there's still only one road into town, a two-lane divided highway running along a causeway from Chatham.*
>
> *But things are changing. With the fishing industry hit hard a decade ago by state regulations, the native-born population has begun to drop precariously. Most sons no longer following their fathers out to sea, heading instead to college and out of Falls Church, many moving off-Cape entirely. Parents worry that the local school system might be shut down, merged with other regional schools.*

"Inevitable destiny," Sargent murmurs. He's just glad his own kids will probably make it through the school system before it comes apart.

> *The annual Town Meeting last night was a hotbed of roiling viewpoints on just what constitutes the best path for the future of Falls Church. For the past few years the town has increasingly gone after the tourist dollar. After all, it's worked elsewhere on the Cape; why not here? Accordingly, trendy little shops have sprung up along Main Street, most of which close for the winter. Homes that have been in families for generations are being sold and converted to condominiums. These, too, are often only occupied during the high season.*
>
> *Those who want Falls Church to remain the close little village they knew are concerned about what they call a "conquest" by outsiders. They say a few are getting rich and longtime residents are being squeezed out. These passions were evident at Town Meeting, when an outburst disrupted proceedings . . .*

"Yeah, yeah, yeah," Sargent says, pushing the paper aside. He's tired of hearing about Hiram Silva's outburst. He has no patience for any of it. These self-righteous native-born folks squawking about being squeezed out! *Give me a fucking break,* Sargent thinks. Okay, so maybe some of them feel they were gypped, but he can name half a dozen families for whom he's sold properties way over market value. Off-Cape, they'd maybe have gotten a third of what they got here. They took the money and bought themselves nice homes up in Orleans or Brewster. What do they have to complain about?

Okay, so many of the old neighborhoods are dark most of the year; the old blocks no longer resound with the laughter of children, the yapping of dogs, the camaraderie of neighbors. Sure, it's too bad—but that's the way it is. *Should we just wither up and die? Should we not try to adapt?* The house on Center Street where Sargent himself had been born and raised is now a duplex condo owned by a couple of wealthy New Yorkers. Sure, it's sad to see it closed up and dark from October to May, but the sale has allowed Sargent to build a castle for himself on Cliff Heights. Better to sell and bring in the tourists than let the town slip into decay.

Yvette Duvalier, for all her annoying airs, was right: Falls Church needs to open up as many swank boutiques and restaurants as it can if it hopes to compete with places like Chatham and Provincetown. *We've got to find a way to make people get off Route 6 and head down here,* Sargent tells anyone who listens. *Nobody passes through Falls Church; it's the last stop on a lonely road.*

Sargent took over his father's real estate business when he was twenty-seven. Sargent senior dropped dead of a heart attack while giving a speech on the Town Green on Veterans Day, 1994. Son was standing behind father, both of them emblazoned in their uniforms: Sargent senior had fought in Korea; Junior had served in the Gulf War. Sargent watched as his old man went down, like a great old oak felled by the lumberjack's saw, and at first he could do nothing. He just stood there, a blubbering, trembling soldier. A girl from the audience, a teenager with braids and freckles, jumped up on the podium and attempted some clumsy CPR. But it was too late: Sargent Crawford Sr. died right there in front of 106 people, and his son just stood there with his hands in his hair.

Since then, Sargent has worked hard to foster a more forceful image in town. Convincing the old fishing families to sell off their homesteads had been difficult at first; but as Falls Church spruced up its Main Street, opened up its beaches and hung out the welcome banner for more and more tourists, property values surged. Now weatherworn fishermen, once worried about surviving, can retire early by selling their homes to rich Bostonians and New Yorkers.

"You've got to move with the times," Sargent mutters to himself, finishing his egg salad, "or they'll move right past you."

He wipes his mouth and looks at his watch. He has an appointment in five minutes. If he hurries, shows them the old Duarte place on the beach and makes the deal, he can swing by the school afterward and pick up the kids.

He stands. *Damn this headache.* He rubs his temples again.

That's when he has the heart attack. It throws him back against his desk as if he's been pushed. He clutches his chest.

He loses his footing, falling into his chair, crashing to the floor. He spits up his egg salad all over his shirt. Then Sargent Crawford lies still.

3:00 P.M.

"Thank you for coming by, Reverend Miller."

Marcella Stein stands aside so he can enter. She's wearing the same blue jeans she wore at Town Meeting, some generic brand that showcases her enormous ass.

"No, thank *you*, Ms. Stein. I'm so pleased you asked me to meet with you."

She gestures for him to sit on the couch. Her house on Beach Road is small, but recently renovated and very modern. Lots of exposed brick and spun glass.

"May I get you something to drink?" she offers.

"A glass of water would be nice," Mark Miller says. "I walked out here on foot. I'm kind of thirsty."

"Don't you have a car?" she asks, moving into the kitchen.

"Yes," he calls. "But it's such a nice day, I thought I'd walk. I like learning the layout of the town."

She returns with a glass of water, a couple of ice cubes tinkling inside. "Falls Church is never so small as it first appears."

He takes a sip, looking at her over the glass. "Yes, it can be quite deceiving, can't it?"

She sits down opposite him in a large overstuffed chair. The room is filled with midafternoon sunlight. She's not an unattractive woman, just oddly proportioned. Nice teeth, dark brown eyes, brown hair dyed with a hint of red cut in a pageboy style. But her arms are short, her hips are wide, and her thighs resemble the sandbags used to prevent the town dikes from flooding over during hurricanes.

She smiles. "The reason I wanted to meet with you personally, Reverend Miller, is that I have some concerns about your plan to buy the old church."

He smiles back at her. "Well, I hope I can allay them, as I certainly need your vote among the selectmen."

"I'll be frank, Reverend," she says, settling back into her chair. "Even without my vote your offer will likely be approved.

You seem to have won over everybody else. It's quite a generous offer. I didn't know ministers made such good pay."

His smile doesn't falter. "It's family money, Ms. Stein. I admit that's how I'm able to make an offer to the town."

"I was going over your letter," she says, barely waiting for him to continue. "You say you graduated from divinity school just a year ago. So you've never led a congregation on your own."

He keeps smiling at her. "I think I make up with enthusiasm and dedication what I lack in experience."

"Maybe so." She crosses her arms and narrows her eyes at him. "Where did you get your degree?"

He doesn't miss a beat. "Yale Divinity School."

She makes a little laugh. "Well, no one can say you weren't educated by the best." She leans back in her chair. "I see you call yourself nondenominational."

"Yes, ma'am."

"Meaning what?"

"That I welcome people of all faiths, and no faith, to my church."

Her eyes narrow still further. "Statements like that trouble me, Reverend Miller. Even the Universalist-Unitarians, for all their good intentions, aren't really nondenominational. They can't disguise their Christian origin, and neither can you."

For the first time his smile fades. "I'm afraid I don't understand."

She studies him. "I have no prejudices, Reverend, but as one of the few Jews in a town unrelentingly Christian, I have many suspicions. Your proposal, as you have outlined it to the selectmen, is to create a kind of community center for the town. Yet it will still be a place of worship. My concern is the type of worship you will be leading. Too often when people say nondenominational, they mean generically Christian."

"This will be a faith-based center, Ms. Stein. We come together as a community, and together we will find a common place for faith."

She locks her eyes on him. "I trust that you will recognize that faith can come in many varieties, and not only from a Judeo-Christian perspective. There is a Muslim family in town. And pagans—"

"Pagans in Falls Church?" He smiles. "How exciting."

She says nothing, just keeps looking at him intently.

"Ms. Stein," he says, breaking the stalemate, "I'm hoping to create a vibrant, eclectic space that becomes whatever its congregation wishes. I have no quarrel with those who wish to attend my church while continuing to attend the services at the Methodist church or mass at St. Peter's, or continue worshiping at their own synagogues or mosques." He leans forward in his chair. "I guess I'm asking you to trust me."

Marcella Stein looks at him. His face, so youthful, is earnest. His cheeks have that high flush of youth, his eyes clear and crisp. No lines mar his forehead; no shadows color his eyes. She could fall in love with a boy like this: earnest young goyim have always been her downfall, ever since college when Brad Bennett broke her heart.

Strange, she thinks. She hadn't thought of Brad in years. Why now?

She stands up and goes to the window. "The other night at Town Meeting, you were wearing a UMass sweatshirt. Do you have any affiliation?"

He smiles. "Not directly. But I was in love with a young woman—a student there, while I was at Yale. We were going to be married—but—"

Marcella turns to look at him. "But?"

"She broke my heart." Mark Miller gives her a sad smile. "She left me—"

Just as Brad had done. Left Marcella for that blue-eyed dimwit Kristy Petersen. "I'm sorry," Marcella tells him, and she suddenly feels a tremendous wave of sympathy for the young Reverend Miller.

But even as she walks him to the door, agreeing that he will have her vote, she remains on guard. She might feel his pain, but, in truth, he remains like all the Waspy boys she'd ever trusted over the years—only to have her heart stomped on and her dreams dashed. *Oh, Mark Miller,* she thinks, *you'd better not be like the rest of them. I'll be watching. I know what to look for. I've seen it all too many times before. I'll be watching you, Mark Miller—every step you make.*

5:15 P.M.

"Let me go, you fucking pig."

Rusty McDaniel has Kathy McKenzie by the arm, taking her out of the lockup in the basement of the police station. He's squeezing it too hard.

"You son of a bitch—you're hurting me!"

He ignores her, just leading her roughly down the hall.

"Hey," Job Emerson says, coming around the corner. "Go easy, Rusty."

"Don't try talking to him," Kathy sneers. "He's so fucking stupid that they had to bring in Nate Tuck all the way from goddamn California to be the chief's assistant."

Rusty backhands her across the face. Kathy goes flying into the wall.

"What the *fuck*, man!" Job is suddenly on Rusty, grabbing his shirt, pushing him away from her. "Rusty, you can't do that!"

"Stupid cunt," he growls.

"Lay off, will you?" Job barks.

"Drug-addicted slut."

Job glares at him. "Man, what has gotten into you?" He moves over to Kathy. "You okay?"

"Shut up, you cocksucker," she says, holding her face in her hands.

Job can't grasp what's happening. His buddy Rusty McDaniel, good-natured and easygoing, hitting a prisoner—and a *woman* at that. A woman he's known all his life. Kathy McKenzie, the closest friend of his wife, Berniece—who just called him a cocksucker.

"Okay, back to the lockup, Kathy," Job says, leading her back and securing her in the cell.

"What's the matter?" Rusty goads him. "You gonna let her get away with calling you that?"

Job ignores him. He looks through the bars at Kathy. "You're just going to have to wait in there because you're out of control. But we're gonna get you some help. Nate's called a doctor and we're going to be transporting you over to Cape Cod Hospital."

She says nothing.

"And in case you're worrying about Josh, he's with Pat Crawford."

Kathy's eyes widen. "The bitch," she snarls. "The fucking rich bitch!"

Job just shakes his head, turning around to Rusty. "Did you get her father's number like Nate asked you to?"

Rusty's eyes are dark. "I don't have to jump at every fucking order that college boy spews out."

"What is going *on* with you, man?" Job snaps. "What is up your *butt*? Do you know Kathy can file charges against you for police brutality? What is *wrong* with you?"

"I just don't know why we're coddling her!" Rusty shouts. "We pick her up a day ago for disturbing the peace, and she's strung out on God knows what—and we sit here all day, making her coffee and buying her lunch. The chief was in there earlier holding her hand. She's a drug addict and a criminal!"

"She's Kathy McKenzie," Job says. "We've all known her for years."

"Fucking trash is what she is."

Job's had enough. "Buddy or not, you say shit like that again and I'm writing you up. Now I'm the officer on charge and I'm telling you to get upstairs and work those phones. Call Cape Cod Hospital and see about transferring Kathy down there."

Rusty glares at him. In his eyes there's a darkness, an absence of light that for a second knocks the breath out of Job. They aren't the eyes of his best buddy. They are the eyes of a man thwarted by life and made bitter from it. Job knows Rusty's story: he's heard it a hundred times over a few beers down at Dicky's. He knows how Rusty had wanted to be a cop ever since he was a kid, how he'd dreamed of someday being named the chief. But that wasn't to be: after twelve years of fine service, Rusty watched as Nate Tuck—college-educated, decorated hero—was brought in out of nowhere and appointed to the number two position.

"That should've been me," Rusty had said to Job one night, his words thick, both of them a little buzzy after a pitcher of Heineken. Rusty had really wanted to go to college, but his parents hadn't been able to afford it. His little sister was sick with leukemia for several years, and her medical bills ate up everything his father made as an electrician. After high school Rusty worked for his dad for a few years, but then old Will

McDaniel developed rheumatoid arthritis, and most of the town's electrical business went over to Tom Longstaff. Then Rusty really loused things up: he went and got Gladys Jawinski pregnant, so they had to get married. Soon Teddy was born and then came Steven and Ann Marie, and Rusty figured his life was pretty much scripted out for him.

The truth was, as good an officer as he was, Rusty wasn't in Nate's league. Job knew this, although he'd never articulate it, and he assumed Rusty knew it, too.

But Job had never seen Rusty like this. He'd seen him wistful; he'd seen him disappointed; he'd seen the first foam of bitterness appear with increasing mugs of beer. But he'd never seen him so cold, so cruel. He'd never seen his eyes so dark.

Rusty stands there, still glaring at him.

"Rusty," Job says. "Please, man. Go get on the phone."

Rusty grins. "All you had to do was say the magic word," he says sarcastically. "*Please.*"

Job watches him go. He walks out with a swagger Job's never seen on his pal before, a thrust of his guns on his hips. *Who does he think he is? John Wayne?*

Job turns his eyes back down to Kathy McKenzie. She's crying softly now.

"Buck up, kid," Job tells her. "It'll be all right."

"No," Kathy tells him, not looking up. "It's only just begun."

Outside, it's started to rain again.

10:17 P.M.

Teddy McDaniel is having a dream. And not just any dream. It's the dream his mother, Gladys, told him about this morning, when she woke up all jittery and anxious, unable to make breakfast before he went off to school. It's the dream his father Rusty had had, too, the one he woke up screaming over in the middle of the night, disturbing the whole house. It was the dream Rusty had hastily whispered to his wife, Teddy's mother, who'd then proceeded to have it herself and tell her son about it over the kitchen table. How relieved Mom had seemed after she'd relayed all those horrible details. How strange, how twisted, coming from her mouth.

Teddy's dream starts just like his mother's, a man in a black coat and top hat sitting on a bench on Main Street. But in Mom's dream, the man had asked her to get up on top of a car and deliver a speech. Public speaking was Mom's worst nightmare. Instead, in Teddy's dream the man challenges him to a ball-throwing match, and suddenly the whole town is lining the street watching, Jamal Emerson front row and center.

"No way will you be able to beat *him*," Jamal taunts Teddy.

"Oh, yeah?" Teddy snaps. "Just watch me."

He turns to the man, who's grinning a really nasty smile.

"I know what you've got in your mouth," Teddy tells him. "My mom told me."

The man laughs. And sure enough, worms drop from his tongue and fall onto his lap.

"You're gross, man," Teddy snarls. "And I can whip your ass throwing a ball."

But when he tries, he finds he can't prevent himself from throwing like a girl, and the ball lands only a few feet away from his feet, the wimpiest pitch he could ever imagine.

The whole town erupts in laughter, especially Jamal.

Then the man throws his ball. It is a powerful, impossible pitch: the ball flies through the air as if shot from a cannon, smashing through the front window of Drucker's general store and setting it ablaze. Soon the whole town is on fire, Teddy's house included, and everybody he knows and loves—his mother and father, his brother, his little sister, his grandfather, even Jamal—are burning alive, screaming and writhing in the flames.

Teddy doesn't know where to turn. He begins to cry.

"There, there," comes a voice, and suddenly he's being embraced, protected from the blaze. He looks up. He knows that face.

It's Mark. Reverend Miller.

"Stay with me, Teddy," Mark whispers in his ear. "I'll keep you safe."

He wakes up. His heart thuds in his chest. His sheets are damp. He's still terrified, still sick to his stomach, and knows he won't feel better until he tells someone else the dream.

And he knows who he'll tell.

If only he can last that long . . .

Sunday, May 19, 11:30 A.M.

Ellen Hutchins refills Nate's cup of coffee. "More eggs, Nate?" she asks.

He pats his belly. "No, thank you. I'm quite full."

"Not too full for a homemade raspberry croissant?"

He grins. "Never too full for that."

The chief's house is filled with the fragrances of cinnamon, fresh baking bread and coffee. Nate loves these Sunday-morning gatherings. Sometimes the chief will invite Job and Berniece and the kids, or Rusty and Gladys and the kids, or Dean and his mother and sister. But today it's just Nate, and he suspects it may be so they can talk about Ellen's trip to the doctor last week. She looks drawn, tired, with dark circles under her eyes. Still, she whipped up a fabulous breakfast, as always.

"Well, your friend certainly did a thorough job," the chief says, setting down the *Cape Cod Times* as Ellen places a croissant in front of Nate. "Really detailed both those unsolved cases. Maybe the article will produce some new leads."

"We can hope," Nates says.

The chief takes a sip of his coffee. "You know what's odd, Nate? As I read her account, I was struck by how much I'd forgotten. How much I guess I'd pushed out of my mind." He grins over at Nate wearily. "Not a good sign for an old cop."

"You're not so old," Nate says, smiling.

"Old enough to think about retiring soon." He gestures for

Ellen to sit down and join them. "I've promised this good lady here to finally take her on the trip we've always dreamed about. To the fjords of Norway."

Ellen smiles. "My mother was born in Bergen. She was always talking about the beauty of the fjords."

Nate looks from Ellen back to the chief. "You're serious? You're retiring?"

"Thought maybe by the end of summer. Norway's spectacular in August."

Nate doesn't know quite what to say. Ever since Nate arrived in Falls Church, the chief has been like a father to him. He's what Nate imagines his own father would've been like, had he had the chance to live to that age. Solid, weathered, with big bushy gray eyebrows and a twinkle in his blue eyes. Nate can't imagine the chief being gone.

Even more, he can't imagine replacing him.

"You're the man for the job," the chief says, as if reading Nate's mind. "That's why I brought you in. As good as Rusty and Job are, you're the man who I want to replace me, and I'll be telling Alan Hitchcock that."

Nate knows the town manager likes him, and feels confident the Board of Selectmen would approve his taking over as the chief. But he doesn't feel ready. Not yet . . .

"Look, Nate," the chief says. "You need to let go of what happened in Oakland. You weren't to blame."

Nate sighs. "You always know what I'm thinking, don't you, Chief?"

"You saved an officer's life. You did what you needed to do."

He shakes his head. "Yeah. I did what I needed to do."

And what was that? Shooting and killing the kid who was aiming at his partner. Little Jesus Ramos was just fourteen years old. Sure, Jesus would've killed Nate's partner if he'd had the chance, but why hadn't Nate aimed for his leg? *Why hadn't I just disabled him, instead of killing the poor kid?*

Nate sees again the photographs in the newspaper of Jesus's crying mother. Some in the community called Nate a killer, but an investigation proclaimed him a hero. Those cracked-out gang members had been shooting at them, after all, and in the course of that raid, three officers had been killed. No one doubted that little Jesus Ramos wouldn't have pulled that trigger.

Except Nate.

*Maybe he wasn't going to shoot. He was just fourteen. . . .
Why hadn't I aimed at his leg?*

I killed a sad, mixed-up, little kid—named Jesus, to boot.
That's why, when Siobhan was gunned down, only days later, Nate took it as some kind of terrible retribution. It was a drive-by shooting that ended Siobhan's life, just like the one that had killed Nate's dad. It would never be proven that it was a gang member's revenge for Jesus's death, taking out the cop's girl-friend as she left her job at a homeless shelter at one in the morning. An investigation concluded it was a random act, but Nate would never be sure.

God took Siobhan from me for killing Jesus.

He knows that's ludicrous, but somewhere deep down in his gut he believes that. How can he be a cop, he's reasoned with himself, and not be able to live with killing a gun-wielding gang member? It came with the territory.

But Jesus had been just fourteen.

And maybe Nate wasn't really meant to be a cop. Maybe he went into criminal justice simply to make his father proud. To live his father's unfulfilled dream. In truth, Nate would rather be just an electrician like Tom Longstaff, or a mechanic like Dave Carlson, or a barber like Fred Pyle, or a fisherman like Claudio Sousa.

And here he was: being given the job of chief of police.

That wasn't what he'd been looking for when he moved here to Cape Cod. He'd already found what he came here for: a quieter, simpler life, away from the drug lords and crackhouses and drive-by shootings. A place where he could forget all the crime and misery of big-city life. Forget, too, the pain that had racked him in the weeks following Siobhan's death. In that, he'd been less successful. Every morning Siobhan was still the first thing he remembered, and the last he thought of before falling asleep at night.

That's why, as pleasant as dinner with Monica Paul had been, Nate knew he wasn't ready to date anyone else seriously yet. It would take a very special woman to help him past his grief over Siobhan. And he hadn't met her yet. He's going to have to break that news to Monica. He doesn't want to string her along.

He's about to respond to the chief, telling him that he's honored, of course, to have his trust, when a loud rapping at the front door disturbs them. Ellen walks over and opens it.

"Rusty," she says.

"Sorry to intrude on your little private party," he snarls sarcastically. He's in uniform; Nate knows he's on duty today. "Just thought Chief would like to know the doctor down in Hyannis has let Kathy McKenzie go. Says she's doing better."

"Please," Ellen Hutchins says. "Come inside, Rusty. Have a cup of coffee."

He ignores her, not moving from the front step even after she's opened the screen door. "She's got a court date set," he says, "but is there any reason to keep her?"

"No," the chief says, walking over to the door. "Rusty, why don't you come inside?"

Nate feels his fellow officer's glare. His eyes are black holes. Nate actually has to turn away from their hostility. "No, thank you, sir," Rusty says. "Wouldn't want to crowd the place."

"Now stop this, Rusty," Chief scolds. "You've been surly and moody for the past two days. Come inside and let's talk."

"Afraid I can't, Chief. I've got to get back to the station and relieve Dean. And let him know that the Reverend Miller is coming by to pick up Kathy."

"The Reverend Miller?" Nate asks, standing up now himself.

"Kathy's asked to be released into his care," Rusty says, not looking at Nate. "Anything else, Chief? Or can I go?"

"I'll want to talk with you tomorrow morning, Rusty," Chief says. "I'm not pleased with this sudden change in attitude."

Rusty says nothing, just turns and walks back down the sidewalk. Ellen lets the screen door swing shut.

Nate looks over at the chief. "Job said something bad went down with Rusty on Friday," he tells him. "He won't say what, but it had to do with Kathy McKenzie."

"Is there something in the water?" Chief laments. "First there's Hiram Silva at Town Meeting. Then Kathy McKenzie. Now Rusty."

Nate scratches his head. "And Betty, too. Didn't you notice how ornery she was at the station all day Friday? She practically bit my head off when I asked her about Hiram."

Ellen shivers, grabbing ahold of the back of the chair. "That wasn't Rusty. That wasn't the boy I've known since he was a toddler. The polite young man who has sat here countless Sundays eating Belgian waffles, holding little Ann Marie on his lap." She starts to cry. "His manner was just so—so hostile."

The chief is quick to put his arms around her. "Don't get upset, sweetheart. You know what the doc said. Stress isn't good."

"Think happy thoughts," she whispers.

Nate watches them. Ellen seems so frail, so frightened.

Suddenly she lifts her eyes to him. "The cancer's come back, Nate. It's all through my body. I'll be lucky to see Christmas."

Nate's jaw just drops. He can't respond.

"Don't think that way, Ellen," the chief scolds gently. "We beat this before; we'll beat it again. We're going to Norway. We'll see the fjords in August. . . ."

Nate still doesn't know what to say. But he understands now Chief's hurry to retire.

Ellen sits down at the table. "You know, I went down to the hospital in Hyannis last night. I wish I'd realized Kathy McKenzie was still there. I'd have gone to see her. I made the trip to see Sargent Crawford—you've heard about his heart attack?"

Nate manages to nod.

"He looked so drawn, so pale, lying there in that bed. Hooked up to all sorts of tubes and machines. Pat says he'll have to have a quadruple bypass. Poor man may never be the same. And so young, too."

"I didn't want her to go," Chief tells Nate. "But she insisted."

"Life is so fragile," Ellen says.

"I'm—I'm so sorry, Ellen," Nate finally manages to say, reaching across the table to place his hands over hers.

The chief starts to fluster, standing up and pacing across the room. "Why so much misery now? Everybody sick, everybody angry—"

"Just like it was, both times, back then," Ellen says, gestur-

Robert Ross

ing to the newspaper on the table. "When the Googins girl was killed. When little Petey McKay disappeared and the Kennelly house burned to the ground. Reading the story made me remember. My mother's cancer came back the same week Priscilla was killed. And all those angry people at Town Meeting when they tried to kick those boys with AIDS out of school. That was the night before Petey disappeared and the fire."

Nate looks from her over at the chief. "That Reverend Miller came in to talk with you yesterday. What did you make of him?"

Chief shrugs. "A pleasant enough young man. A bit idealistic perhaps. Eager to do a good job with the old church."

Nate sighs. "And word is all the selectmen have signed on?"

"Yes. I'd imagine he could be up and running in a matter of weeks, if the closing goes quickly. Of course, there's a lot of renovation that's going to be needed—"

"Don't let him move in there," Ellen says in a very soft voice.

"What?" Chief asks.

"Don't let him take over the old church."

"Why not, Ellen?" Nate asks.

"I don't know. I don't know why I said that. I don't know him. I just—"

"You just what?"

She places a hand over her heart. "Suddenly I'm just very afraid."

Monday, May 20, 1:30 P.M.

Victoria left the university at eleven o'clock this morning. It was an early end to the semester; her colleagues would be on campus through Thursday or Friday. But she couldn't wait any longer to get on the road. She'd spent the whole weekend reading every single final paper, staying up until three o'clock in the morning to tally up final grades. Dropping them by the registrar's office this morning, she left a note for the dean saying she'd been called away early by an emergency. She told him that she was sorry to have to miss end-of-the-year departmental meetings, but she'd call in sometime during the week. She needed to attend to "urgent family business" on Cape Cod.

Yeah, she thinks now, driving over the Sagamore Bridge, the sun struggling to emerge behind fast-moving gray clouds, *family business. Like finding out who killed my parents and my sister.*

Victoria had been fifteen before her aunt had revealed to her that Chipper Robin, fire chief for Falls Church, had determined the blaze had been arson. Deliberately set. Yet there was never any evidence of who might have done it—none at all—and in all this time no one has ever been charged. Just as no one has ever been charged with Petey McKay's disappearance.

She pulls off the rotary on the other side of the bridge to fill her Honda Civic up with gas. She raises her eyes to the sky. *It wants to be beautiful,* she thinks. *The sun wants to shine. But something just won't let it.*

What did she expect to find in Falls Church? How could she find out who killed her family after all this time? What hope did she have of finding out what happened to Petey?

She's not sure, but she couldn't have stayed away even if she'd tried. In the last few days her commitment to returning had consumed her. It was all she thought about. It seemed not to matter so much what she'd do once she got there. It was merely the act of returning to Falls Church that drove her every thought.

Because it is happening again.

That much she's sure of. What "it" is she doesn't know. But it's happening. Again. The evil that had destroyed her world has come back.

And this time she's strong enough to stop it.

Last time she hadn't been as strong.

It's night. She knows he's behind her. He's got Petey. She had seen his claws reach out from under the sheet and grab Petey around the neck. She turned, her terror consuming her, and ran. She runs now, a scared little girl in a Devil costume, her feet crunching the leaves, sending them flying. She falls, skins her knee, gets up and starts running again. She runs in and out of the trees, but everything looks the same. She can hear the surf from out at Lighthouse Point—*crash, crash, crash*—never changing, endless. She falls facedown into the leaves again and her breath is magnified in her ears.

In the distance she hears a sound. Sirens. Horrible screaming sirens.

She gets to her feet and begins running again. She passes cottages boarded up for the winter, empty summer houses left cold and dark. The sirens become louder and she spots a light. A streetlamp. She recognizes Lighthouse Road ahead of her. She stumbles out of the woods and onto the street. She turns as great burning holes in the darkness approach her. Headlights. She waves down the car.

The car, an old Pacer, slows to a stop. It's Mr. Drucker, of the withered hand, from the general store.

"Who's that?" he rasps.

"Victoria Kennelly," she tells him. "Please, you've got to help. Petey McKay's been kidnapped!"

"What? What are you saying?"

Even in the moonlight Victoria can make out his deformed hand on the steering wheel. Sometimes Mr. Drucker could be friendly, especially when parents were around, handing out free gumballs to the kids in his store. Victoria never liked to eat the gumballs that had been in his hand, but she was always afraid of offending him—and she'd seen him yell at kids who came into the store unescorted, watching them suspiciously with little brown eyes under black bushy eyebrows.

And she remembers all too well how hostile his wife had been to her when she'd tried trick-or-treating at her door.

"Please," Victoria begs him through his car window. "We've got to help Petey."

His little eyes narrow at her. "You're the little girl who likes to speak out of turn."

"Please!" She's crying now. "He's being kidnapped!"

He scowls. "What do you mean, *kidnapped?*"

"By a kid dressed as a ghost," she tells him.

Mr. Drucker makes a face. "Is this some kind of Halloween prank?"

"No! Please! Help me!"

He stiffens. "Get in the car and I'll drive you to the police station."

She looks back into the woods. They're dark, quiet.

Find me, Victoria.

She gets into the car with Mr. Drucker.

"What are all those sirens?" she asks.

Then, over the trees, she sees the red glow of flames.

Dear old Father Roche, pastor of St. Peter's Church, where her family had been parishioners, tried to do what he could, taking Victoria in that night at the rectory. He and Chief Hutchins had sat with her all night. Eventually Victoria was sent to live with her mother's divorced sister, a lawyer in Boston. Aunt Joyce was bright and capable, encouraging Victoria in her studies, but she was never very affectionate or warm. Victoria would finish her high-school education at a posh girls' school in Connecticut, seeing her aunt only at holidays. Her parents had provided well for her in case of their deaths. Victoria went on to college in Boston, receiving both a bachelor's and a master's degree in education. School became her life, her refuge against the horrors of the world.

The best thing Aunt Joyce did for her was to introduce her to Caroline. For only through recognizing her own strength— an ability Caroline taught her—did Victoria find a way out of her fear. For a year after the twin tragedies in Falls Church, she had been haunted by the ghost, stalked all day and all night by the relentless figure under the sheet. She would have gone mad, had it not been for Caroline's quiet, persistent admonition that Victoria was stronger than that which haunted her. It is an admonition that keeps her driving ever onward up Route 6 now, heading toward Falls Church.

Beside her on the seat of the car rests Michael Pilarski's final paper. She'd made a photocopy before sending him the original back, marked A. He'd done a good job. A very good job. Victoria takes her right hand off the wheel and places it down on the paper. Even the photocopy feels warm to the touch, pulsing with life.

Fire and Brimstone:
The Story of Father John Fall
and the Founding of Falls Church, Massachusetts

"I do not like thee, Father Fall," Victoria whispers.

She'd been a history buff all her life, so she knew the rudimentaries of her hometown's history: how a group of strict Puritans had broken away from an Orleans congregation sometime in the late seventeenth century, marching south through the marshlands to the little claw of land that jutted off the Cape into Nantucket Sound, where they set up their own church and town. It was named Falls Church because that was the name of the minister who headed the congregation. Reverend John Fall, whom everyone nontraditionally called "Father" Fall.

But Michael had revealed much more of the story, having combed through the journal left by Father Fall. The minister's words had been terrifying to read. "Man had originally Dominion over the creatures Below,'' Fall wrote one day in the fall of 1690, before marching off to establish the town. "But Sin hath inverted this Order, and brought Chaos upon the Earth. Man is dethroned, and become a servant to those things that were made to serve him, and he puts those things in his heart, that God hath put under his feet."

How outraged John Fall had grown over the "sinful" ways of his original congregation, too many of whom wore "bright and various Colours." The women laughed openly with men not their husbands, and boys "drank ale and hath friendly association with the heathen Indians." How John Fall fantasized about the punishments that surely awaited these sinners in hell. He would write three- and four-page-long passages describing in lurid detail how he imagined their flesh burning, how their eyes were being plucked out, how they would cry for mercy. But such cries, he wrote, seemingly gleefully, "would go unheeded, echoing against the dark caves of Hell." In his grusesome imagination, John Fall seemed to take great delight, even—in Michael's words—"getting off on it," releasing his daily pent-up outrage each and every night by candlelight in his journal.

Ultimately, however, such fantasies proved insufficient for Fall's gratification. His journal records his thrill at being able to recruit others to his way of thinking: "To find these Souls amid the ruins, to pick them out of the heap of foulness, all to Followe me." Father Fall must have been incredibly charismatic, Victoria imagines, for he drew dozens, then hundreds, to his sermons, promising them the angry hand of a vengeful God: "For he would smite thee with plagues or fires or floods, destroying Puny man with no more thought than Man kills a mosquito."

Victoria shivers. She wonders why people have always been so eager to believe such pessismistic messages, accept such unkind images of God.

Michael had earned his A by offering historical context, positioning Father Fall as a predecessor of such Great Awakening orators, like Jonathan Edwards, who would be, in the next half century, numerous throughout New England. Like Edwards, Fall seemed to believe that human history was merely proof of Man's innate depravity. Virtue could only arise from faith in God—and in Fall's case, that God came to be synony-

mous with himself. In his sermons Fall upheld the Calvinist
belief that men could not find salvation "by any manner or
goodness on their Own." Salvation came only through God—
and, given that no other minister seemed to understand this
truth quite as well, Fall came to believe that only through
himself could a sinner find God. Only *he*, in other words, had
gotten God's law *right*.

Such had been the foundations on which the village of Falls
Church had been founded. But Father Fall's reign had lasted
only a few years. In December 1697, having charged one of
the young women of his congregation with being in league
with the Devil, the minister ordered her burned at the stake.
As the girl was the daughter of a much-loved family, most of
the congregation rose up in protest against Fall. The governor,
not wanting a repeat of what had happened in Salem, sent down
a posse to prevent the execution. But Father Fall would not be
so thwarted. Taking the girl to the basement of the church, he
set fire to her himself, and in the process burned the whole
place down. He, too, perished in the blaze. Although the girl's
body was reclaimed from the ruins, Fall's was left to rot.
Eventually a new church was built on the site; Michael added
in a footnote that that one, too, would burn. In all, four churches
were built and then burned on the site. Even the present one
almost went up in flames, having been hit by lightning in 1967,
but the Falls Church volunteer fire department had kept the
blaze confined to the steeple, which Victoria remembered as a
charred, twisted finger pointing up at the sky.

So much fire, Victoria thinks. *Fire and brimstone.*
What did it all mean?

It's begun to rain. Just a sprinkle. She flicks on her wipers.

Ahead of her she sees the exit for Chatham and Falls Church.
Near the sign is a hitchhiker, dressed all in black.

Sorry, buddy, she thinks as she passes him. *This is where I
get off.*

Immediately the scenery tickles her memory. A farm stand,
not yet open for the season, where she and her father used to
buy corn in the summer. A little farther along she spies a water

tower with a happy face drawn on its side. Still the same after all these years.

But then she spots a shopping plaza that wasn't there fifteen years ago. A Stop & Shop and a CVS drugstore and a Pizza Hut. The area used to be a swamp.

It's starting to rain harder now. Standing by the side of the road under the Pizza Hut sign is another hitchhiker, also dressed all in black. She's past him before she can look too closely, but she could swear it was the same guy.

She takes the turn for Falls Church. It's a long, straight road cutting through the federally protected marshlands and sand dunes. In the winter this road sometimes ices over, she remembers, effectively cutting Falls Church off from the rest of the Cape—and the world.

Victoria can see up ahead the first houses of Falls Church. The yellow sign of Dave's Sunoco at the corner of Main Street and Cranberry Terrace gradually comes into view. She begins to tremble. Her hands grow a little clammy on the steering wheel. The sky darkens; the rain pounds harder on the roof of her Honda; thunder rumbles over the town in the distance.

And there, on the side of the road, is the hitchhiker. Dressed all in black. He's drenched.

It *is* the same man she saw before.

Except it's not a man.

It's not even alive.

Don't pull over, a voice tells her.

Why not? she asks it. *I am stronger than whatever haunts me.*

She slows down beside the hitchhiker. The man in black is looking at her. He's smiling.

She gasps.

Even in the rain she can make out the grisly sight.

There are worms—worms in the man's mouth!

Monday, May 20, 5:30 P.M.

The windshield wipers squeak across the glass as Rusty Mc-
Daniel heads the cruiser up Pearl Street, then takes a right onto
Main.

"Shut up!" he barks at the kid in the seat next to him.
Goddamn brat keeps mouthing off, and it's driving Rusty crazy.

He barely avoids hitting that stupid retard, Danny Correia,
hobbling along in the rain. Part of him would've liked to have
just run the dumb fuck over. Even though he always liked
Danny before, now he thinks getting rid of him would just do
the whole town a favor. Rusty hates watching him eat French
fries at Clem's Diner, making a mess of ketchup on his face.

Squeak, squeak, squeak.

Rusty keeps his eyes on the wipers. It's like they're hypnotiz-
ing him. He doesn't look much at the road; he drives from
memory. He could find his way around this town blindfolded
and drunk: he knows Falls Church better than anyone. *Better
even than the chief,* he thinks—*certainly better than that frig-
ging golden boy, Nathaniel Tuck.*

He glides through a red light in front of Dave's Sunoco and
heads out along the causeway leading out of town. The rain is
coming down heavy.

"You ran a red light, you fucker," the kid next to him says.

Rusty reaches across the seat and backhands him, sending
the kid crashing into the passenger-side door. *Goddamn brat*

deserves it, Rusty tells himself, *talking filthy like that, just like that mothercunt of his.*

"I'm gonna run away from my grandfather's and just come back, you know," Josh McKenzie tells him, rubbing his reddened cheek.

"I don't give a fuck what you do," Rusty snaps. "Just keep quiet."

Right about now, Rusty hates everyone. He hates the kid; he hates the kid's mother. He hates the chief; he hates Nate. He even hates his own family: his fucking father for getting all crippled with arthritis and ruining the family business, his nagging wife and all her endless complaints, his rotten kids— who have gotten even more rotten since he's had the dream.

The *dream.* It's always there, isn't it? He thought by telling Gladys, it would go away. But only for a little while did he have peace. Then the fear came back, roaring back, and along with it this anger. This feeling of being ready to snap. This feeling of being out of control.

The stars have disappeared. The night falls dark. In the distance there is the low roll of thunder. The rain lashes furiously at the car; the wipers can't seem to catch up. Yet through the torrent Rusty spots a man up ahead, walking along the road, heading into town. He can see him only intermittently, when the sheets of driving rain clear for a tenuous second. The glimpse he gets is of a man bedraggled, hunched over, drenched in the rain.

He rolls the cruiser to a stop alongside him. *What kind of idiot would be walking in this rain?*

Rusty tells the kid to keep quiet and gets out of the car. He shines a flashlight at the guy on the side of the road.

It's a black guy. Probably no more than nineteen or twenty.

"What are you doing out here?" Rusty barks.

"Walking to town," the man responds.

"What business you got in Falls Church?"

The man turns defensive. "What business is that of yours?"

Rusty is on him in a second, his face only inches from the young man's nose. "Listen, punk, don't mouth off at me."

The guy takes a few steps back. "Don't call me punk."

"I'll do one better than that," Rusty snarls. An unholy grin stretches across his teeth. *"Nigger."*

The man reacts, pulling back his fist as if to punch Rusty in the face.

"That's your last mistake," Rusty says calmly. He pulls out his gun and shoots the man straight through the chest. His body flies backward, splashing into the rain-soaked gutter on the side of the road.

Watching out the car window, Josh McKenzie laughs, like it's a Saturday-morning cartoon show, the Road Runner shooting the coyote. The little boy looks down at the dead man and laughs as if it's the funniest thing he's ever seen in all of his six years.

Tuesday, May 21, 7:48 A.M.

"What I worry about the most, frankly," says Miranda Pierce, "is the effect on tourism. I mean, Memorial Day is *this* weekend. The big kickoff to summer."

Her husband looks up over his newspaper. "You can't mean that, Miranda. A white police officer has just shot a black man to death—a *college kid*, for crying out loud, walking back from a party to his rented cottage because his car wouldn't start. Yet again, the presumption is that a black man walking along a street in a predominately white town must be up to no good."

"Oh, Cooper, spare me the bleeding heart," Miranda says, sipping her coffee. "Rusty says the man threatened him. Don't make this about race."

"The kid was unarmed, nineteen years old, a foot shorter than Rusty and at least thirty pounds lighter—a *poet,* for crying out loud! Here on the Cape to finish a manuscript. Tell me how *that* can be threatening." Cooper finds himself feeling indignant, a condition that makes him distinctly uncomfortable. He despises confrontation, even with his own wife. But something about the story, already spreading like wildfire throughout town, has touched a chord inside him. A long forgotten chord. "And Rusty shot him at close range directly through the chest."

"Well, if *you* don't care about our business, I'll have to watch over it on my own." Miranda sniffs, standing and clearing off the breakfast plates. "I am less worried about racism right now as I am about our livelihood. How many tourists are going to want to venture into Falls Church if they think there are gun-toting cops running around?'' She huffs off into the kitchen.

Cooper glances down again at the headline in the *Cape Cod Times:* POLICE OFFICER KILLS MAN IN DISPUTE. Why had Rusty stopped him? What had the young man done? What kind of dispute could there *possibly* have been between them?

Cooper closes his eyes. He sees again his own father, on the day after they'd moved into their house in suburban Connecticut. He was out walking with Cooper, then just ten, pointing out the different types of trees that grew in the neighborhood. Oak. Maple. Elm. A police cruiser had pulled up alongside them.

"Whatcha doin', boy?" the cop had asked, getting out of his car, his hand on his gun. He didn't address the question to Cooper, but to his father. He had called his father "boy."

Cooper's never forgotten the look on his father's face. A look of shame, of humiliation, of anger. Nor has he forgotten the feeling the policeman's words elicited in himself: a sick, sinking feeling down in his gut, as if—try as he might—he'd never make it in this world. Not with people like this cop around.

Cooper's father died almost twenty years ago. He never saw his son's success as a businessman. *Would he be proud of me?* Cooper wonders. He just doesn't know.

He stands, sighs, folding the paper in half. He can't think of it anymore. He has to get ready to open the shop.

8:20 A.M.

Over at Clem's Diner, the shooting is all anyone can talk about. Dave Carlson, who runs the nearby Sunoco filling station and mechanic shop, heard the shot and hopped in his truck to check things out. He tells Marge Duarte he came upon Rusty looking like an "animal—grinning like a vulture over his prey" and the little McKenzie kid "laughing like a hyena in the police car."

"That just gives me goose bumps," Marge says, shivering, pouring cups of coffee all down the counter of customers.

Old Smokey Buttons, who runs the package store, scratches

his head. "Don't know what musta come over Rusty. He was always such a good boy, ever since his daddy would bring him by the shop when he was just knee-high and I'd give him free root beer outta the coolers. Always so polite. He never failed to say, 'Thank you, Smokey.' "

Cliff Claussen, attorney and town moderator, shakes his head. "I think we need to give Rusty the benefit of the doubt. If he shot that kid, there must have been trouble."

"Oh, come on now, Cliff," says Isabella Sousa Cook, town clerk, just now leaning in over the counter to pick up her morning bagel. "What kind of trouble could there have been? The man had no gun. It was pouring rain and he wasn't drunk or on any drugs."

"We don't know that yet for sure," says Hickey Hix, trash collector, done with his job for the day and still smelling slightly of rotting banana peels. "You know these people—they bring in the drugs to Cape from Providence and Boston."

Marge gives him a look. "Hickey—"

But his words—especially *these people*—have already been overheard in the booth against the wall, where postmistress Bessie Bowe and her boyfriend, Noah Burt, are having their usual morning breakfast of poached eggs and home fries. Marge sees Noah put down his fork, Bessie touch his hand. Marge prays there won't be a scene.

Dave Carlson, Noah's boss at the mechanic shop, is quickly over to the booth. "You want a ride up to the shop, Noah?"

The black man shakes his head.

Marge is refilling coffees for Noah and Bessie. "Least the rain's died down," she chatters, making light. "Looks like the sun might actually come out today."

Fire chief Chipper Robin walks in then, the little bell over the door tinkling. He's with Harbormaster Sandy Hooker and Selectman Richard Longstaff, who still seems embarrassed to be seen in public after Hiram Silva revealed publicly the relationship between his daughter and the principal Martha Sturm.

"The news crews have arrived," Chipper tells Marge as he slides into the booth behind Bessie and Noah. "Channel seven and Channel three, with their big satellite dishes outside the police station."

"The poor chief," Marge says.

"I feel sorriest for Rusty's wife, Gladys," Sandy Hooker says. "And his kids."

Noah Burt has had enough. He stands, though Bessie tries to restrain him. He walks around to the booth behind him. "You feel sorriest for Rusty's wife? What about the kid he shot? What about his mother? The fiancée he expected to marry in September?"

"Noah," Bessie says, coming up behind him. "Let's go."

"And *you*, Hickey," Noah says, turning around. "If *those people* are bringing drugs onto the Cape, where do *they* get them? From white drug lords making a killing smuggling them in from Colombia or God knows where."

"Noah, he didn't mean—" Marge tries.

"Bah," Noah says, storming out of the diner. Bessie follows with Dave Carlson.

"Well," Hickey snarls, "ain't he uppity."

Clem's waddled out from the kitchen. "What's all this shouting?"

Marge sighs. "Never mind. It's over, Clem."

"It's just that Noah Burt," chimes in old Cliff Claussen. "I'm sorry, but he's got a temper. He hauled off on me once when I brought in my car for not having the oil changed often enough." He shakes his head, taking a sip of his coffee. "And Bessie's dad was a friend of mine. Old Judge Bowe. A more upstanding, honorable man you'd never find. I can only imagine how he'd feel seeing his daughter running with a . . ." His words trail off.

Isabella Sousa Cook is suddenly behind him. "A what? Say it, Cliff. Show everybody here your true colors. Show 'em what a bigot you really are."

"Leave me alone, Izzy."

She snorts. "Forget the bagel, Marge. I've had enough of these people." She pauses on her way out of the diner. "It wasn't all that long ago that my people were being called '*those people*.' My father remembered when he first came to Falls Church, there were signs in the windows of the stores that said *No dogs or Portuguese*."

The bell jingles as she hurries out the door.

"Come on, folks," Clem urges. "Eat your breakfasts before they get cold."

"Easier said than done," Chipper Robin observes. "Look out the window. Here comes a news crew now. No doubt to get some local flavor."

Clem pokes a fat finger into Marge's face. "Don't talk to them," he tells her. "It's no comment, you hear?"

"Stop stressing, Clem, or you'll have a heart attack."

"I'da worn a tie if I'da known I'd be on television," Smokey Buttons says.

1:15 P.M.

Carolyn Prentiss is opening up her windows, airing out the place. Shuttered the whole winter, the house has that unmistakable musty smell of all closed-up beach houses. "Actually, I kind of like it," she tells Edmond. "The smell reminds me that I'm home."

There are two things Carolyn Prentiss still wants out of life: an Academy Award and a chance to live here—on Cape Cod, in Falls Church—year-round. She bought the place three years ago, but every winter she's had to be on location or—God forbid—Los Angeles. This past winter had been spent in Athens and North Africa, making some trifle with Mel Gibson. All the while, what she really wanted was to be here, sitting on her deck, watching the wind and the snow over Lighthouse Beach.

"You're home, darling, but don't get too settled," her manager, publicist, agent and lover, Edmond Tyler, reminds her. "We've got to be in Cannes in a few weeks."

"Oh, yes," she mumbles, standing on her deck, looking down on Nantucket Bay. "The Côte d'Azur." In Carolyn's mind, the South of France is nothing compared to Cape Cod.

But why should she love the place so? Precisely because it *wasn't* fabulous. Beautiful, yes, but not fabulous in the way the Hamptons are, or Martha's Vineyard—or indeed the Côte d'Azur. There were no other famous names in Falls Church, and while Hyannisport and the Kennedys weren't far away, Carolyn could feel completely removed from the world of celebrity when she was here. She keeps a low profile, never venturing into the town without kerchief and sunglasses. She wants no adultation while she's here. Just quiet. Just refuge.

She'd been a star since she was eighteen, and now, at thirty-

Robert Ross

one, she wants to retire. She has enough money for several lifetimes, enough to allow her to do nothing more than sit here on her deck and read, write and think. If only Edmond agreed. He's bound her by contract to so many projects she can't even think about retiring until the year 2010.

"Darling," he says in his polished British accent, cultivated despite being born in Cleveland, "there are news crews in town. Apparently there was some kind of killing. You'll want to keep a low profile."

"A *killing?*" Carolyn asks, stretching out on a lounge, grateful for the sun on her face. "In *Falls Church?*"

"A cop shot a kid." Edmond shrugs. "Who knows what it was about."

Carolyn closes her eyes. "I just want to hide out here for as long as possible. Whatever's going on down there can't touch me here."

Here she's safe—the only place on the planet she feels totally and completely safe.

2:00 P.M.

At Town Hall, Mary Silva is banging her old fist on Town Manager Hitchock's desk. "We've got to close any loophole that allows that developer Richie Rostocki to build any more houses on Cliff Heights! He's destroyed enough of this town's character as it is!"

Alan Hitchcock lets out a long sigh. "Mary, Mary, always quite contrary. Can you let it go for a day, please? We've got other things to worry about today, with Rusty and all these news crews running all over town."

"You see what's happening?" Mary scolds. "Do you see what Falls Church is becoming?"

"Mary, in heaven's name, how is this tragedy related to overdevelopment?"

The old woman folds her thin arms across her chest. "Fine town manager you are if you can't see the connection. All this development brings in too many tourists. We used to be a quiet community. We kept to ourselves. Few outsiders ever came here. Our police officers are understandably jumpy. Come on, Alan, you know what goes on down at Dicky's Bar in the summer, the way these tourists start acting up! Girls half naked prancing around! Couples having sex on the roofs of cars!''

"Mary, the kid Rusty shot was a *poet*. He wasn't an out-of-control tourist down at Dicky's. He was renting a cottage so he could write *poetry*."

"I don't care what brings 'em here. There's too many."

Alan sighs. "Mary, when are you going to accept that we are now dependent on a tourist economy? I know your family ran the biggest fishing fleet for years, but the fish are all gone."

She draws herself up tall. "They most assuredly are *not* gone. It's just that the state and federal governments put too many restrictions on our fishermen. How can you fish with those kinds of limits?"

He decides to change the subject. Mary Silva is seventy years old. She's never going to see the world any differently. "Mary, how's Hiram?" he asks. "Any better?"

She sniffs. "My brother simply cracked under the strain we've all been going through these last few years as our town is sold off, piece by piece, and these—these *people* start moving in. And while Hiram may have been out of place at Town Meeting, I think in truth *a lot* of good folks in this town have been feeling a little leery about a *lesbian* running our school."

"Martha's done an exemplary job," Alan tells her.

"Regardless. I think we're in the midst of a wake-up call. To think about the future of Falls Church, and what kind of a town we want it to be."

Alan Hitchcock runs a hand over his thinning hair. Mary Silva could sap the power out of an electric plant. He's weary just sitting here across from her. There's no way he's going to tell her the real reason for his fatigue. He'd gotten no sleep after finding that intruder in his living room, planning to make off with the stereo or TV set. Pidge had nudged him awake around two A.M., telling him she'd heard a noise. Alan heard it, too, and went to the top of the stairs with a flashlight. In the glare staring up at him was the face of Jamal Emerson, Job's son.

Alan still can't figure it out. Job was a good kid. He'd been part of a student team at Town Hall last fall, spending a few days in Alan's office learning about local government. Jamal was a friendly, smart, polite kid—not the kind who broke into people's homes. When Alan had recognized him, he threatened to call his father—who was on duty down at the police station. Jamal had simply snarled, "Fuck you!" and had run off into the night.

After checking to make sure nothing was missing, Alan decided against making an official report. He'd talk to Job privately—a decision now tabled with all the commotion over Rusty shooting that kid. Alan hates to sound like Mary Silva, but there's a part of him this morning that's asking a similar question to the one she usually poses:

What is happening to our little town?

2:30 P.M.

"Sargent?"

Pat Crawford touches her husband's clammy forehead. So many tubes are stuck up his nose and down his throat, but the doctor says he came through the bypass surgery with flying colors.

If only he'd wake up, Pat thinks. *If only he'd open his eyes and see me standing here, say my name.*

"Sargent," she says again.

"I'm sorry," a nurse tells her gently, "but he'll be out for several hours. You may as well go downstairs for some coffee. I'll call you when he wakes up."

Pat looks at her. She can hardly focus. She's hasn't had more than a few hours' sleep any night for a week. First there was Josh McKenzie to contend with, who suddenly erupted into the brat from hell. Then came Sargent's heart attack and surgery. Pat feels sapped of all strength. She tries to smile at the nurse but can barely move her lips.

"Thanks," she manages to say, "but I think I'll just sit here."

The nurse shrugs. Pat settles down into a chair opposite her husband's bed. What a hulk he looks lying there—how stiff, cold and hard. She rests her head against the wall and thinks maybe she'll rest, but as soon as she closes her eyes, she opens them again.

Don't close your eyes, comes a voice in her head.

A voice that sounded like Sargent's.

Pat stands and approaches her husband again. She touches his cheek. He's so cold. If not for the monitor assuring her that his heart is beating, she'd swear he was dead. He looks so gray and bloated. He looks like a corpse.

She shivers. She hates the smell of hospitals, the artificial light. She wants to be home. Her kids need her more than Sargent at this point.

Especially her daughter, Melissa.

Just eight years old, Melissa was already turning out to be the beauty Pat always wished she could have been. Blond, delicate, with wide green eyes. Bright too, and determined, looking up at the dinner table last month with eyes ready to do battle with her parents if they objected to her "going steady" with Jamal Emerson.

"I don't object to you going steady with Jamal," Pat had told her, "just to you going steady. You're only eight years old, Melissa."

Still, the budding friendship between Melissa and Jamal took off, as childhood crushes do. Jamal was always polite when he called on the phone; Pat had found it cute how Melissa would laugh coquettishly at the boy's silly jokes.

But Melissa hadn't been laughing last night when she came running into her mother's room, pouncing on her bed and hiding under sheets.

"Mommy!" she screamed. "I had a dream! I had a dream!"

Pat would later blame her daughter's night terror—and the surly, jumpy behavior she'd exhibited all the next day—on the fears she had about her father's health. But what a strange dream Melissa had had. And how determined she was to tell Pat each and every little disgusting detail—right down to the worms that fell from the man's mouth.

Why have I been unable to stop thinking about it? About a little girl's silly dream?

She feels so tired. She grips the guardrail around her husband's body for support. *I just need to close my eyes for a little while. Just a little while . . .*

No, Sargent tells her, insistent in her mind. *Don't close your eyes.*

She studies his face. There's no sign of agitation there, and none on the monitor.

"I'm overtired," Pat whispers. "That's what it is. I'm overtired."

Just the same, she thinks she *will* go downstairs and get a cup of coffee. Better that than sit back down and close her eyes again.

She might just fall asleep.

3:13 P.M.

Sandipa Khan stops by the general store after school lets out. She needs to buy some laundry detergent and a quart of milk. She's not surprised by the crowd gathered outside, all talking about Rusty McDaniel's suspension and the investigation that's now begun over the shooting last night. But what she *is* surprised by are the looks she gets from those gathered. No one says good afternoon to her; they just glare at her as she walks up to the steps to the store.

It's like it was after the terrorist strikes at the World Trade Center, Sandipa thinks. *That's the way they looked at Habib and me then, because we're Muslims, originally from Pakistan.*

"Hello, Sam," she says, bringing her purchases to the counter. He just grunts, placing the detergent and milk in a brown paper bag with his withered hand.

Sandipa sighs. She's always known there's been an undercurrent of suspicion in town against them. She might be the school's kindergarten teacher, and the children might draw her pictures and bring her apples and lilacs from their gardens, but underneath all that, underneath all the outward signs of affection and tolerance, Sandipa knows there's a reserve of mistrust. When her husband, Habib, an author of mystery novels, gave a reading at a bookstore in Orleans a few months ago, the only locals to come were Nate Tuck and Catherine Santos, the librarian. Habib brushed it off, saying it was a busy night for people, but Sandipa had stewed. Not even their next-door neighbors Joe and Ann Silva had come by.

She steps outside the store. She's not sure what's prompted this latest apparent hostility, but she won't give in to it. "Good afternoon, Claudio," she says to Claudio Sousa, fisherman. He nods. "Good afternoon, Sandy," she says to the harbormaster, who also nods. "Good afternoon, Tess," she says to Tess

Woodward, whose family has owned the local pharmacy for some eighty years. Tess doesn't even nod.

Sandipa returns to her car, where Alesha, her daughter, is waiting. "Mama," the little girl says. "There's a funny-looking man in that car over there."

"Where, pumpkin?"

"Over there."

Sandipa looks where her daughter is pointing. It's an old-style yellow Volkswagen bug. There *is* someone sitting behind the wheel, though Sandipa can't make him out. "Why is he funny-looking, Alesha?" she asks.

"He was making faces at me," the child says.

"What kind of faces?"

"I don't know," the girl tells her. "But I got scared."

Sandipa's defenses rise. Was the man harassing her daughter? Was this some kind of racial thing?

She calms herself. Maybe he was trying to be friendly. Or maybe Alesha was just imagining things.

Something compels her to find out. She sets her purchases in the back of her car and tells her daughter she'll be right back. She approaches the Volkswagen.

"Hello?" Sandipa calls.

A young white man reading a newspaper looks up at her with wide blue eyes.

"Hi," she says haltingly. "My daughter said . . ."

The man smiles. "Are you Mrs. Khan?"

She pauses. "Yes, I'm Sandipa Khan."

"Oh, my." The man gets out of the car quickly. "I was just sitting here reading a review of your husband's latest book, hoping I'd get a chance to meet him now that I've moved to town. I'm a *huge* fan of his."

She looks at him blankly.

"Allow me to introduce myself. I'm Mark Miller. I've just bought the old church."

Sandipa shakes his hand. "Oh, yes. Reverend Miller. I recognize you now from Town Meeting."

He claps his other hand on hers as well, holding her now with both hands. "It wasn't just because I'm a fan that I wanted to meet you and your husband, Mrs. Khan," Mark Miller tells her. "I also wanted to talk with you about perhaps helping me arrange a series of educational and religious services at the church. I understand you're of the Muslim faith.''

"Yes," she says. "Yes, we are."

"Well, I really want this to be a multifaith project. Could I at least come by some evening and talk with you and your husband to maybe get some ideas?''

"Mama!"

Sandipa turns. Alesha is out of the car, gesturing wildly to her. The little girl looks terrified about something.

"Mama! Please! Come back!"

"I'm sorry," Sandipa tells Mark Miller. "I've got to go—"

"Of course."

"But yes, do give us a call." She smiles as she hurries off. "I think what you're suggesting would be very good for this community.''

Mark Miller beams.

Back at her own car, Sandipa finds she needs to console a shaking Alesha, who can't describe her sudden paroxysm of fear or the tears that inexplicably fall from her eyes. Sandipa just holds her arms and assures her that everything is going to be okay.

4:45 P.M.

Nate Tuck sits across from the chief, the state police investigators having finally left. They're quiet for several minutes. Finally the chief speaks, his voice thick with emotion.

"What the hell is going on in this town, Nate?"

Nate looks at the older man. His old eyes are red and bleary. Nate thinks he's close to tears. The chief has known Rusty McDaniel all his life. He hired him, taught him everything he knows about being a cop. And he's just spent the whole day with investigators from Boston asking Rusty why he shot an unarmed man at close range. Cliff Claussen had been there, as Rusty's attorney, cautioning him not to say a word. Rusty just sat there, grinding his teeth like some mad dog. Which is how Nate can't help but think of him. He's not the guy he's gotten to know these last several months.

"Wish I knew," Nate says. "Wish I knew what was happening, Chief, but I don't.''

"I had to suspend Rusty without pay. Gladys was in here screaming at me, but I had to do it. Until the investigation is complete."

"You did what you had to do, Chief."

The old man runs a hand over his head. "I hated to do it. It killed me. I know they've got bills. I keep thinking about those poor kids—"

"Yeah," Nate says. "Me too. Especially Teddy."

He and the chief make eye contact. This afternoon Teddy had come running into the station, demanding that his dad be released. "All he did was kill a black guy, probably a faggot," Teddy had shouted. "A faggot writing poetry."

Nate had ordered Teddy out of the station, telling him that being upset over his father gave him no excuse to talk in such a way. But then Gladys had come in, too, hurling invectives at the chief like she was some barmaid from the Old West, punctuating everything with *motherfucker* and *asshole-licker*.

"Gladys wasn't herself," Chief says.

Nate manages a tiny grin. "An understatement. What's happened to that whole *family*?"

"And *Betty*," Chief says. Shock had piled upon shock today: their faithful secretary quit this morning, telling them she was through being bullied by them.

"That's it," Betty had said, standing up in a huff when Dean asked if she'd made any coffee yet. "You think that's all I'm good for? I ought to sue you all for sexual harassment. *Make the coffee, Betty. Pick me up a bagel, Betty.* That ain't in my job description, fellas. Well, as the song goes, *You can take this job and shove it*—wherever you want to shove it."

Dean had followed her out of the building, offering mea culpas and considerable wringing of his scrawny hands. But the chief and Nate had sat there mute, too stunned to say anything, still dumbstruck by the news that Rusty had killed a guy and he might be charged with murder.

"I'll call her in a bit," the chief says. "She was upset. We're all upset."

But Nate knows Betty won't be consoled by a few words. She had *changed* in the last few days—changed like her husband, Hiram, had changed—changed like Kathy McKenzie, like Rusty and Gladys and Teddy. And, according to Job, like his own son, Jamal.

"I got a call here at the station last night from Berniece, who woke up and saw Jamal wasn't in his bed," Job told Nate in between breaks of talking with Rusty and investigators. "I went out to look for him."

"You found him?"

Job nodded. "Yeah. Trying to break into Hornet."

"Jamal?"

"What should I do, Nate? He hadn't gotten into the store when I found him. He was only out in back, trying to figure out how to get up on the roof. He wouldn't explain to me what he was doing, but it was obvious to me. *He was trying to break in and rob the place.*"

Nate just shook his head. This wasn't like Jamal—just as the behavior of all these other folks wasn't like them, either. *What the hell is going on?*

"Excuse me."

Nate looks up. It's a woman addressing the chief.

"Chief Hutchins?"

The chief moves his tired eyes over to her. "Yes," he says. "What can I do for you?"

"I heard about the officer who killed that boy."

He sighs. "I'm not speaking anymore about it. Who are you?"

"My name is Victoria Kennelly."

Nate sits up. That name. *Victoria Kennelly.*

"I used to live here in Falls Church."

That's right, Nate thinks. *She was the girl with Petey McKay when he disappeared. The girl whose family died in that fire the same night.*

The chief narrows his eyes. "Dear God, little Victoria Kennelly all grown up."

"I wonder if I could speak with you about Officer McDaniel—"

He makes a face in annoyance. "Do you have any information about it?"

"Well, not about that specifically—"

The chief shakes his head firmly. "Then no. Absolutely not.

There's an investigation going on. I can't speak to you about it."

"But it's happening again," Victoria Kennelly says, her voice breaking. "Just like before."

"Miss Kennelly, I really can't speak to you now," the chief insists.

"You can't *ignore* it," she says, her voice taking on an edge. "Pretend it's not there. People tried to ignore it before, until it was too late and we were powerless to stop it."

"Miss Kennelly, *please*. I'm having a meeting here with Detective Tuck."

The woman sighs. She makes eye contact with Nate. She has intense green eyes—and something more. Something behind them. She turns and leaves.

"Chief," Nate says after she's gone. "Maybe we should've talked to her. If she knows something—"

Chief Hutchins cuts him off. "Victoria Kennelly went crazy after her family died in that fire. I followed her progress for a while. She was a witness to Petey McKay's disappearance, after all. I was always hoping she'd remember something to help the investigation. But all she ever did was talk about ghosts and goblins. I gave up on her after a couple years. She'd always been a high-strung girl. Her weird theories are the absolute *last* thing I want to hear tonight."

He covers his face with his hands.

Nate stands and looks out into the station. Just Dean at the front desk. Nate strides across to the front door and opens it. The street is dark and empty. Victoria Kennelly has vanished back into the night.

Why was she here? Why had she come back to Falls Church? What did she know? Not only about Petey, but about what's happening *now*?

It's happening again, she had said.

Nate vows to find her tomorrow. Wherever she's gone, he'll find her.

He wants to find out what Victoria Kennelly knows, and how she knows it.

Wednesday, May 22, 12:00 A.M.

That night, just as the bells from Town Hall chime twelve, Monica Paul hears the singing. She looks around.

Singing—drifting through the still night.

She had been getting ready to call it a day, planning to hop in her car and head back down the Cape. She'd spent the day getting reactions to the shooting from the townsfolk for a profile of a community in crisis. Monica's looking forward to writing the piece: it has all sorts of angles—local boy in trouble, the changing character of the town, the issue of race. She's rolling the words around in her head, settling on a lead, when she hears the singing.

Her car is parked in a lot off Church Street near the wharf, behind the old fish market. She'd parked it here earlier, when she interviewed the market's owners, Joe and Angela Sousa, who told her what a good kid Rusty had been, how sad everyone was when his father developed arthritis and couldn't work.

Then, after the interview, Monica had met Nate for dinner at Wong's Chinese. Despite her extravagant praise for Sam Wong's steamed dumplings, Monica found Nate seriously distracted—not surprising, she supposed, given the events of the day.

"Please," Nate begged her as they left the restaurant. "Don't write about all this weirdness yet. It'll make Falls Church sound—I don't know, crazy."

"I'm the press, Detective." She smiled at him. "Writing is what I do. I don't ask you to stop fighting crime, do I?"

He said nothing in response. And although he made no move to pull away when she reached up and kissed him, neither did he really kiss her back. He was equally noncommital when she asked him for another date. So Monica just shrugged and let the matter drop. They simply walked in silence along Main Street for a long while.

Finally Nate had turned to look at her. "I love this town," he said plainly. "It gave me a place to come to when I needed it. I'm not going to let anything happen to it."

"Good for you, Detective," she said. "That's what I like about you."

They said good night, and she headed back to her car, fighting the damp wind that whips off the harbor. That's when, unlocking her car door, she heard the sound of *singing* mixed in with the wind.

She looks up now, caught by it, straining to hear.

Hymns. It sounds like hymns, coming from the old church several yards up the block.

From here Monica can see the old charred steeple looming up beyond the trees. She listens carefully. She hears it again. There's no doubt about it. That's *singing*.

She relocks her car and heads up the street toward the church. The townsfolk have been complaining about this for weeks. Clem Flagg says he's been awakened nearly every night by it, but when the police investigate, they find nothing.

A grin stretches across her lips. Maybe Monica Paul, ace reporter, can do better.

She loves being a reporter. Ever since she was a kid, she's had this insatiable curiosity. She used to read Lois Lane comics not for Superman's exploits but for Lois's undercover pursuit of scoops, often beating out Clark Kent for the byline in the *Daily Planet.* But Lois had it lucky, running after smugglers and space aliens. Too often Monica's editor assigns her boring tasks like covering Wetlands Commission meetings. So when she gets the chance to play investigative journalist, she jumps at it.

Her eyes follow the rise of the boarded-up church. The

singing is louder now. She smiles. What will she find inside—
a bunch of renegade Jehovah's Witnesses?

For a moment the night breeze carries the fragrance of blossoming lilacs. Oh, how she loves Cape Cod in the spring. Her decision to move here had been the absolute right one. There's such a different pace of life here. When she and Al had lived in Washington, she had seemed unable to ever catch her breath. Moving to Boston had been just as bad, maybe even worse. She was consumed by his world of political schmoozing, trapped by Sunday-morning breakfasts with clients and vacations taken with fax machines and cell phones. Not once has Monica ever regretted leaving him, not after finding a sense of peace in her life here for the past three years.

She stops in front of the church. Just beyond lies an old cemetery, with crooked, broken brownstone slabs dating back to the 1600s. Nate had walked her through it when she was writing the piece on Priscilla Googins, who was murdered right here in this church. In the daylight the place had been creepy enough. Now, in the dark, with the wind howling through the trees and that persistent singing, it's downright eerie.

Maybe a place can be too calm, too peaceful, Monica thinks idly.

She looks up at the windows of the church. Many are boarded up. From behind the wooden planks peek broken shards of glass, catching a glint of moonlight. The front doors at the top of the stairs are similarly covered with plywood; graffiti mars the surface, especially several large words spray-painted in red. Monica approaches to read them:

PRISSY GOO LIVES.

She shudders. How do those kids get *in* here? The plywood is securely nailed in front of the doors. She walks back down the steps and around to the side of the church through the tall, damp grass. There's a door there she remembers from her earlier visit with Nate. It had been padlocked then. Her breath catches a little as she realizes the padlock is gone.

"Someone must have a key," she whispers to herself.

She turns the knob. With a sudden shiver the old door opens in her hand. She peers inside. Blackness. The foul smell of rotting wood.

The singing abruptly stops.

Why should I be afraid? Monica laughs. *Why should I be afraid of a group of kids singing hymns?*

Still, maybe she ought to call Nate on her cell phone. She fumbles in her pocketbook for it, but she is distracted suddenly by movement inside the church. Instead of her phone she withdraws a flashlight, shining it into the darkness. It illuminates a child's face. She recognizes him. It's Teddy McDaniel. She'd met him when she went out to Rusty's house, trying unsuccessfully to get an interview.

"Teddy?"

He runs off into the church, his footsteps echoing against the old wooden floorboards.

With her flashlight Monica looks around, making out what appears to be an old church hall, filled with torn-out pews and chairs piled one on top of each other. She steps inside. The place smells musty and damp. The beam of her flashlight follows Teddy's echoing steps out a door. They fade away, only to return above her, running along the church's main floor.

She follows him, out the door and into a stairwell, using her flashlight to sidestep fallen beams and at least one languid old rat. She shudders, emerging into the rear of the church's nave. To her left are the front doors, sealed from the outside, and to her right, stretching up to the altar, are the pews. Many are broken or missing. The odor of decay mingles with that of incense, so thick that Monica chokes a little, covering her mouth with her hand.

"Teddy?"

Her voice echoes in the darkness. She begins to walk down the central aisle, keeping her flashlight ahead of her. The altar is bare. She reaches it and scans the altar floor with the flashlight. At her feet is a large dark stain. Revulsion grips her. Is it the blood of Priscilla Googins?

All at once the singing begins again, loud and fervent, startling Monica. She shouts out, dropping her flashlight.

"Hallelujah! Hallelujah! Hallelujah, hallelujah, hal— leeeee—lujah!"

She scrambles to retrieve the flashlight, gripping her hand around it and swinging its beam up through the darkness at the choir loft. There's no one there, but the singing continues.

*"Hallelujah! Hallelujah! Hallelujah, hallelujah, hal—
leeeee—lujah!"*

It seems to come from everywhere, from every board and
every beam of the church. It seems to come through the walls
and up from the floorboards. Monica swings her flashlight from
spot to spot but illuminates no one.

Until she makes out voices closer to her, little voices singing
the words but separate from the rest, not part of the choir. The
voices of children.

Monica moves the beam to the front pew just a step down
from the altar. Three children. Two boys and a girl. Teddy
McDaniel and a black boy. She thinks it's Jamal Emerson. The
girl looks familiar, too: hadn't she met her with that woman?
What was her name? The wife of the real estate agent. Crawford?

The children are singing. Sitting there, staring up at her,
singing along with that ghostly choir.

Monica Paul is suddenly terrified.

That's when she turns and sees the man in the black hat.

He has a knife in his hand. He grins. Worms slither from
his lips.

Monica screams.

The knife punctures her flesh once, then again. And then
again and again and again.

The children keep singing. The choir raises its voice in glory.

*"Hallelujah! Hallelujah! Hallelujah, hallelujah, hal—
leeeee—lujah!"*

Memorial Day Weekend

And so the dream progresses. Little Josh McKenzie had started it all by telling his mother, Kathy, who told Hiram Silva, who told his wife Betty. Betty Silva told Rusty McDaniel, who told his wife, Gladys, who told her son Teddy, who told his best friend, Jamal Emerson. Jamal told Melissa Crawford, the girl he had a crush on, who then told her mother, Pat, who, finally falling asleep after getting home from Cape Cod Hospital, dreamed her worst fear: her husband, Sargent, had died and she'd have to go on all by herself.

No, that wasn't her worst fear, but Pat Crawford would be hard-pressed to describe what was worse than even her fears of Sargent's health. All morning she was a frightful bundle of nerves, terrified of every little creak in her house, screaming out loud every time the phone rang. Finally she could take it no more and hurried over to her neighbor Yvette Duvalier, who was just getting ready to head down to her restaurant. Pat told the dream to Yvette, who listened indulgently, touching her hand and telling her to go home and get a good rest.

Women with no lives outside the home are prone to breakdowns, Yvette had thought condescendingly, slipping behind the wheel of her Jaguar and starting the ignition.

That night Yvette had the dream: a man in a black hat stood on the steps of Town Hall and shouted to everyone who passed by that Yvette's real name was Erma Flopp and that she wasn't born in Montreal but in Saginaw, Michigan, and that she and her husband were planning to file for bankruptcy, their restaurant soon to be in receivership. And then he laughed, having revealed Yvette's worst secrets, and worms had fallen from his mouth.

Yvette awoke screaming. She ran out to the kitchen and told the dream to her husband, Paul, who then had his own visit from the man in black the following night. Paul then passed on the whole sordid tale to his golfing partner, town attorney Cliff Claussen, who that night dreamed his wife had found his collection of little-girl porn (*Baby Chicks in Heat*) hidden in the basement. Cliff actually wet the bed he was so upset. He got up, dried off and headed straight over to Town Manager Alan Hitchcock's house, passing along the dream to him. Alan thought Cliff mighty bizarre for telling him such a tale in the middle of the night, but a couple of hours later he dreamed that Selectwoman Mary Silva discovered how long he'd been embezzling funds from the town treasury. Alan woke up in a cold sweat, shaking his wife, Pidge, awake to tell her the dream.

"Oh, Alan, you're such an alarmist," Pidge grumbled, turning her shoulder to him. "No one in this hick little burg would ever be wise enough to figure that out."

In the morning the first real crush of tourists arrived in Falls Church, in numbers that allayed Miranda Pierce's fears that the shooting would deter the crowds. They came in station wagons and trailers and all manners of sport utility vehicles, piling into the cottages along Lighthouse Beach, filling the condos along the main drag and crowding into the True Value to buy their beach chairs and suntan oils. It was a gorgeous weekend, filled with sun, the mercury rising into the high 70s. Aggie Duarte opened the Clam Shack, a traditional sign of the start of the season, and was immediately deluged with folks ordering fried calamari and steamed mussels. Already, at five in the afternoon, there was a crowd swilling beer on the patio out back at Dicky's Bar, throwing fried clams to the seagulls. The town's two guesthouses, The Beach Plum and The Rose, both hung out signs stating NO VACANCY. Another summer had begun.

And on Monday morning Pidge Hitchcock, looking as if a train had hit her, staggers into the Seaside Realty office, looking for Laura Millay.

"My *God*, Pidge, you look a *wreck*," Laura tells her.

"Listen to me, please, Laura, I've got to tell you. I had a dream. . . ."

Laura smirks, leaning against her deck and crossing her arms over her chest. "Must have been a nightmare judging from how you look."

Falls Church was home to many snobs, but Pidge Hitchcock had them all beat. Laura can't deny gloating a little. She's never seen Pidge without her hair perfectly coiffed, her makeup expertly done, her nose in the air and her eyes looking down at all the common slobs around her. But she's standing here now, with no makeup at all and her hair sticking up from sleep, yesterday's spray still hard and stiff.

"Laura," Pidge pleads, "please let me tell you my dream."

Laura Millay laughs. She's never cared much for Pidge, but she puts up with her. All of those who move among the Falls Church upper crust have to put up with each other. Sargent keeps her on staff here because he needs Laura's husband, Roger, at the bank. Roger insists they have dinner once a week with that uncouth Richie Rostocki because he's the biggest developer in town. They all eat at Duvalier's and shop for clothes at Hornet because they wouldn't think of stepping foot into a place run by one of the natives. They keep to themselves, the Falls Church elite.

Except for Laura, who's already almost forty-five minutes late for a rendezvous with Claudio Sousa out at the beach.

"Please, Laura!" Pidge is begging. "*Please!*"

"Oh, go ahead, Pidge. Just make it quick."

So Pidge tells her, about being forced to scrub floors at the Laundromat and serve lobsters to tourists at the Clam Shack and being laughed at by all the common people in town, nasty folk like Mary Silva and Gyp Nunez and Tess Woodward and Smokey Buttons and Hickey Hix. Laura can hardly keep from laughing herself, watching Pidge shudder with each name she says. *Has the old bitch been at the sauce?* Laura can't help but wonder.

"But the worst part of all," Pidge says, trembling, "was

the man. The man in black. He was coming for me, Laura. Coming for all of us."

"Okay, Pidge. Calm down."

The other woman does indeed seem to relax. "Thank you, Laura," she says softly. "Thank you." She turns to leave.

"Pidge, you really ought to go see a doctor."

"No. I'm all right now. I feel better now." She closes the door to Laura's office behind her.

Almost immediately there's a knock again at the door. The secretary Cassie Beaumont peeks in her head.

"Mrs. Millay? There's a gentleman here to see you."

"Gentleman?"

The door is pushed open abruptly. Cassie shrinks back as the man makes himself seen.

"Claudio," Laura says angrily. She looks at the secretary. "That's okay, Cassie. I'll see him."

"You're damn right you'll see me," Claudio says.

"Close the door," Laura scolds.

He obeys, but is quickly in Laura's face. She backs away.

"Were you planning on standing me up?" he shouts.

"Keep your voice down." Laura walks around behind her desk and sits, assuming the guise of a professional business-woman. "I've been running late all day. For Christ's sake, Claudio. Since Sargent had his heart attack, I've been practically running this place myself."

"I'm through sitting around waiting for you, Laura."

She's had enough of his childish rantings. He's been getting far too possessive, far too demanding. "Then *fine*, Claudio. Don't wait anymore. Let's just end this whole thing."

"Sure," he says, grinning malevolently. "I'll just stop over at the bank on my way home and say hello to your husband."

She glowers at him. "He'd never believe your filthy lies."

Claudio rushes behind the desk and grabs Laura by her shoulders, forcing her to her feet. She tries to push him off, but he's too strong. He smells of fish and sweat, an aroma that once excited her but now nauseates her. He kisses her hard on the mouth. She keeps struggling in his arms.

Finally he pushes her away from him. She wipes her mouth with the back of her hand.

"You'll regret doing this, Laura," he snarls.

"Get out of here," she says. "Never put your filthy stinking fish hands on me again!"

He seethes, looking for a moment as if he'll lunge at her again. But he doesn't. He merely stalks out of her office, slamming the door behind him.

Good. That little tryst went on way longer than it should have.

Laura tries to concentrate on her next appointment but finds herself shaking. She can't even write any notes. She pulls out the files for the old Winn place on Center Street. She's scheduled to show it to a bunch of tourists here for the weekend, who came into the office yesterday insisting they'd fallen in love with Falls Church and just *have* to own a part of it. Laura slips the folder out from the rack but drops it, papers fluttering everywhere.

"Goddamn it," she says, almost in tears.

On her hands and knees, her pearls dangling below her chin, she can't understand her sudden nerves. Had Claudio really rankled her so much?

Or was it Pidge, with that silly dream of hers?

He was coming for me, Laura. Coming for all of us.

"Here," says a voice, startling her. "Let me help you."

She looks over. A man has entered and is now stooped down, helping her retrieve the papers. Their eyes meet. It's the Reverend Mark Miller. Their shoulders brush. Laura feels a tingle throughout her body.

"Thank you, Reverend," she says.

They stand. He hands her the papers he's gathered. "Please," he says, "call me Mark."

She smiles, staring into the bluest eyes she's ever seen.

I could get lost in those eyes, Laura thinks. Suddenly her nerves are calmed. *Oh, yes,* she tells herself. *Very lost.*

Monday, May 27, 3:12 P.M.

Victoria Kennelly looks down at the business card Caroline had given her:

KIP HOBART. TRANSPERSONAL PSYCHOLOGY.

What had Caroline said about him? *We had a long conversation about—well, about some interesting things. . . . He's someone you might want to talk to.*

She takes a deep breath and punches in Kip Hobart's number. It's a holiday weekend, but Victoria prays his office will be open.

A woman answers the phone. "Center for Holistic Health," she says.

"Uh, hello, I was calling to—make an appointment with Dr. Hobart."

"Have you seen Dr. Hobart before?"

"No, I haven't. I was referred by my therapist in Boston, Caroline Jenks."

"All right. May I get your name?"

Victoria tells her. She listens as the woman explains that Dr. Hobart doesn't take insurance, but that he does have a sliding scale. *None of that matters,* Victoria thinks. *All I care about is that he believes me.*

"When were you looking to come in?"

"As soon as possible."

"Is this an emergency situation?"

Victoria considers the question. She's seen the man in black now every day since she's been here, and today she saw him twice. "It's getting close to one," she says.

"Okay." The woman on the other end of the phone seems to be flipping through some pages. "How about tomorrow morning, then, at eleven o'clock?"

"That's good." Victoria glances out her guesthouse window. There's a police cruiser parked out front. "Thank you."

"We'll see you then," the woman chirps.

"Yes, thank you. Good-bye."

She hangs up the phone. She looks in the mirror and concentrates on the dark circles under her eyes. She's barely slept in days.

Her first day in Falls Church she'd walked down Center Street to Beach Road, intending to visit the site where her house had once stood. But she couldn't bring herself to walk farther than the end of the block. She stood in the very place she had stood that night, watching from a distance as the furious flames licked their way higher and higher, consuming the house in the blackness of the night, the roof finally caving in. Despite the entreaties of neighbors and dear old Father Roche, Victoria had refused to budge, watching until the bitter end, when all that remained of her house and her family—indeed her entire life— was a pile of black smoldering ash.

She realized then she was standing on Petey McKay's front lawn. Here his mother still lived, a sad, lonely old woman. Standing there, Victoria saw the curtains shiver, falling back into place.

She was watching me, Victoria realized. The whole town will now know I'm back.

She's suddenly startled by a knock at her door. "It's Lydia Atkins," comes a voice. The guesthouse proprietor. "You have a visitor."

"A visitor?"

For a moment Victoria's frightened. What if it's *him*—the man dressed all in black, the man whose teeth are rotting and filled with worms? The man who's replaced the ghost in her visions, the man she feels certain was the one under that sheet—the man who took Petey away and killed her family.

You're stronger than he is, Victoria, she reminds herself.

She opens the door.

Lydia stands there with a policeman. Victoria recognizes him from the other day in the chief's office.

"Miss Kennelly," the policeman says. "I'm Detective Nate Tuck. I was hoping maybe we could talk—about what you came to see the chief about."

"It's okay, Miss Kennelly," Lydia tells her. "Nate's a good guy. I wouldn't be disturbing you if I didn't think he could be trusted."

"Yes," Victoria says. "Yes, please come in."

Lydia leaves them alone. Victoria gestures to a small table beside the window. Nate sits down in one of the chairs, taking off his hat. Victoria sits opposite him.

"How did you find me?"

He smiles. "I'm a detective. And there are only two guest-houses in town."

She smiles back. "Well, I'm glad you found me."

"I would've been here sooner except that—well, there's been a lot going on."

"Yes," Victoria agrees. "I heard about that reporter who's missing."

Nate nods. Something in his eyes tells Victoria there's a connection there, that the reporter isn't just any old missing-person case for the detective. She feels a sudden swell of compassion for Nate Tuck.

He sighs. "I was curious about what you were going to tell the chief the other day. We'd been a through a lot just then, you understand. I don't think he was—open to hearing anything else at that point."

"I understand," she tells him.

Nate fidgets with his hat in his hands. "You're from here, originally," he says.

She nods.

"I know about the tragedy you went through," Nate tells her. "One of the things I've been trying to do ever since I got here is to find out what happened to Petey McKay. And the identity of the arsonist who set fire to your house."

Victoria sighs. "I read the piece in the *Cape Cod Times*. It must have dredged up a lot of unpleasant memories for people in this town."

Nate casts his eyes down to the floor. "Monica—she was trying to help me solve those crimes."

Victoria reaches across the table and rests her hand on Nate's. "You're not going to find her, Detective Tuck. I'm sorry. But you won't."

He pulls his hand back defensively. "How can you say that? What do you know about her disappearance?"

She smiles kindly. "Only what I've read and what I've heard around town. That her car was found down near the wharf, locked, and that you were the last one to see her. She was supposedly heading home. But she never reported in to work the next day." She pauses. "She was working on an article about the shooting."

"What are you saying, Miss Kennelly?"

Victoria closes her eyes. "Only that you're not going to find her, just as no one ever found Petey."

She can see a certain distrust growing in Nate Tuck's eyes. A disbelief. She's learned to recognize that in people. All her life, whenever she's talked about the ghosts, people either believed her or didn't, and she could always tell by looking in their eyes. None of her boyfriends had believed her. She realizes now that was the reason, more than anything else, that none of them ever lasted very long.

"If people could only *remember*," Victoria says all at once, looking pleadingly across the table at Nate Tuck. "Remember what it was like last time. I've seen what's happening in this town. People suddenly going mad. Filled with rage and hatred. Deep-seated resentments bubbling to the surface. This morning in town I saw a fight between two women. I don't know who they were, but one slapped the other across the face, right on Main Street. One of your men had to break them up. Do you know the incident, Detective?"

He nods, seeming to study her. "Yvette Duvalier and Pidge Hitchcock. Officer Sousa had to issue them both warnings."

"Society ladies, right? Not the kind to be brawling on the street." Victoria looks at him intently. "Have other people been acting out of character, too, Detective Tuck? The officer charged in the shooting, perhaps?''

"What does all of this have to do with Monica?''

Victoria puts a hand to her face. "I don't know. I just know that there are *forces* here. Things that have wreaked havoc here before. Brought *evil*.''

He makes a face. "What kind of forces?''

"Detective, I can see you are a rational man. You probably did well in mathematics, didn't you?''

He just grins at her, clearly not understanding why she asks.

"To you, there's always a logical explanation for things, isn't there? One plus one is two. Two plus two is four. With that kind of mind-set, you'll never understand what's happening here.''

He sighs. "Miss Kennelly, if you can't be specific about what you suspect—''

"I'm sorry, Detective. I wish I could be.''

"Are you suggesting there's something *organized* going on? Something—*brainwashing* people? Something—I don't know—something *supernatural?*''

"I'm not making any specific suggestions, Detective. I just know that something is happening here again, something that happened once before, something that *killed my family.*''

There: she sees it in his eyes again. The disbelief. *Her grief has made her crazy.* That's what he's thinking. It's as if she can read his thoughts.

Nate Tuck stands. "Well, I appreciate your input. Thanks for your time.'' He replaces his hat on his head. "If you *do* get any specifics, let me know, okay?''

She nods. She says nothing more. To try to persuade him is pointless. She watches him go, not blaming him for his reaction. She's sure Chief Hutchins told him she was mad. Everybody thought so after she left Falls Church. She got a few cards for a while, a few letters from school friends. "My mother told me you're crazy now,'' one little girl had written. "Is it true? What does it feel like to be crazy?''

Victoria presses her fingers into her temples. *It feels horrible,* she thinks. *Simply horrible.*

When she looks up into the mirror, the man in black is there, grinning his hideous smile.

Tuesday, May 28, 1:03 A.M.

Laura Millay is finally drifting off to sleep. Her husband, Roger, snores beside her. She's been tossing and turning for the past two hours, her mind unable to relax, to stop thinking.

His eyes . . . his lips . . .

There had been something so exciting about seducing a man of the cloth. And one so young, so fresh out of divinity school.

She had found Mark Miller a place to live, a small efficiency in the Grand Avenue Apartments, across the street from the old church. "Perfect!" Mark had exclaimed. "Mrs. Millay, I can't thank you enough!"

Exciting, yes, the way she had looked at him, the way she had playfully tapped his nose with her finger, the way she had smiled, pursing her lips.

But frightening somehow, too, the way he had looked back at her, realizing her intent, the way she could almost suddenly *smell* the sex in the air, as if the hormones released gave off an aroma. Thick and pungent, like incense. All at once, Mark had reached over and kissed her; his trembling, eager hands found their way up inside her blouse; his hot, wet lips moved from her mouth over her chin and down her neck. "Easy, baby," she whispered as he tore her buttons and ripped off her bra—as if it had been a very long time since he had satisfied his carnal urges.

She still hurts a little from the sex, so fast and fierce had it been. But she hurts in a *good* way.

She had orgasmed *twice*—shattering, powerful climaxes that left her shaking on the bed as Mark stood, pulling up his pants, almost shame-facedly looking away from her.

"That was—*incredible*," she managed to say with a gasp.

"You're a married woman," he said, trembling himself, looking in the mirror.

She stood, slipping back into her dress. "It's our secret, darling." She kissed the back of his neck. How sweet his skin was, how soft and young. "I'll never tell."

She remained shaky the rest of the night. As good as the sex with Claudio had been, she hadn't experienced anything this intense in a long time—if ever.

She could barely look at Roger all night, certain he'd see the truth right on her face. Even after he had fallen asleep, she kept her distance from him in bed, tossing and turning, unable to sleep.

Or was she, rather, for some unknown reason, *unwilling?*

It doesn't matter now, she thinks, in those last few moments of consciousness before sleep takes hold. *I'll sleep, and in my dreams I'll see Mark again. The best lover I've ever had in my life.*

But it's not Mark who's waiting for her in dreamland.

It's a man, in a black coat, beckoning to her from the little beach cottage where she used to rendezvous with Claudio. She's hesitant to go inside, but she can't help herself. She looks around to make sure no one has followed her. All she sees is a yellow Volkswagen.

"Who are you?" she asks the man inside the cottage.

He gestures for her to come closer. She can see at least three dozen Polaroid photographs are spread out on the bed. The man in the black coat motions for her to look at them.

Laura gasps. They're of her—her and Claudio. Graphic sexual shots, the two of them in every imaginable position. Laura with her legs spread and Claudio between them, licking away.

"How did you get these?" Laura demands.

The man gestures to someone behind her. Laura turns. Her three children, David, Amy and Nora, are standing there.

"No!" she screams.

But the children run eagerly to the bed, where the man begins gleefully showing them the pictures. They pick them up, bring them close to their faces.

"Is this your cunt, Mommy?" David asks.

She tries to rip the photograph from his hands, but he pulls it away from her, laughing.

"Show us how you fuck, Mommy," Amy chirps.

"Yes, show us!" Nora adds.

The man is suddenly on her, pushing her down onto the bed. Laura screams. The man is on top of her now, his face revealed as a decomposing corpse. He opens his mouth and worms begin falling onto her face. When he brings his cold lips to hers, Laura can feel—and *taste!*—the wet, juicy, horrid things squiggling down her throat.

Worst of all, he rapes her, and her children watch.

"Laura! Laura! Wake up!"

She open her eyes. Her heart thuds in her chest. Roger is shaking her.

"You were having a nightmare!"

"Let me go," she says, throwing back her blankets and jumping out of bed.

"Are you okay, darling?"

"I—I just want to go downstairs. Take some aspirin."

Roger slumps back in bed. "You never let me try to comfort you anymore."

"I—just need some aspirin." She pulls on her robe and heads downstairs into the quiet house. She's shuddering so much she can hardly keep her balance, so she keeps a tight grip on the banister.

Dear God, I need to get this out of me. I need to tell it to someone. I need to pass it on. Get rid of it.

But why not Roger? Why not just tell Roger?

"No," she mumbles. "Someone else ... I've got to tell someone else."

And she knows who. She feels as if she may have a nervous breakdown right there, waiting until she's sure Roger is back to sleep. Then she tiptoes out to the garage and slips into her car.

In minutes she's in town, down by the wharf. She still has a key. They didn't meet here that often, fearful of too many prying eyes, but a couple of times Laura had surprised Claudio, waiting for him in his own bed in the middle of the afternoon, when he'd come trundling in from a morning out on his boat. She parks her car now behind the apartment building, not really caring if anyone sees her, barefoot with her robe flowing behind her. She lets herself in, hurrying up the stairs to the second floor.

Marge Duarte, the waitress from the diner, opens her door as Laura passes. She glares at her, surely having caught her here before, but Laura pays her no mind, slipping her key into Claudio's lock and turning the handle. She enters the apartment and closes the door behind her.

The room stinks of fish and beer. His underwear and socks are strewn everywhere.

"Claudio," Laura says.

He sits up in bed. He's bare-chested, his powerful shoulders and big arms covered with hair. He squints his eyes, recognizing Laura.

"Baby, you came back to me."

She sits down on the edge of his bed. "I had to see you," she tells him. "I had a dream. . . ."

And so the dream is passed from the exclusive homes of Cliff Heights down to the apartments along the wharf, from the wealthy newcomers to the old fishing families. Claudio Sousa is thrilled to have Laura back in his arms, but once she tells him her nightmare, she's gone, back into the night. He rolls back over, cursing her, and when he finally falls back to sleep, he, too, is visited by the man with worms in his mouth.

He's a trembling bundle of nerves when he shows up at his boat at four-thirty, unable to untie his nets until he's told the dream to his uncle Manny Duarte, who experiences it himself the next night, waking up his wife, Aggie, to tell it to her. Aggie tells her daughter Susan, who runs the Clam Shack with her, and Susan tells her father's cousin Joe Sousa, from whose fish market she buys the clams for the Clam Shack. Joe Sousa has the dream and he tells it to his wife Angela, who tells

Selectman Gyp Nunez when he stops by the market to pick up some fresh cod. At Town Hall the next day, Gyp tells the tax collector Max Winn, who tells Selectwoman Mary Silva, who tells the town manager's secretary, Mary Jo Hooker, who tells her husband, Harbormaster Sandy Hooker, who tells Gerry Garafolo at the pizza joint, who tells his wife, Barbara, who tells son Nicky, who tells his friend Billy Hix, who tells his father, Hickey, who tells Lucille Pyle at the True Value, who tells her husband Fred, the barber, who tells his first customer the next day, Clem Flagg from the diner.

And the summer is only just beginning.

Wednesday, June 12, 8:09 A.M.

"Mornin', Nate," calls Smokey Buttons as Nate enters the diner.

"Mornin', Smokey," Nate replies.

But the usual chorus of voices greeting him doesn't join in. Nate looks around. Joe Sousa sits glumly in one booth with Gyp Nunez, neither making any attempt to say hello. Behind them Max Winn and Town Manager Alan Hitchcock are arguing about something, hunched down and whispering hard, oblivious to Nate or anyone else. Even Hickey Hix, usually happy to strike up conversation after hauling garbage all morning, just sits at the counter, solemnly drinking his coffee, grunting and pulling away when Nate sits down beside him and brushes against his arm.

"What's the matter, Hickey? The quality of Falls Church trash got ya down?"

Hickey turns on him. "You big-city types like to make fun of us low-income folks. Everybody's got to make jokes. Hickey the trash hauler. Well, screw off, copper."

With that, he stands, pushing his way out the diner door.

Marge is in front of Nate, filling his coffee. "What's up with *him*?" Nate asks.

Marge shrugs. "Wish I knew. Wish I knew what was up with everybody."

Just then, Alan Hitchcock shouts, "That's *slander*, Max Winn!"

The sour-faced old tax collector is on his feet. "Is it now? You won't be so high and mighty, Mr. Town Manager, when the whole town learns what a lying thief you are!"

"Slander, I say!"

Winn storms out of the diner.

"Alan," Nate calls over. "What's wrong?"

"Ah, just let me be," the town manager says, brushing him off with a wave of his hand.

Marge shakes her head. "Oh, Nate. It's like the whole town is eating itself alive, ever since Rusty and the shooting." She looks as if she'll cry. "I haven't seen the town this keyed up since . . ."

She stops. Nate looks at her. "Since when, Marge?"

"No, I shouldn't get into all that. Who wants to think of those days?"

Nate takes a sip of his coffee, keeping his eyes on her. "You're talking about your niece, aren't you? Priscilla Googins."

Marge shudders. "Poor Priscilla. Funny how I can go for so long not thinking about all of that. But then, all at once, she's in my mind constantly." She leans in over the counter at Nate. "It was like this then, too. We don't like to remember, but it was. Everybody at each other's throats."

Nate remembers Victoria Kennelly's words: *If people could only remember what it was like last time. There are forces here. Something is happening here again, something that happened once before, something that killed my family.*

"Marge, was it also like this when Petey McKay disappeared? When the Kennelly house burned? I know there was that Town Meeting trying to get those boys with AIDS expelled. . . ."

Marge closes her eyes. "Yes," she says in a soft but steady voice. "It was the same kind of feeling in town. Everbody nasty to each other. Finding fault, placing blame . . ."

Nate sighs. There's no question that in the past three weeks the little town he'd grown to love had changed. Oh, sure, some of it was the coming of the tourists. Main Street was clogged with traffic; the beaches were filled; out-of-towners asked stupid questions like *How come there's no McDonald's around here?* Folks were rude to each other because lines at the post office and the general store suddenly multiplied twentyfold. Girls walked down the street in bathing suits too revealing for some of the old locals; kids carried CD players blasting out rap music. Nate had been warned that tempers often grew short in the summer.

But not in June. Maybe late in the summer, when the dreaded "Augustitis" set in, when the locals just couldn't take any more lines or clogged traffic or rude tourists demanding a place for their kids to pee. Nate could maybe understand some of this in August—but not now. And not to this degree.

Things were bad. Two nights ago, Claudio Sousa had beaten up a guy down at Dicky's, knocking out three of the guy's teeth. Habib Khan threatened to charge Fred Pyle with discrimination when the barber refused to cut his hair. Pidge Hitchcock was arrested for disorderly conduct and public intoxication when Job found her staggering along Main Street a couple of nights ago. Both Sandy and Mary Jo Hooker were almost arrested after Nate was called in to break up a domestic squabble. Both had tried to hit the other, Mary Jo with a wooden hanger and Sandy with a frying pan. Their two little boys were crying their eyes out watching their parents' struggle.

And good old Betty and Hiram Silva had started a petition asking for the resignation of Martha Sturm as school principal. What was even more alarming and surprising was that they'd already collected almost *fifty* signatures, according to what Hiram told his sister, Selectwoman Mary Silva, who was eagerly supporting the drive. Alan Hitchcock had made no public comment. From town government, only Marcella Stein had voiced any objection to the petition.

What is happening to this town? And where is Monica? What happened to her?

For the first two days after her disappearance, Nate didn't sleep, keeping a twenty-four-hour search going. He checked all her last stops, all the people she'd spoken with that day. He even got the key to the old church and looked in there. But she was nowhere. Gone.

It eats him alive whenever he thinks about it too long. He can't help but think of Siobhan. *Any woman who gets involved with me is in danger. It's my fault. If I hadn't asked Monica to write that article—*

But what was he thinking? That the killer—or killers—of Priscilla Googins and the abductor of Petey McKay had swooped down on Monica, fearing she'd uncover the truth? Somehow he didn't think it was that simple.

There are forces here.

Nothing makes sense anymore. People he'd once thought of as family have been turned into things outside themselves. Betty hasn't been back to work since the day she stormed out, slamming the phone down on Nate whenever he's called. When Nate tries to visit, Hiram shouts curses at him from their front door.

Down at the station, a bleak depressing atmosphere permeates everything. The chief is glum and mostly silent, torn by the twin griefs of Ellen's illness and Rusty's investigation. Everybody's working overtime; Nate's even filled in on a couple of Rusty's shifts, putting in the overnight hours he'd once felt guilty for not working.

"What's happening with Rusty?" Marge asks, reading his mind.

"The investigation is almost over. I've been working with the state police. We'll have a decision very soon."

She nods. Nate knows it's plain on his face: they're going to have to charge him. The kid had been unarmed. There was no evidence of a struggle. He was shot at close range. And Dave Carlson, first on the scene, swears Rusty had been laughing when he came upon him.

Laughing!

I just know that there are forces here. Things that have wreaked havoc. Brought evil.

"Evil," Nate mumbles to himself. It's the only word he can use to describe what's happening all around him.

"You okay now, Clem?" Marge is asking. Nate looks up. The diner's owner comes out from the kitchen, holding a chubby hand against his head.

"Yeah," he says weakly. "I guess I'm okay now."

"What's wrong, Clem?" Nate asks. "Those hymn singers at the old church still keeping you up at night?"

"The old church," Clem says blankly, his eyes meeting Nate's.

Marge leans on her elbow against the counter. "Oh, poor

old Clem was probably putting away too many Little Debbies last night.'' She gives Nate a smirk. "Poor baby had a bad dream.''

"A dream?'' Nate asks.

"Yeah.'' Marge laughs. "And what a corker, too. Some guy all in black—''

"Please, Marge,'' Clem begs. "Don't bring it up again. Once I told you, I felt better.'' He puts his hand to his head again. "Sort of.''

Marge winks at him. "Not better enough that you've filled all these orders.'' She spins the wheel where she tacks up her customers' checks. "Back in that kitchen, lard pants. People are hungry! Get that waffle maker sizzling!''

Clem obeys, robotlike.

Nate just watches him, then turns his eyes back to Marge, whistling as she strides down the counter to take a couple of new orders.

He had a dream, Nate thinks. *Clem had a dream. . . .*

Thursday, June 20, 8:47 A.M.

The Board of Selectmen gave final approval for the sale of the old church and things moved quickly after that. Mark Miller received permission to get into the place even before the final closing and start fixing things up. A number of folks from town volunteered to help: Claudio Sousa was up on a ladder painting the trim; Hickey Hix and his son, Billy, were cutting the grass; Fred and Lucille Pyle were replacing broken windows; Pidge Hitchcock, of all people, was sweeping out the nave.

"Never thought I'd see that woman do anything more strenuous than lift her nose in the air," remarks Sam Drucker at the general store.

"It does seem a bit odd, all these folks volunteering to help," says Cooper Pierce, buying dog food for his wife's French poodle. "Even Yvette and Paul Duvalier have been over there, buying all sorts of fabric to make curtains and such. And Gladys McDaniel, too, even with all the worries she's got about Rusty. Makes me feel a little guilty for not being down there myself."

"I'm a Methodist," Drucker says, shaking his head. "I'm not going to get messed up in any other church, no matter how popular."

That wasn't always the case—now, was it, Sam?

He grunts, trying to ignore the sound of his late wife's voice, as he puts the dog food in a bag for Cooper and nods good-bye.

*Don't you remember when we joined that Bible study group
with Grace West?*

The store's empty. Sam begins wiping down the counter
with a sponge. His missing fingers tingle. Funny how he can
still feel them, even after all these years.

We would meet at Grace's house, don't you remember, Sam?

It's as if his wife, Alice, dead these last six years, was
standing right beside him.

*How excited we were to join. Oh, yes, it was you and I and
Florence Reich and Frank and Anne Winn and Tommy Longstaff
and Chipper Robin—oh, Chipper was just a kid then, so bright-
eyed and fervent. Remember how proud Grace was of him?
Told him what a good God-fearing young man he was.*

The bell over the door jingles. Sam looks up. A woman
enters the store, a young woman. Dark, pretty. She disappears
down one of the aisles.

Who is it, Sam? Who is that woman?

Sam tries to get a glimpse of her in the overhead mirror he
placed to ward off shoplifters. But all he can make out is dark
hair and a good figure. He keeps his eyes on her until she walks
up to the counter, a tube of toothpaste and a box of sanitary
napkins in her hands.

"Hello, Mr. Drucker," she says.

He just looks at her.

"Do you remember me? I'm Victoria Kennelly."

"Oh," he says. And of course, he does.

So does Alice.

The girl who made Grace go away!

"You've come back," Sam says, not ringing up her purchases yet.

"Yes," she says. "I've come back."

He scans the toothpaste, then the box of napkins. He gives
Victoria her total and she hands over the cash.

She takes her bag, preparing to leave. She's a few steps from
the door when Sam speaks again.

"You ought to go check out the old church," he tells her .
"They're really fixing it up."

She looks back at him. For several seconds she just holds
his stare. "Thank you," she finally says. "I think I'll do just
that."

* * *

The next couple of days it rains. Officer Dean Sousa is walking the Main Street beat. Gone is the usual spring to his step, the cheery good mornings he'd call out. This thing with Rusty has really gotten him down. Rusty was like a big brother to him. And now poor Job, too: every day, especially now that school's let out, his son, Jamal, has just gotten worse. Yesterday Dean found Jamal spray-painting nasty words about Principal Martha Sturm on the pavement of the municipal parking lot.

"Mornin', Aunt Marge," Dean says as he passes the diner. Dean's aunt—and everybody's favorite waitress—is hunched in the door frame under the awning to keep from getting wet, smoking a cigarette. Dean never knew she smoked.

But Aunt Marge doesn't answer. When Dean stops to see if she heard him, she simply blows smoke in his face and goes back inside.

"What's eatin' *her*?" Dean asks out loud.

The same thing that seems to be eating everybody in town these days. Everybody's so surly that Dean thinks it's affecting tourism. More than one visitor has stopped to tell him they're never coming back to Falls Church because the people are so rude. Dean's never known the locals to be this unpleasant. Aunt Marge's always got a smile for anyone who comes by.

She wasn't the only one of his relatives to sit there glumly at his mother's birthday party last weekend—heck, at least half of them refused to sing when his sister Diane dragged out the cake. His uncle Joe nearly got into a fistfight with his uncle Manny, and his cousin Claudio insulted his cousin Susan, calling her a fat cow.

"What's going on with everybody in this town?" Dean asks Miranda Pierce, shaking the rain off his hat as he stops by Hornet.

"Shhh," Miranda tells him, her finger to her lips. She nods in the direction of the hand-made jewelry. There's a woman there trying on some earrings. Even with her dark glasses and kerchief, Dean knows who it is: *Carolyn Prentiss,* his favorite movie star in the entire world.

Gosh, ever since she'd bought a house in town, Dean's been hoping to run into her. Hoping for just a glance, just a touch—

oh, God, how he has dreamed about her! He's seen every movie she's ever made. Especially that one where she played a space villainess and got to run around in that skintight shiny silver spandex—

"Dean," Miranda warns, breaking his reverie, "don't make a scene."

"Of course not." He stiffens, drawing up his chin and setting his puny shoulders back in a hilarious assumption of dignity. "What do you think I am? I'm an officer of the law. And, after all, she's just a person like anybody else, just somebody shopping. . . ."

Carolyn Prentiss moves past him, a whiff of her perfume tickling his nose.

"Holy—holy—holy," Dean stammers, losing his balance, stumbling backward and knocking over a whole pile of shoe boxes. They clatter down into a heap. Carolyn looks over in surprise.

"Oh, Dean," Miranda grumbles, stooping down to pick them up.

"It's okay, situation under control!" he shouts to Carolyn, moving his hand up to tip his hat to her, then realizing he'd taken his hat off. "Just a little accident here! Don't worry, no one's seen you! No one knows who you are!" He laughs awkwardly. Miranda rolls her eyes. Carolyn Prentiss disappears behind a rack of summer dresses.

The door opens. A muscular man in a tight black shirt and khaki shorts enters, looking around. He spies Carolyn and makes a beeline toward her.

"Oh, no, you don't," Dean shouts, rushing up to the guy and taking his arm. "We just don't let anybody off the street harass our citizens. I'll have to ask you, mister, to back off. Miss Prentiss wants to be left alone. No autographs, no pictures, please!"

"Get your hand off me, pip-squeak," the man snarls. "I'm her manager."

Dean gulps.

"It's okay, Officer," Carolyn Prentiss says in that same syrupy voice Dean knows so well from the movies. She pushes her sunglasses up on her head. "This is Edmond Tyler, and he's always barging in on me. I appreciate your intentions."

"Well, I just—I—uh—"

She smiles. "What's your name?"

"Um—um," he stammers.

"It's Dean," Miranda calls over from the floor, where she's still picking up boxes. "Officer Dean Sousa." She pauses. "One of Falls Church's finest."

"Didn't know the local police had a high-school auxiliary," Edmond Tyler snaps.

"I think he's *very* fine," Carolyn says, winking at Dean. "Law enforcement is a noble career for a young man to pursue. You must be very brave."

"Well," Dean says, laughing, "I've had my moments."

"And this ain't one of 'em, buddy," Tyler says. "Carolyn, we have to hurry. You've got that conference call with Spielberg and Geffen in half an hour."

"*Spielberg*," Dean says in wonder. "Like in Steven?"

"No, like in Bertha," the manager quips.

Carolyn heads up to the counter, where she buys a silk scarf. Miranda beams. Tyler impatiently drums his fingers against each other near the door.

"It was good to meet you, Officer Sousa," Carolyn says, turning to give him a smile.

"Oh," he says breathlessly. "You can call me Dean."

"Okay, Dean," she says, reaching over and kissing him on the cheek. "Thanks again."

He stands there like that, not moving for several minutes, just staring at the door after she's gone.

"She called me Dean," he says dreamily.

Miranda just shakes her head and goes back to work.

Father Jim Roche has been pastor of St. Peter's Church for the past twenty-nine years. When he was first assigned to the parish, he was a young, bright-eyed priest filled with idealism and hope for the future. But as the years have passed, he's grown old and tired, and he's watched as his parishioners have fallen away. At one time he had two priests with him at St. Peter's. Now it's just him and rotating visiting priests from elsewhere on the Cape.

He lives alone in the rectory, shuffling down the stairs every morning at five-thirty. Dear devoted Agnes Doolittle, his house-keeper and cook, is already there, and the heady fragrance of coffee always greets him by the third step down. He says a morning mass at seven o'clock, often with only old Mr. and Mrs. Sousa and the Reich sisters in the pews. On Sundays it's not much better, with a handful of families in regular attendance. Weekly collections have dropped over 70 percent in the last five years, and the bishop is considering shutting down St. Peter's, sending Father Roche over to Hyannis.

Much of his time now is spent in the church garden, tending the roses and planting annuals. That's what he's doing now, down on all fours, digging holes with a small spade to plant four boxes of smiling yellow pansies he picked up at the True Value this morning. Dear Lord, wasn't Lucille Pyle in a better mood than she's been all month? She greeted him warmly again, the way she always used to, even though she was a Methodist. Father Roche was pleased to see the change in her; so many folks in town had gotten so surly, just as the warm weather arrived. He couldn't understand it.

But as he presses the pansies down into the soil along the walkway, he's not sure how happy he is about the *reason* behind Lucille's renewed cheeriness.

"I feel so *worthwhile*, Father," she told him, "helping the Reverend Miller set up his church. It's really true what they say. The more you do for others, the better you feel." She smiled at him from behind her cat-eye glasses. "You must come to our first service, Father. You know it's open to all faiths."

Father James Roche snorts as he stands, brushing off the dirt from his pants. This newfangled religion is something alien to him. In the old days you stood for something. Everyone knew what the Catholics believed. There was no mistaking them for Methodists or Lutherans or certainly not Jews. Now he's heard that guy Miller's got pictures of Jesus, Moses, Muhammad, Buddha and Siva, all up on his altar together.

Father Roche looks off down Main Street. He sees the trucks rumbling down the road, taking a right onto Church Street. He knows where they're heading. All week he's seen them going down there, to the old church, fixing it up, bringing in new glass, new shingles, new paint. His own church could use some sprucing up, but he doesn't see the town flocking to help *him* out. Why, he's even seen Aggie Duarte and Sally-Ann Amato, two of his most loyal parishioners, down at the old church, carrying in carpeting and gilded cups. Meanwhile, neither one of them has made Sunday mass in *two weeks!*

"Father, you shouldn't be getting down and up like that," says Agnes Doolittle, coming out of the rectory, shaking her head. "I'll plant the flowers for you later."

"Oh, for pity's sake, Agnes, my joints aren't that bad," he tells her, bending down to dig another hole, grunting a little as he does so. "Besides, I don't see a whole army of helpers around here the way that guy Miller has."

"And it's mighty odd, too, don't you think?" Agnes asks. "I mean, I know he's a charming boy. He's been by here a couple times, very sweet. But I'm not going down there to help him paint."

Father Roche looks up at her. "He's been by here?"

"Oh, yes. Twice. Just to say hello."

The priest shakes his head. "He's never come to see me. The only time I met him was at Town Hall that night. Seemed a little aloof, if you ask me."

"Oh, no, he's been very charming. Father, here, let me help you."

He'd been struggling to stand again, but his knee caught on him, so Agnes has to help him get his balance. It's at that moment that his eyes catch sight of a young woman walking with a man down the sidewalk past the church. He knows her. By the Lord Jesus, it's—

"Victoria!" he shouts. "Victoria Kennelly!"

She turns up the walkway to St. Peter's. The man, someone Father Roche thinks he recognizes from town, walks a few steps behind her. "Hello, Father," she says. "Hello, Mrs. Doolittle."

"Little Victoria Kennelly?" Agnes asks. "I can't believe my eyes."

She smiles. "I'm surprised you recognized me, Father."

He smiles in return, clapping her hands warmly in his. "Oh, Victoria. How often I've thought of you all these years."

"And I you." She smiles, looking up at the church. "Without you, I'd never have survived those first few days."

"Oh, my dear," Father Roche says thickly. "What brings you back to Falls Church?"

"I'm not sure," she tells him, looking deep into his eyes. "I was hoping you might be able to help me figure that out."

"Me?"

She nods. She gestures to the man behind her, who comes up to join them. "Father, do you know Dr. Kip Hobart?"

The priest looks at the young man. Handsome, green eyes, with a cleft in his chin. "I've seen you in town—"

"Yes," Dr. Hobart says. "I have an office on Green Street. I'm a psychologist."

Victoria smiles. "And much more than that." She looks from Hobart back at Father Roche. "Could we speak with you for a few moments? I was hoping maybe you could help us."

"Help you?"

"Yes," she says. "Could we go inside and . . . talk?"

There's something in her eyes that frightens the old priest. Something he can't pinpoint, but it's there nonetheless. Frightens him in a way he hasn't felt in a long time. Not since . . . not since he saw the thing that killed Victoria's family, the thing that most likely also made off with little Petey McKay.

The thing that he knows was the face of the Beast.

Father Roche suppresses a shudder, clapping off the soil on his hands and leading them into the rectory. Agnes Doolittle puts on a pot of coffee. Then they all settle down to talk.

Sunday, June 23, 10:55 A.M.

On the day the old church is finally reopened, it seems as if the entire town turns out for the event. The renovation work is remarkable, everyone agrees, with new stained glass and all the old wooden pews polished to a high shine. The grass has been cut, the front steps repaired, the walls all given a fresh new coat of white paint. Much still needs to be done: the downstairs hall hasn't yet been touched and there are still some broken windows high up in the nave and, of course, the steeple remains a burned ugly stub sticking up into the sky. But all in good time, Reverend Miller assures folks. All in good time.

Nate arrives a few moments before the welcoming service is about to start. He's come with the chief and Ellen, who's making a rare public appearance. She looks drawn and pale, walking a little slowly, but she's determined to keep up. The chief holds her by the arm with the utmost gentleness and solicitation. Her earlier apprehension about Miller and his church has given way to a deep curiosity.

"I had to see for myself what the fuss is all about," Ellen says. "Helen Twelvetrees stopped by with a casserole—so sweet of her—and she told me what a stunning change had come over the place."

Nate takes one arm and the chief another as Ellen makes the climb up the front steps. Nate hadn't wanted to come, but the chief asked him to as a special favor, so he could serve as

added support for Ellen. Of course Nate agreed, but he would
have preferred staying on the hunt for Monica Paul. He's spent
the last few days questioning all her coworkers, friends and
neighbors down in Barnstable. He hasn't been able to sleep
since she disappeared. Where is she? How could anyone vanish
without a trace?

"Mrs. Hutchins! Chief!" The Reverend Miller meets them
halfway. "How pleased I am to see you both."

"Quite a face-lift you've given to the old place," the chief
tells him, shaking his hand.

Mark Miller beams. "Oh, it hasn't been me. It's been my
flock."

He gestures around. Nate has reached the top of the steps
and peers into the church. He sees the reverend's flock all
right: everybody hustling and bustling around, welcoming their
friends and neighbors, passing out programs, arranging flowers
on the altar. People who just days before had been part of the
grumbling mass of Falls Church. People like Cliff Claussen
and Sandy Hooker and Pidge Hitchcock. Even perennial nasties
like Mary Silva and Max Winn are here, showing people to
their seats.

"Good morning, Nate," says Marge Duarte.

"Marge," Nate says, smiling. "Sorry I haven't been by the
diner in a few days. I've been overwhelmed." He looks around.
"What a turnout, huh? I can't imagine what's gotten into all
these folks. I mean, Gerry Garafolo? Hickey Hix? You'd think
they'd be home watching the Red Sox."

Marge looks at him as if not comprehending his remark.
"It's an honor, Nate, to do the work of the Lord."

His smile stretches into a broad grin. Surely that's one of
Marge's cracks. In a second she's going to roll her eyes.

But she doesn't. She moves off to welcome other curious
arrivals. And Clem's with her. *Clem*—in a blue suit and his
hair combed.

What the hell is going on here?

Nate looks around. There's Laura Millay, the ice queen of
Cliff Heights, passing out programs. Mark Miller comes up to
her, whispers something in her ear and watches as she moves
off to take care of whatever task he's assigned. Since when
has Laura Millay taken orders from *anybody?*

Nate looks in another direction. There's fisherman Manny Duarte and developer Richie Rostocki, a more unlikely pair Nate can't imagine, setting up some extra folding chairs together.

"What's going on here?" Chief asks, coming up behind Nate.

"That's what I want to know," Nate says.

Ellen tries to smile, but it's clear she's troubled, too. "Such disparate people coming together in a common cause. I suppose we should be impressed."

The chief looks around at the church. "But what's the cause? That's what troubles me."

"Look," Nate says, gesturing with his head.

They all turn. Rusty McDaniel has just come into the church, followed by his wife and children. It's the first time he's been seen in public since the shooting. He'd been under orders to stay at home until the investigation is complete.

"Jesus H.—" Chief sputters.

Several townspeople look at Rusty but quickly turn their faces away. But others—Nate's detective eye notes all part of the Reverend Miller's "flock"—approach him, shake his hand, welcome him kindly and gently to the church.

"Should I go over to him?" Nate asks.

"No," Chief says. "It would cause too much of a scene. Let him be for now."

Laura Millay is showing the McDaniels to a pew in the back of the church. Ellen, meanwhile, has taken a seat herself, her legs starting to give out on her. The chief slides in next to her. Nate is about to follow suit, when there's a hand on his shoulder. He looks up.

"Detective Tuck?" It's Kathy McKenzie, but he almost doesn't recognize her. She looks different.

"Yes?" Nate braces for a scene.

Kathy smiles. "I just wanted to apologize if I was any inconvenience down at the station. I don't know what came over me. But I'm doing better now."

For a moment Nate doesn't know how to respond. Kathy stands there smiling up at him, her hair combed neatly, her face scrubbed clean of any cosmetics. The Kathy McKenzie he knew wore a lot of makeup: eye shadow, rouge, lipstick.

Her hair was usually big and sprayed. Now she wears it flat to her head, parted simply in the middle.

"I'm glad to hear that, Kathy," Nate says. "Are you—back to work? Is Josh with you?"

"I'll be getting Josh from my father this week. And I've quit my job. The Reverend Miller helped me so much during this crisis. He's given me a job here, at the church."

"At the church?" Nate looks across the room. Mark Miller has his back to them, still greeting people at the door, but Nate feels certain the good reverend knows that Kathy is talking to him. Had he instructed her to do so? As part of her rehabilitation, perhaps?

"Yes. I'm going to be helping with the cleaning, and also working as a secretary." She smiles again. "He really saved my life, Reverend Miller did."

Until you went crazy, I wasn't aware it needed any saving, Nate thinks to himself, but he just smiles at Kathy and then takes his seat next to the chief.

"What the hell is going on here?" he asks again.

But before the chief can answer, Ellen shushes them. The Reverend Miller is walking down the aisle toward the altar. Everyone starts to applaud.

Nate doesn't join in.

Victoria arrives with Kip Hobart and Father Roche just as the applause begins. They slip into the back pew relatively unnoticed. They sit quietly, listening to Reverend Miller's words.

"This is a home for all of you, for all good people," he is saying. "You will see that on our altar we have symbols of all the world's great faiths. Judaism. Christianity. Buddhism. Hinduism. Islam." He gestures into the audience. "My deepest thanks go to Habib and Sandipa Khan for donating a copy of the Koran brought with them from Pakistan."

There's a smattering of applause. Victoria looks from the Khans, smiling modestly, to Kip and then to Father Roche.

He speaks with words coated in honey, the ghost had told her.

Not the ghost who had taken Petey, not the one who had

haunted her all these years. But another ghost—a woman—a woman who appeared to her in Kip Hobart's office the first day she went to see him.

Dr. Hobart had *believed* her. Victoria had been so relieved—thrilled even—by that fact. Kip Hobart had believed her when she told him about the ghost. Caroline had known what she was doing when she recommended Victoria see Dr. Hobart. He was a young man, but his words were old and wise. On entering his little office in a redbrick building on Green Street, Victoria had picked up a brochure. *Past-Life Regressions. Hypnotherapy. Channeling.* Dr. Kip Hobart was no ordinary psychologist.

"They used to call what I do parapsychology," Kip had explained to her. "You know, the guy who's always brought in to offer the rationale for the supernatural in all those poltergeist and demon possession movies." He smiled at her. "Usually—although he or she puts up a valiant fight against the forces of the dark side—the parapsychologist gets killed in those films, leaving the way open for the hero or heroine to save the day."

Victoria laughed. But then she added plainly, "This isn't a movie."

Kip Hobart nodded. "I can see that. I sensed something different about you the moment you walked in."

He called in his assistant then, Alexis Stokes, a pretty blond woman with large round eyes. She took one look at Victoria and nodded her head. "There's someone with you," Alexis said. "A little boy."

"Alexis can see the dead," Dr. Hobart explained matter-of-factly.

Victoria didn't react. She knew who the little boy was. Petey had been following her ever since she abandoned him that night in the woods.

Dr. Hobart's assistant studied Victoria carefully. "The boy is saying, 'Find me,' " she said, her eyes moving a couple feet away from Victoria. "He's being really insistent. 'Find me,' he's saying over and over."

"That's why I'm here," Victoria said. "That's why I came back to Falls Church."

Dr. Hobart nodded, listening intently.

''Whatever killed my family,'' Victoria said, so grateful at finally being *heard*, ''whatever took Petey away, is *back*. It's returned, and I'm trying to stop it.''

Dr. Hobart took her hand. ''Okay, Victoria. I'm going to ask you to trust me.''

She had no choice. Caroline had sent her here. She trusted Caroline. And she needed an ally. She couldn't go on alone.

So Dr. Hobart hypnotized her. It was nothing like the hypnosis she'd seen on television, with all sorts of hocus-pocus and snapping of fingers and deep trances. The hypnosis Dr. Hobart conducted was just a heightened state of both relaxation and awareness. Victoria sat there on his couch and suddenly became aware of time and space in a way she had never been before.

She saw Petey, just where Alexis Stokes had been looking. The boy was indeed mouthing, over and over, ''Find me. Find me.''

But she saw someone else, too. A woman sitting in a chair across the room. A young woman whom Victoria thought looked vaguely familiar, but she couldn't be sure. Dark-haired, dark-eyed, plain. Probably no more than eighteen or nineteen. She wore a cashmere sweater and a little gold cross. She looked so sad.

''He speaks with words coated in honey,'' the young woman told Victoria. ''But there is venom beneath.''

''Who?'' Victoria asked.

''We believed him,'' the ghost told her. ''He had many followers. He said we could end the war if we only believed.''

Then the young woman stood and walked across the room. Victoria saw the chair she had been sitting in was covered in blood.

''It was the girl who was killed!'' she screamed to Kip Hobart. ''I saw her! Priscilla Googins!''

Prissy Goo had been killed years before Victoria had been born, but of course she'd heard the tales while growing up. She'd taken part in the schoolyard ghost stories. *Tell me tall or tell me true; tell me what happened to Prissy Goo.*

And on her first day back in Falls Church, Victoria had seen the article in the *Cape Cod Times*. Priscilla's photo had been paired with that of Petey McKay. The two unsolved murders of Falls Church.

"It's happened not once before, but *twice*," she explained to Kip afterward, sipping a cup of herbal tea that Alexis had brewed for her to calm her nerves. "Petey and Priscilla both. It was the same evil."

Kip Hobart nodded. "Then it's probably happened even more, too. I suspect this may just be a recurring pattern for Falls Church."

That's when Victoria remembered Michael Pilarski's final essay. She reached down into her bag, gripped its pages and pulled it out, scalding hot.

Kip Hobart took the essay and set it down on the coffeetable in front of him. It was literally steaming as he turned each page, glancing through it.

"The old church," he said quietly.

"Father Fall," Victoria said in return.

Their eyes met.

He believes me, Victoria thought, feeling as if she would cry in gratitude. *He believes me!*

"This is a home for all those who look to God for answers, a home for all those who cherish rightness, and goodness, and the true path that leads to the light of truth and wisdom."

Many in the congregation rise to their feet as Reverend Miller finishes his remarks. Suddenly Alan Hitchcock is up on the altar, shaking his hand heartily, clapping him on the back. "As the town manager," Hitchcock says, taking the podium, "I want to officially welcome Reverend Mark Miller to our community and to thank him for all he's done with this historic old church."

Mary Silva is fluttering behind him, angling for her chance to speak. "And for the Board of Selectmen, I second that," she says. "Thank you for your inspiring words, Reverend Miller. Thank you!"

Nate sees Marcella Stein stand up and walk out of the pew she was sitting in, heading to the back of the church. "Apparently not all the selectmen agree," he whispers to the chief.

Mark Miller has reclaimed the podium. "Please join us in the back for coffee and refreshments. We hope soon to have our church hall renovated downstairs. Anyone who'd like to volunteer, please see Kathy McKenzie and she'll take your name.''

People begin sliding out of their pews and heading toward the back. The chief helps Ellen stand. She gives him a small smile.

"You doing okay, sweetheart?" Chief asks.

"Maybe I ought to skip the coffee. I'm feeling a little tired."

The chief nods. "You'll give folks my regrets, Nate?"

"Of course."

He looks at him sternly. "And keep your eye on Rusty."

Nate agrees. He watches them leave by the side door. Nate's heart breaks when he sees Ellen so frail, the chief so solicitous of her. They've been married thirty-some years. He thinks fleetingly of Siobhan, of what life might have been like had they been able to spend three decades together. Thinking about Siobhan inevitably makes him think about Monica, and vice versa. His heart aches. In both cases he still blames himself.

He turns, only to nearly walk smack-dab into Catherine Santos, town librarian, who's been waiting to talk with him. "Miss Santos," he says in surprise.

"Nate," she says, "what in blue blazes is going on in this town?"

He grins. "So you've noticed it, too."

"Yes. All these people—*Mary Silva*, for God's sake—kow-towing to this guy like he was—I don't know—the Second Coming!"

"It does seem odd, doesn't it? Guess that's what happens when folks find religion."

"But Laura Millay?" Catherine asks in disbelief. "Marge Duarte? *Clem?*"

Nate looks up. His fat friend from the diner is huffing and puffing up on the altar, rolling up the cord for the microphone.

"As if Clem has ever done anything more physical than fry eggs," Catherine Santos remarks.

Nate just scratches his head.

"Well, I've got the willies after all this," Catherine tells him. "I'm not staying around any longer. I want to go home."

"Okay, Miss Santos." Nate smiles at her as she hurries away, but he's quickly scouting out someone else in the crowd.

He spots her. Marcella Stein. He's glad she's still here. He walks over to her.

"You looked as if you weren't too happy about Mary Silva conferring the selectmen's blessing on this place," Nate says.

She eyes him coldly. "She had no right speaking for us."

"What did you think of the speech the good reverend gave?"

Marcella studies him. "I'm not sure I want to say, Nate. I just offered my opinion to Cliff Claussen, who acted as if I were blaspheming. Suddenly this town isn't in the mood to listen to any dissent."

"Try me," Nate says.

Marcella sighs. "Oh, Miller said all the right words. He's got the Koran and the Star of David up there. But there was something troubling. Something underneath the words."

"What do you mean?"

" 'This is a home for all those who cherish rightness, and goodness, and the true path that leads to the light,' " Marcella quotes. "But what does he mean by rightness? Goodness? *Whose* rightness and goodness? And what is the *true* path?" She pulls in close. "Did you notice who *wasn't* here tonight, Nate? Nearly the whole town, but no Martha Sturm."

Nate looks around. That's right. He hadn't seen the school principal all night.

"Several of Reverend Miller's biggest boosters are the ones petitioning to get Martha Sturm fired, and he's made no attempt to distance himself from that. For all his honeyed words preaching tolerance, he said nothing tonight about the persecution of Martha Sturm."

Just then, Nate feels a hand on his shoulder. He turns. It's Victoria Kennelly.

"I just wanted to say hello," she says.

"Uh, hello," Nate says. "Victoria Kennelly, this is Marcella Stein."

The women nod at each other.

"I couldn't help but overhear your remark, Ms. Stein," Victoria says. " 'For all his honeyed words.' Do you think Reverend Miller might be insincere?"

"I'm finished offering my opinion for tonight," Marcella replies. "Come to the next Board of Selectmen's meeting if you want to hear what I think."

She says good-bye.

"I didn't mean to scare her off," Victoria says.

Nate grins down at her. "So what did *you* think about the reverend's words? Did *you* think they were insincere?"

She's about to answer, when the door to the church opens and in comes Dave Carlson—town mechanic, all-around nice guy, father of two and the informant on Rusty McDaniel. It was Dave who found Rusty laughing, smoking gun in his hand, standing over the lifeless body of that poor kid. Now it's Dave's eyes that are wild. He staggers into the church, making a beeline toward Rusty, shouting something unintelligible.

Nate's on the scene instantly.

Victoria watches him. He's a good man, this Nate Tuck. They need him.

Their first ally had been Father Roche. Victoria knew he could be trusted, and besides, the old priest had been in Falls Church for many years. He would know things that she, Kip and Alexis wouldn't. He would remember Priscilla Googins. Yes, they needed Father Roche.

At first, the priest had been reluctant to listen to their story. Catholics were funny like that, Victoria thought: They believe selectively in the supernatural. Jesus could rise from the dead, could transform bread and wine into his flesh and blood, Padre Pio could exhibit the stigmata and the Virgin Mary could appear to little girls in the French countryside. Even the Devil could make cameo appearances, which is why the Catholics alone kept the ritual of exorcism on the books.

But suggest to a Catholic that the ghosts of a little boy and a murdered woman might appear, and they throw up their hands, telling you that you're crazy.

"You can't deny it, Father!" Victoria had said to him. "That night, when you took me in, you saw it, too! You saw the ghost!"

The thing that would haunt her for so many years had made its first appearance that night, just hours after she witnessed the flames dancing through her house, as she shivered under a blanket in the rectory. Father Roche had been sitting on the side of her bed, consoling her, while the ghost stood just a few feet away, beckoning to her with its long skeletal fingers. From Father Roche's expression Victoria could see that he saw the apparition, too, and that it terrified him as much as it did her.

"Admit it, Father," she said the other day when she and Kip met with him. "You saw it, too."

He covered his craggy face with his old hands. "I looked upon the face of the Devil," he croaked. "And not for the first time."

And so he told them about Priscilla.

"I got the call that she'd been found stabbed," Father Roche explained, "and I rushed over to the old church to give her last rites. Her family was deeply religious, and I knew they'd want that. Even though Priscilla had turned her back on the faith—well, it was the times, you know. So many of the young people in the 1960s were experimenting with all sorts of new ideas."

Kip had leaned in toward the priest, fascinated by his account. "What kind of new ideas was Priscilla experimenting with, Father?"

"It's so hard to remember. There was a group of young people—they met in the old church. It was a kind of cult. They were hippies. I suppose you're both too young to remember what it was like."

"So what happened when you went to give Priscilla the last rites, Father?" Kip asked.

He shuddered. "I saw the Evil One. In the face of a young man. One of those in the cult. His eyes were black. He had . . ."

The old priest was unable to speak for a moment.

"Go ahead, Father," Kip urged.

"He had worms in his teeth!"

Victoria steadied him with her hand on his. "Who was he, Father?"

His face had drained of all color. "I can go years without thinking about all of that. I think everyone just pushed it out of their minds. Because it wasn't just Priscilla, you know. Just as it wasn't just the McKay boy's disappearance, or the deaths of your family, Victoria. There was so much horror going on besides that."

"Exactly. The whole town had gone mad, just as it has again today."

The old priest nodded. "I remember the boy who was killed by the police shortly before Priscilla was found dead. I remember how more and more, people began doing terrible things. I remember watching it affect people, this evil, one by one—"

"That's how it happened when I was a girl, too," Victoria said as Kip Hobart took it all down in his notebook. "People just started acting weird, turning on each other. Lots of people joined with Grace West trying to get those little boys with AIDS kicked out of school—"

"Yes," Father Roche said. "Grace West. The things she made people do!"

"Somehow," Dr. Hobart said, looking at both of them, "whatever evil was here in 1967 and again in 1988 has returned. And both times, it takes hold of people, one by one, spreading like a terrible cancer."

Something jars Victoria back to the present. She looks up. Not three feet away stands the Reverend Mark Miller, surrounded by several adoring townsfolk. But the young minister is staring directly at her.

His eyes. So blue. So mesmerizing.

Eyes Victoria has seen before.

But those eyes had been black.

Victoria sees the face of Grace West turning around to glare at her when she had had the nerve to stand up at Town Meeting and say what was happening was wrong.

She staggers backward as if she's been struck. She grips the edge of a pew. Mark Miller keeps staring at her. She feels as if the life is being sucked out of her. She feels as if she'll crumble to the floor in a heap.

But then, Dave Carlson lets out a loud, agonizing scream, and even Mark Miller is forced to turn his eyes to him.

"You've gotta listen to me!" Dave is shouting, being restrained by Nate Tuck and Job Emerson. "You've gotta lock him up! You've gotta put him away!"

"Easy man," Job is saying, gripping Dave by the shoulders.

Victoria gathers her wits to concentrate on the scene. She sees Nate Tuck turn to Rusty McDaniel and suggest he leave. She overhears him say Rusty shouldn't have come anyway, that his presence is clearly upsetting people. She watches Rusty and his family leave without protest, Nate escorting them out.

Her eyes turn back to follow Job Emerson escorting Dave Carlson to the side door.

"But you've gotta listen to me," Dave is blabbering. He's trembling, as if he's scared for his life. "I've gotta finish telling you my dream!"

Job scowls. "Dave, in all the years I've known you, I've never known you to get drunk and stagger into a place upsetting everyone!"

"You've gotta listen! At the end, at the end of the dream, the man in black opened his mouth—"

"Whatever," Job is saying, hustling him out the door.

"*He had worms in his mouth! There were worms!*"

Job Emerson closes the door behind them. Victoria stares at it for several seconds.

The church is emptying out as she realizes what she's heard.

That's how he does it.

That's how his evil gets passed on.

Through people's dreams.

She hurries out of the church, not wanting to catch the eye of Reverend Miller again. She sees Kip and Father Roche standing on the front steps, talking with Nate Tuck. Perfect. She rushes up to them.

"Listen to me, Detective," she says. "What I'm about to say is going to sound crazy, but you have to listen."

He looks at her oddly.

"We have to prevent your fellow officer Job Emerson from going to sleep tonight."

"Dear God," Father Roche intones.

"What are you talking about?" Nate asks.

"Whatever you do," Victoria insists, "you mustn't let Job close his eyes."

Monday, June 24, 10:05 A.M.

But there was no way to stop it. Even if Nate had fully believed them, fully trusted their ridiculous rantings, there would have been no way to keep Job from going to sleep. He told them just that, but when old Father Roche had placed his hand on Nate's shoulder and looked him straight in the eye, telling him, "I need you to believe," Nate had gotten into his cruiser and driven over to Job's house.

He caught him just as he and Berniece were heading upstairs.

"It's been a long day, Nate," Job told him. "You really need me back at the station?"

Nate felt like an idiot. "No, buddy. Go on to bed. Sorry to have bothered you."

He was being crazy. Job had been through a lot, what with his best pal, Rusty, cracking up and his son, Jamal, turning into a juvenile delinquent. What was Nate supposed to say? *These three crazy folks are convinced you're going to have a bad dream, Job, a dream that's going to put you under the power of some evil force. Stay awake, Job. Don't close your eyes.*

Nate puts his hands over his face now and wishes to God he *had* said those words.

It seems crazy—unbelievable—but hadn't Betty Silva reported to them that *Hiram* had had a dream, and hadn't everything started from that point? Part of Nate isn't surprised when he gets into the station this morning and discovers Job is absent. When he calls the house, he gets Jamal, who says his parents are gone.

"Where are they?" Nate demands.

"They need to find the Lord," Jamal had says eerily calmly, and then hangs up on Nate.

Nate is in his cruiser within seconds, tearing out down Pearl Street and racing around the block to the old church. He finds Reverend Miller supervising a painting job of the eastern wall, Hickey Hix and Fred Pyle up on ladders.

"Have you seen Officer Emerson?" Nate asks, not offering any cordialities.

Mark Miller smiles his boyish grin. "No, I haven't, Detective. Was he planning on coming by here?"

"Maybe *you* can tell *me*," Nate challenges.

The young minister raises his eyebrows. "I'm not sure what you mean."

Nate feels ridiculous then, but he has to follow through on whatever lead he's been given, even one as crazy as Victoria Kennelly's theory. "Let me ask you, Reverend," Nate says. "How have you managed to get these folks so devoted to your church? I've never known Hickey up there to climb a ladder for anybody. And Fred should be cutting hair."

Mark Miller smiles again. "The Lord works in mysterious ways, doesn't he, Detective?"

Nate says nothing in response, just hops back into his cruiser and resumes his search for Job and Berniece. He has not found them. Jamal hasn't been lying: they are indeed not home. Their house is a mess; their son sits quietly with his hands clasped in a living-room chair. In town Nate inquires at the diner, at the True Value, at Woodward's Pharmacy, but no one admits to having seen either Job or Berniece. Looking at the faces of the townspeople of Falls Church, Nate suddenly realizes he trusts none of them. So many had been among the Reverend Miller's flock yesterday. And this morning Marge Duarte looked at him with cold, unspeaking eyes, Clem turned his shoulder, and Tess Woodward appeared to be lying through her teeth.

Nate feels frightened. Not even exploring the crackhouses in Oakland had made him this uneasy.

"I need you to believe," Father Roche had urged.

From the pay phone at the corner of Pearl and Main, Nate calls the nursing home where Berniece works. "Can you tell me if Berniece Emerson showed up at work?"

"No, she hasn't. It's not like her at all."

Nate hangs up the phone.

Okay, this is just too weird. I'm not going to start believing some wacky tale spun by a crazy woman, a senile old priest and some New Age psychologist.

"Excuse me, Detective?"

He turns. Behind him is the hunched figure of old Agatha Reich, retired schoolteacher and eighty-seven years old.

"I heard you were looking for Berniece Emerson."

"Yes," Nate says. "Both she and her husband."

"Well," the old woman says, "Berniece comes by every morning to help me get dressed and up and around. She's a wonderful nurse's aide, you know."

Nate's nodding. "And she didn't show this morning?"

"Oh, she *did*," Miss Reich tells him. "She was at my house bright and early. But in such a *state*. Something about a dream she'd had."

"Dear God," Nate says in a small voice.

"She insisted on telling me. A horrible thing. I tried to get her to sit down, have a cup of tea, but she was out the door. Her husband was waiting for her in the car."

"Miss Reich, please try to forget what she told you. She wasn't . . . well. She's . . . not herself. That's why I'm trying to find her."

The old woman shivers. "Oh, but I can't forget it. I wish I could. It was so horrible that I can't repeat it. But I haven't been able to think about anything else since."

And tonight you will dream the same dream, Nate thinks, *and tomorrow you will tell your sister, Florence, who will tell someone else, who will tell someone else. . . .*

He hops back into his cruiser and speeds over to Kip Hobart's office.

Monday, June 24, 11:58 A.M.

"So according to your theory, we have to stop Miss Reich from falling asleep," Nate tells the group.

Kip Hobart sighs. "Yes, I suppose. Though I think that will be very difficult to do, given that she's an eighty-seven-year-old lady."

Nate bangs the table with his fist. "This is too crazy!"

Father Roche, clearly upset himself, stands and walks across the room, wringing his hands. "The Reich sisters are my most devoted parishioners," he laments. "Those poor dear ladies . . ."

"I'm afraid," says Victoria Kennelly, letting out a long sigh, "we may have to concede a few more will fall under his spell before we figure out how to stop him."

"Look," Nate says, angry now, "I'm sworn to protect people. If you honestly believe something is going to happen to that old lady, I can't just sit back and do nothing."

"I'm afraid there's nothing you *could* do, Nate, except haul her into jail and pump her full of No Doz."

Kip Hobart shakes his head. In all his years as a transpersonal psychologist, he's never run across anything like this. During his two years in Falls Church he's dealt with pretty standard psychotherapeutic issues: grief and loss, depression, identity crises. A number of clients come down from the Upper Cape for past-life regressions—he's one of the few practitioners in the area to offer such service—and he's used hypnosis to help several locals quit smoking.

He hasn't had a paranormal case since living in northern California, where he worked with several clients who claimed to be possessed by evil spirits. Most of them, Kip believes, were simply delusional psychotics, but at least two had been authentic: there was some kind of entity living within them, and only through the exorcisms he'd learned from Alexis's father had he been able to heal his clients.

Sometimes Kip feels as if he'll never be able to live up to the example set by Dr. Timothy Stokes, Alexis's father and Kip's mentor. Dr. Stokes had been the most amazing teacher Kip had ever had, a no-nonsense, old-fashioned parapsychologist, who taught Kip the difference between poltergeists—spirits determined to stick around and cause trouble—and ghosts who were merely confused dead people simply needing directions to the afterlife.

Oh, Kip knows there are some who think him odd, who roll their eyes at his embrace of the supernatural. His last boyfriend, in fact, had finally walked out on him, fed up with Kip's "wavy gravy" ways. But to deny what he saw—what he truly believed, deep down in his soul—would have been a disservice not only to himself but to the relationship. He was sorry Tom never understood that. He needed someone in his life who would *believe.*

After Dr. Stokes's death, Kip took to traveling around the country with Alexis. Most people assume they're lovers, which makes both of them laugh. In a way, he supposes, Alexis *is* his lover: although they're not sexual with each other, no one has ever really understood or believed in him the way she does. There's a bond between them, a kinship forged forever by the death of her father in a battle between the spirits of this world and the next. In that moment, when Dr. Stokes's heart stopped in the midst of an exorcism, Alexis became Kip's only family and he hers.

He looks over at her now, sitting off to the side, listening to their little band of ghost hunters discuss the mysterious occurrences in Falls Church. Who would have thought they would find such a situation here? This was supposed to be a place where they healed, put the grief of Dr. Stokes's death behind them. Cape Cod was supposed to be a place of peace, removed from the cruel pace of the rest of the world. But this evil they are confronting—it seemed to *thrive* here, to have taken root long ago. It would not be easy to dislodge it.

"Nate," Kip says, trying to reassure him, "I don't think long-term damage is necessarily done to any of these people. We've been going over this. Remember, what we're postulating is that this is not the first time something like this has happened here."

"That's right," Victoria says. "In the weeks leading up to the fire at my house, there were many people who began exhibiting irrational behavior. I remember my father commenting on Mr. Drucker at the general store. His wife, too. And even the Reich sisters, who you're worried about now. They were all part of Grace West's group trying to expel those boys with AIDS. But when she was gone, they all reverted back to their normal selves."

"Oh, but it was a terrible time," Father Roche adds. "I remember how people picked quarrels with anyone they met. I remember being called down to break up a fight between Chipper Robin and Sam Wong down at the Chinese restaurant. Chipper had called him some racist name."

"*Chipper?*" Nate looks astounded. "The same one who's fire chief today?"

"Yes." The priest sighs. "He was just in high school then."

"The point is," Kip says, "that all of these people came out of the horror eventually. Today Chipper's no racist. And I can't imagine the Reich sisters, sweet as they are, going after two sick little boys."

Father Roche is nodding. "And the same was true some twenty years earlier, around the time of poor Priscilla's death. I remember Joe and Angela Sousa almost got arrested for assaulting one of those hippies who dared to walk barefoot into the fish market." He shudders. "Strange, how I'd repressed so much of this—the Sousas, Chipper, Grace West, Priscilla—"

"I think that's part of the pattern," Kip says. "Whatever force is doing this, it becomes only a vague memory after the horror is over and the town returns to normal."

Nate doesn't seem convinced. He's pacing the room. "Look, I'm not saying I buy your crazy ideas, but I know this much."

He looks at them. "Not everyone came back to normal. Not Priscilla Googins or Petey McKay or"—he turns to look at Victoria—"your family."

"You're right about that," Kip says quietly. "There have always been victims. Like that poor man Rusty McDaniel shot."

Nate closes his eyes. "And Monica Paul." He opens his eyes again, looking out the window. "And Rusty himself. I don't care what made him do it—he'll still have to live forever with the fact that he killed an innocent kid."

Kip has a sense that Nate feels Rusty's situation personally— that it's a private hell Nate knows only too well. He's often been able to intuit such things—Dr. Stokes had called him a genuine "intuitive"—but of the particulars in Nate's case Kip can only guess. But he admits that Nate has a point. There have already been casualties in this war against the evil in Falls Church, and there will likely be more.

"Whatever this thing is," Kip says, "it seems to draw strength from hostility between people. Death and destruction is what it thrives on, what it needs to stay alive."

"That's it," Nate says. "I'm going over to the old church and bringing Mark Miller in for questioning."

"For what, Nate?" Kip laughs. "For suspicion of consorting with evil spirits?"

"I'll think up something," Nate growls.

"That would only provoke the flock," Alexis says suddenly. It's the first time she's spoken. They all look over at her. She's a soft, blond, beautiful woman with enormous eyes. "That's not how to beat him."

Kip listens. Alexis is a wise woman, having inherited much from her father.

"The way to beat him," she tells him, "is not to arrest him, not to meet violence with violence." She's a study of calmness and decision. "Think how he was beaten before."

"Well," Victoria says, "I'm not sure what happened in previous attempts, but I know everything changed from the moment I stood up at Town Meeting and declared what they were doing to the Denny boys was wrong. The evil may have taken revenge by kidnapping Petey and killing my family, but the spell itself had been broken. People dropped out of Grace West's group.

There were letters to the editor saying the Concerned Citizens of Cape Cod were nothing but a bunch of bigots.''

Kip rubs his chin, thinking. ''Victoria, what happened to Grace West after that?''

She shrugs. ''I was sent to Boston to live. I don't know.''

''Father?'' Kip asks. ''Do you remember?''

The priest scratches his head. ''Strange, how I don't recall so much of that time—Wait! Yes, I *do* remember. Again, it's one of those memories I seem to have shoved way in the back of my mind, but if I force myself, I can bring it back. I seem to remember there was talk that Grace West left town with many of her bills unpaid. People didn't speak of her much after all that happened. It was as if they were just glad she was gone. I remember now that Sargent Crawford Senior told me that he'd rented an apartment to her, and that she left without paying her last month's rent. She just disappeared into the night. Sargent figured she was so humiliated by the way the town had turned against her that she just hightailed it out of here.''

Nate is looking at Father Roche strangely. ''She was renting from Seaside Realty?''

''Yes.''

The police detective leans forward intently. ''Where, Father? What apartment was she renting?''

''Oh, I'm not sure I know—Wait, I do. Funny how these things keep coming back to me once I try to remember them. It was in the Grand Avenue Apartments down by the wharf—opposite the—'' His voice fades off as fear overtakes his features.

''Opposite the old church,'' Victoria finishes.

''Exactly where the Reverend Miller is living now,'' Nate says.

''Dear God,'' Kip says breathily.

Nate stands up and paces the room. ''This is too goddamn loony for me! What are we thinking here? That Mark Miller and this Grace West are in cahoots with—with ... I don't know what?''

''That's exactly what we're thinking, Nate,'' Victoria says. ''Only *more* than that.''

She reaches down into her bag and withdraws three manuscripts, each held together in the upper left corner by a clip. She seems to wince as she touches them.

"I had copies made of a student's final paper," she tells them. "I've mentioned this to you already, Kip. I thought we all ought to read this together; though I caution you, it's hot stuff."

She passes the manuscripts around. Kip's fingers burn as he takes his copy from her. "You're not kidding," he says.

Nate drops his on the floor, pulling his hand back with an *ouch*. Father Roche looks at her fearfully. "What *is* this, Victoria?"

She holds up her hands. There are blisters on her fingertips. "It wasn't easy getting this copied," she says with a small smile. "I short-circuited two of the three copy machines at Staples in Orleans."

Alexis has moved closer to read over Kip's shoulder. He places the document down on the table in front of him. "I suspect this may point the way toward some answers," he tells the group. "I suggest we all take a moment to read it."

Fire and Brimstone: The Story of Father John Fall and the Founding of Falls Church, Massachusetts

by Michael Pilarski

The image of the strict Puritan minister preaching damnation, fire and brimstone to his congregation could have started with the Reverend John Fall (1650–97), better known as "Father Fall" and the founder of Falls Church, Massachusetts, on Cape Cod.

The youngest son of English parents who arrived in Massachusetts Bay Colony in 1642, John Fall was born in Northampton, later moving with his family to Roxbury. He was educated at Harvard College, where his surviving notebooks show a distinctly conservative approach to theology. "In Adam's fall, we sinned all" is prominently written at the top of every page in his elaborate, spidery handwriting.

In his rigid interpretation of Christian theology, John Fall was a spiritual descendent of the beliefs of the first Pilgrims, who, appropriately enough given Fall's later career, had made their first landfall in 1620 on Cape Cod. Unlike the later, more moderate immigrants to the New World, the Pilgrims—and indeed John Fall's particular Puritanism—practiced a rigid, austere asceticism. Shortly after graduation from Harvard in 1674, John Fall began keeping a series of journals. In the earliest, dated October the 2nd, 1675, Fall wrote about his increasing dissatisfaction with what he perceived to be a "trend favouring secularism" in much of colonial society. Paraphrasing William Bradford, leader of the Pilgrims, Fall sermonized:

> Of all sorowes most heavie to be borne is that many of our children, by the great licentiousness of youth and the manifold temptations that have arisen, are drawne away by evill examples into extravagante and dangerous courses, getting the raines off their necks, and departing from their parents. The colonies are tending to dissolutnes, and the danger of their soules, to the great greefe of our founders and the dishonour of God.

In 1680, John Fall married a woman named Abigail Trout in Boston. But it was not a marriage of much duration. Abigail was killed in a fall down the stairs at their home only a week after their marriage. The magistrates ruled that her death was accidental.

Curiously, John Fall wrote very little about his wife in his journal. She is mentioned only on the day of their marriage, for which Fall recorded only the simple statement, "On this day, I entered into the covenent of Marriage with the grace of God." The next day—on the morning after apparently consummating said covenant—Fall wrote at length about the "evills of the carnal flesh," how "sanctity cannot be given to profanity no matter how necessary its function." Was he guilt-ridden about engaging in sexual relations with his own wife?

On the day of his wife's death, Fall made no entry in his journal, but on the day of her burial, he wrote, "There is no sin in finding freedom from temptation." It is an enigmatic statement. What sin was he justifying by claiming through it he had freed himself from temptation?

Already it would appear that Fall was forming

his own theology, for by this time he had stopped quoting his teachers and used Bible passages only when they supported his own particular obsessions. Usually he seemed to be composing his own set of rules and strictures, not referenced by any specific biblical text. Soon after his wife's death, he wrote: "And if a man shall lye with a woman, no matter how sanctioned by Societie, if he is determined to live by purity alone, the act shall be a sinn."

Fall's rejection of sexuality, even within a sanctified marriage, would appear to be nonsensical, given that its logical conclusion, if followed, would mean the end of the human species. Yet "no matter how necessary its function," the sexual act still left the participants somehow tainted, less pure. In this, Fall was actually harking back to the old Catholic traditions of a celibate priesthood. It is not surprising, then, that John Fall, who would not remarry after Abigail's death (an unusual situation in Puritan New England), would eventually become known as "Father" Fall—a title with further resonance of Catholicism.

In the summer of 1687 John Fall accompanied a group of settlers from Boston to Orleans on Cape Cod, apparently to serve as minister. But his views had become increasingly rigid and moralistic, with an emphatic repugnance toward sin and earthly experiences that set him apart from the religious leaders already on the Cape. Due to its remote location and seafaring tradition, the Cape embraced a more tolerant and free-spirited religious tradition. Fall's journal of January 1688 records his alienation from much of the Orleans congregation:

> Our thoughts and feares growe very sadd to see such multitudes of idle and profane young men, and even the women cavort with profanity. If it not be yet remedied, we and many others must not only say, with greefe, that we have made an ill change, even from licentious

Boston, but we must meditate some safer refuge, if God will afford it. . . .

It is tempting to bring twenty-first-century psycho-
analysis to the journal of John Fall, for he recorded
with extreme care and precision the sins he saw being
committed around him. In the spring of 1688, he
recorded the trial of Martha Mayes for adultery, writing how Martha's hands must have "caressed the
flesh of Daniel Alden's buttocks" and how Daniel's
"stern member pierced woman's soft and yielding
crevisse." Clearly, John Fall had a vivid imagination
when it came to such vices and their punishment.
Fall was convinced Daniel and Martha (and others
like them, equally recorded in his journals) awaited
their true punishment in hell. In passages three and
four pages long, Fall described in lurid detail how he
imagined their flesh would burn, how their eyes
would be plucked out, how their cries for mercy
"would go unheeded, echoing against the dark caves
of Hell." In such gruesome imaginations, John Fall
seemed to take great delight, apparently "getting off
on it," to use current lingo.

"Man had originally Dominion over the creatures
Below," Fall wrote one day in 1690. "But sin hath
inverted this Order, and brought Chaos upon the
Earth. Man is dethroned, and become a servant to
those things that were made to serve him, and he
puts those things in his heart, that God hath put
under his feet."

By 1692 John Fall had become outraged by the
"sinful" ways of his congregation. Too many wore
"bright and various Colours." The women laughed
openly with men who were not their husbands, and
boys "drank ale and hath friendly association with
the heathen Indians." Fall wrote, "Acts too
unspeakable have become commonplace," but not
so unspeakable that he couldn't record them in his
journal, like the lengthy account of two teenage boys
found in "sinful embrace" in the barn.

His angry denunciations of such behavior had brought him a following, for which he was grateful. "To find these Souls amid the ruins," he wrote, "to pick them out of the heap of foulness, all to Followe me." He drew dozens, then hundreds, to his sermons, promising them the angry hand of a vengeful God: "For he would smite thee with plagues of fires or floods, destroying Puny man with no more thought than Man kills a mosquito." In this way, Father Fall—as the crowds came to call him—was a predecessor of such Great Awakening orators as Jonathan Edwards. In his sermons, Fall upheld the Calvinist belief that men could not find salvation "by any manner or goodness of their Own." Salvation came only through God—and, given that no other minister seemed to understand this truth quite as well, only through Father Fall could a sinner find God.

In 1692, Father Fall and two hundred of his faithful followers received a grant to start their own church and community on a sandy, marshy peninsula southeast of Chatham, which they quite logically named Falls Church. The first year of the congregation appears to have been peaceful, but in his journal Father Fall lamented "how easy it be for Saints to fall into Sinn." Apparently, the "Saints"—when not preoccupied with the sins of others—went about their lives with a degree of comfort and prosperity, and some of their fervid allegiance to Father Fall faded. In early 1693, he recorded in his journal: "Yesterday they listened but today they looke askance at my words and prefere fishing to my sermons." Without any sin to preach fire and damnation against, Father Fall feared a loss of his authority.

In 1697, he charged one of the young women in his congregation, Constance Ward, with being in league with the Devil. Without a trial, Father Fall ordered Constance burned at the stake. Unlike the witchcraft trials in Salem, there was no evidence presented of witchery on Constance's part. There was only Father Fall's insistence of it. In his journal, he wrote:

> She has bewitched many of the Saints of our communion, even attempting her Wiles upon my own pious Selfe. The look of the Devill lives in her great black eyes and in the movements of her small, soft hands. She has been sent by the Evil One to Provoke sinn and so she must suffer the fire of damnation.

So great had Fall's dictatorship become that many of the congregation simply accepted Constance's fate, but a number rose up in protest. Constance's father, Benjamin Ward, was a much-loved farmer, with many friends and influence in the town. Ward appealed to the governor, who, not wanting a repeat of what had happened in Salem, sent down a posse to prevent Constance's execution.

But Father Fall would not be so thwarted. Taking the girl to the basement of the church, he set fire to her himself, and in the process burned the whole place down. He, too, perished in the blaze. While Constance's body was recovered, Fall's was left to rot in the ruins of the church. Eventually a new place of worship under a more tolerant minister was erected on the site. (That church, too, would burn, in a mysterious fire in 1778. Over the ensuing decades, four churches would be built on the site, each one burning in its turn. Even the present one was almost consumed by flames, having been hit by lightning in 1967.)

Beset by his own demons, Father John Fall offers an example of religion used as tyranny by one man. In the end, what seemed to matter most to Father Fall was not sin but his own power. The punishment of sin was a tool he used to gain authority; unrest was necessary for the maintenance of his power.

Tuesday, June 25, 12:12 A.M.

"Poor man," says the night nurse, resting a hand on Sargent Crawford's forehead.

"His family used to be such dutiful visitors," says another, behind her, checking his chart. "But no one comes anymore."

Sargent Crawford trembles in his unnatural sleep. Since he slipped into the coma some days ago, his doctors have notified his wife that his condition, once thought to be improving after the heart surgery, was now gravely serious.

"Is he going to die?" Pat Crawford had asked, and Dr. Kendall had been surprised at the lack of passion in her voice. He told her he couldn't offer a prognosis, not yet anyway—but he thought the family would want to be with him. Yet so far—and that was days ago—there have been no visitors to Cape Cod Hospital to see Sargent Crawford.

None that can be seen, that is.

In the dark reaches of his mind, Sargent Crawford is awake. He's walking down Route 6 in his hospital johnny, heading toward Falls Church. The only cars on the road are big black hearses, and from behind the curtained windows he occasionally catches glimpses of people he knows: Laura Millay, Yvette and Paul Duvalier, Sandy Hooker, Richie Rostocki, Tess Woodward, Alan Hitchcock, even Sargent's wife, Pat, and their kids. None seem to think it odd that Sargent's walking on the highway with his butt exposed. No one stops to offer him a ride. Not even Pat. That bothers him most of all.

When he finally makes it to the outskirts of Falls Church, it's snowing. A fierce blizzard. He's afraid that the road into town will be iced over, cutting it off from the rest of the Cape. But then he remembers that he's on foot, and that it won't matter. Not unless he freezes to death. But despite the wind and the nearly obliterating snow, Sargent doesn't feel cold. He just trudges along, his bare feet making deep prints in the powdery drifts.

At the top of Main Street, not far from Dave's Sunoco station, he spies a body, facedown in the snow. It's a young kid, a black kid, shot in the chest. He walks on, with downtown Falls Church soon becoming visible through the blowing snow. Suddenly Sargent feels frightened. Nothing up until now has caused him any fear, but the sight of Falls Church in the distance fills him with dread. He knows if he turns around he'll see something horrible behind him. Had it followed him all the way here?

He turns and sees the horribly burned figure of a woman. Charred purple flesh drips off her face as if liquid.

"He's in the church," the things rasps.

"The church," Sargent Crawford repeats.

Then everything goes dark.

Thursday, June 27, 8:35 A.M.

"Thanks for agreeing to talk to me, Miss Santos," Nate says as the librarian ushers him into her private office, closing the door behind her, glancing out suspiciously as she does so.

"I'm glad you're here," she tells him. "Things are happening that I can't quite fathom."

Nate notices the look that passes between Catherine Santos and her assistant, Helen Twelvetrees, just before the door closes. It's one of distrust, suspicion, even hostility. He remembers that Helen had been one of those hustling and bustling around at the opening of the old church.

"Why don't you start then by telling me what you've been noticing," Nate suggests.

Catherine Santos sighs. She pulls her long gray braid over her shoulder and holds it, almost for balance. "I'm not sure what to say, Nate. It's like I told you the other night at the church. People have just been acting so strangely. For weeks everyone was at each other's throats. Now the whole town seems to have found religion."

"Like Miss Twelvetrees out there?"

Catherine nods. "She keeps trying to get me involved, keeps trying to persuade me to go over to the old church with her. But I can't, Nate."

"Why not?"

"Well, partly because that church is filled with people who

are trying to get poor Martha Sturm kicked out of her job. They claim to care so much about the community, yet that petition is splitting this town apart."

Nate nods. He's seen them standing with their clipboards out in front of the True Value and Woodward's Pharmacy. They're people he once respected, even loved—Betty Silva, Gerry and Barbara Garafolo, Dave Carlson. They stand there asking passersby, even tourists with no stake in the town, to "take a stand against the homosexual agenda in our schools." A lot of ignorant, frightened people have been corralled into signing.

"But it's not just that, Nate." Catherine Santos seems clearly distraught. "It's—it's even more than that."

"Talk to me."

She sits down behind her desk. "It's like it was before. I've seen this happen before."

Nate sits down opposite her. "That's exactly why I came here, Miss Santos. I'm trying to understand things, make sense of what's happening, and no one knows this town's history better than you." He looks at her directly. "I want you to tell me about the period when Priscilla Googins was murdered."

She smiles weakly. "They say I have an encyclopedic memory when it comes to this town. But for certain things—like poor Priscilla—I have to force myself to remember. I have to pull the memories out like they're jars of fruit stuck far back in a cabinet I'm too short to reach."

"That seems to be the case for most folks," Nate observes. "Did you ever come across the name of Dexter Coffin in the police files?"

Nate thinks. "Yes," he says. "He's mentioned in the files on the Googins murder. One of the suspects, though there was never any evidence."

Catherine nods. "Yes, they suspected Dexter, and do you know why? Because he wore his hair long and had a beard and protested the war in Southeast Asia. They suspected all of us in that group of peaceniks who started meeting at the old church—and well they might have, I suppose."

"Why was that?"

She shrugs. "We started out as peaceniks. That's what drew us all to the group. We had no name, no mission except that

we wanted peace and love and all that groovy kind of stuff.''
She laughs. "I remember the boy who suggested we all meet
at the church. He was a friend of Dexter's. A young man with
a bright orange Afro. What was his name? Tommy Keegan,
that's it. We met at the church and prayed for peace.''

"But something changed," Nate says.

"Oh, yes. Something changed. We started calling for revolu-
tion. For overthrowing every tradition our parents had taught
us, by any means necessary. It was the curse of the idealism
of the 1960s. How a generation crying out for peace turned
into violent radicals like the Symbionese Liberation Army. I
used to tell my father he had nothing to fear from the group
of hippies I was hanging out with. And then one night, listening
to Tommy Keegan rant from the pulpit in the old church—
calling for blood to be shed, if necessary, to rid the world of
the old Establishment—well, I sat there and realized my father
did have something to fear. We *all* did.''

"This Tommy Keegan," Nate says, remembering, "he was
also a suspect in Priscilla's murder.''

"Yes, he was.'' Catherine Santos looks over at Nate with
surprise. "Yes, I had forgotten that. Priscilla was his girlfriend.
I remember her now, sitting up there next to him on the altar.
Everything ended when Priscilla was killed. Tommy tried to
keep us together, but people were turning against us in town.
And then I—''

She stops, as if frozen.

"And then you what, Miss Santos?''

She seems unable to continue for a moment. "Well, I only
did what I did because—because Dexter—''

"Dexter Coffin," Nate says.

"Yes, Dexter.'' Catherine Santos has started to cry. "I was
in love with him, Nate. We were going to get married. He was
such a good boy. He was so young, just eighteen when we met.
I couldn't let the police go on thinking he killed Priscilla.
Because he was too gentle. Not like—''

"Not like Tommy Keegan," Nate says.

"Yes.'' She looks at him intently. "It was Tommy Keegan
who told the police he suspected Dexter killed Priscilla. He
lied, Nate! Oh, dear God, how had I forgotten this?''

She stands, suddenly shaking, overcome with a memory.

"Take it easy, Miss Santos," Nate says.

"Tommy Keegan." She gasps. "Tommy Keegan—who persuaded all of us he loved peace and tolerance—was in reality a horrible creature, Nate! He was a horrible man who lied to cover up his own—" She stops, unable to put her lips around the word.

"His own what, Miss Santos?" Nate's at the edge of his seat. "What are you remembering?"

"I saw him," she says in a small, terrified voice, gripped by the sudden memory. "I saw him with blood on his hands. *Priscilla's* blood . . ."

"When was this?"

"The night she died. Oh, dear God, it's all flooding back to me now. He wouldn't let me into the church. I was looking for Dexter." Catherine's face has gone white. Her lips tremble. "He said he had cut himself, but I pushed past him, walked into the church, and I saw—I saw—"

"Priscilla," Nate finishes for her. "You saw her body. I remember now, that it was you who called the police. But you never told them about Tommy Keegan, about seeing him leaving the scene with blood on his hands."

She looks at him with stark terror in her eyes. "Because I never—I never *remembered*, not until just now. Oh, Nate, you must believe me!"

He just stands, unable to say *what* he believes.

"Tommy suggested to the police that it was Dexter who killed Priscilla," Catherine says, "and when the police went to question him, Dexter pulled a gun on them. Oh, you've got to understand, Nate. It wasn't loaded. Dexter had no intention of killing anyone. He was far too gentle for that. He was just so conditioned—we'd all been brainwashed into thinking the Establishment was out to get us. It was instinctive, pulling that gun. It wasn't loaded! And they shot him, Nate! They killed Dexter, and it was all Tommy Keegan's fault!"

She shatters into a horrible wail of tears. Nate moves over to place his arms around her. Her grief, her sudden recollection of this long-buried horror, touches him. He knows all too well the pain she must be feeling. He thinks of that scared little boy, Jesus Ramos, pointing that gun at him. He thinks of Jesus, facedown in a pool of blood from Nate's own gun.

God took Siobhan away from me for killing Jesus.

"Take it easy, Miss Santos," he tries to console her. "It's okay."

"No," she sobs. "It's not. And it's happening all over again."

"What do you mean?"

She looks up at him. "After Dexter was killed, when I heard that it was Tommy who had suggested the police question him, I stormed over to the church to confront him. The memory of seeing him that night with blood on his hands must have returned then, because I remember shouting at Tommy, calling him all sorts of names in front of all of our friends, all of our group. I called him the Devil! And soon others had joined me! People who had loved Dexter. It was as if we had broken out of some kind of spell, and we saw Tommy for what he was."

"Which was?"

"A *demon*. A demon in the body of a boy." She looks up at Nate. Her tears have stopped. "When he started shouting back at us, he had become something else. A thing—a walking corpse—his face eaten with maggots."

He pulls back a little. Was this whole town as crazy as Victoria and her group of ghostbusters? How much of this could he take at face value? *I mean, come on,* Nate thinks, looking down at the earnest face of the librarian. *A walking corpse? His face eaten with maggots?*

Still, it's his duty to warn her. Especially after what has happened to Job and Berniece.

"Miss Santos," he asks awkwardly. "Did Miss Twelvetrees mention at all a—a dream she may have had?"

"A dream?"

"Yes. A dream."

Catherine considers the question. "As a matter of fact, yes. A few days ago. Helen was very agitated, and she stopped the first person who came into the library. Barbara Carlson, who was returning her kids' library books. Helen took her aside and talked to her. I didn't realize they were so close, but afterward Helen seemed better." She pauses. "Except it was that afternoon that she went over to start volunteering at the church."

And so Barbara Carlson told her husband, Dave, who told Job Emerson, who told his wife, Berniece. . . .

Oh, Christ, Nate thinks. Now he's getting as bad as Kip Hobart, who called it "an epidemiology of evil."

But how long could he keep discounting the dream theory? Nate had interviewed both Reich sisters and had found them—predictably—quarrelsome and discontent. He tried to keep them in the house all day, but his quarantine proved ineffective. Florence Reich simply called Paul Stoddard on the telephone. Stoddard, the local repairman, was always lending a hand to the two old ladies; he was the one they called whenever they blew a fuse or their toilet backed up. Nate deduced that the phone call had been placed when he spotted Stoddard the next night, cursing out a bunch of tourists on Main Street, accusing them of bleeding the town dry.

Nate arrested the irate repairman for breach of peace, but he wasn't the only one in the family acting out of control. Nate was called out the next day to the Stoddard house on upper Church Street by neighbors upset over an outdoor tussle between Paul's wife, Joan, and her sixteen-year-old daughter, Liz. When he told this to Kip Hobart, the psychologist determined that Paul must have passed the dream to Joan, who passed it on to their daughter, and that by now Liz Stoddard would have passed it on to someone else. It could be anywhere in town once again. If they had hoped to contain it, Kip said, they had lost. "It's escaped from our grasp like a slippery eel," Kip observed.

Nate just shook his head. Could he dare to believe it? Could he dare *not?*

This week had been one long nightmare. Job and Berniece were still nowhere to be found. Jamal—surprise, surprise—had been taken under the wing of Mark Miller, who managed to get Town Manager Hitchcock's blessing in letting the boy stay with him. Nate tried to get the chief to protest, but the chief's been consumed with his own worries. The night before last, Ellen took a turn for the worse; she's once more lodged at Cape Cod Hospital, with the chief at her side at all times. That left just Nate and Dean to run the station. Thank God the summer temporary cops started next week to give them a hand.

So far, Nate had been reluctant to share with Dean much of what Kip, Victoria and the others suspect is happening. It was still too bizarre for him to comprehend even on his own. "Until we make direct linkage between these occurrences," Kip had said, "until we can document the patterns, we won't be able to fully understand this adversary we face. We need to all do more research, more investigation, before we can make a move."

Nate had bristled at that, fired by a determination just to barge in and throw Mark Miller in jail.

"Look, Nate," Kip told him, "I know you want to find out what happened to Monica Paul and what caused your friend Rusty to go berserk. But we need more ammunition for this assault. You're an officer of the law. You know you have to enter into your assignments carefully, with deliberate planning. We don't want to be ambushed here."

"That's right," Nate agreed. "I'm an officer of the law. I'm no ghost hunter. All of this seems too far out in left field for me."

"So do your own research," Victoria suggested, sounding almost dismissive. "If you don't believe, Nate, then you can't help us. Go out and talk to people on your own. You'll see we're not crazy."

So Nate had determined he'd start by finding out more about the murder of Priscilla Googins. After all, he'd made that his cause ever since coming to Falls Church.

And now Catherine Santos has practically solved the case for him, in just a few minutes of conversation here this morning in the library. The killer was a hippie named Tommy Keegan.

"What happened to this Keegan guy?" Nate asks her. "From the records I see the police tried to keep tabs on him, but given as there was never any evidence to link him to the murder, he seems to have just slipped away."

Catherine shakes her head. "I don't know where he went. The last time I saw him was during that horrible confrontation— so horrible I've banished it from my mind all these years." She wraps her arms around herself. "Oh, Nate, I have a terrible suspicion."

His eyes meet hers again. "Tell me."

She shivers. "That young man who's renovated the old church. There's something about him. He came here, trying to win me over, I think. And he almost did. He was very charming. He made me think of Dexter. So young, so idealistic."

"So what stopped you from being won over completely?"

"I realize now it wasn't Dexter he reminded me of. Maybe his youth, but that's where the resemblance stops. In truth, he reminded me of someone else."

Nate knows who she means. "Tommy Keegan."

She nods. "At the church opening the other night, seeing the way people responded to him, ran around doing his bidding, it reminded me of the way so many in our group had treated Tommy."

"So what is your suspicion?"

"I think Mark Miller is doing just what Tommy tried to do. Turning the people of this town against each other, despite all his honeyed words."

Honeyed words. Marcella Stein had used the same phrase to describe Mark Miller's speech, and Victoria had reacted to it. Nate would have to ask her why.

He stands up and looks down at Catherine Santos. "I'm going to ask you to help me," he says. "What I'm about to ask you to do is very important."

"I'll do whatever I can."

"You know the history of this town better than anybody. Would you put together something for me? An outline of the months Tommy Keegan's group of hippies met at the old church, right up to and including Priscilla Googins's death."

"Of course. I'll go through all the old newspapers."

"And see if you can find other periods in this town's history when other such episodes occurred. Local unrest. A pattern of violence followed by some kind of organizational development." He pauses. "There's one other time that I know of . . ."

She meets his gaze. "Yes. Grace West's Concerned Citizens of Cape Cod. The time of Petey McKay's disappearance and the arson at the Kennelly house."

"Precisely."

Catherine stands behind her desk. "Consider me your deputy, Nate. I'm going to start my research this morning."

"Thank you. I'll stop back toward the start of next week. In the meantime, call me with anything urgent." He starts to leave, his hand on the doorknob, when he turns back. He *has* to say something. Whether he truly believes it or not, he *has* to tell her.

"Another thing, Miss Santos. If anyone starts to tell you about a dream they had, stop them. Refuse to listen. Walk away if necessary, even if you feel you're being rude. Under no circumstance should you allow anyone to tell you about their dream. Do you understand?"

Catherine Santos's face once again drains of all color. "Nate," she says, "I'm not going to ask any questions of you right now because I suspect you don't have any answers. But I don't mind telling you that I'm frightened."

Nate looks at her. "It will be okay, Miss Santos."

When he opens the door he notices Helen Twelvetrees scurrying back to the front desk. Had she been eavesdropping? Suddenly Nate realizes once more there are very few people left in Falls Church he can trust.

Friday, June 28, 9:37 A.M.

"Reverend Miller, my name is Victoria Kennelly."

His eyes reflect warmth and welcome. He grasps her extended hand. "How very nice it is to meet you, Ms. Kennelly."

He gestures for her to enter the church. She steps inside. "Ever since coming back to Falls Church," she says, "I've felt as if I needed to connect somewhere spiritually. I'm sure you understand what I mean."

"I do indeed." He smiles kindly. "And how pleased I am that you chose our church."

"Well," Victoria says, a small grin ticking the corners of her mouth, "I'm actually checking out all three churches in town. When I was a girl, my family attended St. Peter's. I've become a bit of a lapsed Catholic, I suppose, but I'm going to attend mass on Sunday and see if I feel any pull to go back."

"A good idea," Mark Miller says. "In a spiritual journey one must be open-minded and inclusive, for an awakening may occur anywhere."

"Yes. That's why I called you and asked if I could meet with you. Your church *seems* to be the most comfortable fit— being nondenominational and all—but I'm going to give the Catholics another shot, and indeed the Methodists as well."

"Of course." He looks at her intently. "So what can I do to help you in your quest, Ms. Kennelly?"

She smiles. "Well, maybe you can tell me what your services

here are like. I attended your opening and was very inspired by your sermon that night. Is that the kind of thing I could expect on a regular basis?"

Mark Miller doesn't answer for several seconds. His bright blue eyes remain transfixed on hers, and for just a quivering second Victoria feels fear.

"Actually, yes," he says. "We're very community oriented. It's really up to the congregation how we run things. We're not beholden to any particular ritual or format. I usually talk about some topic, and others take the podium as well. We might sing, but only songs that are universal, not in praise of any specific religion, onlt those that honor the search for the light of truth and wisdom."

"I like that."

He presses his palms together in the gesture of a prayer. "It's the only way for many people these days," he tells her. "There's a yearning to embrace the spiritual, to find through a community rather than any ritual or dogma a greater connection to the infinite—and to one's own soul. I respect and admire all religions, but they are increasingly not the path many people feel comfortable taking these days."

"So you have no name, really, for this congregation?"

He smiles. "They've called it the 'old church' for decades. If anything, perhaps we will simply evolve into being the people of Fall's Old Church, a reflection of the town and community, not of any particular sect."

Victoria eyes him. "A nice honor for the town's founder, the Reverend John Fall."

She waits to see if there is any reaction in his eyes. There isn't.

"Father Fall, he was called."

Mark Miller smiles. "Yes, of course. Though I admit to being a little behind in my local history. Is it a particular interest of yours?"

"Well, I'm a history teacher, and being a Falls Church native, I made it a point to find out what I could."

Again she watches his eyes for any reaction. Again there is nothing.

"I'd be fascinated to learn more," Mark Miller says. "Come. Let me show you how we've fixed up the nave."

He leads her into the center of the church, where the walls shine with light blue paint. On the altar are symbols of the world's religions: a menorah, a Koran, a statue of the Buddha. In the center of the back wall an illustration of a dove, a remnant of the days of Christian worship, has been restored against a purple background.

"My, you've done a wonderful job of fixing up the place," Victoria says. "I can remember as a girl sneaking in here once. Everything was so dilapidated and broken. We thought it was haunted."

He smiles indulgently. "Haunted? Really, now. A place of worship."

"Well, surely you know that a girl was murdered here years ago." Victoria holds his eyes. "Right up there, on the altar."

Does he know I'm testing him? How far should I push?

"Yes," Mark Miller says sadly. "I know that much. Such a horrible, blasphemous act. But all the more reason to restore this as a holy place, to return the church to its former glory."

"You certainly have done that."

"Oh, we still have a great deal of work to do." He places a hand on her shoulder. "If you have any special talents, Ms. Kennelly, we would welcome them."

There's something about his hand on her shoulder that troubles her. Victoria feels a terrible coldness. She looks up at him. He's smiling at her.

Part of her simply wants to run. Break away from him, run for her life. She had known this was a risk coming here. *Does he know who I am? Doe he see through my ruse?*

But just as she's about to succumb to her fear, the spell is broken. Kathy McKenzie enters the nave from a side door, carrying some folded linen. She spots Mark Miller with his hand on Victoria's shoulder and stops where she is, glaring.

"Sorry to interrupt," she says curtly.

"Not at all," Mark says smoothly. He removes his hand and motions for Kathy to join them. "We may have a new member of our community. Kathy McKenzie, this is Victoria Kennelly."

Victoria tries to smile but feels her lips are trembling. "Nice to meet you. But I haven't officially decided—"

Mark Miller clasps his hands in front of him. "I understand, Miss Kennelly, but we *are* hoping."

Victoria looks at Kathy McKenzie, who is staring at her. "I think I've seen you around town," she says. "You have a little boy."

Kathy says nothing. Mark Miller takes up the awkward slack in conversation. "Yes, yes, indeed she does. Our spirited little Josh. Where is he now, Kathy?"

Finally Kathy's eyes flicker. "He's—he's downstairs in the church hall, helping Jamal and Teddy and some of the other children."

Mark Miller beams. "Ah, yes. The children of our flock are as dedicated as their parents. They're helping clean out the debris downstairs so that we can finally have a church hall again."

"How wonderful," Victoria says.

"Well," Mark says, "I hope you decide to be with us at a service soon. I can guarantee you that you will be warmly embraced by our community."

"Do you have any materials? Any literature I could take with me to read?"

Mark looks at her. He's not smiling anymore.

"No," he says. "We have no literature. Only ourselves. Our community. Isn't that right, Kathy? Wouldn't Ms. Kennelly be embraced by our community?"

Kathy moves her eyes over to Victoria. *They're empty,* Victoria thinks. *She's like one of those dolls with glass eyes and lids that close automatically if you lay it down.*

"The community would embrace you," Kathy repeats to her.

"Well, that's something to look forward to." Victoria manages a smile. "Thank you so much, Reverend Miller. I'll be back." She turns to leave, then looks over her shoulder. "Nice to meet you, Kathy."

"Thank you so much for coming by, Ms. Kennelly," Mark Miller says, walking with her to the door. "I am sure you will make the right choice, whether it be us, or the Catholics, or the Methodists."

"I'll keep you posted."

"Good-bye," he says warmly.

Once he's closed the door, Victoria hurries around to the side of the church. She makes her way inside through the half-opened door there, peering into the darkness of the hall. She spies Jamal Emerson and Teddy McDaniel, just as Miller had told her, carrying out debris. She manages to slip into a closet just as they head toward her, hauling the pieces of charred wood and broken furniture outside to a Dumpster. She's grateful that the closet has wooden slats on the door so she can make out their forms moving back and forth. The boys speak not a word to each other, just go about their tasks. They're joined by other children whom Victoria strains to recognize through the slats. There's the Crawford girl. And Nicky Garafolo, the little boy she's seen at his father's pizza joint. And Billy Hix, the kid who often helps his father pick up the trash at the guesthouse. And others she doesn't know.

"I won't tolerate such behavior," comes a voice.

Victoria holds her breath, standing as still as possible. It's Mark Miller. He's scolding someone. He sounds very angry.

"Rudeness is a *sin*," he's saying.

She hears a horrible crack—hand against skin. Has he struck one of the children?

No, not a child—

"I'm sorry," a woman's voice is saying from somewhere in the darkness of the church hall. "Please, Reverend. I'm sorry. I was jealous of her—"

"Jealousy is also a sin," Mark Miller says again, and Victoria hears another crack.

It's Kathy McKenzie, Victoria realizes. *And he's hitting her across the face.*

Suddenly the closet door is yanked open. Victoria manages to suppress a scream. There's no one there. It must have swung open on its own, but now she's revealed if anyone walks by—

All at once, her eyes drop downward. There *is* someone there, someone who opened the door, who knew she was inside.

A child. She recognizes him as Josh McKenzie.

His eyes are big and round, unblinking, staring up at her.

He's under his power, Victoria thinks. *He'll turn me in.*

But instead, the little boy whispers:

"Will you help my mommy?"

Victoria makes a mad dash, running past him and out the side door into the daylight. She runs all the way to the police station, and collapses into Nate's arms.

"I just left him there!" Victoria cries. "Left him and his poor mother, too . . ."

Nate eases her down into a chair, then closes the door to his office.

"You did the right thing for now," Nate assures her.

Kip is there as well. "Absolutely, Victoria," he tells her. "To have revealed yourself then would have tipped him off to how closely we're watching him."

"I knew that instinctively," she says. "That's why I ran. But he was *hitting* her! The child wanted me to help his mother, and I *ran*." Victoria starts to cry again.

Nate's blood boils. "Look, there's nothing I want to do more than go over there and arrest him for assault. But you didn't *see* him hit her. You only heard it. So it would be your word against his."

"And I have a strong feeling Kathy McKenzie would deny it if confronted," Kip says. "All we'd do is lose our strategic position against him."

Nate sighs. "Poor Kathy," he says. "This is her worst nightmare come true. This is what she lived with when that ex-husband of hers was around. He beat her, had her completely under his thumb, the way this fucking minister has her now." He runs his hands through his hair. "Whether he's some supernatural demon or just a Svengali, I'm going to have to make a move soon. I can't just let him go on abusing people."

"If we make a move too soon, Nate, things could get far worse," Kip cautions.

"Like how?" Nate asks, clearly getting fed up. "What kind of power do you think he really *has*?"

"That's what I've been trying to determine." Kip looks over at Victoria. "The fact that Josh McKenzie asked you to help his mother is an encouraging sign. It means there exists in these people some connection to their humanity, to their individual spirits. A part of them is struggling to break free from his control.''

Nate feels as if his head is going to crack open. ''But what are we dealing with here? How does he manage this control?''

''Look, Nate,'' Kip says. ''Both Alexis and I have been taught how to *see*—see beyond what is tangible or obvious. But it's as if there's something in the way whenever we try to see Mark Miller or anyone connected with the church.'' Kip pauses. ''It's as if he anticipated we'd be looking, and so he set up some kind of barrier.''

''Well, he's had practice,'' Victoria says. ''This isn't his first time launching an attack on Falls Church.''

''I'm at the end of my rope, people,'' Nate says. ''So you're thinking he's the *same* as Father Fall? Mark Miller is Father Fall reincarnated or something?''

''All I know is, now that I've looked directly into his eyes, I've seen him before.'' Victoria shivers. ''Grace West staring back at me at Town Meeting. Different, but the same.''

''I'm heading over to talk with Father Roche,'' Kip says. ''I think we need to consider conducting an exorcism.''

''Christ Almighty,'' Nate moans.

''Nate, just give us a little time. *Please*. You've seen what's happened in town. You told us what Catherine Santos revealed. Please, Nate. Give us some time and maybe we can figure out what's going on,'' Kip pleads.

The police officer just glares at him.

Kip continues. ''If Mark Miller is simply in the power of Father Fall or some other malevolent force, then he will be freed. If he is, in fact, merely that malevolent force manifested, then he could be destroyed.''

Nothing more is said as Kip stands and leaves the office. Nate just lets out a long sigh and rubs his temples. He looks over at Victoria.

''We've all gone mad,'' he mutters.

She says nothing.

Nate remembers the chief's words the day Victoria first walked into the station: *Victoria Kennelly went crazy after her family died in that fire. All she ever did was talk about ghosts and goblins. I gave up on her after a couple years. She'd always been a high-strung girl.*

If the chief knew the theories Nate's been entertaining these last few days, his confidence in his number two man would evaporate on the spot. Here the chief is, sitting at his wife's deathbed, believing Nate's got everything under control back in Falls Church, and what's Nate doing? Planning an *exorcism* to deal with the town's problems!

The chief would be handling this much differently. The chief would take Mark Miller in for questioning. He'd get a search warrant and look through every last room in the old church, as well as Miller's apartment, for any trace of Monica Paul.

"You're doubting yourself," Victoria says.

He looks over at her. "I'm doubting everything."

"I did, too, for a long time."

Victoria Kennelly went crazy after her family died in that fire.

"It wasn't until I came to the realization that I was actually stronger than whatever it was that haunted me that I finally, truly, accepted that it was *real*." She smiles weakly. "Rather a surprising development. You'd think that once I felt strong enough to face my demons that they'd disappear. But they didn't."

"I'm an officer of the law," Nate tells her simply. "They didn't teach this kind of stuff at the police academy."

"You're taught to evaluate evidence. What do you make of that student's report? Even as a photocopy, it burned your hands."

Nate sighs. Yes, indeed it had. And he saw with his own eyes the changes that had come over the people of this town. But maybe it was a trick. The paper could have been coated with some kind of low-grade acid by some crazy lady who's persuaded a dotty old priest and a wavy gravy New Age shrink to believe her stories. And maybe there *was* a madness being spread in this town—but not by dreams but rather by some good old-fashioned germs, the way anthrax had spread so easily through the mail a year ago. Maybe there are *microbes* loose out there, spores that produce not flu and fever but madness and intolerance and bigotry—

Nate laughs to himself. As if *that* theory is any less crazy than the one Victoria Kennelly is proposing.

"I just don't know," he admits to Victoria. "I'm left here with one officer and myself. I'm trying to do what's best, trying to handle this the only way I know how."

"I know it's hard, Nate." Victoria's eyes hold his, deep dark eyes. So beautiful. "All my life I have been running away from Falls Church. But now, I know that every path I took simply led me back here. I stood up to him before, and he was defeated. Alexis was right. That's the only way we will win here. Not by throwing him in jail, but by standing up to him. Standing up for what's right."

He looks at her. She's really a beautiful woman. He doesn't just mean that physically, though certainly she's lovely with a lithe, gym-toned figure. But Victoria Kennelly's beauty, Nate realizes, comes from something else. He sees it in the circles under her eyes, the years of struggle etched on her face. It's in the set of her jaw, the straightness of her shoulders and back.

"You can see goodness in a person as much as you can see the color of their eyes," Siobhan once said to him.

She was talking about the people she worked with at the homeless shelter in Oakland. How she could see goodness and wisdom and experience in the tilt of someone's head, how she could see nobility in someone's eyes as they thanked her for a plate of food. And Nate had believed her, for he saw it in Siobhan herself, every time he stopped by the shelter, observing her hunched down, talking to some withered husk of a human being, laughing with them, touching their hair, holding their hand.

He can see goodness in Victoria Kennelly. He can see strength. He can see wisdom and determination. What he does not see is madness.

"The most important weapon a police officer has in his arsenal," the chief has told him, "is instinct. Trust your gut, Nate. It's the first course of action."

He sighs. But these theories—a curse of dreams . . . the walking dead . . .

"Tell me," he says, trying to believe her. "How do you propose to stand up to him this time?"

She smiles. "I just became a voter again here in Falls Church.

I've notified my dean that I need to take a leave of absence next semester. I'm putting down some roots.'' She smiles. ''And as a Falls Church citizen, I'm starting my own petition, in favor of keeping Martha Sturm as school principal. Will you sign?''

Nate laughs. ''You think it will be as simple as that? First you tell me we're dealing with some malevolent ghost and now you tell me it can be defeated by *collecting signatures?*''

She shrugs. ''All I did last time was speak out at Town Meeting.''

Nate smiles. ''So Kip and Father Roche and all their hocus-pocus won't be needed?''

''Oh, I think they should do everything they can. We all need to do our parts.''

''And what's mine?''

Victoria smiles. Their eyes hold. ''I think that will become obvious, Nate. I think you'll know soon enough.''

Thursday, the Fourth of July, 11:45 A.M.

High season peaks on Cape Cod on July 4. For the past three days tourists have packed themselves onto Falls Church beaches, baking themselves red under unrelentingly sunny skies. All week, Duvalier's Restaurant hasn't had a table open for breakfast, lunch or dinner for longer than it takes to change silverware. Ladies in sunbonnets and halter tops from as far away as Kansas City and Vancouver have crowded into Hornet and Jazzy and Precious Moments, dragging their husbands in checkered Bermuda shorts and kneesocks behind them. An army of kids have taken over the boardwalks with their skateboards, and many a visitor has been heard to grumble about the failure of the Falls Church police force to keep a handle on the little hooligans.

The workforce in Falls Church has also undergone its annual change, from local year-rounders to seasonal workers. A few college students from Boston mix among the waiters and houseboys, but these days it's mostly foreigners from Jamaica or eastern Europe who are serving the food and cleaning the guesthouses and driving the shuttle buses. They've been a particular concern of Town Clerk Isabella Sousa Cook's for the past few years, ever since they first started arriving in town.

"Let's face it," she's saying to Selectman Richard Longstaff as they make their way down Main Street to the noontime Fourth of July ceremony on the Town Green. "We like to pat ourselves on the back as the land of freedom and opportunity, but these seasonal workers get here and, frankly, they get the raw end of the deal.''

Longstaff says nothing as they walk.

"Come on, Richard," Izzy says, irritated by his silence. "You know as well as I that business owners like Yvette Duvalier hire these people because they'll accept less money than American workers. They'll live in those run-down shacks Sargent Crawford keeps up in the woods off Beach Road—places so dank and unsanitary even the college kids turn their noses up at them.''

"Don't go making waves, Isabella.''

"Making *waves?* Richard, you and Marcella have been the only two selectmen I've ever thought had any conscience. What's our job as elected officials if not to make waves?'' The saucy old town clerk stops on the street and stabs her finger against Longstaff's chest. "What's gotten into you these past few days, Richard? It's like you've had the fight knocked out of you.''

He looks at her with blank eyes, with dark circles surrounding them.

Izzy leans in close to study him. "Have you been sleeping, Richard? Is it worrying about Kim that's got you down? Look, I know it's tough what with that petition going around against Martha Sturm and everybody knowing about her and Kim's little affair of the heart. But there's another petition just started in support of Martha. I just signed it this weekend.''

"I've asked Kim to move out of the house if she continues in her sinful ways.''

Isabella Sousa Cook is stunned. She's never known a father as doting and devoted as Richard's been to Kim. His daughter has been Richard's whole world ever since his wife died.

"Don't be so rash, Richard! Come on! I might be sixty-two years old, but I try to keep up with the times. It's the twenty-first century, Richard. It's not a big deal anymore if two gals or two fellas want to—''

"Stop it, Isabella!'' Richard Longstaff covers his ears with his hands. "You speak *filth.*''

"Filth?'' Isabella Sousa Cook stares at her old friend. They have much in common. They're both from the old school. They

both lost their spouses at relatively young ages, choosing not to marry again in honor of the memory of their lost loved ones. They could both be traditional, sentimental old fools—but both were also open-minded people. *Forward thinkers*, Isabella always thought. "The times are never going to pass *us* by," she'd say with a laugh to Richard as they sat in Town Hall.

Now she takes his face in her hands, studying his eyes. "Where are you, my friend? I can't see you in there."

She's serious. Those aren't the eyes of Richard Longstaff. Those aren't the eyes that have laughed at her antics at the town's Christmas parties, where she's been known to come out in a red-and-green grass skirt and Santa hat doing a hula dance just for the heck of it. Those aren't the eyes that have told her in one good-natured look that she may have crossed some line, cracking a joke in the middle of a hearing or telling a new voter he had a cute ass.

"Isabella, let me go," Richard says.

She withdraws her hands. "This town has gone a little mad, Richard, what with the petition against Martha and all sorts of other things. People aren't themselves. Please don't fall into lockstep with them."

He simply turns his face and walks away from her, heading toward the Green.

"Mrs. Cook?"

She turns. It's Tim Lipnicki, the town assessor, and his wife, Sarah, leading their brood of kids up to the Green. He's a nice young man, barely thirty years old, always unfailingly polite. He's one of the few people in town not to call her by her first name.

"Hello, Tim, Sarah." She waves with both hands down at the children, who look up at her with timid little faces. Isabella notices Tim seems just as timid. Even anxious.

"Go ahead," his wife says, nudging him. "Tell her."

"Tell me what?"

Tim Lipnicki swallows. Isabella notices Sarah Lipnicki's features are hard. She's gathering her children, looking back at Tim. "We'll meet you at the Green," she says.

Isabella watches them walk away. Then she turns back to Tim. His face is ashen.

"Are you all right?" she asks. "You look sick, honey."

"Mrs. Cook, I need to tell you something."

"What is it, Tim?"

He summons the strength. "I need to tell you a dream I had."

11:55 A.M.

Bessie Bowe steps out of her little house on Cranberry Terrace. It's a beautiful day. The sun is streaming; the sky's an umbrella of brilliant blue. She loves the summer, the days of lemonade and flip-flops. She's not one of those year-rounders who grumbles about the return of the summer tourists. Every Labor Day, when Aggie at the Clam Shack hangs out that sign announcing THANKS FOR A GREAT SEASON, SEE YOU NEXT SPRING, Bessie's heart sinks a little. The winters can be so long and so bleak.

Despite the crush of customers coming through the post office in July and August, Postmistress Bessie loves the summer months, and the Fourth of July is her favorite holiday. It's a rare day off in the middle of the week. Ever since she was a girl, she's loved the ceremony down at the Green and the fireworks later in the evening over Nantucket Sound. She and Noah will watch them tonight from the wharf together, just as they have these past four years, sipping hot cocoa out of a shared thermos.

Speaking of Noah, where is he? Bessie checks her watch as she walks down her steps toward her driveway. *We'll miss the opening remarks if he's much later.*

Bessie has a suspicion that tonight Noah is going to ask her to marry him. He's been hinting about it. Bessie smiles. Of course she'll say yes. She thinks only briefly what her sister up in Brewster might think: *Bessie, you can't marry a black man.* But of course she can. She's forty-eight years old; it's time she found a little happiness. Her sister, Mavis, had always been the pretty one, the one who got everything she wanted, the Bowe sister who had all the boyfriends in high school. Mavis married the school quarterback, of course, and now has five kids and a big house. Bessie simply shakes her head. She's no longer concerned with what Mavis might think. She will marry Noah.

Bessie, it's not so much that he's a black man, she can hear Mavis saying. *But he pumps gas for a living. He fixes cars. What kind of lifestyle is that?*

Bessie puts her fingers to her temples. If she doesn't care what Mavis thinks, why is she still hearing her voice? She loves Noah, and she doesn't care if there are still some petty minds in this town that turn away when they see them walking into Clem's Diner or the Clam Shack together. *I don't care what people think. Noah is good to me. We have fun together. He makes me happy.*

She looks down. There are chalk marks scrawled across her driveway. *Words.* She can't make them out. . . .

She takes a few steps back. The words pop out at her. She gasps.

NIGGER LOVER.

Noah's pickup rumbles down the street just then.

"Bessie, baby, sorry I'm late!" he calls from the open window. "Dave's been in such a foul mood these past few days down at the station. He barely let me have the afternoon—"

He stops. Bessie would do anything to keep him from seeing those words. If she'd only spotted them a second or two earlier, she would've made a dash for the garden hose and sprayed them off. . . .

But Noah sees them. He falls silent. He simply sits there in his truck staring at the words.

Bessie puts her hands over her face and starts to cry.

Who would do such a thing? Who, in this little town where she grew up? Who was filled with so much hate?

12:30 P.M.

Father Jim Roche isn't feeling much Christian charity this afternoon. Standing there on the Green, clapping politely when Alan Hitchcock finishes his address and the old cannon is fired, he realizes these are not good people. Oh, they may have been—once—but not anymore. And he has a hard time simply accepting the fact that they're possessed by some malevolent force. *God gave us free will,* Father Roche thinks. *You can't be made evil without some foundation already in place. Even a hypnotist can't force a person to do something against his own true nature.*

So what are they dealing with here? How have the citizens of Falls Church become so—so *corrupt?*

He's trying to find compassion, he really is. *It's your vocation, James,* he scolds himself as he watches these people mill around him on the Green. *You're supposed to be more understanding. More sympathetic to their plight. These people need your help, not your scorn.*

But he can't help himself. He may have been a priest for nearly forty years, but he's still human. He resents the fake piety suddenly shown by people like Max Winn, who all his life has been a nasty old curmudgeon. Now he stands up there at the podium introducing Alan Hitchcock with words that are as grating as fingernails on a blackboard for Father Roche. "When one sees the light of wisdom and truth," Max Winn had said, "one understands one's purpose in this life." As if the old fool even knew what he was saying. As if Max Winn had ever studied the Bible, taken a catechism class, been to Sunday mass, listened to what Father Roche might have to say about seeing the light.

Maybe that's what has him so rankled. All of these people trooping over from the old church, with the Reverend Miller leading the way. People like Manny and Aggie Duarte, and Gyp Nunez, and Marge Duarte, and the Amato family, and the dear old Reich sisters—all parishioners of St. Peter's whom Father Roche hasn't seen in weeks. People like Yvette Duvalier, who suddenly cared more about what color to paint the shutters on the old church than what to serve for dinner at her posh restaurant. He should be glad that someone—anyone—has awakened some greater spiritual awareness in the hearts of people like Yvette—and Richie Rostocki and Laura Millay—but he knows it's not *real* spirituality. This is about as far from spiritual truth as one can get.

It's a *cult.* That's what his housekeeper, Agnes Doolittle, has called it. She's right. And Father Roche has never had much patience with cultists. "You cannot brainwash those willing to listen," he has said more than once. Try as he might to do otherwise, he blames the flock as much as their leader—Pat Crawford and Claudio Sousa and Sandy Hooker and Lucille

Pyle and Clem Flagg and Musty Moore and Hickey Hix were just as responsible as the Reverend Mark Miller.

"Hello, Father."

He looks down. It's a boy, little Eddie Moore, whom Father Roche baptized and whose first Holy Communion he served. He's not even eleven years old yet, but he's with them. Father Roche saw him walk over with the group from the old church, holding his mother's hand.

"Hello, Eddie," he says carefully.

"Father," the boy asks, "do you think it's possible you, too, might ever see the light of truth?"

The child's words chill the old priest's soul. "I believe I have, Eddie. I have accepted Jesus Christ as my light of truth."

Eddie Moore just smiles, a tight little grin that seems far too old for his unblemished face, a grin that devastates Father Roche in its patronizing glare.

"Come," the boy whispers, reaching out his small hand. "Join us."

"Never," snarls Father Roche. "And you can tell that to your master, whoever he is."

Eddie simply laughs, a tinkly little sound, and scampers away into the crowd.

The children, Father Roche thinks. *How can I blame the children? Maybe their parents . . . maybe the adults bear some responsibility . . . but the children?*

Dear Jesus. What forces are we dealing with here?

Father Roche turns around suddenly. From across the Green the deep blue eyes of Mark Miller are staring at him. Father Roche looks quickly away and hurries back to St. Peter's.

9:04 P.M.

The first fireworks explode against the night sky. Nearly the entire population of Falls Church has gathered at the wharf. The crowd seems curiously subdued to Carolyn Prentiss. While there are pockets of applause and the usual yips and yahoos, whole stretches of people seem simply to stand and watch, the expressions on their faces solemn and withdrawn. Carolyn just pulls the brim of her straw hat down farther over her face and continues her walk along the beach.

"I'm going into town to watch the fireworks, and I want to go alone," she'd insisted to Edmond.

"You can see them perfectly fine from here," he protested.

"I need a little break, a little journey into the real world," she snapped. "Just to remind myself that it exists."

Ever since getting back from Cannes, they'd been fielding calls from Woody Allen, trying to persuade Carolyn to take a part in his next ensemble production. She likes Woody—even if she *did* side with Mia in their breakup—but she can't even *consider* his offer right now. The idea of committing to another project after working her ass off for two solid years is anathema to her. Edmond's been feverish in his attempts to cajole her into doing the Allen film, trying to convince her of what an honor it is to be asked. Maybe so, but she simply doesn't have the heart to commit to another picture. Even when Spielberg asked, she said no.

What would it be like to be married to one of these guys? Carolyn's thinking, eyeing the fishermen and the mechanics in the crowd as she passes, their faces lit up alternately red, blue and gold from the fireworks. She was married once, to America's top male adventure hero—a disaster from the start, given that he's gay—but the association *did* give her the name recognition to jump to the top of the box office. Now Edmond expects she'll marry *him* sooner or later. She laughs. She lets Edmond keep his delusions.

I have enough money never to work again, she tells herself as she walks, the surf lapping gently at her feet. *I never wanted to be a movie star. It just happened. I was just an actress because I'd dropped out of college and had nothing else to do.* But then America's biggest matinee idol spotted her in some silly TV show and married her and gotten her the cover of *Vanity Fair.* Her parents back in St. Louis were dumbstruck. Their lazybones daughter, the one they predicted would make (at best) a mediocre housewife, was now the country's most exciting new star.

If I get an Oscar for that stupid picture with Mel Gibson, I will retire. She's made her decision. She doesn't care what Edmond thinks. It just might be time to get him to move on anyway. So she'd break her contracts. Let them sue her. It would give her the chance to just be alone, hidden away from

all the trappings of celebrity. She could live here full-time.
Maybe meet a local guy and settle down. . . .

*Hell, I'm not going to end up like one of those gargoyle old
movie stars who don't know when to quit, who just keep on
year after year, gradually going crazy, living in gilded squalor
when Hollywood stops calling. . . .*

"Miss Prentiss?"

A police officer has approached, whispering low. It's the
guy she met at that store in town, that young geeky guy who
knocked over the display.

"I just want to caution you that the crowd sometimes gets
a little rowdy," he tells her, "and I wouldn't want any trouble
for you, if people recognize you."

She tries to remember his name. *Dan,* she thinks. And one
of those Portuguese names so common in town.

"I appreciate the warning," she tells him. "But this crowd
seems a little less lively than I'd have expected."

"Yes," he says, making a face, "but you never know."

"No," she says, giving him the smile that's charmed mil-
lions. "You never know."

Even in the dark she can tell he's blushing. What a sweetheart
this guy is. Not bad-looking, either, even if he's as skinny as
a pencil and still has traces of teenage acne on his chin.

Dean, she remembers. *Not Dan. His name is Dean.*

"Dean," she purrs, "would you mind if I stood here with
you, just to be safe?"

"Uh—uh—of course not." He straightens up comically,
throwing back his shoulders. "In fact, that's probably a good
idea."

An enormous explosion of red, white and blue rips through
the sky above them. There's scattered applause throughout the
crowd.

"I imagine it's a hard job policing all these folks here on
the wharf," Carolyn says into Dean's ear.

"Sure is." He's assumed an air of importance that amuses
her to no end. "Especially with all the out-of-towners who pile
in. You know what happens when folks on vacation have a
little too much beer."

"It must be horrible."

"It can be." Dean juts out his chin. "We've brought in

several extra temporary officers for the summer. You see, we've been a little . . . short staffed."

"Yes, I understand so. That officer who shot that poor boy. What a tragedy."

"Yes, it certainly is."

"What's going to happen to him?"

"Well," Dean says, sliding in conspiratorially toward her, "off the record, the chief is going to formally charge him next week. There's nothing else to do. The investigation by the state police leaves little other recourse."

"What a shame."

"I'll say. And now another officer has gone AWOL." He sighs dramatically. "These are surely trying times for Falls Church's finest."

Carolyn suppresses a giggle. "So long as you're still on patrol, Officer, I feel safe."

He's completely tongue-tied by that one. "Call me Dean," he manages to say.

"Dean," she says. "So long as you'll call me Carolyn."

She thinks he might faint. The finale has started, a dozen fireworks shot into the sky at the same time, a dazzling display of red-and-green pyrotechnics against the blackened sky.

9:30 P.M.

She has to get away from Roger. How much longer will it be before he joins them? Not that she wants him to, necessarily, but it would make life easier.

Life is not about ease or convenience. Mark has told her that.

Laura puts a hand to her head. The fireworks are too loud, too bright. Her head throbs. She staggers away from Roger and the kids, their chins lifted into the air as they watch the finale of colors. She just has to be alone, away from them, away from the noise in the sky.

And in her head.

"What is wrong with you?" Roger has demanded. "I ask you a question and you don't answer. The children say you forget to make them lunch. What's going *on* with you, Laura?"

"You can't understand," she's told him. "When you see the light, you'll understand."

"Stop with that kind of talk," her husband has snapped, many times now, whenever she tries to tell him that he's lost, that he needs to be saved, that he needs to follow the light of truth. "You speak nonsense. You spend all your time down at the old church. You're supposed to be running the office while Sargent is in the hospital, but whenever I call, you're not there."

Laura stumbles through the sand in the darkness, finally resting against a pulpy post holding up the town pier. Roger never once suspected a thing when she was cheating on him. Never once did he challenge her, question her, provoke her. But now, ever since she's been saved, he's been a thorn in her side, a grating, unnerving presence.

"Go ahead," he's insisted. "Explain to me the theology of that church. Explain to me what you find so compelling."

"I have accepted the light of truth and wisdom," she's responded.

"But what does that *mean*, Laura? What kind of theology is that? Give me specifics."

Oh, how she *hates* him. She hates Roger because he asks her questions like that, questions for which she has no answer.

"All in good time, my dear," Mark has said to her. "All men will see the truth eventually."

She doesn't care about the truth. All she cares about is that Mark touches her, presses his lips against hers, places his malehood inside her—

"Laura."

She turns, startled.

It's Claudio.

"What do you want?" she snaps. "Leave me alone."

"I still love you, Laura."

She turns, running under the pier in the heavy, humid darkness. The stink of rotting wood and old fish assaults her nostrils. Claudio follows.

He grabs her arm in the dark and tries to kiss her. She pushes him away. "Don't be a fool," she says. "He's forbidden it."

"I know he has, but I cannot help myself. I love you!"

She can barely make him out, it's so dark. A tiny glint of moonlight catches the whiteness of his eyes.

"I try to fight it, Laura," Claudio says. "I tell him I think only of the truth, of following the light. But it's a lie. I still love you, Laura. I can't put it aside."

She recoils when he tries to touch her. "I will tell him, Claudio. I will tell him and he will not be happy with this."

"Let's go away, Laura." Claudio's face looks desperate in the faint moonlight. "We can escape. You and I. We can get away from here—from him."

"Escape," she says, almost as if not understanding the word.

"Yes, *escape*. We can escape him, Laura. . . ."

The moment freezes. It's as if all sound has ceased. The rumblings of the crowd moving over the pier above them are gone. The steady wash of the surf has been silenced. Only in the far distance does the sound of the foghorn persist.

"Laura," Claudio says.

"Shh," she orders him. "Be quiet."

She feels the fear then, in the split second before she sees him. Despite the near pitch darkness, she can see Mark Miller clearly. He approaches them, suffused with an unearthly light.

And as Laura predicted, he's not happy with this.

"Please," Claudio says, falling to his knees. "Forgive me. It was a weakness. It was—"

"I have no time for weakness," Mark Miller says. "I hate weakness."

Claudio screams. For a second Laura wonders if the people on the pier above will hear, if someone will come running down to investigate. But she knows the reverend wouldn't permit that. Claudio can scream all he wants, but no one is going to hear him.

Laura covers her face with her hands. She hears Claudio continue to scream. She hears his flesh being ripped open, the snapping of his rib cage, the horrible sound of his blood hitting the sand like a waterfall. She hears the crack of his neck, the final twisted sound from his throat, the thud of his body as it falls lifeless to the ground. Only when it's over does she remove her hands. Mark Miller is standing no more than an inch from her face.

"I refused him," she insists, terrified. "I told him that I'd tell you everything."

"You're mine," the minister says to her, placing his blood-soaked hands against her cheeks. "You are mine."

"Yes," she agrees meekly. "I am yours."

He kisses her. She can feel the plump, cold worms move from his mouth to hers. She swallows them. It's what he wants. And what he wants, *she* wants.

It's the only truth she has left.

Sunday, July 7, 3:11 P.M.

Dean Sousa and the four summer-temp cops are doing their best to control the riot, but it's not easy. The crowd is getting more agitated by the minute.

"Give us back our town!" the rioters start to chant. "Give us back our town."

Nate watches from the window of the station. "There's got to be over a hundred locals out there," he tells the chief. "People you'd never believe. There's three selectmen out there and the town manager!"

The chief shakes his head. "They've been acting odd for weeks. What surprises me is Isabella Sousa Cook—our much-loved town clerk—calling us traitors!"

Indeed, Mrs. Cook is out there, elbow to elbow with people like Mary Silva and Max Winn and Tim Lipnicki and Richard Longstaff and Pidge Hitchcock, brandishing a sign: HUTCHINS AND TUCK ARE SELLOUTS.

Photographers and newscasters representing media as far away as Providence and Boston are out there, too. The riot's been growing steadily ever since this morning, when it was announced that Rusty McDaniel would be formally charged with murder. A few townsfolk tried to prevent him from being taken away to state police headquarters in Barnstable. Clem Flagg, Hickey Hix and Manny Duarte stood in front of the police car with their arms folded over their chests until Nate threatened them all with arrest. "You're a traitor, Nate Tuck," his old pal Clem charged, shaking his fat fist. "We won't forget it!"

Actually, passions have been high in town since Friday morning, when the body of Claudio Sousa was found horribly mangled under the town pier. Nate thoroughly investigated the crime scene and has spent all his time since questioning everyone he can, but so far he has no suspect or motive in the killing, just the nagging feeling that it's connected to everything else. The murder was gruesome, reminding them all of the death of Priscilla Googins so many years before. It looked as if poor Claudio had been mauled by some animal. His guts had been ripped out through a hole in his torso.

"Yeah, animal, all right," Fred Pyle had snarled at the barbershop. "One of these crazed tourists who come here every summer and destroy our way of life."

With Rusty being formally charged, something seemed to snap in town. Two of their local boys were victims of what they saw as the evil outside world. Tess Woodward was outside the station right now shouting through a megaphone, calling those outside Falls Church limits "godless, sinful people!"

"What the hell has happened to this town?" Chief asks Nate, his face contorted with grief and worry.

Nate can't explain. How can he burden the chief with more than he already had?

Oh, yeah, by the way, Chief, while you've been sitting at your wife's deathbed, an evil supernatural force has taken over the citizenry of Falls Church, and I've been just twiddling my thumbs, unable to do a damn thing. Nate can just imagine Chief's response to *that.*

But the chief isn't waiting for an answer. "I do believe that people are basically good, Nate, but they're also basically frightened. You tap that fear, and people will do anything. That's where all of this nonsense comes from."

Nate's listening intently. "What do you mean?"

"All of this craziness, I'm just trying to understand it." The chief looks thoughtful. "For the last few years folks in this town have been afraid of losing what they think is most precious to them. You heard Fred Pyle say it the other day. Their *way of life.* They think all these new developments and new shops and new people are going to mean the end for them. People always think there's not going to be enough of the pie to go around, so they lash out. It's the root of all intolerance. It's called *fear*.''

Nate looks back out the window. It was a theory that sure as hell seemed easier to grasp than Victoria's mumbo jumbo about ghosts. ''Shall I go out and try to disperse them?'' Nate asks.

The chief sighs. ''Freedom of assembly, Nate. Freedom of speech. Let them have their rally. Let them get it out of their systems.''

Nate watches as Clem Flagg clamors up to the top of the steps to take the megaphone from Tess Woodward. He's out of breath. ''We won't forget Rusty or Claudio,'' he booms. ''They are our heroes. They are the sons of Falls Church!''

The crowd cheers.

''I say to you,'' Clem shouts, ''*you*, you tourists over there who are watching us today, swilling your beer and munching your potato chips, thinking we're all a bunch of ignorant rubes—*you* are the problem! We don't need you or your dollars! There's blood on your money! You are responsible for Claudio being dead and Rusty taken away!''

A group of tourists has gathered opposite the station to watch the crowd. Just a bunch of innocent young people, a couple of them eating ice-cream cones. Nate watches as they realize Clem has been addressing his tirade to them. Manny Duarte spits at them. Betty Silva approaches to wag a finger at them. Nate can't hear what she's saying, but he knows that Clem's inciting a riot.

''I'm going out there,'' he tells the chief.

''Be careful, Nate. Don't make things worse.''

At the sight of him opening the door, the crowd boos. It stops Nate in his tracks. These are people he's come to *love*. Falls Church gave him a home when he needed it most. ''Go back to California!'' shouts Marge Duarte. *Marge*—his pal!

He tries to ignore it. ''Clem,'' he says sternly, ''I could book you on inciting a riot. Now lay off that stuff, you hear?''

The chorus of boos grows louder. Clem stands defiant. Nate is about ready to take him into the station, when suddenly a roar goes up from the mob. A roar that turns into a cheer. Nate turns. Walking up the steps of the station, his flock parting obediently for him, is the Reverend Mark Miller.

"Clem," he says gently, "Officer Tuck is right. We can't be causing a riot here. Especially on the Sabbath."

"All right, Reverend," Clem says, dropping his chin in obedience.

Mark Miller smiles at Nate. "Please. May I try to calm the crowd?"

Nate says nothing as Miller takes the megaphone from Clem. "Good people of Falls Church, in our hearts today there is great sadness." His voice echoes against the brownstone buildings of Pearl Street. The mob falls utterly silent. "There is sadness, and there is anger. Righteous anger. But let us move from this place to our church. Let us move to our church and pray. Pray for our fallen brothers. Pray for our town. Pray that all may one day find the light of truth and wisdom."

He sets down the megaphone. "Thank you, Officer," he says, and walks back down the steps.

Clem follows. So does the crowd, orderly now and silent. They follow Mark Miller as if he were the Pied Piper all the way down Pearl Street, making a left onto Grand Avenue and then a right onto Church. Nate follows at a respectful distance, watching as each and every one of the mob walks solemnly into the old church. Then Gerry Garafolo closes the door on Nate and his officers.

Dean has walked up beside him. "Nate," he says thickly. "My mother and sister were in that crowd."

Nate looks at him without speaking.

"My whole family has been acting strange for weeks." The skinny little officer looks as if he might break down and sob. "My aunts, my uncles, my cousins. My mother commented on it. She said they were being outrageous, ridiculous. And today I saw her *with* them in that mob, and my sister, too, chanting for blood. Maybe it was my cousin Claudio's death that did it. Maybe that pushed them over somehow. But my mother isn't a rabble-rouser, and neither is my sister. *They make cakes and pies, Nate!* That's what they do. They run the bakery, that's all. They don't hate tourists. They don't riot in the streets."

The poor kid looks so stricken. Nate wants to tell him everything he's heard, all the theories he's been considering, crazy or not. He needs all the help he can get to stop this thing. But just what *is* it that he needs to stop? The chief is right, isn't he? This is America. People have the right to assemble, to follow whomever they choose. They can believe whatever they want, hate whomever they want to hate. All this unrest is about the fear that lives deep down inside everyone, the urge to scapegoat others for problems that seem too big. The chief is right. People are lashing out because they're afraid of losing what they think is most precious to them. You don't need a ghost or some supernatural evil to explain that.

For the moment Nate says nothing, just puts his arm around Dean's shoulder as they head back to the station.

Monday, July 8, 11:11 A.M.

Please, Miss Santos, I need to talk to you.

Catherine can't get the words of that poor boy out of her mind. He had clearly been in so much pain. She hadn't even realized what he was doing until it was almost too late—and then suddenly Nate's warning came clanging back at her.

If anyone starts to tell you about a dream they had, stop them. Under no circumstance should you allow anyone to tell you about their dream.

"I'm taking an early lunch," she tells Helen Twelvetrees, who, as usual these days, says nothing, just looks at her suspiciously.

Why am I so frightened of her? Catherine wonders. *Why do I feel as if Helen is always watching me, spying on me?*

She looks around, making sure Danny Correia isn't waiting for her, and slides into her car. She starts the ignition. The poor boy's words are still ringing in her ears.

Please, Miss Santos, I gotta tell ya a dream. . . .

Catherine knew Danny's mother. A good woman. Catherine had grown up with Doris Correia, gone to school with her. How worried Doris had been at the end about leaving Danny. She knew she had cancer, that her time was short, and Danny, though an adult, was retarded, and had never lived on his own. He had never held a job, never known what it was like to take care of himself.

"You'll watch out for him, won't you, Catherine?" Doris asked.

Catherine had done what she could. She talked to Alan Hitchcock about finding Danny a job with the town. Danny was slow, but he could handle simple tasks. Alan gave him a position as janitor at Town Hall, and the young man had taken to his duties with great responsibility and cheer. For the past seven years anyone heading into Town Hall has been greeted by Danny Correia, pushing his broom, offering a broad smile and a little nugget of wisdom overheard in those hallowed halls: maybe *Don't take any wooden nickels* or *A smile is just a frown turned upside down.*

He's a good soul, Catherine thinks. *I'm sorry, Doris. Sorry I couldn't help him this time.*

For Danny was trying to lure her into something that she had been warned against.

"Miss Santos," he said. "I saw a man in my dream last night. He was a very bad man. He came into my house and—"

"Stop, Danny," Catherine ordered. "Stop right now!"

"But I gotta tell you—"

What would have happened if Catherine hadn't hurried to the ladies' room, hiding out in a stall like some frightened child? She felt foolish, but something compelled her to do it. Maybe it was discovering that peculiar pattern in Falls Church's history, the odd confluence of events seemingly repeated every fifteen or twenty years. Every generation. It unnerved her, made her anxious, given what she sees happening in town—given what she remembers has happened in the past.

So she ended up waiting in the ladies' room until Helen Twelvetrees came in looking for her, a mix of confusion and contempt on her face. Assured that Danny was gone, Catherine emerged, but she's remained on her guard ever since. She called Nate Tuck, who arranged to meet her at the rectory of St. Peter's. Better there than at the station, he said, what with that bizarre riot from yesterday.

As she drives, Catherine reaches over to the passenger's seat to pat the photocopies she'd made, reading through dozens of old newspapers on the library's microfilm machine. Strange. The papers are *warm*.

Victoria Kennelly greets her at the rectory door. "I'd heard you were back in town," Catherine says as she embraces the younger woman.

"Miss Santos, it's good to see you again. Thank you for helping us."

Catherine looks at the faces in the room. Seated around the round dining table are Father Roche, Nate Tuck, that young Dr. Kip Hobart, and a woman Catherine doesn't know. Father Roche's housekeeper, Agnes Doolittle, is pouring tea.

"I'm still not sure what it is I'm helping you all *do*," Catherine says, "but I think I have some interesting information."

"Please, Miss Santos," Father Roche says, gesturing. "Have a seat."

"Miss Santos, this is my friend, Alexis Stokes," Kip Hobart offers. The two women smile in greeting. Catherine settles herself opposite Nate, who watches her with concern. She spreads the photocopies in front of her on the table. Now they're more than warm. They're *hot*. She withdraws her fingers quickly.

Victoria places a hand gently on Catherine's shoulder. "Here," she says. "Try these."

She hands her a pair of leather gloves.

"But how did you know?" Catherine asks. "Why are these papers this way?"

"Because they must indeed contain information that, as you suggest, is *interesting*." Victoria smiles. "Information that we need to know."

Catherine feels cold terror race down her spine. "What's going on here? You must tell me. This morning Danny Correia tried to tell me a dream, but I wouldn't let him, Nate, because you warned me not to."

Nate sighs.

"Are you sure you didn't hear it?" asks Kip Hobart.

"I'm sure. I stopped him." She smiles ruefully. "I hid in the ladies' room."

"And that's your salvation," Kip tells her.

"Should we go try to find poor Danny?" Father Roche asks.

Kip shakes his head. "What's the point? He's surely told someone else by now."

"We don't know that for sure." Nate stands, pulling out his

phone from the loop on his belt. "If it's true he's passing something on that warps people's minds—however it manages to do that—we can maybe gain an edge." He quickly calls Dean at the station, tells him to pick Danny Correia up and bring him in. "Hold him there until I get there," he instructs. "And under no circumstances are you to allow him to tell you anything, Dean. I mean *anything*. He'll take orders from you. He'll do what you say. Tell him to stay quiet until I get there. Don't allow him to say *anything*."

"Please," Catherine says. She feels near tears. "Won't someone tell me what's going on?"

Victoria sits beside her. "Why don't you present us with your findings? Maybe it will begin to add up to you."

Catherine sighs. She slips on the gloves that Victoria has given her. "I did what you asked, Nate. And you were right to suspect what I think you were suspecting. The tragedies involving Petey McKay, Victoria's family and Priscilla Googins weren't the only ones in Falls Church's history. During World War Two there was the death of a young man out near the lighthouse. He was a Chinese American, but it seems some of the town leaders thought he might be Japanese and accused him of being a traitor. The papers are filled with articles and letters to the editor questioning his motives in setting up a business in town. A special Town Meeting was called, and the town eventually denied him a license."

"May I see these?" Victoria asks. Catherine nods, watching as Victoria winces just a bit picking up the top sheet of paper. "Yes. The charge against Mr. Lee was organized by a Peter Colson. Does anybody know who he was?"

They're all too young to remember, even Catherine, and Father Roche hadn't arrived in Falls Church until the 1970s. "Colson isn't a local name," Catherine tells them. "So I looked him up in the town directory."

"You *are* a good detective," Nate says with a small smile.

"Peter Colson is listed as living here only one year, 1943. It would seem he came to town, got things all stirred up and then left."

"Recognize a pattern?" Kip asks. "Isn't that what happened with Grace West and Tommy Keegan?"

Catherine looks at him. "Yes," she says, starting to understand. "That *is* what happened."

"How did poor Mr. Lee die?" Father Roche asks.

"His throat was cut. He was found on the beach."

Victoria's still reading the photocopies. "It says here he was found the day after Miss Florence Reich stood up at Town Meeting and said the town's persecution of him was wrong. She was just a young girl then. Eighteen, it says here. She seems to have changed a lot of people's minds by speaking up."

"Just as you did, Victoria," Catherine says, starting to recognize the pattern they're talking about.

Victoria looks as if she might cry.

"Just for curiosity's sake," Nate asks, "did the directory give an address where this troublemaker Peter Colson was living?"

"Why, yes," Catherine says. "He was at the Grand Avenue Apartments down by the old church."

Nate nods. "Just like Grace West."

Catherine shivers. "Tommy Keegan lived there, too."

"As well as our good reverend," Kip adds.

Catherine looks around at all of them. "You're suspecting Reverend Miller—he's the problem, isn't he? He's doing what Tommy Keegan did. What all of these people throughout Falls Church's history did."

"Except he's far more clever now," Kip muses. "He's seen what went wrong before. My guess is he wants this town under his domination, the way Father Fall once held sway here. So this time he's going about it differently."

"What do you mean?" asks Father Roche.

"Each time, the person we shall call—to use Nate's good word—the *troublemaker* has utilized current trends or contemporary fears to gain control. During World War Two, it was the nation's xenophobia and fear of the Japanese. During the 1960s it was the distrust of the counterculture, the hippies. In the 1980s it was fear of AIDS."

"And now?" asks Catherine.

"Now none of that would work. Now he must be much more clever. He mustn't come across as hateful or intolerant. As a society we've become much too wary of bigots and extremists. He has to sneak in, under cover of night—"

"And catch us in our dreams," Father Roche says, trembling.

"Precisely. And as near as we can trace it back, the dream started with one of our most vulnerable citizens, a little boy, Josh McKenzie. Only once a significant number of the population was under his control did the troublemaker actually appear. And then he presents himself as enlightened and tolerant." Kip looks at each of them. "But we've seen what his enlightenment and tolerance has produced. The petition against Martha Sturm. The murder of that poor man walking into town. Neighbor turned against neighbor. Locals pitted against tourist."

"And you blame Reverend Miller for all that?" Catherine asks incredulously.

"What else did you find?" Kip asks. "Tell us the rest of it."

So Catherine does, relating as best she can the results of her findings. There was a scandal in 1920 involving a band of moonshiners, a ruckus in the street in which three people were killed, all instigated by a "reformer" named Millicent Peabody, who, breaking the pattern, turned up not once but for *five* consecutive years in the town directories. Kip speculates that this may have been one of the more successful excursions for "the troublemaker," as the Roaring Twenties in Falls Church were anything but. Catherine explains that while the rest of the country engaged in all sorts of rules-busting activities, Falls Church was known as a haven where alcohol, cigarettes and even dancing were banned by the town fathers. And *mothers*—for Millicent Peabody was elected selectwoman and ruled the town manager with an iron fist for five years. Until that day in 1925 when she was defeated at the polls and quickly disappeared from town.

"That kind of evil, that kind of repression, cannot endure," Kip surmises. "Each time it has gained a foothold, no matter how long it took, eventually the people rose up and brought it down."

Before that period the record grows spotty. The library is missing many newspapers between 1888 and 1912, Catherine explains, but she found some tantalizing hints. In 1898 there was a rally of the town's Yankee population against the rising numbers of Portuguese fishing immigrants. It was led by a man named Willis Parker Polk, of whom no reference can be found in either town directories or census records.

"A less successful venture," Kip speculates, although that was also the year of one of the many horrific fires at the old church. The conflagrations were certainly keyed to activities of "the troublemaker." In 1851, when another blaze destroyed the structure on the old church site, a woman was found raped and murdered on the wharf. The minister at the time, a firebrand named Gabriel Collins, accused her and many of the women of Falls Church of immoral acts. Material on Collins was scant; Catherine estimates he didn't hold the position long.

The last germ of information she could find was a notice in the old town records of a campaign in 1783 to rid the town of "heathens," presumably Indians but apparently expanded to include many white townsfolk. A magistrate named Ezekial Starr held public trials on the Town Green of all those who "violated God's divine laws," and at least two men and three women were executed.

"I suspect," Kip concludes, "if the records were extant, that such activity could be found all the way back to the death of Father Fall."

"So do we think finally they are all the same?" Father Roche asks, his old eyes weary and sad. "Is this merely the same malevolent spirit of the town's founder, rising every generation to continue his vendetta against sin?"

"I suspect that is the case," Kip says. "He won't surrender his control over this town."

Nate lets out a long sigh and walks over to the window.

"You're not sure you believe all this, are you, Nate?" Catherine asks.

"I—I don't know what to think," he tells her.

Catherine doesn't know what to think, either. She wishes Nate would say something more. If he believes, she'll believe. But he won't look at her. He simply sighs again and then walks out of the room.

"Thank you, Miss Santos," Kip says. "You have been a tremendous help."

"But what can be done?" she asks in desperation. "If this is true, we can't just let Reverend Miller continue like this."

She sees Kip look over at Father Roche. Their eyes hold. They seem to have come to a conclusion.

"No," Kip promises her. "We won't let him continue. It's time Falls Church is finally free of Father Fall."

Monday, July 8, 6:30 P.M.

Nate didn't want to bring her here. All of this is just getting too incredible for him, and it's turning more bizarre by the minute. Kip and Father Roche are back in Falls Church planning an exorcism—an *exorcism*, for Christ's sake! Like in that movie with Linda Blair that scared the shit out of Nate as a kid with all its mumbo jumbo and swiveling heads. And, meanwhile, here he is—with a strange woman he barely knows—at the coroner's office in Bourne looking at the mangled corpse of Claudio Sousa.

Alexis had insisted it was important to their investigation. Nate grumbles under his breath as poor old Claudio is wheeled out on a gurney. Since when did he let some civilian call the shots in investigating a crime? There was no evidence tying Claudio's murder to Reverend Miller; in fact, the minister had been on the beach with several members of his flock watching the fireworks at the time Nate estimates Claudio was ripped apart under the pier. Miller was the first person Nate investigated after the crime, and found he had a solid alibi.

But he can't deny the coincidence: Claudio had been, after all, one of those painting walls and repairing the roof at the old church. So he's agreed to Alexis's odd request. And now, here they are, standing in the morgue, inspecting the rutted, pulpy corpse. It was their last chance to do so; the body will be turned over to the family for burial tomorrow.

"What are you looking to find?" Nate asks, not for the first time, as Alexis stares down at the dead man.

She's an odd bird, this one, Nate thinks. For most of their discussions, she always just sits there, not saying a word, just listening, with those big round eyes of hers watching them all. In the car all the way down here, she had refused to answer Nate's questions beyond vaguely reassuring him that she hoped to help the investigation. Neither does she answer him now. Alexis simply stares down at the corpse, seemingly unfazed by the gruesome sight of Claudio's pale and purple body, his head nearly severed, his torso ripped down the middle. She rests her hand on his head and closes her eyes.

"What are you doing?" Nate asks.

"Yes," she says. "It is just as I thought."

"*What* is?"

She turns her enormous eyes up at him. "This wasn't a random act. This wasn't part of his plan."

"How do you know?"

Alexis smiles. "My father taught me how to listen. Really listen. Claudio may be dead, but that doesn't mean he isn't still able to communicate with us."

Nate sighs. "So what did he tell you?"

"Claudio was a follower. Father Fall only kills his followers when they betray him, or do something against his wishes." She's silent, apparently listening for more details. "He tried to get away. He tried to break out from his control, and so Father Fall killed him."

"Meaning Reverend Miller. But he was on the beach. He has an alibi. Witnesses who aren't members of his congregation saw him far off down the beach."

Alexis isn't listening to him. She places her hand against the corpse's bloodless white cheek. "Fly free, my good man. Fly free."

Heading back to Falls Church, neither Nate nor Alexis say a word. They know what awaits them: the ritual Kip and Father Roche are preparing. The hocus-pocus that will supposedly cast the Devil back to hell. Nate wishes he could believe the way they all do. He wishes he didn't keep reacting the way he's been reacting for the past few days. *This is crazy,* he thinks. *This isn't police work. This is insane.*

Dean had reported that Danny Correia had been silent when he picked him up. He said not a word, just whimpered a little, a scared little boy in the holding cell. Kip concluded that meant he'd already passed on the dream.

Maybe, Nate thinks. *And maybe all this is a crock of shit, and the real killer of Claudio Sousa and maybe Monica Paul is laughing his ass off at all of us.* Maybe Rusty just cracked when he shot that kid. Maybe Job and Berniece just cracked, too, disappearing and leaving their son behind. Maybe the whole town just cracked and found religion.

"I just want this to be over," Nate says, finally breaking the silence as they head down the causeway that links Falls Church to the rest of the Cape.

"I have a feeling it will soon be over indeed," Alexis says. Her big eyes seem filled with a sudden and terrible sadness. "But not in the way any of us would want it to be over."

Tuesday, July 9, 12:01 A.M.

"Now."

Father Roche holds aloft the cross. They're standing in the grass of the graveyard just beyond the old church. The moon is high overhead, a silver fingernail. The town is quiet. Kip Hobart steps forward with a book open in his hands.

"Spirits of hatred and intolerance, of greed and ego," he intones, *"you are not welcome here."*

His voice sounds so tremulous to his ears. So young. So untried. Kip remembers hearing his mentor, Dr. Stokes, speak these same words. The first time was at a house in New Orleans, where he rid the family of the unclean spirit that had plagued them for years. How strong Dr. Stokes had been. How assured.

You're simply playacting, comes a voice. *You're nothing like him.*

Kip tries to ignore it, concentrating on the next line from the book. *"Spirits of vengeance, spirits of malice, spirits of cruelty,"* he says, his voice cracking, *"you are not welcome here."*

Go home, little boy. You know not what you are up against.

Kip clears his throat. He looks over at Father Roche, who stands behind him, trembling, his old hands clasping the jeweled crucifix.

It had been Kip's first thought that Father Roche should conduct the ritual, using the Catholic rites. But the old priest had objected, saying he needed the bishop's permission, and he knew it would never be granted. "An unsanctioned exorcism would have no power," Father Roche had said, but Kip suspected the old man was simply too terrified to try.

And why shouldn't he be terrified? The demon is taunting him. *Remember, Kip Hobart, that eventually even Dr. Stokes succumbed to powers greater than he.*

"He had a heart attack," Kip whispers into the night. "He still succeeded in driving out the unclean spirits."

There's laughter in the night air that tickles the long grass of the old cemetery, though Kip is certain only he can hear it. Laughter that mocks him.

Ah, but I know all about you, Kip Hobart. As I know the secrets and the fears of all who come to live in Falls Church.

"You are not welcome here!" Kip shouts.

Laughter again. *Little boy. Are you pretending to be your great hero, Dr. Stokes? How pathetic.*

Kip tries not to listen to the taunting, but this devil's right: He *does* know his thoughts and his fears. Since moving to Falls Church, Kip has kept far away from the horrors that he'd once fought alongside Dr. Stokes. He's settled into a comfortable existence as a psychologist—even with his past-life regressions and psychic channeling, he hasn't had any serious contact with forces from the other side. His days of traipsing around the world helping Dr. Stokes exorcise demons from houses are over.

Or so he thought.

You let yourself get soft, the voice tells him. *You have no power. You can barely read the words.*

"Here we welcome the only—" Kip pauses, then starts over. He is indeed mixing up words. "*Here we welcome only the spirits of good, of truth, of compassion, of—*"

A scream cuts through the night air. Kip's words catch in his throat. He gasps out loud. Out of the corner of his eye, he can see Nate, at the edge of the graveyard with Victoria and Alexis. The policeman reacts to the sound. It appears to have come from the old church.

Alexis has come up behind him. "We have to go inside," she tells him urgently.

"But that's what he *wants* us to do," Kip protests, aware

of how fast his heart is beating in his ears. "He's trying to lure us inside, onto his turf. We can't—"

"It is the heart of the possession," Alexis says. "You remember my father's teachings. That's where the exorcism must be performed."

"She's right," Father Roche says. "Performing the ritual outside the church will not be effective. Even the Catholic ritual places you on the spot."

Kip looks up at the old church. A small light has appeared in an upper window. He had hoped this could be done from out here, with Reverend Miller safely asleep in his room at the Grand Avenue Apartments. But Kip should have known he'd be here waiting for them. Ever since Catherine Santos refused the dream, he's surely been aware of their attempts to stop him. Perhaps he's known even longer than that.

"Maybe *you're* not going inside, Hobart," Nate says, approaching him, "but I am. That was a scream from inside. Someone may be hurt. I'm calling for backup and going inside. Enough of this hocus-pocus."

"You *can't*, Nate!" Kip shouts. "You'll destroy everything if you get this place swarming with cops. We've got to be able to perform the ritual!"

Nate cocks his gun. "Then I'm going in on my own." He bounds off past them, up the front steps of the church. The door, to none of their surprise, is unlocked.

The church is deathly quiet. The moonlight flickers across the pews, reflecting off the gold goblets and silver menorah kept up on the altar. Father Roche follows Nate and Kip inside. Nate had said he'd give them ten minutes for the ritual; otherwise, someone might come along and accuse them of trespassing. The Reverend Mark Miller, not the town, now holds the lease on the old church.

But first Nate wants to check for the source of the scream. Father Roche watches as the police detective scans his flashlight across and under the pews. There appears to be no one in the nave of the church.

"It was not the scream of the living," Alexis tells him,

approaching him calmly. "It was an echo of one of the screams of the many who have died in this place."

Nate seems annoyed by her. He pushes past her abruptly and continues his search. Father Roche can see Nate's struggle. He doesn't want to believe in all this supernatural nonsense. The old priest can understand. He, too, once wanted to disregard it. It borders on heresy: *Thou shalt have no strange gods before Me.* To acknowledge the power of demons and evil spirits is not what James Roche was taught in the seminary.

But then why hasn't the Church ever officially disavowed the rites of exorcism? They've been kept on the books all these centuries. Once, when he was a young priest, Father Roche met a wise man, Monsignor du Clerc, from a parish in Quebec. The good monsignor told him why the Church had never repudiated the rites of exorcism: "For when you've been in our line of work for as long as I have, you will see at some point, maybe more than once, the face of the Beast. Up close, so you can smell his breath. And you must have the means to fight him."

Father James Roche has seen the face of the Beast. He saw it that night when Victoria Kennelly stayed at the rectory. But that wasn't the first time. He had believed Victoria's story because he had seen the Beast before, in the eyes of Tommy Keegan. He hadn't wanted to believe it then, and he had prayed to God to tell him that he was wrong, that he'd been mistaken, that He would never allow the Fallen One such leeway upon the earth. The old priest prayed and prayed and prayed, begging God to tell him if indeed he had seen the Beast, but until now God has remained stubbornly silent. It has taken nearly fifteen years, but finally Father Roche has his reply from God.

That was indeed the face of the Beast I saw and he has now returned to finish what he started.

So why had he balked at performing the exorcism himself? *Because I'm an old man. Because Kip Hobart is young, and he's done this before.*

But with the tools and the words of pagans. Father Roche tries to stifle the doubt in his chest. *Only Christ can drive out the Devil—*

No. It is precisely such parochial thinking that provides the handiwork for the Fallen One. If anything has come out of this, it is Father Roche's newfound understanding that no faith is greater than any other. To elevate any one belief—any one god or ritual over another—merely sets the stage for the Devil to dance. Father Roche would raise his cross in support of Kip Hobart's words, but they would work together, combining their faiths, to rid this place of its evil.

"All right, go ahead," Nate tells them after a brief tour of the unfinished church hall below. "Cast your spells. Do whatever it is you need to do and let's get out of here."

They assemble on the altar. Kip and Father Roche stand in the center, on the spot where the old priest knows Priscilla Googins was murdered. He trembles, lifting the crucifix high. Once more, Kip recites their complaint, proclaiming that spirits of evil and intolerance are not welcome here.

"John Fall!" Kip shouts, his voice steady now, echoing horribly against the walls of the church. *"Your time has come! You must face the reckoning of the living!"*

He raises his hands into the air.

"I abjure thee; I repudiate your power! Your hold over this place is ended!"

There's nothing. No sound.

"Odious and contemptuous spirit, I command you to depart! By the judge of the quick and the dead, by your Maker and the Maker of all things, depart this place in haste! Your restless, hostile spirit shall no longer hold power here!"

Suddenly there's a ferocious sound from outside, a terrible thud, a great wind hitting the front wall. But the night is calm and clear; they all know that. Still, shutters begin to bang against the church, and the menorah that stands upon the altar table falls to the floor. Father Roche's grip around the crucifix tightens.

"Hear me, John Fall!" Kip continues. *"By your Maker be cast back into the outer darkness!"*

A terrible scream is heard again. But this time none of them move. It comes from nowhere, from everywhere. It seeps up from the floorboards, hurls itself down from the rafters.

"Spawn of hatred!" Kip shouts. *"I cast you back into the darkness where you must stay, never to shame us with your intolerance and vengeance again!"*

The church shakes. Father Roche sees it then.

The face of the Beast.

"Sweet Jesus, Mother of Mercy," he mumbles in prayer.

A horrible hiss fills the church. Something emerges from the darkness in front of them, great red eyes and snapping jaws. Father Roche can smell—*taste*—its hideous breath just as Monsignor du Clerc had described. Putrid and foul.

"Come with me, priest!" the thing bellows.

Father Roche trembles in its sight. He lifts the cross in defense.

"Puny man! Do you think such symbols hold any power over me?"

"Begone," the old priest croaks. "Back to the darkness!"

The Beast laughs. Its claws tear the crucifix from Father Roche's hands. It looms over him now, its rancid stink making him vomit all over himself.

"You are mine, priest! Mine!"

Father Roche screams as he feels this demon overtake him.

And at that moment a section of the floor of the altar gives way. Alexis plunges down into the dark depths below.

"Alexis!" Kip screams.

After the deafening crash into the hall below, the church falls eerily silent, except for Father Roche, who has dropped to his knees, his hands covering his head, vomiting onto the floor, sobbing and shaking uncontrollably. Nate and Kip bound to the front of the church to take the stairs down to the floor below, three steps at a time. Kip is the first to reach Alexis, who lies among a twisted pile of floorboards at the far end of the hall.

"Alexis! Dear God, Alexis!"

He begins pulling away debris to free her, even as it becomes clear that she's not moving, and will never move again. A sharp piece of wood has staked her through the heart, impaling her as if on a spear.

There's surprisingly little blood at first. It trickles down the broken floorboards slowly, gradually covering Kip's hands and arms as he digs. Nate finally has to pull him away. "More of the floor could come down," he tells him. "It's not safe here."

Kip spins on him, feeling himself slip into hysteria. "Not safe! No, not safe, Detective Tuck! And it never will be! We don't have the power to stop him! We were foolish to even try! Can't you hear him laughing at us? Laughing! Laughing!"

Kip Hobart collapses to his knees, his bloody hands covering his ears.

Tuesday, July 9, 7:49 A.M.

They agree that for now, to implicate as few as possible, it will be said that only Kip and Alexis had been in the church, and that Nate, passing by, had heard the crash and investigated. Kip, despite his grief and hysterics, quickly pulled himself together and determined it would be the only way for them to continue to operate.

"*He* knows we were all in there," Kip said, "but we can't let his flock know. Not yet."

Nate agrees to the plan but doesn't like it. This whole wacked-out ghost-hunting has made him uncomfortable from the start, and now he's withholding evidence. He himself had been trespassing—breaking the law. But Victoria had urged him to please go along, just to give them a little time to regroup. He reluctantly agreed, but already he was hoping to wash his hands of all of them. Even if he can't get Victoria's beguiling eyes out of his mind.

Father Roche was inconsolable, having had some kind of hallucination, a vision only he saw. All that the rest of them had witnessed was his screaming and then collapsing, followed by Alexis's falling through the floor.

They're all a bunch of hysterics, Nate thinks. *Even Victoria. Maybe especially Victoria.*

When the Reverend Miller arrives to survey the damage, he

seems both concerned about his church but also genuinely saddened by the girl's death. "Does she have any family?" he asks Nate. "Is there anything I can do?"

At the station Nate goes through the motions of charging Kip with illegal trespass, but Mark Miller, arriving with Kathy McKenzie, insists he doesn't have the heart to press charges, given the tragedy of Alexis's death. "This town has been through too much of late," he says. "Far be it from me to add to any suffering."

Kip professes to be grateful. To Nate, Mark Miller expresses his willingness to cooperate with any investigation. "We had contractors in there who assured us the floors were safe," he said, producing documents signed by none other than Richie Rostocki, the town's own developer. "I am just *horrified* by this."

Kathy McKenzie looks quizzically down at Kip sitting in the chair beside Nate's desk. "I remember you," she says. "I went to you so that you could help me quit smoking."

Kip's eyes flicker up to hers.

"Why were you inside the church?" Kathy asks. "Why were you trespassing, Dr. Hobart?"

"We thought—we thought we heard a scream." Kip shifts in his chair. "And the front door was open."

"Yes," Nate agrees, pleased not to have to lie this time. "There doesn't appear to have been any forced entry."

Mark Miller's eyes brim with tears. "That such a tragedy should occur again in such a holy place. . . ." His voice breaks off. "I'll speak to my caretakers. I don't know who could have left that door unlocked. It could have been me. I'm so . . . sorry. . . ."

He walks away, clearly distraught.

Nate watches as Kathy McKenzie pauses beside Kip. "You said you heard a scream?" she asks quietly.

Kip looks up at her again. He nods.

"From where? Where did you hear it?"

Kip seems to consider his answer. "From everywhere, it seemed. From everywhere and nowhere at once."

Kathy says nothing. She takes in his answer, lowering her eyes.

Has she heard it, too? Nate wonders. Then Kathy hurries off to follow Mark Miller out of the building.

When the chief gets in, drawn and ragged from another night sitting at Ellen's bedside, Nate fills him in on what's happened. But he can't lie to the chief. He just can't.

"I was in there, too," he says quietly, "when the floor went down."

The chief looks at him sharply. "I didn't hear that, Nate."

"Chief, I have reason to suspect that Mark Miller is . . . Well, I was there doing an investigation."

"With two civilians?"

Nate sighs. "I needed their input. They had information—"

He's cut off by the chief. "Nate, I can't process this. I am tired; I am upset; I could get a call at any time that my wife is dead. And we've just had the second death in Falls Church in a week. This has not been a good summer. Don't make it worse."

"Chief, I was just—"

"I trust you, Nate. If you need to conduct an investigation, you have my support. I just can't handle details yet. I just want to be sure you don't do anything that's going to come back and haunt all of us later." He narrows his eyes at Nate and lowers his voice. "The three of you didn't *cause* that crash, did you?"

"No. It was an accident we had nothing to do with." Nate's not sure how true that is. How much had Kip's mumbo jumbo caused the floor to collapse? Victoria certainly made a lot out of the wind that suddenly hit the church right before it happened. Nate's not sure it was as strong as she made it out to be— again, he's starting to think they're all a little hysterical—but maybe it was enough to dislodge some post, some beam. . . .

"Look, Nate," Chief says, letting out a long sigh. "Don't disappoint me. I'm counting on you. This is the worst period I can ever remember. Murders, accidental deaths, the situation with Rusty . . . Please hold down the fort as best you can. I need you, Nate. *Please.*"

The older man places his hands on Nate's shoulders. Nate feels his throat tighten, the emotion coming from his gut. Chief Philip Hutchins is the closest thing to a father he's known since his own dad was gunned down so long ago. There's no way Nate would do anything to let this man down.

"I'll keep the peace; I promise you, Chief," Nate tells him.

The chief nods and lets out another long sigh. He heads back out to his car so he can return to Ellen's bedside and wait for the end.

Wednesday, July 10, 7:05 P.M.

But keeping the peace isn't easy. That week, the police blotter has been filled with incidents. On Monday night a fight between a couple of fishermen and some tourists from Philadelphia down at Dicky's Bar. On Tuesday afternoon a complaint from a couple renting one of the cottages out at Lighthouse Beach that local kids were egging their car. On Tuesday night Sam Wong at the Chinese restaurant had to call the cops on two teenagers, Liz Stoddard and Billy Hix, who were harassing his customers.

But the worst came on Wednesday morning, and everyone is still talking about it. Sometime during the night, a small cross had been hastily banged into the ground in the front yard of Job Emerson's house on Beach Road and set ablaze. The house has, of course, been empty since Job disappeared three weeks ago, but Sam Drucker, who lives next door, noticed the burning cross at seven o'clock in the morning and called police. A reporter from the *Boston Globe,* in town to cover the series of unexplained deaths, was quickly on the scene to get a photo, and a crew from Channel 7 was also able to get footage of firefighters putting out the fire for the noon news.

"Who would *do* such a thing?" asks Marcella Stein, her face red with anger. The Board of Selectmen has gathered to discuss the petition against Martha Sturm. There's quite a crowd packed into the selectmen's chambers at Town Hall. Off to the side sits the object of the town's scorn, Martha herself, supported by her partner, Kim Longstaff. Their faces are masks of studied dispassion. Reporters from as far away as New York are crushed in around the sides of the room, and television cameras wait like crocodiles outside of the hall.

But first Marcella has seized the opportunity to condemn the cross-burning on Job's lawn. "This is beyond anything we have ever experienced! Some have suggested it was a prank by some kids. It is no prank! It is a hate crime, and should be treated as such."

She and Cooper Pierce seem to be the only ones on the selectmen board to be outraged by the incident. Gyp Nunez, Richard Longstaff and Mary Silva sit there expressionless, seemingly bored by all the talk. Finally Gyp even gripes, under his breath, "Well, Job had it coming by running off and leaving his kid. Typical of those people. No responsibility."

Marcella is stunned. She immediately asks that Gyp be given a formal reprimand, but she's voted down. Even Cooper, always trying to keep the peace, votes against her. "Let's just move on," he pleads. "Leave the cross-burners to the police."

Marcella glares at him. "As an African American yourself, Cooper, I am flabbergasted that you want to dismiss this so quickly."

"This whole town is coming unglued," Cooper says. "I just want some peace."

Marcella's aghast. "I cannot for the life of me understand what's come over all of you. We've had a killing in this town with racial overtones and now a cross-burning on the lawn of an African American citizen. And you all act as if you don't care. What kind of image of Falls Church is being given out to the world by your indifference?"

Photographers snap a dozen pictures of Marcella as she speaks.

"What I am concerned with *tonight*," insists Mary Silva, sliding the microphone down in front of her, "is that we get to the business at hand. Which is considering this petition that has been circulated by so many of our good and decent citizens."

"This petition is a travesty," Marcella says. "Martha Sturm has done an excellent job."

"May I ask that the petition be presented?" Mary Silva

looks around the room and smiles. "I recognize Hiram and Betty Silva."

"I think you ought to recuse yourself," Marcella objects. "Hiram is your brother."

Hiram raises his chin in defiance. "I am merely one of the many who are expressing our rights to gather signatures as citizens of this great community." His wife, Betty, is busy handing each board member a copy of the petition. "At least two dozen of us have been out every day circulating this—"

Marcella looks at the names and throws it down in disgust. "These names aren't even all voters."

"Which is precisely why it holds no legal authority," comes a voice. A tall woman with tortoiseshell glasses approaches the board members. "May I speak, please? I am Attorney Nancy Schaefer of Boston, representing Martha Sturm."

"Please," Marcella says. "It's about time Martha is allowed to present a defense."

Nancy Schaefer levels her eyes at the board. "This petition is mean spirited and has no legality whatsoever. It is merely an attempt to discredit my client, who from all accounts has been a superlative principal. Even on the night of Town Meeting, the night Mr. Silva so rudely attacked my client, this town confirmed by a voice vote its support for Martha Sturm's work as principal. Even Mr. Silva's wife spoke out in support that night; although I see now, for whatever reason, she and others have changed their views."

"I saw the truth!" Betty Silva says loudly. "I saw the light of truth!"

The attorney eyes her coldly. "May I remind this board that in this state we have a law forbidding discrimination on the basis of sexual orientation. I have worked with the Massachusetts Commission Against Discrimination and I assure you I will—"

"Make no threats to us!" Selectman Richard Longstaff suddenly barks. "If we want to fire that filthy dyke, we can do so!"

The crowd gasps.

"Father!" Kim Longstaff is on her feet. "How could you?"

"You shame me," he snarls. "Sitting there beside that abomination—"

"This is outrageous!" Nancy Schaefer shrills. "This is slander! I will bring charges—"

"Enough!" Marcella shouts as the reporters run around, taking it all down, the photographers snapping their cameras. People in the crowd are now hooting, some in outrage over Longstaff's remark, others cheering him.

"What has this town come to?" Marcella begins banging the gavel. "Order! Order! This petition has no legal weight. I move that it be thrown out and all of this disregarded—"

Mary Silva is on her feet. "It may carry no legal weight, but we can't ignore the will of the people it so obviously represents!"

A loud cheer explodes from the audience.

"I move that we fire Martha Sturm," says Gyp Nunez, leaning his head on his hand, his lip curling.

"You can't do that!" Nancy Schaefer bellows. "This isn't procedure. This is a farce!"

"Fire her!" starts the chant from the crowd. "Fire her!"

A dozen people surge on the board. Marcella bangs her gavel futilely. "Order! Order!" Cooper Pierce simply covers his face with his hands. The reporters are frantically calling in their stories on their cell phones. Martha Sturm starts to cry.

And in the back of the hall, standing among the roiling crowd, watching impassively as all of this unfolds, is the handsome young minister, the Reverend Mark Miller. He's quoted the next day in many of the articles, saying how much he regrets the turmoil and unpleasantness and hurt feelings, but, after all, the will of the people must be done.

When it's noted that many of those who led the petition were members of his church, he simply calls them good and decent citizens who have the courage to act on their convictions. "I admire them," he tells the *Boston Globe*. "They can teach us all a lesson. It is time all of us start standing up for what is right and good and moral." When he is asked whether that means he would consider Martha Sturm immoral, he says simply, "I think Selectman Longstaff spoke for many when he called her an abomination." And then he referred the reporter to the chapter in Leviticus that he said proved his point.

Thursday, July 11, 2:15 P.M.

"I think he's tipped his hat at last," Victoria says. "By coming out against Martha Sturm, Mark Miller has revealed his true colors. He's no open-minded nondenominationalist. He's a bigot, a fundamentalist."

Nate makes a face. They're standing in his office, in front of his desk, face-to-face. "So you're saying just because he's a fundamentalist, that's proof he's really Father Fall, returned from the grave?"

"Look, Nate. It's adding up." Victoria looks at him with wide, passionate eyes. "I've been studying the research Catherine Santos did for us. I realize now that Fall reappears in town at the point when discontent in town is already at its peak. When I was a girl, it was when there was a lot of fear and suspicion around AIDS. When Priscilla Googins was killed, it was when there was all sorts of social unrest over the Vietnam War. This time, tensions between Falls Church natives and the newcomers—the summer people—had reached a crisis point. It's fertile ground for him. He appears when people's souls are primed for hate."

Nate sighs, crossing his arms over his chest. "So tell me what he wants from all this."

"He wants the town back under his thumb again, the way he had it for those few short years after he founded the place." Victoria looks at him as if it's simple mathematics to figure it out. "And he's being very crafty this time, starting off slow. He invades people's dreams, gets them even more anxious and scared. Then he can play savior, giving them sanctuary and hope through his church. It's the classic strategy of any cult. Then, as his first target, he chooses homosexuals—the petition against Martha Sturm. See, homosexuals are the last minority in this day and age that it's still okay to demonize in public. So he can start there. But you can be sure he won't end there."

"You know what, Victoria?" Nate is shaking his head. "All of this simply reveals Miller to be some Jerry Falwell wanna-be, not some devil from Falls Church's distant past."

Victoria smiles. "Your skepticism is helpful, Nate. It keeps us in check. But at the very least I think all of this proves Miller isn't what he says he is, and I think sooner or later he's going to reveal more about himself, until he's finally Father Fall, truly and completely, once more."

"Before you write that in stone," Nate says as he walks around behind his desk, "take a look at these."

He hands Victoria a file folder. She accepts it, opening it up to look at the papers inside. "What are these?"

"Transcripts, to start," Nate tells her. "From Yale Divinity School. Look at them. He was a good student."

Victoria studies them. Yes, these are transcripts for Mark Miller. All As and Bs. Behind the transcripts she glances at a letter from the dean, who comments on Mark's "extraordinary commitment" as a student. Behind the letter is a photocopy of a page from some newsletter or yearbook: Mark Miller in cap and gown, receiving his diploma.

"So he went to school," Victoria says, her voice trailing off just a little.

"Keep looking," Nate tells her.

At the back of the file are several more photocopies. The first is a newspaper article from Mount Pleasant, Michigan: ST. ANN'S HIGH SCHOOL GRADUATES FORTY-THREE, reads the headline. Below, among all the names, Nate has highlighted in yellow: *Mark Bartholomew Miller.*

"I'm not sure what you're suggesting this proves," Victoria says softly.

"Look at the last piece of paper in there," Nate instructs. She does. It's a copy of a birth certificate. *Mark Bartholomew*

Miller, born January 5, 1977, Mount Pleasant Hospital, Mount Pleasant, Michigan. Father: Randolph B. Miller. Mother: Hazel Winslow. Six pounds four ounces at birth.

Victoria just looks at Nate without saying anything.

"So if he's Father Fall," Nate says, "he spent an awful lot of time living somebody else's life before getting here to Falls Church."

Victoria sets the file back down on Nate's desk. "I admire your detective work. But nothing in these papers undercuts my theory. Maybe that's how he operates. Maybe he gets reincarnated in people. Maybe only after he graduated from divinity school did Mark Miller realize he was really John Fall and—"

"And maybe he's just what I said," Nate tells her, his eyes hard. "A Jerry Falwell wanna-be."

Victoria is speechless. "I thought you believed us. I thought you wanted to help."

"I just think we all ought not to get hysterical."

She paces across the room. "How do you explain everything that's happened, then? The personality changes? The deaths? How do you account for what happened in that church the other night?"

"I admit there's something freaky going on, and I want to find out what it is, too." Nate tries to keep his voice level. "But people's personalities change for a lot of reasons. And as far as what happened in that church, I have to be honest with you, Victoria. I was there, too. All I can say for sure is that the floor fell in and a girl got killed—when we shouldn't have been in there in the first place."

"You heard the scream, Nate. You heard the wind."

"If it was as windy as you say it was, who's to say that scream wasn't the wind howling through the broken old steeple?"

Victoria sits down, unable to respond. "And to think I'd been starting to trust you, Nate."

He walks over to her, takes her hands. "You *can* trust me."

She takes her hands away from him. "No. All my life, I've only been able to trust those who *believed* me."

Nate says nothing.

Victoria looks up at him. "None of the men I've ever been involved with ever believed me. That's why none of them lasted. The aunt who raised me never believed me, either, when

I told her what I saw. Do you know what that was *like,* Nate? Do you know what it was like to grow up with images of the dead in your mirror? People called me crazy. My aunt sent me to all sorts of shrinks. But the only one who helped me, the only one who made a difference, was the one who *believed* me.''

Victoria's mind goes back to those early days in Caroline's office, those days where she would cry and insist what she saw was real. She's not sure, to be honest, if Caroline ever *really* believed her. Even at the end, when Caroline referred her to Kip, Victoria's not sure her therapist ever *truly* accepted that the supernatural was real. But Caroline accepted that it was real to Victoria, and she taught her that she was stronger than it. Caroline never tried to dissuade her, to prove her wrong, as Nate was doing now. Caroline started from a place of belief in Victoria and went from there.

''Look,'' Nate says, ''I'm not ruling out anything. Enough weirdness has happened that I can't do that. But as a good cop, I have to keep all possibilities open. Even the possibility that Mark Miller may be innocent—at least innocent of the charges you're making.''

''Fine.'' Victoria stands. She wants to get out of here. Nate may be just doing his job, but she feels disrespected somehow. Patronized. And she hates that feeling. Caroline would say this was ''her stuff''—baggage she carried from years of always being on the defensive. Whatever it was, she wants out of Nate's office. She wants to get away from him and his doubts. ''I should go over and check on Kip,'' she tells him. ''Since Alexis's death he's been pretty distraught.''

''They were very close,'' Nate says.

Victoria nods. ''Her father was Kip's mentor. After the father's death, Kip assumed a kind of brotherly protection of Alexis. He's taken this very hard. I'm not sure how soon he'll be up to doing battle again.''

''And Father Roche?''

Victoria smiles sadly. ''He's not much better. Whatever it was that he saw, whatever vision appeared to him, it frightened him badly. His housekeeper reports he hasn't been out of bed in days. The bishop has sent a visiting priest to fill in for him at Sunday masses—not that many are still showing up these days. It's mostly tourists filling the pews. Most of Falls Church citizens can be found Sunday mornings at—'' She pauses, looking over at Nate. "Well, you know where."

"Wait, Victoria. Don't go just yet."

She looks at him.

"Look, I just want you to know . . . I don't think you're crazy."

She gives him a small grin. "Well, thank you very much, Officer Tuck."

"No, I don't mean to sound condescending. I really don't. Look, Victoria, I know something about what it's like to grow up confused and separate from everybody else, scared to look over your shoulder. My dad was gunned down by gang members who vowed to come after my mother and me. I never got to play with kids my own age. I grew up thinking I was trapped, that I was different, that I—"

Her grin melts into a smile. *He* is *trying, in his own way, to understand.*

"I appreciate what you're trying to do, Nate." She approaches him and places a hand on his arm. "Have you had lunch yet?"

"No, I—"

"Come on. Let me treat."

They head over to Wong's Chinese. Nate tells her that these days he avoids lots of places in town: Clem's Diner, Duvalier's, the Clam Shack, Gerry's Pizza. "They're all members of the old church," Nate says. "They've changed."

"They're under his control," Victoria says as Margaret Wong places a plate of snow peas, bamboo shoots and black mushrooms in front of her.

Nate has ordered the General Tso's Chicken. He grins at her. "And maybe they've just found religion," he argues. "Maybe Miller has done exactly what you say—tapped into their fears and anxieties and deep-rooted prejudices—but there's nothing supernatural about it."

She shakes her head. "So explain what pulled me back here. Explain Petey's message on my bathroom mirror. Explain Rusty McDaniel and Kathy McKenzie and Job Emerson's disappearance. Explain all these dreams people are having. Explain what Catherine Santos found, over and over, in Falls Church history.''

"I can't. Except what Miss Santos found could, in truth, just be the stuff that happens in any town. Why do we have to attribute the supernatural to hatred and persecution? It's very much a human trait, sorry to say.''

"Explain Monica Paul's disappearance.''

Nate looks at her. Victoria raises her eyebrows. Again she realizes that the missing reporter means something more than an unsolved case to the detective.

"You were friends with her,'' Victoria says.

"Yes.''

He says nothing more, just returns to his meal. He's having trouble using his chopsticks. He finally gives up and grabs a fork. Victoria can't help but smile.

He's a good man, she thinks. *Even with his doubts, he's a good man.* And she's surprised at the tiny little pang of jealousy she feels when Nate reveals that he and Monica Paul had been friends. *Lovers?* she thinks. *Were they lovers?*

"We went on a couple dates,'' Nate says, almost as if reading her mind. "I got her involved in all this. Asked her to write a piece about the unsolved murders. In a way I feel responsible.''

"Do you think she's . . . ?''

"Yes.'' Nate takes a sip of tea. "You told me that yourself. That I wouldn't find her. Yes, I think Monica's dead. But I can't imagine how or why.''

Victoria reaches across the table and touches his hand.

"I won't give up until I find out what happened to her. I owe her that much.''

"Nate, I'm sorry.''

He gives her a tight smile.

Just then, Sam Wong approaches the table to ask if everything is okay. They tell him yes, but he lingers. "Detective Tuck, I am sorry to intrude. . . .''

"What is it, Sam?''

"But I hear stories. I hear that they are talking about me and my wife at that church.''

Victoria watches the man speak. His hands move over and over each other.

"What do you mean, *talk about you*?'' Nate asks.

"Yes," Sam Wong tells him. "The teenagers who come in here to harass me and my customers. They were good kids once, but now they say things. They say things like my statue here is offensive. An offense to God."

He gestures. Beside the door is a large Buddha made out of jade. Sam and his family are Buddhists, and always have been, since the day they arrived here from Taiwan in 1964. Victoria can remember eating here on Christmas night with her parents. It became a tradition in their house, in those happy years before the fire destroyed their lives. After turkey with all the trimmings, served at two in the afternoon, they'd all sit around, waiting for hunger to sneak up on them again. It usually hit around seven in the evening. Then they'd pile into the station wagon and head over to Wong's, never failing to bring Sam a little gift: a slice of fruitcake or a popcorn ball or a cupcake with red-and-green frosting. Sam would accept it with great thanks, then tell them the story of Siddhartha, a lesson in multicultural religious expression Victoria's parents always welcomed for their children.

Nate's looking up at Sam with concern. "You're saying that these teenagers tell you they've heard these things at *church*?"

"Yes. That's what they say he tells them at Sunday services."

Victoria looks over at Nate.

"Thanks, Sam," Nate says. "I'll look into it."

The proprietor gives a little bow and moves away from the table.

"I think it's time I made another visit, don't you?" Victoria asks. "Whether I'm right or you are, Nate, it's time we learned exactly what he's preaching, exactly what keeps these people coming back to him." She takes a sip of tea. "After all, dreams last only so long."

Sunday, July 14, 11:05 A.M.

"And I say to you—to all of you—to each and every one of you—God lives in your hearts. Listen to Him!"

Mark Miller is indeed passionate, standing at the lectern. Behind him a part of the altar is roped off, covered with a green tarp, a jarring reminder of the latest tragedy that occurred there. The minister has promised his congregation they will repair it soon and move beyond destruction and fear to a new way of life.

"Yes, my brothers and sisters, you can hear God speak if you listen. You can hear Him tell you what to do! You can hear His promise of a new life, led by the light of truth and the light of wisdom!"

"Amen!" Clem Flagg calls out from his pew.

The old church is packed. Nearly every row is filled. Gerry Garafolo and Yvette Duvalier and Max Winn and Musty Moore and the Reich sisters and Paul Stoddard and Cliff Claussen and Alan Hitchcock and Tess Woodward and Isabella Sousa Cook and Gyp Nunez and Mary Silva and Sandy Hooker and Connie Sousa and Dave Carlson and Hickey Hix and so many more, each with their families, each shouting *Amen!* in their turn, each with their eyes set hard and steady on their minister, each glowing with the light of truth and wisdom.

"Yes, you know what God tells you. You know it in your hearts. You know that He has said He will have no strange gods before Him. You know He has written it all here, in His book."

He pats the Bible on the lectern. Behind him the symbols of other religions have been pushed to the side, to make room for the construction work. The Star of David and the Koran are still there, but no longer in the center.

"God's word is universal," the Reverend Miller says, his words echoing against the stained-glass windows. "We are all God's children. All of us!"

"Amen!" calls little Jamal Emerson, seated in the front pew.

"Amen!" calls Sandipa Khan, behind Jamal, her husband, Habib, and her daughter, Alesha, at her side.

"All of us, sinners," Mark Miller continues, looking down at them, "sinners who must examine our lives—examine our ways—and examine the ways of those around us! We must root out the false gods! We must stand up, as so many of you have, and call evil by its name! We are a good and decent people—tolerant of sinners, but not of sin!"

"Not of sin!" echoes Helen Twelvetrees.

"Man had originally Dominion over the creatures Below, but sin has inverted this Order, and brought Chaos upon the Earth. Man is dethroned, and has become a servant to those things that were made to serve him, and he puts those things in his heart, that God had put under his feet!"

"Amen, my father!" Richie Rostocki shouts. "Amen!"

Mark Miller lowers his voice. "The thoughts of good and decent men grow sad to see the multitudes of idle and profane young men in this world, and even the women have come to cavort with profanity. If such is not remedied, we and many others will suffer the wages of their sin—"

From the back of the church, a small flutter, like the sound of pages being turned.

The minister appears not to notice but continues on with his sermon.

"Of all the sorrows most heavy to be borne is that which we feel for our children, who are drawn away by evil examples into dangerous courses—the music they listen to, the celebrities they idolize, the pursuits they follow. The reins are off their necks, so to speak, and they are departing from their parents' values."

The page fluttering again. Danny Correia, up until now managing to keep his simple eyes trained upon Reverend Miller, finally succumbs to his curiosity and turns around to look into the pew behind him. It is the very last pew in the church, and there he sees a pretty, dark-haired woman. She's wearing gloves, and she's flipping through several papers that are stapled together in the corner. She trails her finger along the words that are printed upon the page, as if she's following what Reverend Miller is saying.

"What is that?" Danny whispers.

"Our children are being led toward dissoluteness," the minister continues, his voice booming through the church, "being taught by those God would find abominations to his name. There is danger to their souls and—"

"To the great grief of our founders and the dishonour of God," the woman behind Danny whispers, reading along. Her words match Reverend Miller's exactly.

"What *is* that?" Danny asks again.

The woman looks up at him. "He tells you lies," she whispers. "Don't believe him."

With that, she slips out of the pew and hurries out the door.

The disturbance has caught the attention of Reverend Miller. He stops speaking. The congregation sits in a stilled hush. Like an angry teacher, Miller moves around from his pulpit and strides forcefully down the center aisle. He stands over Danny Correia.

"Your little mind has appeared to wander," the minister accuses.

Danny just hunches down in his pew, frightened.

"Brothers and sisters," Mark Miller says, "this—this boy— is the face of sin!"

There is a murmur throughout the congregation. They've known Danny all their lives. He's such a happy, simple young man, always ready with a greeting, a happy remark about the day. How can he be the face of sin?

"Do you know why he was born with such a simple mind?" The crowd remains hushed.

"Surely some of you know. You knew his mother. You knew she never married the boy's father. Who his father is, no one even knows."

No one says a word. Yes, indeed, some of them know the story of Danny Correia's mother. Aggie Duarte knows. Barbara

Garafolo knows. Lucille and Fred Pyle know. Doris Correia was a friend, a good woman, a decent woman, who made a mistake once. Everyone makes mistakes. Everyone . . .

"Those thoughts are blasphemy!" Mark Miller bellows, as if reading the minds of everyone there. "This is the result of sin! This simpleton! This creature—one of God's pathetic rejects!"

"You lie," Danny Correia says plainly, and his voice, though even, echoes throughout the church. "You tell lies and I don't believe you!"

Mark Miller glares down at him. "God has rejected you, and so must we."

"Yes!" shouts Mary Silva. "So must we!"

It takes a few moments, but soon the whole church is filled with a chorus of rejections of the poor boy. "Reject! Reject! Reject!" they chant.

Mark Miller stands back, pleased. He lifts one arm and points with a long finger toward the door.

Danny Correia stands, tears falling down his cheeks as the crowd turns on him. "You all lie!" he shouts. "I don't believe any of you!"

He runs from the church. His mind can make no sense of any of it. He just keeps running until he reaches the point, where the sand crumbles away into the foamy surf. He falls against the old lighthouse, covering his face with his hands, and cries.

Monday, July 15, 1:30 P.M.

Chief Philip Hutchins is tired. Bone tired. He's slept maybe eight hours max in six days. Sitting at Ellen's bedside, he waits for some sign that she's ready to go, but her little fits never last too long. Mostly she just lies there with her eyes closed, shallow breathing, hanging on to life by the slenderest thread he can imagine. She's so frail, so thin, such a shadow of the woman she was. How can she still live? How has she the strength?

"I'm just going to the station for a little bit," he told her before he left. "I'll be back in a couple hours."

He kissed her warm forehead. She made no reply.

Pulling his car into the lot behind the station, the chief realizes it's been days since he'd been able to communicate with Ellen at all. She opens her eyes occasionally, looks at him—but she never speaks. He has no idea if she can hear him or understand him. But each time she opens her eyes, he promises her that he'll be there right with her until the end.

It's like one long nightmare to him. A couple of times he's picked up the newspaper as Ellen drifts in and out of consciousness. The headlines sear his soul: HAVEN FOR INTOLERANCE ON CAPE COD. HATE CRIMES MOUNT IN COMMUNITY BY THE SEA. Several editorials have attacked Falls Church for fostering a climate of fear and bigotry. The murder of a black man, cross-burnings, racist graffiti, the resignation under pressure by

Martha Sturm, which, of course, was followed by promises of a lawsuit against the town. This isn't the Falls Church Phil Hutchins knows. This isn't how he wants his last days as police chief to be remembered.

He nods to a couple of summer cops as he walks up the steps to the station. He wonders briefly where Job took off to, and why. Money? Debt? Or did it have anything to do with that "climate of fear and bigotry" described by the *Boston Globe*? But to leave Jamal behind is simply unthinkable. The chief's heart is broken by the plights of his two men Job and Rusty. They were good cops. Good men. What had happened?

And Betty. Once upon a time the chief never walked into the station without smelling Betty's wonderful coffee. Now the place is heavy, sterile.

He looks up and sees the Reverend Mark Miller sitting in Nate's office.

"Hello," Chief says, approaching the door.

Nate sits behind his desk. His face is tense.

Mark Miller's face is equally tense. "Well, Chief, am I glad to see you," he says. "Maybe you can make some sense of all this."

The chief squints his eyes at Nate. "What's going on?"

"I'm just asking Reverend Miller some questions," Nate tells him.

"Apparently I'm suspected of something," the young minister says. "But he won't tell me what it is."

The chief looks from Miller over to Nate. "Reverend, will you wait outside a minute? Let me talk with Detective Tuck."

"Please," Miller says, standing, his face indignant, and then huffing out of the room.

The chief closes Nate's door. "Okay. What's going on?"

Nate sighs. "Look, I told you I'm conducting an investigation."

"Into what?"

"Into what's been happening in this town. Into Rusty's madness. Into Job's disappearance and the disappearance of Monica Paul. Into Claudio Sousa's murder. Into the hate crimes that are popping up and the change in people's characters and the fights and the riot out in front of the station and the—"

"Enough, Nate. I know what's going on in this town. But what has Mark Miller to do with it?"

Nate lowers his voice. "You were at the opening of the church. You saw how people flocked around him, did his bidding. You saw how he led the people from the riot over to his church as if he had cast some kind of spell over them."

"Nate, get to the point. I'm very tired. I'm in no mood for riddles."

Nate sighs and closes his eyes. "Chief, I can't explain it. I simply wanted to ask him what he knows."

"About what?"

"I was asking him—well, I asked him why he encouraged his congregation in their petition against Martha Sturm."

The chief rubs his temples, sitting down in the chair in front of Nate's desk, the place so recently vacated by Mark Miller. "As repugnant as I might find that petition," he tells Nate, "it's not illegal. And as much as we might want to think that church and state don't mix, many churches take political stands. There's no law against that."

"But he's preaching intolerance. He went in there saying he'd do one thing and he's doing another."

The chief can't believe what he's hearing. "Nate, have you lost your senses like everyone else in this town? Have you ever heard of a little document called the Bill of Rights? It guarantees freedom of speech. Freedom of religion. You can disagree with what the man says, but you can't be calling him in here trying to police what he preaches—"

"I know." Nate seems exasperated. "I wasn't trying to do that."

"Then what *were* you trying to do?"

Nate pulls open the top drawer of his desk. He tosses a sheet of papers, stapled in the corner, in front of the chief. "Read this."

The chief looks down. *"Father John Fall and the Founding of Falls Church,"* he reads, skimming. "What the hell is this, Nate? I don't have time to read a student essay."

"Touch it, Chief."

The chief does. It's hot. He pulls his hand back. "What did you have that on, the radiator?"

"No, Chief. It's always hot like that."

The chief looks at him strangely.

"Look," Nate says. "What I'm going to say will sound bizarre. It does to me, too. But I have to follow up on all leads. There are some folks in town who think that maybe—maybe Mark Miller has some—some *supernatural* connection to this Father Fall."

The chief just looks at Nate. He wants to go to sleep so badly. This feels like a ridiculous dream, one of those nightly exercises in futility, where nothing makes sense and you're involved in inexplicable tasks and people around you say the most absurd things.

"Nate, I'm very tired," he says. "Do you understand? I have to return some calls and get back to the hospital."

"I know you think I'm being crazy. But these people—"

"Who are these people?"

"Well," Nate says, hesitating, "Kip Hobart, for one." He pauses. "*Doctor* Kip Hobart."

"Right. The one who hypnotizes folks into reliving their past lives as Cleopatra and Charlemagne."

"And Father Roche," Nate adds.

"I've heard he's angry that Miller's stolen much of his congregation."

Nate sighs. He looks defeated. "And Victoria Kennelly," he says, almost under his breath.

The chief laughs. "A stellar group, Nate. Rock solid, grounded individuals."

"Victoria sat in on Miller's service yesterday. Word for word, his sermon at times followed exactly words used by Father Fall over three hundred years ago."

The chief lets out a long sigh. "Most of today's fundamentalist preachers sound the same as the old fire-and-brimstone guys from Puritan days. I've listened once or twice to Pat Robertson when I'm flicking through the TV channels." He slaps the student essay. "And if this—this Michael Pilarski—was able to come upon John Fall's writings, why couldn't Mark Miller find them, too? He's preaching in his church, after all."

"Then why is it *hot?* Why do the pages burn to the touch?"

"I was never good in chemistry, Nate. Send it out to be analyzed. We have investigators who do things like that. But maybe you've forgotten that little bit of basic police procedure."

"Chief, I think it's my job to consider all the evidence and all the charges. . . ."

Philip Hutchins gets angry. He likes Nate Tuck, he trusts him—or at least he did, until now. This is the man to whom he hopes to turn over his post, the man he hopes will carry on for him. And now Nate's talking about ghosts and the supernatural.

"Goddamn it, Nate," the chief says, raising his voice and pounding his fist down on Nate's desk. "Don't we have enough troubles? We've got two murders and a disappearance in town for you to be investigating!"

"Just as we had murders and disappearances in the past! My investigation has found a pattern—"

"A pattern that you blame on the avenging ghost of Falls Church's founder. A pattern you're trying to pin on this guy because you don't like what he preaches! I'll tell you this much, Nate. It wasn't some ghost that tore out Claudio Sousa's insides!"

Nate backs down. The chief can see Nate's struggling with this, too. He doesn't fully believe all this nonsense himself.

"Look, Nate. If it ever got out that you were in that church the night the floor buckled in, we could all be in a lot of trouble, and more trouble is the last thing I need right now. I've let it go because I trusted you. You said you were investigating something and that to reveal you were in there that night might jeopardize your investigation. So I let it go. Reluctantly, but I let it go. But now that I see what you're doing—now that I see what your investigation *is* . . ."

He shakes his head, unable to continue. Nate says nothing, just sits back in his chair.

"You keep this up," Chief tells him, "and the next thing you know we'll have the *Globe* editorializing against us for going after freedom of speech. That is *not* what you do in time of crisis, Nate. You know that. Just because we're facing some problems, we don't shift into a police state. We don't clamp down on people. You just can't haul somebody in here because you don't like what he says. This isn't the old Soviet Union. This is America. This is Falls Church."

There's a light tap on the door. The chief stands and opens it. It's Mark Miller.

"Chief," he says, "I'm sorry to interrupt, but I wanted to know if Detective Tuck needed to ask me any more questions. I've already told him about my background and my beliefs, and that I never met Monica Paul and that I have no idea who killed poor Mr. Sousa or where Officer Emerson might be or for what reason Officer McDaniel might have shot that boy. So may I go now? I do have responsibilities at the church."

The chief looks over at Nate. "Anything else you have for him?"

"No," Nate says sullenly. "That'll be all."

"Okay, then," Chief says. "You can go."

"Thank you," Miller says.

Just then, Officer Dean Sousa appears. His thin face is more pinched than usual. "Chief," he says in a small voice. "There's a—a call for you—on line two."

The chief looks at him. Dean's face says all he needs to know. "It's the hospital," Chief says, his voice cracking. It's not a question. He lurches toward Nate's desk and lifts the phone to his ear.

The doctor tells him Ellen has died.

The chief hangs up the phone.

"Is Ellen—" Nate's voice catches in his throat.

"I wasn't there." The chief's voice shatters. "I told her I'd be with her until the end, but I wasn't there."

The chief slumps back down into the chair.

"Oh, Chief," Nate says, getting up and coming around to him, touching his shoulder.

"I didn't get a chance to say good-bye."

With that, Philip Hutchins begins to cry. He knows none of his men have ever seen such a sight before, but there's no way he can hold back his tears. So many years he and Ellen have traveled down this road together. For richer, for poorer, in sickness and in health. The laughter, the joy, the crushing sadness of two stillborn babies. The hopes and the dreams, the ambitions fulfilled, the realities settled for. Always together, the two of them. And now he was alone.

The chief covers his face and sobs. His body shudders with grief.

"May I?"

Through his tears he hears a voice. Mark Miller gently moves around Nate and crouches at the chief's side.

"She's with God," Miller says kindly. "May I pray with you?"

The chief looks at him. His eyes are soft, comforting. "Yes," Chief Hutchins croaks. "Pray that she's found peace."

Mark Miller takes his hand. They each close their eyes and begin to pray.

Monday, July 15, 2:11 P.M.

Sargent Crawford sees a woman. Not the one whom he sees all the time, the horribly burned woman with the flesh dripping off her body like red-and-purple wax. This is a different woman. One he thinks he knows. She's ahead of him on the road, the road to Falls Church.

In his coma Sargent Crawford stirs. A nurse looks down at him pitifully. Never any visitors. His family seems to have forgotten him. He trembles like this frequently. The machines show brain activity. The doctors tell her he's dreaming, and that's a hopeful sign.

Hopeful for what? the nurse thinks. *I wouldn't want to wake up if my family didn't care whether I lived or died.*

"They *do* care," Sargent tells her, but he knows she can't hear him. How he manages to hear *her*—he has no idea. But he does. He seems to be able to do so much these days. He's discovered he no longer needs to walk all the way up Route 6, his hospital johnny flapping open, revealing his ass. He can *fly*. He decides to do so now, so he can catch up with the woman on the road, the woman he thinks he knows.

But try as he might, he can't fly fast enough to catch her. She's in a hurry, walking very fast.

"Hey," Sargent calls. "Slow down!"

"Oh, I'm just not used to this, not at all," says the woman, finally stopping.

Sargent alights next to her. "I do know you! You're Ellen! Ellen Hutchins!"

Ellen smiles at him. "Oh, Sargent, have you *seen*?"

"Seen what?"

"The horrible woman. How badly burned she is."

"Yes. Oh, yes. I have seen her. Were you trying to get away from her?"

Ellen sighs. "I was trying to get home. To get back to Falls Church. You see, I wasn't able to say good-bye to my husband. I know Phil must be very distraught."

Sargent sighs. "It's not easy getting to Falls Church. I walk and I walk and walk and I can only get so far. I've even learned to fly, but I never seem to make it past the outskirts of town. I get to where I can see the buildings, but I barely make it to Dave's Sunoco." He lowers his voice, looking around. "There's a body in the road there, Ellen. You should tell the chief to look into it."

"Oh, he knows about it, dear. So much tragedy. But who's the burned woman?"

Sargent looks around to see if she's there. The coast is clear. "I'm not sure. I see a lot of people along this road, but usually I don't recognize them. Some of them are pretty banged up." He pauses. "Like poor Claudio Sousa. I *did* see him, but he was like you, hurrying very fast."

"Probably had someone he needed to say good-bye to," Ellen says. "Just like me."

"But I'm *telling* you, Ellen. This road only *looks* as if it leads to Falls Church. It doesn't, really. It only goes so far."

Ellen looks at him kindly. "Dear Sargent. This road will take *me* to Falls Church, but not you. Not yet, anyway, dear."

"Why is that, Ellen?"

"Because you're not dead yet, Sargent. You can only go so far along this road."

With that, she's gone. Sargent suspects she's back in Falls Church, looking for Phil. He turns. Of course the burned woman is there. One eye swings precariously by a slender tendon in front of her pulpy black face. She tells Sargent what she always tells him: "He's in the church."

"*Who* is in the church? *Please* tell me what you mean."

"If you go back, you must make sure you tell them. He's in the church. In the basement. That's where they'll find him."

"But what do you *mean?*"

She says nothing more. And, just as it always does, everything then fades to black.

Wednesday, July 17, 11:30 P.M.

Cooper Pierce can't sleep. He tosses and turns until finally Miranda tells him to go take a sleeping pill. "Tomorrow we open the shop early," she reminds him groggily. "Thursday is our early day."

Not that it much matters, Cooper tells himself as he stands and heads into the bathroom, opening the medicine chest. As if they've done any real business all season. What with all the trouble in town, their profits are down. *Way* down.

He swallows a Unisom. Usually he has no trouble falling asleep. But there's no question he's been under a lot of stress lately. Never have they had this bad a season. The whole town is hurting. Every day some new hostility breaks out in Falls Church. Half the cottages along the beach are empty, their renters having packed their bags and gone home. "Why be harassed by locals when you're on vacation?" one irate woman from upstate New York had complained to him. "You can tell your town fathers our family will *never* come back to Falls Church."

"I can't understand it," Cooper said to Miranda just the other day. "It's as if the locals are deliberately sabotaging tourism."

Miranda sniffed. "Well, we know how a lot of them feel. Mary Silva's made no bones about it. She's said for years that she thinks Falls Church should go back to being a quiet little fishing village."

"But there aren't any fish left!" Cooper has become exasperated by the town's attitude. "As bitter as she and a lot of folks might be, they know our only industry left is tourism. It's our only source of revenue. But I saw Fred Pyle over at the beach picking a fight with a couple of seasonal renters. One of them threw a punch at him and the cops had to be called. But he was *goading* them into it, Miranda. I saw it. He was calling them squatters and trash and carpetbaggers—all because they had put their blanket down on a section of the beach he claimed his family owned. But, Miranda, *there are no private sections of the beach!* Fred made that up, simply to pick a fight!"

"Calm down, Cooper. You'll get high blood pressure."

"What's *truly* bizarre—I mean just *totally* beyond comprehension—is that it's not just the old natives who are doing it. It's newcomers, too, people like you and me. Yvette Duvalier has insulted so many customers at her restaurant that the seasonal folks I know say they won't step foot inside, ever again!"

"Well, Yvette's always been a bit of a snob."

Cooper shook his hands in the air. "Our business is suffering because of the actions of these ridiculous people!"

That much Miranda agreed with. "And if we don't have a fabulous August to make up for July," she said, "I can't see how we can reopen next year."

"The strangest thing of all," Cooper said, "is that all of these people—Mary Silva, Fred Pyle, Yvette, so many others—they all belong to that church."

"I know," Miranda agreed. "I was thinking maybe we ought to start going on Sundays, Cooper. I mean, *everybody* seems to go—"

"How can you even *suggest* such a thing? It's a racist place, Miranda. They don't *want* us."

Miranda made a face at him. "Oh, pooh, Cooper. It's not racist. If it was, they wouldn't have accepted Sandipa and Habib Khan as members. I mean, they're not even Christians!" She pauses, considering something. "Though it's odd. Sandipa came into the store the other day, and she was wearing a cross around her neck."

"You *see?*"

Miranda waved her hand at him. "Oh, it could have just been a piece of jewelry with no meaning to it."

Cooper was adamant. "Mark Miller runs a racist church."

"Why do you say that? Just because of the petition against Martha Sturm? Look, Cooper, just because they might be opposed to the blatant promotion of homosexuality in our school system doesn't make them racists."

Cooper glared at her. "So you've bought the spin, too, Miranda. Since when was Martha Sturm promoting anything other than a good education?"

"Cooper, it's not like you to get so passionate about things!"

No, it wasn't. It wasn't like him at all. All his life Cooper Pierce had avoided confrontation at all costs. He believed it was the best way to get ahead. *You get more flies with honey than vinegar.* All that sort of thing. But he was frightened. Sometimes it felt to Cooper as if the whole world was closing down around him. Getting smaller, tighter, choking off his wind.

"Mark Miller took poor Jamal Emerson in when his parents disappeared," Miranda reminded him. "He wouldn't have done that if he was a racist."

"Have you seen how he treats the child? He has Jamal running errands for him, sweeping out the church, polishing his shoes! I actually saw that, Miranda! Out in front of the church. Jamal was *polishing Miller's shoes.* Miller even called him *boy.*"

His wife smirked. "Cooper, Jamal *is* a boy."

"Besides, Miller has made no public condemnation of the cross-burning on the Emersons' lawn," he told his wife. "Or about what was written on Bessie Bowe's driveway. Or the sudden rise in the use of the N word among Falls Church teenagers whenever black tourists drive through town."

Again Miranda sniffed. "Just because he issued no public condemnation——"

"Father Roche did! Our own Methodist minister, Reverend Shanker, spoke out forcefully in the press. But not a word from Reverend Miller." Cooper pauses, thinking of something else. "Nor from our esteemed town manager, either."

Miranda nodded. "I *do* think Alan should have said something. Just telling that reporter *No comment* seemed a cop-out."

"It's the attitude the whole town has taken. I can't believe we live in a community where crosses are burned on people's lawns! What *is* this—Memphis in 1955? Are we next, Miranda? And who will speak out for us?''

Except for Marcella Stein, none of Cooper's colleagues on the Board of Selectmen have seemed at all concerned with the rise of racist incidents in town. Maybe they were afraid that by speaking out they'd be seeming to confirm the guilt of Rusty McDaniel, who would be tried on a charge of hate-motivated murder.

Yet Cooper couldn't condemn his colleagues too severely. He himself had been reluctant to speak up. At the board meeting, he had let it pass. He felt some shame in that. No wonder he couldn't sleep. Marcella Stein was right to be angry with him.

"No wonder I'm awake all night," Cooper grumbles to himself now, flicking off the light in the bathroom and heading back to bed.

But in the darkness he knows it's not just his conscience that's keeping him awake. It's also that stupid, idiotic dream Roger Millay told him this afternoon. Cooper can't even remember all the details, but it's been there all day, nagging away at the back of his mind.

The sleeping pill works quickly. And Cooper's last waking thoughts are about a man in a black hat, worms and burning crosses.

"Who are you?"

It's Cooper's brother, Albert, looking at him strangely, scrunching up his nose as if he doesn't recognize him.

"It's Cooper," he tells Albert.

"You ain't Cooper."

"And you ain't Albert," Cooper says. "Albert be forty years old. You be still a kid."

He looks around. He's in his old Harlem neighborhood, up near 128th Street, before they moved up to Connecticut. God, he hasn't been back here since they left. How many years ago was that? So many he could no longer count. . . .

Everybody on the street is looking at him queerly. "What's the matter witcha?" Cooper asks, realizing he's using the inner-city dialect he studiously gave up after getting to college. "Whassup witch you all?"

He approaches his old house. And there, sitting on the front stoop like he always used to do, is his father, the best man in the entire world. The man who inspired Cooper to achieve, to work hard, to make his way in a world that wasn't always so happy to make room for him. Cooper's heart fills with a sudden gladness to see his father, but he pulls back all at once.

Daddy's dead, Cooper realizes. He died a long time ago. He never saw Cooper's success, never lived to be proud of everything Cooper achieved, never knew about everything Cooper left behind. . . .

"No, no, I didn't leave it behind, Daddy, not really!" He starts to run, as fast as he can, finally falling at his father's feet on the stairs, joyfully calling out, "I didn't leave nothin' behind, Daddy, not really. I would never be 'shamed of where I came from, never—"

But his father glares down his nose at him and asks, "Who are you, boy?"

"It's *Cooper,* Daddy! It's Cooper!"

"You ain't no son of mine," his father says.

"But, Daddy!" Cooper reaches out his hands toward his father. Suddenly he stops, horror gripping his entire body.

His hands are *white*.

His father starts to laugh. But it isn't his father anymore. It's a man in a tall black hat, and there are worms in his teeth. "Watch this, *boy*," the man says, raising a hand and snapping his bony fingers.

Suddenly Cooper's whole house—the place where he was born—is in flames. Roaring, crackling, enormous flames, red and orange and blue and yellow. It turns into the shape of a giant burning cross.

Cooper Pierce screams.

"Wake up, Miranda, wake up!"

"Oh, for God's sake, Cooper—"

She switches on the light. She turns to look at her husband. His face is contorted in terror. He's drenched in sweat.

"Dear Lord, Cooper, what is it?"

"Let me tell you my dream, Miranda. Please, please! I need to tell you my dream!"

Thursday, July 18, 1:30 P.M.

Nate watches as Ellen Hutchins's body is lowered into the plot of the town cemetery. Beyond him stretches a view of Nantucket Sound. It's a sharp, clear day, with a brilliant blue sky, a couple of gulls gliding lazily overhead. The temperature is in the mid-90s, but the humidity is low, making it a day perfect for sitting at the beach, for sipping iced tea on a front porch, for laughter and bike riding and cold frosty beer. What it is not is a day for funerals. It should *rain* during funerals. It should be dark. It should be cold.

Nate keeps his eyes on the chief. He looks like a little old man in his dark civilian suit, his shoulders heaving with sobs as he watches Ellen's coffin disappear from view.

"Ashes to ashes, dust to dust," intones Reverend Wilfred Shanker, the Methodist minister. Nate doesn't listen to the rest. He keeps his eyes glued on the chief. Beside him stands the Reverend Mark Miller, the chief's new best friend and confidant.

Nate moves his eyes across the rest of the crowd. All people he knows, people he had come to care about, people who— over the last few weeks—have become strangers to him. But today they look the same as they always have, their faces turned in grief. Betty Silva warmly embraces the chief. Marge Duarte wipes away tears as Reverend Shanker delivers his final prayers. Clem Flagg's van is loaded with homemade lasagna and custard pies for the gathering afterward at the chief's house. Gladys McDaniel, even with all her own personal torment over Rusty, had still managed to show up. She clasps the chief's hand and kisses him on the cheek.

What was I thinking? Why did I think all these people had turned into monsters?

Nate watches as the mourners file away. He watches Mark Miller help the chief into the waiting limousine and then slide in beside him. Nate might still have some lingering doubts about the message Mark Miller preaches in his Sunday sermons, but he can't deny the comfort the young minister has given to the chief over these last few days.

"Hello, Nate."

He looks up. Victoria approaches him. She looks spectacularly beautiful in the sun, her brown eyes reflecting the light, her skin glowing, her auburn hair blowing in the gentle breeze. She wears a dark dress and flat shoes. Her face is free of any makeup.

"Victoria," he says.

"It was very moving to see how much he loved her."

Nate can't speak for a moment. "They were as devoted as any two people I ever knew."

They're quiet, watching the cars follow the limousine out onto Main Street. Musty Moore, part-time gravedigger, stabs the mound of earth with his shovel and begins filling in the site. Victoria looks up at Nate. "Aren't you going back to the house?"

"In a bit. I just needed a little time by myself."

Victoria touches his hand. "I understand. I need a moment, too."

He watches her as she walks some feet away through the cemetery, stopping to look down at a pink marble marker. Even at this distance Nate can tell she's crying.

Nate gives her some time, then gently walks up behind her. He reads the names on the stone:

WILLIAM KENNELLY SYLVIA KENNELLY WENDY KENNELLY
1949—1988   1950—1988   1974—1988
TOGETHER IN HEAVEN

"They're together," Victoria says, "and I'm still here. Alone."

Nate places a hand on her shoulder.

"I think of how my sister and I used to fight." She smiles sadly. "I'd give anything for a sister right now."

Nate's not quite sure what to say. "Uh, Victoria, do you need a lift—a ride?"

She sighs. "Thanks, Nate. But I'm not going back to the guesthouse. I'm . . . going over to the woods."

"The woods?"

She nods. "Ever since I've come back to Falls Church, I've been meaning to go there. The woods where Petey disappeared. My family's house once stood on the edge of the woods. I haven't been able to bring myself to go back there, but I feel strong enough finally."

"Let me take you."

"That's not necessary, Nate."

"It's on the way to the chief's house. Let me drive you."

They head over to Nate's car. They don't speak as they head out of the cemetery, driving around the block to Beach Road. Nate's not quite sure where to stop, where the Kennelly house once stood. They pass Job's house, where a patch of charred grass remains as evidence of the burning cross. The state police have taken over that investigation, but they have no clues. *Where are you, Job? What's happened to you?*

"Here," Victoria says. "Stop here, Nate."

He pulls up to the side of the road. "I'd like to go with you."

She looks at him. "This is *not* necessary."

"I'd like to. May I?"

She sighs, then nods. They walk up through the grass between the O'Keefe and Drucker houses. There's an indentation in the ground for several feet, like a little gulley covered over with grass. "This was once our front sidewalk," Victoria points out. Gnarled beach plum trees and scrub pines grow in a haphazard fashion all around them. "Here," Victoria says, stopping. "This was our house."

An edge of concrete foundation remains jutting up from the earth, mostly covered now in beach grass and tickweed. Nate spots another piece some feet away.

"They never rebuilt on the site," Victoria tells him.

Her eyes are focused on the woods beyond the house. There's

a darkness within. Shadows seem to move within the branches. A lone crow swoops out from the trees and into the blue sky, an enormous, ragged old bird.

"You're not going . . . *in* there, are you?" Nate asks.

"That's where Petey is. I told him I'd find him."

Nate takes her hands. "Victoria, don't go in there. Spend the day with me. I have the day off. Let's head out to the beach."

She turns her eyes up to him. "Don't you need to go to the chief's?"

"Yes, I need to go. But just for a little while. He's already said he doesn't want people at the house for very long. Why don't you come with me? After that, we'll get a couple of take-out platters from the Clam Shack and head up to the lighthouse. Okay?"

She closes her eyes.

"Okay?" Nate asks again.

"Okay," she says.

At the chief's house the townsfolk embrace both Nate and Victoria. Marge Duarte tells him she misses him coming by the diner. Isabella Sousa Cook winks at Victoria and tells her that Nate's still single. "I've been trying to fix him up since he got here," the sassy town clerk jokes. "Don't let him get away."

It's as if everyone's back to their old selves. Except Nate notes how many of them still fuss over Reverend Miller, who sits there by the chief, patting his knee occasionally, telling him he'll make it through.

If she has any suspicions, Victoria doesn't mention them. She conveys her sympathies to the chief, then withdraws into a corner, looking out the window. Nate claps the chief on the shoulder, telling him not to worry about anything. "I have everything under control now," Nate assures his boss, who just looks up at him with weary old eyes.

Finally they're able to leave. They pick up a couple of baskets of fried clams and then swing by Smokey's Liquors for a bottle of white wine. They park at Nate's house, where they grab a couple of wineglasses, then walk the few yards to Lighthouse

Point. Unlike previous summers, there aren't that many visitors out here. Tourism has been falling off fast in Falls Church this year, a situation that's troubling for everyone.

They pick a spot and spread out a blanket. Nate uncorks the wine and pours a glass for Victoria. They make a toast. "To summer days," he says.

She doesn't say anything in response, just clinks her glass and takes a sip.

He offers her a basket of clams. "Only a couple," she protests. "I haven't been getting to the gym as often as I should, and one of these things is as bad as three slices of chocolate cake."

Nate's mind suddenly jumps back in time a couple of months. Monica Paul. Patting her stomach and protesting that after all that cheese pizza, she'd better forego any dessert.

"What's the matter, Nate?" Victoria asks.

"Nothing."

She sighs. "Were you in love with her?"

He turns sharply to look at her. "Who?"

"That reporter who's missing."

He smiles. "How did you know I was thinking of her?"

"Lucky guess."

Nate pulls off his shirt and stretches back on the blanket, sitting up on his elbows. "No, I wasn't in love with her. She was a terrific woman. Maybe in time I might have fallen in love with her. But I only knew her a week when she . . ." His voice trails off.

Victoria looks down at him kindly. "I didn't mean to bring up anything painful."

"It's okay."

She moves backward so that she's lying beside Nate on the blanket. "Have you ever been in love?"

"Yes," he tells her. "Once."

"Care to tell me what happened?"

"She died." Nate sighs. For the first time it doesn't rip his gut out to talk about Siobhan. In fact, he finds he *wants* to talk about her. "She was killed in a drive-by shooting in Oakland. Not a day goes by that I don't think of her."

"Oh, Nate." Victoria's eyes glow with compassion. "And you carry some guilt about her, too, just as you do Monica."

"You're a very intuitive person."

"And you're a very compassionate man."

He wants to talk. For the first time since coming to Falls Church he wants to talk about his past. So he tells her how much he loved Siobhan, how he had wanted to marry her. She reaches over and takes his hand as he speaks. It's a gesture that comforts him and encourages him to keep sharing. He tells her about Jesus Ramos, the boy he'd killed in Oakland, how he carries his death with him deep in his heart, how a day doesn't go by without his remembering.

Victoria sits up and places both her hands on Nate's face, looking down into his eyes. "You need to try to let all of it go," she says. "Such things weigh us down if we carry them too long. I know that, Nate. I lived with such pain for so much of my life. All it does is weigh us down so that we can't fly. And I believe we were *meant* to fly, Nate."

He feels like some big old sap, wanting to cry, looking up at her. She leans down, her sweet hair brushing his face, and kisses him gently on the lips.

They fall silent. They lie there, holding hands, watching the clouds move across the sky. Out here on the windswept point of the town, where the sand crumbles into the sea, they feel safe, far removed from whatever might be going on only a mile away. Here it's just them, and their memories, and their stories, and their laughter. Here they don't talk about exorcisms or the vengeful dead or the power of evil to warp the minds of men. Rather, they share their pasts, their secret truths—and then fall giddy against each other, the wine lightening their moods. They ask each other their favorite colors. Their middle names. Whether they prefer M&M's plain or with peanuts. They finish the fried clams—fat content be damned—and polish off the wine, just as the sun begins its edge of the horizon.

"Do you know there's a moment right after the sun sets when the sky glows green?" Victoria asks Nate.

"Green?"

"Yup. Keep your eye on the horizon."

The sky transforms into a magnificent palette. Nate watches as the golden orb sinks quickly. He sees lots of colors—reds and oranges and violets—but he's not sure he sees any green.

Maybe because he's become too engaged watching the colors reflect on Victoria's face instead of the sky.

"You see?" she asks, turning to him.

He kisses her. A deep kiss, and she responds. They say nothing, just gather up their things and walk back to Nate's cottage holding hands.

They make love. Afterward, Nate feels good, better than he has in weeks. How long has it been since he last made love to a woman? So long he's not even sure he knows. And the last time he made love to a woman he actually *cared* about—well, that would be Siobhan. He floats dreamily beside Victoria, his eyes closed, smelling her all over his body. What a beautiful fragrance. It intoxicates him. Then he reaches out to touch her again and realizes she's no longer there.

He sits up with a start. "Victoria?"

She's at his stove, wearing just one of his police shirts, scrambling some eggs.

"Hey," he says, coming up behind her, kissing her on the neck.

She rubs her head against his shoulder. "I didn't feel like going into town for dinner."

He murmurs a reply, kissing her ear.

"In fact, I wish I never had to go back into town again," she says, gently breaking contact and moving over to scrape the eggs onto two plates.

"You're sweet to do this," he says. "I haven't had a home-cooked meal since—" He pauses, saddened by the memory. "Well, since before Ellen got sick."

She smiles ruefully. "See what I mean? No matter how we try to stay away from it, the sadness and fear of the real world always seems to find us."

Nate pulls on a pair of boxers and a T-shirt before settling down at the table. Outside, the foghorn calls. They can hear the surf crashing on the beach just a few feet away.

"We have to face the world," he says. "But not tonight."

They eat in silence for a while. Finally Victoria looks over at him. "I like you, Nate. In fact, I could find myself liking you a great deal."

He smiles. "I'm glad. I feel the same."

"But I can't, you know."

He puts down his fork. "Why can't you?"

"Because you don't believe."

"Victoria—"

She shakes her head. "There is an evil in this town, Nate. An evil I came back to Falls Church to confront. As much as I might like to, I can't just stay here out at the point and pretend what's going on in town isn't happening."

"You aren't pretending, Victoria. You *are* confronting the evil. By coming face-to-face with the loss you experienced as a girl, by not allowing that tragedy to define you as an adult."

She makes a face. "That's not all of it, and you know it, Nate. There is a very real evil out there that threatens all of us."

He sighs. "Oh, Victoria. You saw the people at Ellen's funeral. You saw them at the chief's house. So maybe they all got a little crazy earlier this summer. Maybe a lot of them have fallen under the charm of some snake oil minister. But that *happens*, Victoria. I'm convinced now that what we're dealing with here is *not* the supernatural but some plain old human frailties. . . ."

"Human frailties don't explain away all that's happened here, now *or* in the past."

"Maybe not—so it's my job to figure out just what *has* been going on. But from now on, I'm using official police procedure, not hocus-pocus and mumbo jumbo."

She looks at him hard across the table.

He sighs. "I'm sorry. I don't mean to sound so rigid. If I find empirical evidence of the supernatural, I'll investigate. But let's be honest here, Victoria. I *did* investigate the supernatural and all I found were a bunch of theories and, let's face it, some hysterical people."

"Including myself?"

"Not you, Victoria." He stands. He's lost his appetite suddenly. "But Alexis—I mean, God rest her soul, but come *on*. I take her down to the morgue and she places her hands on Claudio's mangled head and claims he talked to her. *That's* supposed to be evidence for me? How am I supposed to write that up in a police report?"

She just closes her eyes. Nate feels terrible. It had been so wonderful between them, a feeling of connection he hasn't felt since Siobhan, and now he's gone and punctured the whole balloon. But he can't go along with her crazy theories. Not anymore.

"If all these people have been turned into monsters, explain to me how they could be out there distributing the milk of human kindness at Ellen's funeral? They're back to normal, Victoria."

She sighs. "I never said anyone was turned into monsters. We're all capable of good and evil. He doesn't drain out the good; he just ratchets up the bad."

"He? You mean Mark Miller."

"I mean Father Fall."

"Whoever. But you saw how good he's been to the chief. How the chief has responded to him. And the chief has had no dream. Look, I'm not saying Miller is a saint, but maybe people respond to him on his own merits with no supernatural pressure. I mean, lots of people get turned onto preachers or gurus or rock stars, becoming completely devoted—and it's all about their own human needs and dreams, not because of any spell or dream curse."

"All that's true, Nate." She stands now, too, clearing off their plates and carrying them to the sink. "I believe that was his modus operandi in the past. But this time he wants to succeed desperately. Each time before, people eventually woke up to his evil and said no. Sometimes it took longer than other times, but eventually Father Fall was always cast back to wherever he came from." She pauses, looking at Nate for emphasis. "This time he wants to stick around."

Nate runs a hand through his hair. He can still smell Victoria all over him. A lovely, sweet scent, like lilacs, though he doesn't think she wears any perfume. He wishes so much they were back in bed together, before all this came bubbling back to the surface. "What's your evidence of this theory, Victoria?" he asks weakly. "Tell me your evidence."

"I have no evidence you could write up in a police report, Nate." She's getting dressed, pulling on her panties and slipping her dress back on over her head. "But I've been trying to fight him in my own way, to turn opinion against intolerance and

hate. It's worked before, but this time he was ready. I started
my own petition in support of Martha Sturm, but I only managed
to get signatures from those few he hadn't yet captured through
their dreams. I wrote letters to the newspapers, denouncing the
racist attacks, but no one inside Falls Church seems to have
read them. People have canceled their subscriptions to the newspapers, claiming they're biased against Miller.''

She sits down on the bed, slipping on her shoes.

"I try to jog people's consciences at the True Value and the
pharmacy, but they just look at me as if I'm mad. I go down
to the seasonal cottages to try to make friends with people and
they look at me with suspicion and fear. Don't you see, Nate? He
knows he can only win through subterfuge, through diabolical
means. He knows the essential goodness of human nature—
so he has to subvert it, abduct it, before anything even starts.''

Nate just sighs. Their eyes hold. They say nothing more.

"It's okay, Nate," she says, standing. "I can go on alone.
Father Roche is out of commission; Kip has lost his confidence;
you no longer believe. Well, I came down here expecting to
do this alone, and so I shall.''

"Don't go, Victoria.''

"Really, I need to. It's getting late.''

"Then let me drive you.''

"No.'' Her hand is on the door. "I'd rather walk. It's a
beautiful night.''

"But we're almost a mile outside of town. And it's dark out
here—''

"No, Nate. I can handle myself.'' She smiles. "I'm stronger
than anything that haunts me.''

He knows he can't stop her. He worries that something might
happen to her—but what? Whoever killed Claudio and Monica
was still out there, but that's not what unsettles Nate at the
moment. It's something else, something intangible. Had he
really stopped believing in her supernatural theories?

"I had a good time,'' she says, a trivial way to end their
day. He moves to kiss her one more time, but she's gone, out
into the night. He watches from his screen door as she pads
through the sand along the beach, the moonlight illuminating
her only so far before she disappears into the darkness.

* * *

I'm not afraid, she tells herself.

But she's never been able to lie to herself. She knows the truth. Out here alone in the dark on this windswept stretch of beach, she *is* afraid.

Because she knows someone—*something*—is following her. She hears nothing, sees nothing, but *feels* it nonetheless.

I'm stronger, stronger than whatever it is.

For a second she considers hurrying back to Nate's. But she won't do that. No, that is *not* something she will do. She will continue to walk forward, back to town, just picking up her pace a little bit. . . .

That's when the white hand thrusts itself from the dark and grabs her wrist.

Wednesday, August 7, 10:30 P.M.

Dicky Sikorski is fed up. This has been one hell of a month at his bar. Hey, he's used to fights—but *every night*?

"Hey, Brian, knock it off, will ya?" he calls from behind the bar across the room. Brian Silva, one of the town's last fishermen, is jabbing his finger at the chest of some tourist in a Metallica T-shirt. "Leave him alone."

Brian just scowls and skulks away.

Sheesh, Dicky thinks, shaking his head, wiping down the bar. It's been bad enough in past years when loudmouthed tourists or seasonal residents came in here and started acting up. But now it's the *locals*—Dicky's year round customers, his old reliables—who are just as often picking the fights.

"What's Brian doin' now?" asks Merry Stevens, one of his waitresses. She wears a halter top with DICKY'S ON THE WHARF printed across her ample bosom. "Last night he pulverized the guy who beat him in pool."

Dicky lets out a long sigh. "All the fishermen seem to have gone a little crazy since Claudio was killed. It's like they blame everyone they see—like anybody who walks in here could be the one who did it."

Merry smirks. "Well, couldn't they be?"

"Don't you get goin' now, too, babe." Dicky looks around his joint. He loves this place. He loves the smell of spilled beer, the amber-colored lamps, the tinny music from the jukebox. Joan Jett is playing right now, singing about how she loves rock and roll. Dicky loves it, too. It was always his dream to open a bar on the Cape. This place started out as just a little beer-and-pretzel place on the wharf, but in the last few years it's taken off as Falls Church has become more and more of a tourist destination.

This summer, however, business has definitely slacked off. It started out strong, but peaked on the Fourth of July, and has been downhill ever since. Tourists tell Dicky that the locals are just too hostile. And then there've been all the deaths to consider, too. Finding a guy under the pier with his insides ripped out has definitely slowed things down a bit.

"Well, we might be slow, but that don't mean we're dead," Dicky says, speaking his thoughts as he refills a customer's Budweiser from the tap. "We've still got enough business to keep my two waitresses hopping. . . ." He pauses, looking around. "So how come I see only one?"

Merry shoots him a look. "It's not like Tandy to be late."

Dicky grunts. "When you see her, tell her to get her ass over here and talk to me."

He places the beer in front of his customer. The guy's been looking down at the bar, his eyes avoiding contact, but Dicky recognizes him anyway. It's Joe Sousa from the fish market. Cousin to Claudio. One of the good guys in town.

"Joey, Joey," Dicky says, tapping the counter underneath his downcast eyes. "I didn't even see ya. Why so glum? Why aren't you over there beating the pants off those fishermen at the pool table?"

Joe shrugs. "Just not up to it, Dicky."

"They're getting mean, those boys. I don't blame you. I'd stay away, too."

"Everybody's getting mean, Dicky."

The bartender leans in on an elbow in front of him. "I know what you mean there, Joe. This town has definitely taken on one nasty edge."

Joe Sousa looks at him plaintively. "I thought things would be different when I started going back to church, but they weren't. I thought all of us at the church would be like brothers, but we're not."

"You went back to church, Joe? Hell, I bet that made Father Roche mighty glad."

"No, no, not St. Peter's." Joe's eyes look sad, bloodshot, with deep dark circles around them. "The old church. A few weeks ago Angie and I started going over there on Sundays."

Dicky squints his eyes at him. "Yeah, you and a whole lot of other folks. Can't say I understand it, but that Miller seems to know how to draw folks in."

Joe takes a sip of his beer. "Well, it just seemed to be the right thing to do. We'd both been anxious a lot, and uneasy about things. So it just seemed right. We didn't even question it. We just went."

Dicky straightens up, folding his arms over his chest. "But it wasn't what you were looking for, huh?"

"At first it was. But now ... I don't know, Dicky." He makes a halfhearted laugh. "The good reverend wouldn't like that I was in here. He takes a dim view of alcohol."

"Well, that's a laugh! As if he'll ever get the folks of Falls Church to stop imbibing!"

Joe looks at him with the strangest expression, as if the idea weren't as far-fetched as Dicky thinks. He just shakes his head. "I never expected those of us who sit in the same pews every Sunday to turn on each other," Joe says. "But we have."

"What do you mean?"

Joe grimaces. "I'll give you an example. Years ago—I'm talking twenty, twenty-five years ago—back when my father owned our property, he and old Mary Silva, who lives next door, got into a disagreement about a right-of-way. There's a shed of ours that you can only reach by walking over a little piece of her property. Well, they fought and they fought about it, but finally my father and Mary got things settled, and for years there was no problem. But now all of a sudden, she's brought it up again and is being a royal bitch. Says she'll have me arrested if I so much as step one foot on her property."

"Mary Silva's always been a tight cunt."

Joe shrugs. "Maybe so, but we always got along. But now she's putting up a fence and bad-mouthing me to everybody." He chokes a little. "Even to Reverend Miller, who suggested maybe I ought to stay away from Sunday services for a while."

"So he's taking her side in it, then?"

Joe looks as if he might actually start crying. "You know what was *weird*, Dicky? He seemed to—I know this sounds strange—but he seemed to *enjoy* our fight. Like he was—I don't know—*getting off* on it. One day, down in the church hall—which I was helping to repair, by the way—Mary starts in on me, and I shout back at her, and Angie starts to cry, and I look over and Reverend Miller's standing there *grinning*. I mean grinning from ear to ear! He seemed to love it when we fought. He'd come up to me and tell me things Mary had been saying about me—as if he *wanted* me to get pissed off, *wanted* to stir up trouble."

"That's fucked, Joe."

"No kidding. It got me thinking, and that's why I'm feeling so out of sorts, Dicky. I feel like I got kicked out of my family. Angie's mad at me because she wants to still go over to that church, but now I feel different about it."

"How different?"

"I don't want to go anymore. The way they're always saying some ways are bad and some people are sinners. I mean, I even got caught up in all that bullshit about Martha Sturm. Hell, I always liked Martha. But I went along like everybody else and signed that damn petition anyway. I don't know why."

"Here," Dicky says, taking Joe's mug and refilling it for him. "This one's on me."

"Dicky," Merry calls. "Look what the cat just dragged in."

The bartender lifts his eyes. His second waitress, Tandy Hotchkiss, has just walked through the door. She looks a wreck, her hair is a mess and she's not wearing her halter top.

"Hey, Tandy," Dicky calls, moving over to the end of the bar. "What's up with you?"

She staggers to the counter. Dicky knows she sleeps during the day; he guesses she overslept. But that's no excuse to come in looking like she just got hit by a bus.

"Dicky, please, I gotta talk to ya," Tandy mumbles.

"So talk to me."

"Dicky," she says. "I gotta tell ya a dream I had. . . ."

Sunday, August 11, 1:30 P.M.

The heat wave started midweek, with the humidity settling over the Cape with a defiant dampness that made everyone even more miserable than they already were. Long-simmering family feuds erupted to the surface. Joe Sousa pulled up Mary Silva's rosebushes. Paul Stoddard kicked in Frank Winn's garage door. In front of the general store, Sophie Sousa, ninety-four-year-old mother of Isabella Sousa Cook, slapped eighty-seven-year-old Agatha Reich across the face—all because, back in 1933, Agatha had stolen Sophie's date to the town cotillion.

All of them congregants at the old church.

Coming out of Sunday services this afternoon, people form little groups apart from each other, casting sidelong glances at those who were once their friends and neighbors, brothers and sisters in the embrace of the church. It's hot, and people are ornery. Children scrap, pushing each other down. Parents slap the backs of the brats' heads. Marge Duarte tells Clem Flagg he stinks. Pidge Hitchcock fans herself with a prayer booklet and tells her husband she thinks Laura Millay is a whore. "Look at her," Pidge spits. "Showing that much cleavage at church."

Alan Hitchcock sees the clevage very well, and likes what he sees. Little beads of sweat dapple Laura's exposed bosom. Pidge sees her husband's lust and, in a huff, rushes over to complain to Reverend Miller. Shaking his head, the minister lectures Alan on the wages of sin, but then hurries over to Laura to squeal that Pidge Hitchcock called her a slut. Laura, enraged, strides over to Pidge and spits in her face. Alan Hitchcock then starts berating Roger Millay for his wife's behavior, and they almost end up in a fistfight right on the church steps.

Mark Miller stands back and watches it all unfold. Like a duplicitous diplomat, he moves from one group to the other, telling secrets, passing stories, spreading lies.

Meanwhile, Jamal Emerson watches *him*—thinking that the minister seems like an old housewife, one of those nasty gossips his mother used to disparage of ever becoming, leaning over their fences with each other and ripping the town to shreds. *He likes this,* Jamal thinks. *He actually* likes *getting them all hot and bothered.*

Jamal knows such thoughts are bad, that he mustn't question or judge the reverend's behavior. But watching him play the village gossip has kindled something in Jamal: it's made him think of his mother.

Where is she? Where is my father? Why did they leave me alone with this man? They'd never do that unless they had no choice. They love me. They—

"Boy," Mark Miller snaps. "Did you wash the car? I'm taking a drive this afternoon."

"Yes, sir, Reverend; yes, sir." Jamal had gotten up early to wash and wax the minister's new car, an awesome Porsche Boxster leased for him by Mr. Millay. The Reverend had given him instructions to have it done by this morning, so Jamal had set his alarm for six o'clock. It was damp and dusty sleeping down in the basement of the church, but that's where the reverend insisted Jamal stay, kicking him out of the Grand Avenue Apartments now that Kathy McKenzie had moved in with the reverend. But nobody talks about that.

Meanwhile, tourists keep leaving Falls Church in droves. The heat wave brought a fresh load of beach-happy travelers who just as quickly hightailed it out of town once the locals turned on their harassment. Fights down at Dicky's have gotten so bad that the town has had to step in, throwing a violation Dicky's way and shutting him down for a week. Dicky himself has started to brawl, with skinny little Officer Dean Sousa trying in vain to pull him and fisherman Brian Silva apart. Dicky

spent the night in jail. Both of his waitresses were also arrested
for throwing beer into customers' faces.

The locals don't have it much better. Laura Millay has had
to lay off all the agents at Seaside Realty since no one's renting
or buying in Falls Church these days. If Sargent Crawford ever
wakes up from his coma, he may find his business in bankruptcy.
Then, last week, Sam Wong's restaurant had a brick thrown
through its window. And poor Bessie Bowe is afraid to walk
down Main Street for fear of being jeered. Dave Carlson fired
Bessie's boyfriend, Noah Burt, and rumor has it Noah's decided
to leave town, whether Bessie comes with him or not.

Editorials continue to be written against the town, lamenting its
hostility to tourists and condemning the hate-motivated incidents
that seem to get worse with every passing week. Now it's overweight people who are being targeted for harassment by the town's
teenagers. Tourists showing too much cellulite are heckled until
they turn around and leave town. Marcella Stein has been called a
"fat-ass" more times than she can count, but so far she hasn't been
able to identify the culprits who sped by in a car. But as soon as she
knows who they are, she says, she plans on slapping charges on
them so fast the little brats won't know what hit them.

Clem Flagg has borne the brunt, too. It's early evening, with
the sun setting, when he sneaks over to Marcella's house and
rings her bell.

"I thought maybe you'd understand," he tells her. "It's
gotten so that I can't walk on the sidewalk without a band of
kids gathering around, calling me names."

Marcella folds her arms across her chest and raises her chin.
"Well, it's *your* church community who's doing it," she scolds.
"All of this hostility is coming from the kids of people in your
church."

Clem seems near tears. "Yes," he says, his lower lip blubbering. "I know."

Even with the sun setting, it's still stiflingly hot, and sweat
drips down Clem's chubby cheeks, staining his white shirt.

"Why?" Marcella asks. "Why this targeting of people?"

"The reverend gave a sermon a few weeks ago about the
sin of gluttony," Clem says. "The reverend said fat people
were as bad as thieves and adulterers. He said that we were
sinners and should be *shunned*."

Marcella is aghast. "There's that concept of *sin* again. I don't know why you Christians are so big on it. And to think Miller had the audacity to come here and tell me he was *nondenominational*."

"Oh, he never speaks of Christ, only God," Clem tells her. "But God is always angry in the reverend's descriptions. We're always displeasing God somehow, never pleasing him."

Marcella shakes her finger at Clem. "Look, I smelled a rat right from the start, but no one listened. So what do you want me to do? He's got the whole town government eating out of his hand."

"Please, Marcella. I'm coming to you as the last sane member of the Board of Selectmen. Even Cooper is attending the church now. He and Miranda both."

At last she invites him in. He settles himself, a little out of breath, onto her couch. She sits opposite him.

"Talk to me, Clem."

"I feel guilty even being here, talking out of school, so to speak." He shivers. "But something's happening. I don't feel safe anymore. I can't go back to the church. Not with all that talk about the sin of gluttony. Even my old friends have turned on me. Marge. Hickey. Sandy." He starts to cry. "And yet I feel so—so lost without Reverend Miller."

Marcella says nothing in response. She just stands, picks up the phone and calls Nate Tuck. Clem just sits there blubbering on her couch.

Nate comes out, listens to all Marcella has had to endure, then listens to Clem. Nate says very little, just takes it all down, and promises he'll look into it. That's all.

"That's all?" Marcella asks.

"That's all," he tells her.

Clem just starts crying again on her couch.

Nate gets into his cruiser and drives off. It breaks his heart, but what more can he do?

There's no law against hating fat people.

Meanwhile, no one has seen Victoria Kennelly in nearly three weeks.

"She checked out weeks ago," Lydia Atkins says. "I have no idea where she went. I've told you that on the phone, and I've told Nate Tuck the same. So why do you keep bothering me?" The guesthouse owner frowns. "In my opinion, good riddance to her. She was just a troublemaker."

Lydia shuts the door to the guesthouse in Kip Hobart's face.

She's one of them now, he thinks. *Lydia Atkins has had the dream.*

Just like most everyone else in town.

Kip looks up at the sky. Not even noon and already it's blazing hot. He feels as if he's living in hell. He estimates that more than half the year-round population of Falls Church is by now infected with the evil. A few of the more prominent seasonals, like Yvette and Paul Duvalier, have also fallen under Father Fall's control.

In fact, Lydia Atkins's move to the other side may have been why Victoria left the guesthouse, although Kip has no way of knowing for sure when either event happened or which preceded the other. But Victoria was smart enough not to stay if the proprietor of the place was able to spy on her and report back to her master.

Still . . . where did Victoria go?

Through all of this, Victoria had kept regular appointments with Kip. She called them grounding sessions. She talked about her fears, her hopes—and not only about defeating Father Fall. But for the last few weeks, she hasn't shown up. Kip considers the possibility that at first Victoria may have been trying to be respectful, giving him a chance to grieve Alexis's death. He admits to not being in much shape to offer effective therapy for a while. But for Victoria not to call, not to leave any message . . .

Maybe she cut out on us, Kip thinks. *Maybe she went back to Boston. Maybe Victoria called the college and withdrew her leave of absence, and soon she'll be back teaching her courses, the horrors of Falls Church far, far away. Who could blame her?*

Yet even having just known her for only a short time, Kip feels certain Victoria would never willingly turn her back and walk away.

If only I hadn't let Alexis's death shoot me down, he thinks. *As if Alexis would have wanted that. As if that's what her father had taught me.*

Still, Kip had needed some time to grieve, some time to reflect on what was happening. His faith was being tested. Kip believed in a strong, compassionate God, a Maker of all things, a collective higher power that lived within all people and in everything around them, natural and man-made. It was this belief that gave him his power. *If you believe,* Dr. Stokes had taught him, *if you truly believe, you will know what to do.*

That didn't mean you always won. That didn't mean you were always safe. It simply meant that you knew what to do. Death was a part of living, and who knew exactly what fate demanded? It was all part of a larger scheme.

So Kip is ready. He woke up one morning last week knowing he could face the Demon of Falls Church once more. This was his own destiny, his own karma. He had been *meant* to come here to Falls Church, to be here, waiting and ready, when he was needed. So he will do battle once more, even if it means he risks his own death. He knows that's how Alexis viewed things. To hide out, to pull back, would be a dishonor, not only to Alexis and her father, but to Kip himself.

But first he needs to find Victoria Kennelly.

He heads back to his place on Green Street. Even as he

unlocks the door, a pang of grief hits him. Every corner of the place holds memories of Alexis. The house still holds her scent.

How she had loved the bay windows that look out onto the street. How she'd insisted from the first moment they walked into this place that this was home. In the front windows her jade plants still thrive in the sun. Her cacti sprout little yellow flowers.

Stay with me Alexis, Kip prays. *Help me fight. Help me win.*

He hears a sound. Coming around the corner, he realizes someone is in his living room. *A woman. Could it be . . . ?*

"Hello, Kip."

"Victoria!"

There's someone behind her. A young man. Kip makes a face in puzzlement. It's Danny Correia. The janitor from Town Hall.

"During our last adventure," Victoria tells him, "you gave me a key to the place. I hope you don't mind that I used it."

Kip grasps her hands. "Of course not, Victoria. I was so worried about you."

"I've been keeping a low profile, which is why I didn't want to camp out in front and wait for you." She smiles. "Do you know Danny?"

"Yes. Hello, Danny."

"It's not the heat," Danny says, pulling something apt from his treasury of quotes, *"but the humidity."*

Kip smiles. "That's for sure. And it *is* hot as blazes up here." He switches on a fan wedged into an open window. It rumbles to life. "So bring me up to date. Where have you been?"

"Well, to start, a while back I was walking out by the lighthouse and I ran into Danny here." They all settle down onto Kip's couches. "Somehow, Danny says, he just knew he could trust me."

"I just knew I could trust her," Danny echoes.

Kip smiles. "Trust you with what?"

"Danny, why don't you explain?" Victoria suggests.

"There was a bad man in my head," Danny says. "A bad man with a black hat and worms in his mouth."

"Was it Reverend Miller?"

"I asked Danny that," Victoria says. "He said it didn't look like Reverend Miller. But once I made the connection, it was as if a light had gone off for him. He was certain they were one and the same."

"One and the same," Danny repeats.

Kip looks at the doe-eyed young man. "But, Danny, weren't you going to his church?"

"Yes." Danny looks suddenly as if he might cry. "But then he started to lie. They all lie there."

"Tell me first why you started going to that church, Danny."

"Because I had that dream and I got scared."

Kip looks from Danny to Victoria and then back again. "Why did this dream scare you so much? Because of the man in black?"

"No. What was *really* scary was what he told me. He said my mother was buring in hell. He even showed me a picture of her in the fire. She was screaming. He said it was because she was bad. She was bad in the way she made me."

Kip pulls back. "Danny, I'm so sorry." He's overwhelmed with compassion for the simple young man. Everyone knows how much Danny loved his mother. "You know that's not true, don't you, Danny?"

"Yes," he says, tears welling in his eyes. "That's why I know now that he lies. My mother is in heaven with Jesus and she is a saint wearing a diamond crown."

"That she is," Kip assures him. "But this dream—you tried to tell it to Miss Santos?"

Danny scratches his head. "I tried, but she wouldn't let me."

"Why Miss Santos, Danny? Why did you want to tell *her*?"

The young man shrugs. "I don't know. It just seemed I *had* to tell her. Her face just came into my mind."

"So he has a plan," Victoria interjects. "Fall has it all scheduled out as to *who* he takes and *when* he takes them."

"But when I couldn't tell Miss Santos," Danny says, eager to finish his story, "I had to find somebody else. So I told Franny O'Keefe, who works at the general store."

Kip nods. "And after that, you started feeling scared, right, Danny? And you thought the only way you'd feel better was to start going to Reverend Miller's church?"

Danny nods. "I liked it at first."

"What happened to change that, Danny?"

Danny's lower lip starts to quiver. "Reverend Miller said I was God's reject." He looks at Victoria, then back at Kip. "And that's not true! My mother always told me I was God's special treasure. So they *lie*. They all lie. I don't want to go there anymore."

Victoria smiles. "You see, Kip? Fall doesn't control them completely. He doesn't totally obliterate what's good in people. Their humanity remains. Free will can resurface."

"That's encouraging," Kip says. "But so far, Danny's the only one I know who's broken free."

Victoria sighs. "Yes, but remember, Alexis felt that Claudio Sousa tried. That's why he was killed. And I suspect others are struggling with it, too. Especially those who can be singled out in any way. Haven't you seen the teenagers taunting poor Clem Flagg on the street?"

"Yes," Kip says. "Those are the people we'd be most likely to win away from him."

Victoria stands, walking over to the bay window and looking out. From here, they can see the burned steeple of the old church. Scaffolding is being erected around it. The steeple is being repaired.

"I think we're entering an even more dangerous period," Victoria says softly. "Fall doesn't just want control. He wants dissension. He wants terror. It's what he thrived on when he was alive."

"So tell me what you've been doing these last few weeks."

Victoria turns around to look at him. "The dream was apparently making its rounds and finally ended up with my landlady. I recognized all the signs. She got edgy and disoriented, then started attending the old church on Sundays. Then she became surly and judgmental of me, calling me a troublemaker. So I decided a strategic retreat was in order."

"Where did you go?"

"I paid a visit to my student, Michael Pilarski, the one who wrote the paper on Father Fall. He lives in Dennisport. I asked to see all of his notes, all his photocopies of Fall's journals, telling him I was thinking about writing a book. That led to a trip up to Boston to the archives so I could read the thing in its entirety."

Kip looks at her in fascination. "And there's more than what your student wrote in his paper?"

Victoria nods. "Oh, yes. It's clear that once he founded this town, John Fall was not satisfied. He had spent all those years reviling what was wrong in society, rooting out evil and sin and calling on fiery punishments from God. So when he finally had created a paradise—where all his followers lived according to his rules and dicates—he was *bored*. If there was no more sin to be discovered, no more evil to be exposed and punished, then there was no reason left for his existence." Victoria makes a small, ironic laugh. "So Father Fall set about *creating* sin so he could continue exposing it, continue punishing it."

From her bag she removes more photocopies for Kip to read. As before, they're hot to the touch. "It's funny," she says. "Michael's hands didn't burn. Neither did the hands of the archivists who brought out Fall's journal so I could read it. It's only those of us who are *fighting* him who feel the heat." She smiles. "Appropriate, I guess."

Kip's looking over the photocopies. It's hard to read Fall's spidery, seventeenth-century handwriting, but he makes out a few phrases that Victoria has highlighted. He reads them out loud: *"In God's name we must smite thy sin of gluttony. . . . For the Goode of this Churche I have told Mistress Stanhope the foul and filthy lie told of her by Mistress Jones and watched the fury take hold of her countenance. . . . For his remark, unintended though it may have been, he shall be lashed."*

"It's obvious," Victoria says. "Fall was finding reasons to keep strife and discord alive in his congregation. He writes of how one young man had difficulty pronouncing words that began with *R*s. So Fall had the guy put in the stocks and publicly humiliated. When his lisp didn't disappear, the poor man was cast from the church and shunned by his family. Fall had managed to get rid of all the sinners, so he had to make up new *sins!*"

"No wonder they finally turned on him," Kip says.

Victoria nods. "It was when he tried to have that poor girl Constance Ward burned as a witch that he went too far. Constance was well liked and her family was powerful, and Fall finally faced a rebellion. After I read his journal, it's clear Constance aroused him sexually. Her sin was simply to be too pretty for him to abide. She brought out the sexuality he'd tried to repress ever since killing his wife for doing the same thing.''

''You think he killed his wife.''

She nods. ''I think it's a fair conclusion to draw.''

Kip agrees. ''It *does* seem apparent from what I've read. That old demon sex. You just can't keep it down.''

The doorbell rings. Kip reacts with a start, but Victoria eyes him calmly.

''It's probably just Catherine Santos,'' she tells him. ''I asked her to meet us here. I filled her in on everything we know. We need her help. She's been doing more research on Fall and his times.''

Kip lets the librarian in, who's eager to share with them what's she gleaned from town documents. She reports no record of any burial for John Fall. She's walked the graveyard of the old church and has found no stone with his name. ''I imagine the reports were correct,'' she says. ''His body was left to rot in the ruins of his burned church.''

Kip makes them all some lemonade. ''Well,'' he says, passing around the glasses, ''it looks as if Falls Church's Ghostbusters are back in business. Shall we call Nate and Father Roche?''

''Father Roche is still too distraught,'' Victoria tells him. ''I went to see him this morning. He's barely left his room in weeks. His housekeeper worries that he's had a breakdown. The bishop is apparently sending a doctor to check on him.''

''Just what *was* it that he saw that night?'' Kip wonders.

''Whatever it was, it affected him deeply.'' Victoria sighs. ''So Father Roche remains out of commission. As for Nate— Nate won't be rejoining us. He may even prove to be an obstacle in what we need to do. We're going to have to be very cautious. Father Fall knows who we are. And he knows what we know.''

''If I can make a suggestion, then,'' Kip says, ''I think our next step must be to track down the dream. We must find out who's had it last and prevent it from being spread any further. We destroy his base, so to speak.''

''And if Danny could wrest himself from Fall's influence,'' Catherine Santos says, ''I believe others can, too. We need to start appealing to their consciences.''

''Yes,'' Victoria agrees, ''although that's not going to be

easy. None of Martha Sturm's old friends jumped to her defense when I started that counterpetition. What we need to understand and address is their *fear*. That's what got them caught in his web. What Danny's dream has proven conclusively, I think, is that he controls them through fear.''

So they agree it's a plan. How to enact it, however—how to fight the fear and track down the dream—remains for now a big unknown.

Monday, August 12, 12:02 P.M.

Nate curses his car's air conditioner. It's barely putting out any air. He rolls down his window and the sticky heat from outside hits him like a physical punch. It's wicked. Summers were never like this in Oakland.

I should really take the car up to Dave's Sunoco and let Noah Burt have a look at it, Nate thinks before remembering that he heard Noah had quit—or been fired—or somehow left Dave's employ.

So they had a dispute. People have disputes all the time. Doesn't mean there's anything sinister behind it.

Except he knows about the graffiti at Bessie Bowe's. He knows about the harassment in town. He actually arrested a couple of kids yesterday, threw the book at them and faced down their irate parents who later came in to complain. "They were threatening some tourists and calling them niggers," Nate said, pounding his desk. "And they will be prosecuted for a hate crime!"

He's got to put an end to these hate-motivated incidents. He's got to show that they won't be tolerated in Falls Church.

That's why he's heading over to see Habib and Sandipa Khan. He remembers hearing there had been some harassment of them last year during the start of the war in Afghanistan. He just wants to check and see if they've had any problems. He's also just a little suspicious: he's heard they've been attending Sunday services at the old church.

He turns onto Center Street, passing St. Peter's on the corner. He thinks of poor old Father Roche in the rectory. Every time he's stopped in to see him, the old priest has been nearly incoherent, just sitting there, wringing his hands. Nate feels some responsibility for his condition. *I was there that night. I encouraged their flights of fancy, their hysterics. I let them into the church, allowed them to walk into private property and indulge all their delusions. . . .*

He immediately thinks of Victoria. How she was so convinced in the truth of her mission. How determined she was. The strange thing is that Victoria's crazy theories are the only ones that offer any consistent answers to the mysteries gripping this town. But he can't be running off chasing the supernatural any longer. With the chief out on leave, Nate's the acting chief of police, and he'd promised to follow a straight and narrow path.

But what *is* that path? Nate has spent the last couple of weeks investigating all of these hate crimes, all of these disputes and brawls that are ripping Falls Church apart and destroying its economy. Each and every one originates with a member of Reverend Miller's church—Reverend Miller, who unfailingly stops by to visit the chief every day, who sits with him and prays for Ellen's soul, who has even brought the chief with him to Sunday services.

Nate wishes he could talk with Victoria. As much as he wants to believe that her theories are crazy—that she's a hysterical, unbalanced woman—he can't help but miss her something *fierce*. That day they spent together had been awesome. The way she had listened to him when he spoke about Siobhan and the death of Jesus Ramos. The insights she offered, the gentleness of her touch. She wasn't unbalanced. He's not sure he's ever met a woman who was so strong and so grounded.

He pulls into the Khans' driveway and turns off his ignition.

But Victoria's *gone*. No one's seen her in weeks. Still, Nate can't believe she's left town for good. Not with the determination he'd seen flashing in her eyes to fight the evil she believes has infected Falls Church—the same evil she believes killed her family.

He sighs and steps out of his car, walking up and ringing

the bell. Sandipa opens the door. The first thing Nate notices is that she's wearing a small gold cross around her neck.

"Hello, Nate," she says softly.

"Sandipa. May I come in?"

She gestures for him to enter. What Nate sees startles him. A statue of the Virgin Mary stands atop the fireplace mantel. A King James Version Bible rests on the coffee table.

"I—I wanted to come by and ask you a couple things," Nates stutters as Habib comes out of the kitchen and shakes his hand. "If that's okay."

"Of course," Habib says. "Sit down, Nate."

The Khans sit in chairs opposite Nate. There's an awkward silence.

"So," Nate starts, "are you writing a new mystery?"

Habib shakes his head. "I'm not writing mysteries anymore. There's no socially redeemable value to them. I'm writing an inspirational text, about finding the truth and following the light."

Nate makes a face. "What do you mean exactly?"

"Just that." Habib looks at him as if his meaning must be obvious. "One day, I hope, you, too, Nate, will follow the light."

Nate shifts on the couch. "Do you mean . . . the preachings of Reverend Miller?"

Habib falls silent. Nate looks over at Sandipa, who fingers the cross around her neck.

"I notice you have some Christian symbols around," Nate says. "And the Bible. Don't tell me you've converted. I thought you were proud of your Muslim faith. I remember how passionately you've defended it—"

"It's not about being either a Christian or a Muslim," Habib says, and Nate picks up on the defensiveness in his voice. "It's about following the light."

"We just wanted . . . to be accepted," Sandipa says in a small voice.

"But you *are*, aren't you?" Nate asks. "Haven't you been accepted here?"

Habib has fallen into a darkness that Nate can't read. "Not always," he says bitterly. "We haven't always been accepted."

Nate gestures with his hands. "But there's no need to fall

into lockstep with the majority. Is that why you've started attending the old church? Why you have all these symbols of a religion not your own?" Nate struggles for the right words. "Look, I'm concerned about a real intolerant turn I see here in town. Our diversity is being threatened. And then I come in and see all this—"

"We just want him to accept us," Sandipa says, an edge of desperation, of fear, creeping into her voice.

Nate looks from her back to Habib. He doesn't want to ask them the question that's on his lips. It's nonsense; it has nothing to do with anything. . . .

But he can't help himself. "Tell me," Nate says. "Have either of you had any dreams that have unsettled you?"

Habib stands. "Nate, I have work to do. I was writing when you rang the bell. I really don't like being disturbed when I'm writing."

"Of course. I'm sorry." Nate stands. Habib nods quickly and strides out of the room. Sandipa shows Nate to the door. He looks down at her. The fear shining from her eyes is unmistakable. He decides to say nothing more. He doesn't know what he would say if he could find the words.

He just wishes Victoria would come back.

Friday, August 16, 4:30 P.M.

"Poor Father Roche," says Agnes Doolittle, turning the squeaking electric fan in his direction. "So hot up here, but he refuses to leave his room."

Victoria wraps her arms around herself. Her eyes rest on the shriveled old man hunched down in his rocking chair. "What did the doctor say?" she asks.

The housekeeper looks as if she might cry. "He thinks Father had some kind of shock. He suggested we send him to a sanitarium that the church runs in upstate New York."

"Oh, dear," Victoria says, feeling the tears in her eyes.

"It's up to the bishop," Agnes tells her. "I keep hoping—praying—that Father will snap out of it."

Victoria approaches him. She falls down on one knee before him and takes his hands in hers. "You helped me when I was a little girl," she whispers to him. "I want to help you now, Father."

His gray eyes move to find hers.

"We're going to defeat him," she says. "I promise you that."

He squeezes her hand.

But in the corner of the room, the Beast is laughing at both of them.

Defeat me? The Devil laughs. *That's impossible, isn't it, priest?*

"No," Father Roche says, his voice weak yet defiant. "Not impossible."

So get up and let me see you walk.

The old priest groans.

The Beast lumbers toward him. Sometimes it takes the shape of a man, other times a reptile, still others a hideous thing of indefinable shape. Father Roche refuses to look upon its face, but he can smell it, putrid flesh and bile overpowering the room.

Soon you will be mine, the thing whispers, close to his ear. *Soon you will be completely mine.*

"No, no, no, no," Father Roche cries, and Victoria caresses his creased face with her hand.

Agnes Doolittle stands behind her. "Some days he'll talk; other days he'll just sit silent like this, occasionally crying out." The housekeeper can't hold back her tears now. "I try to comfort him, but he won't even know I'm there."

"Father," Victoria says, "can you hear me?"

His eyes find her voice.

"It's Victoria. Victoria Kennelly."

"Victoria," he says.

"I'm going to defeat him, Father. You will see. We will win."

"No," he mumbles. "No. Just pray. That's all we can do."

"Then that will be your job, Father. You can still help us. You pray. I'll do the rest."

She stands. Father Roche closes his eyes. Victoria softly kisses his forehead.

Downstairs in the kitchen Agnes Doolittle cries some more. "I have been taking care of him for fifteen years, ever since my husband died. I love that man. I would do anything to make him well."

Victoria embraces her. "He's very fortunate to have you."

They're both startled by a knock at the screen door. They look up. It's Nate Tuck.

Victoria steadies herself as Agnes goes to the door, wiping her eyes. "Oh, hello, Nate. He's no better. There's no point in seeing him."

Victoria considers slipping out through the front door, but it's useless. Nate's seen her. He asks Agnes if he might come in for a moment so he can speak with Victoria.

"Is that okay, Victoria?" the housekeeper asks.

Victoria nods. Nate steps in, a little bashful. Agnes Doolittle leaves them alone to talk.

"Hello, Nate."

He reaches out awkwardly with his hands, wanting to touch, to connect, but Victoria remains impassive. "I've been so worried about you," he finally says. "Where have you been?"

Victoria's defenses are solid. "Doing what I told you I'd be doing. Trying to find a way to defeat the monster that's left Father Roche in the condition he's in."

Nate shuffles his feet. "Victoria, I've—I've missed you."

She softens. "Oh, Nate, there can never be anything between us if you don't believe."

He sighs. "I've been watching things closely. One false move on Miller's part and I'll—"

"You'll what? Throw him in jail?" She makes a little laugh. "There's no law against preaching hate, Nate. You told me that yourself."

"Well, there are laws against hate *crimes* and inciting people to violence or harassment or discrimination." His face shows determination. "I don't like the climate in town, and I don't mean just this heat wave, Victoria. I've made several arrests this week alone."

"That's very good, Nate." She tries to find a way of cutting the meeting short. She's missed him, too, but she's not going to admit that. She has no time for sentiment. "If you'll excuse me, I have an appointment."

"Don't go yet," Nate says, taking her arm gently as she tries to pass. He pulls close to her face. "I've—I've been unable to get you off my mind."

She lingers for just a second, long enough for their lips to find each other, to touch for just a second. But then she pulls away.

"No," she says, agonizing. "So long as you don't believe, Nate, there can be nothing between us. Nothing." She tries to smile, but the effort is too difficult. "Say good-bye to Mrs. Doolittle for me."

Victoria walks out, letting the screen door bang softly behind her.

Sunday, August 25, 11:59 A.M.

The heat wave holds for the rest of the month. Thunder rumbles frequently, like an angry animal in its far-off lair, waiting to pounce. Lightning rends the heavy gray skies, but still the heat and humidity never break. Such torridity inflames passions, crackles into fistfights. Teddy McDaniel beats up a tourist kid on the Town Green and a crowd cheers him on. A whole beach house of college kids is run out of town by locals throwing eggs and rocks. Seasonal workers from places such as Jamaica and Lithuania are told to pack up and leave: not only are there no more jobs for them, but "their kind" are no longer welcome in town. The traditional Labor Day sidewalk sale, an event once promoted to bring in shoppers to Falls Church's trendy boutiques, is canceled.

By the last week in August the locals have what they've claimed to always want: there are no more tourists in Falls Church. Along Lighthouse Beach the rental cottages stand vacant. The shops along Main Street are mostly closed. Duvalier's Restaurant, where last year the rich and fashionable danced, has folded into bankruptcy. An editorial in the *Cape Cod Times* declares: FALLS CHURCH HAS DONE ITSELF IN.

But few seem to care. They're too busy fighting and calling each other names. Now it's not just the tourists who are the problems. Their neighbors are trouble, too. Joe Sousa's shed is torched, and the cops suspect Mary Silva, though they have no evidence. Gerry Garafolo, fed up with Musty Moore borrowing his tools, breaks into his neighbor's house and goes on a rampage, taking back not only his things but pilfering a few other goodies as well. The pizzamaker is arrested and released on bail. Somebody robs the Clam Shack of all its summer earnings, someone who clearly knew the combination to the safe. People begin accusing everyone who ever worked there, and at a selectmen's meeting Gyp Nunez proposes—in all seriousness—that the town reestablish the old tradition of putting citizens in stock for public ridicule. Only Marcella Stein's vow to call in the American Civil Liberties Union dampens the enthusiasm for that idea.

The only time most people are silent these days are the two hours during Sunday services, while the Reverend Mark Miller delivers his stinging orations condemning society and the weakness of the flesh—sermons that have become infamous throughout the area. A profile in the Sunday *Globe* magazine called Miller "an unapologetic, old-style, fire-and-brimstone minister." Indeed, Miller's early exhortations for tolerance and open-mindedness have been completely supplanted with calls for a return to a strict morality. "I have found my calling, I suppose," Miller told the *Globe*. "But I'm only giving the people what they wanted. They were tired of faiths where the rules had become vague and open for interpretation. They want order hammered out of the chaos."

Yet *chaos* was precisely what had befallen much of the town, and the few who did not—as yet—attend those Sunday services merely scratch their heads in puzzlement. Why have so many of their friends, families and neighbors become so devoted to this man who tells them only that they are sinners and that sin is corrupting the world? As far as anyone can tell, Mark Miller preaches no specific dogma: in that area alone he remains ironically consistent with his early promise that he would remain nondenominational. Except for the images embedded in the old stained-glass windows, there is no specific Christian iconography in the church. In fact, all of the various religious symbols have been removed. There is no cross, no Koran, no Buddha, no Star of David. It is only Miller standing alone on the altar now.

He does occasionally cite from the Bible, but only those passages that declare things "sinful" or "abominations." Mostly he rails in his own words, and those few who have attended his services out of curiosity have walked away befuddled: *Is there* no *good in the world? Is there* no one *who leads a good life?*

Such questions, if posed to church members, elicit merely defensive responses, as vague as their minister's sermons. "You must find the light of truth," congregants say. "You must find the light of wisdom."

"And I say unto you," bellows Mark Miller, his fist banging down upon his lectern, "sin waits in the dark to claim you! Sin takes first your children, for it is the idle hands and open minds of youth that are the easiest to enslave. But sin would make all of you slaves to your own unclean desires. The *need* to sin lives deep within all humans, born unclean by Adam's fall. My people, I exhort you! You must remain forever vigilant, waging war against sin, destroying it wherever it exists around you, and then rooting it out from within yourselves!"

"Amen!" calls Cooper Pierce.

"Amen!" calls Hickey Hix.

The church hangs heavy with heat and humidity. A few members dare to fan themselves with prayer books. Pat Crawford had passed out from the heat earlier. Reverend Miller had called her *weak.*

"Sin comes for us!" he shouts now, his voice echoing off the rafters. "Look around you! See the faces of sin! Those who profess to be living decent lives may, in fact, be liars. Sin is *cunning.* Sin is *clever.* But it *can* be spotted. It *can* be recognized, if you only choose to *see!*"

There's a rustle from the back of the church. A few heads dare to turn around, followed by a couple of small gasps. Job and Berniece Emerson have slipped into the last pew. No one has seen them in two months.

Mark Miller notices them, too. His face tightens. Sitting at his feet, their son Jamal's eyes light up when he spots his parents.

The minister strides down from the altar. He glares at the Emersons as he stands in the center aisle.

"We have new faces here today," he tells the congregation.

People crane their necks to look at the Emersons. The couple looks tired, weak, undernourished. The expressions on their faces are pitiful, pleading.

"Why have you come here?" Miller demands.

"Because we want—we want to worship with all of you," Job says, his voice cracking, as if he hasn't spoken in a long time. "It's all we have ever wanted. We have wanted to be here for so long, with you, with our son."

"Dad," Jamal says, walking down off the altar.

"Stay where you are!" Miller demands, turning around and pointing at the boy. Jamal stops in his tracks. Miller turns his attention back to the boy's parents. "How *dare* you disrupt our service!"

"Please," Berniece says, her own voice an unrecognizable shatter of glass, "we want to worship, like all the rest here—please don't force us to stay away any longer."

"Mom," Jamal calls, defying Miller and rushing down the aisle to her.

The congregation watches as mother and son embrace, Jamal clinging tightly to Berniece.

"Let him *go*," Miller growls in a low voice. "He belongs with me now."

"*No*," Berniece says. "I will not. If we cannot stay here, we will take him with us."

Miller glares at her. Then he stretches out his arms, as if calling on the heavens. "Look, people! Look upon the faces of *sin*!"

At that moment thunder rattles the church. People draw in together in fear.

"Sinners! Sinners!" Miller shouts, pointing a long bony finger at the Emersons.

"Shun them!" calls Max Winn. "Shun them!"

"Shun! Shun! Shun!" the congregation begins chanting. The Emersons push out of the pew, hurrying toward the door.

"Begone!" Miller commands. "Sin is not welcome here! Begone, you defilers of all that is good!"

The family pushes through the door, disappearing.

But the rage is still evident on Miller's face. His young, unblemished skin is suddenly red, his ears purple, his brows knotted together like a beast in the woods.

"They are not the only sinners here," he says in a low, ominous voice, swinging his pointed finger across the congregation. "No, not the only sinners!"

"There!" shrills Yvette Duvalier. "There sit more sinners!"

She is standing, pointing at Cooper and Miranda Pierce.

"Sinners!" the congregation echoes.

Cooper tries to protest. "No, we are not . . . We are good; we are loyal—"

Miller looms down at them. "You are *liars!* Yes, I can see the sin in your black eyes!"

"No!" Miranda screams. "Please don't cast us out!"

"Shun them!" Max Winn shouts.

"Follow your sinning brother out of this place!" Miller commands Cooper.

"Shun! Shun! Shun!"

The Pierces run down the center aisle and out into the day.

"Who else?" Miller looks crazed now, an animal that's tasted blood. "Look around you, people! It is time we begin the process of rooting out sinners! Who else do you see?"

Sandipa and Habib Khan have already pulled close together with their daughter, Alesha, fearing the wrath of the crowd will single them out next. They are not mistaken. Alesha cries out when old Agatha Reich, sitting in front of them, stands with some difficulty. "Here are the sinners!" the old woman calls, pointing down at the huddled family. "They would destroy all we cherish! They are sinners!"

Miller has sprung across the aisle to leer at them. *"Yeeeeesssss!* See the sin! It is clear, isn't it? Do you see how it can be recognized? She tries to deceive us by wearing the cross, but we know she stands facing the infidel nonetheless!"

"No," Sandipa cries. "Please don't turn us out."

"Shun! Shun! Shun!"

The Khans hurry out of their pew, following the path of the Pierces, down the center aisle, taunted by the chants and jeers of their friends and neighbors, of readers of Habib's books, of Sabdipa's students, of Alesha's classmates.

"We shall remain vigilant!" Miller exults, throwing his arms into the air, his eyes wide with the fires of passion and righteousness. "We will be triumphant over sin!"

"Amen!" shouts Marge Duarte.

"Amen!" shouts Dicky Sikorski.

"Amen!" shouts the entire church. But each and every one of them is in reality terrified that they will be next.

Sunday, August 25, 7:55 P.M.

Nate sits in his car in the chief's driveway for a moment after turning off the ignition. Habib Khan's words still ring in his ears:

It's like a jihad. He's declaring a holy war against this town, and I am afraid we are all powerless to stop it.

Nate rubs his temples. He's been trying to keep Falls Church from self-destructing, but he's failed. It's happening, and happening fast. Oh, how he had hoped it was all just a bad dream. He remembers Ellen's funeral, when he convinced himself that no one had really become monstrous, that they were all still the same good people he had come to love. But it was a sham, an act.

Nate keeps rubbing his temples. He remembers Betty Silva's compassion for the chief. He remembers Marge Duarte's eyes, looking up at Nate, telling him how much she'd missed him. That wasn't a sham. It couldn't have been.

But in the last few weeks, Betty Silva had started another petition, given that the one against Martha Sturm had worked so well. This time the target was the low-income housing up on Cranberry Terrace. Betty wants to prevent any more of it from being built, to keep out, as the petition says, "any further undesirables from spoiling our town." The first signature on the list was none other than Town Manager Alan Hitchcock, a gross conflict of his position. Yet he was followed by

Selectwoman Mary Silva, Selectman Gyp Nunez, and Selectman Richard Longstaff, not to mention Hiram Silva, Pat Crawford, Yvette and Paul Duvalier and Marge Duarte—who, Nate
has learned, quit the diner because working with Clem was
"akin to condoning the sin of gluttony."

After hearing the latest outrage from Habib Khan, Nate has
decided to confront the chief. At the very least he needs to
know that Job has returned to town.

Ellen's roses still bloom along the trellis, making Nate feel
terribly sad. The chief has barely left the house in the weeks
since her funeral, except to attend services at Miller's church.
Nate wonders if he was there this morning, when the jihad
Habib described was apparently launched.

He rings the bell. It takes a few minutes, but he hears the
chief stir within the house. Finally the old man pulls the door
open. He looks up at Nate with sunken eyes.

"Chief," Nate says. "I need to speak with you. It's important."

The chief says nothing, just steps aside so Nate can enter.

The house hasn't been cleaned since before Ellen died. Dishes
are piled up in the sink; a stink of rotting food emanates from the
kitchen. The television drones monotonously in the background.
Some auto race on ESPN.

"Chief," Nate says, "we need you back at the station."

The old man doesn't look at him. "I'm stepping down, Nate.
You know that."

"Not yet. You haven't retired yet. We need you, Chief."

Chief looks at him with distant eyes. "Ellen and I were
going to go to Norway when I retired. Remember, Nate? She
always wanted to see the fjords of Norway."

Nate takes him gently by the shoulders. "Chief, this town
is coming unglued. Something bad is happening here."

The chief closes his eyes.

"Listen to me," Nate says, raising his voice. "It's the influence of Mark Miller. He's twisted the minds of some good
people—"

The chief pulls away. "Don't start that again, Nate. Reverend
Miller has been very good to me. So have his church members.
They bring me food; they sit with me—"

"To keep you from moving against them," Nate charges.

"Chief, Miller's inciting violence. He's promoting hatred. Today he threw out all his nonwhite church members, and he encouraged the rest of the flock to be on guard against them—"

"Nate, a church has a right to decide who they will allow to join. Even civil rights laws make exceptions for religious organizations—"

"Not if they're encouraging violence."

The chief scowls. "How is he encouraging violence? I've been to those services, Nate. Sure, he's a bit old style, going after sin and bringing down the heavens to punish sinners. I don't pay attention to all that. But it's not about violence."

"Well, apparently his style has changed. Were you there today?"

"No." The chief sighs. "I just couldn't get out of bed."

"Chief, I'm telling you. All of the problems that this town has experienced this summer can be traced back to him. He encourages hostility. According to Habib Khan, he was exhorting his members to go after anyone—*anyone!*—they see as sinful. With that kind of directive, the fights on the beach and at Dicky's Bar and the harassment on the streets all become easy to understand."

The chief looks at him. "Nate, if you can show me any direct link between his sermons and any of the crimes committed in this town, I'll listen to you. But I've told you before. Just because you disapprove of a religion's teachings doesn't give you the right to shut it down!"

Some of Chief's old fire has returned to his eyes. *That's a good thing,* Nate thinks. *But he's got to be made to understand.*

"I think I'm very close to making a direct link," Nate tells him.

"So Habib Khan is giving a statement? Anybody else?"

Nate sighs. "No. Cooper and Miranda Pierce were thrown out, too, but they refused to talk to me." Nate hadn't liked the fear he saw in the Pierces' eyes. Cooper had never been one to relish confrontation of any kind, but something even more ominous was keeping the Pierces from talking. There was raw, genuine terror in their eyes. The same terror that Nate had seen in Sandipa Khan's eyes, pleading with her husband not to say any more to Nate. In the end, even Habib had decided against filing a formal charge against Miller, as much as Nate tried to encourage him.

"One more thing, Chief," Nate says. "Job is back. Habib said he and Berniece were thrown out of the church because they'd come back to claim Jamal."

Chief's eyes grow fierce. "Well, Job better have some answers as to why he disappeared. What has he said?"

"I haven't been able to find him, or Berniece or Jamal," Nate says. "Come on, Chief, you know that Job would never disappear willingly. Clearly something happened between him and Miller. I've got to find out what that was."

"Nate, next you'll be back to accusing Miller of something supernatural, calling him a devil or a warlock or something like that."

Nate's quiet. "Yeah," he says. "Maybe I will."

"For crying out loud, Nate!" Chief yells. "Mark Miller may be old-fashioned, he may be puritanical, but he's been *good* to me! He helps me pray for Ellen! Ellen is trapped right now in a sinner's purgatory, and only our prayers can help send her to heaven—"

"Oh, Chief, you don't believe that. You don't believe in such—"

"Mark Miller is helping me! He is helping Ellen!"

"Mark Miller is *evil!*" Nate shouts, drawing close to the chief. "How can you let him brainwash you? Devil or warlock or just a man, he's *evil*, Chief! You've got to see that!"

Chief says nothing, just walks away from Nate, sitting back down in his chair in front of the television set.

Nate turns to leave. With his hand on the doorknob, he pauses. He's not sure if he believes what he's about to say, but he has to say it. He loves the chief. He would never forgive himself if something happens and he'd never warned him.

"Chief, just do me one favor."

The old man says nothing, just keeps his eyes glued to the race cars zooming around the track on TV.

"If anyone tries to tell you a dream," Nate croaks, "don't let them, okay? Don't let them tell you. Walk away from them, whatever. Just do that much for me, okay?"

Chief Philip Hutchins doesn't reply. Nate sighs, then lets himself out the door.

Thursday, August 29, 6:05 A.M.

The itchy scent of ragwood is in the air. It's a warm morning, promising to be another scorcher. The heat has simply refused to let up. Victoria awakes, her sheets damp and sticky. She tries to hold on to her dreams from the night before as best she can, certain they contain some clue she needs to fight Father Fall. But just as they have every morning of late, they slip from her grasp as soon as her eyelids are open and the light of day fills up the dark corners of her mind.

She sits on the edge of the bed and stretches. Kip has allowed her to stay in Alexis's old room. Victoria is surrounded by the dead woman's things. Her books. Her photographs. Her clothes. Victoria had hoped that being here, so close to Alexis's energy, might help her find inspiration in the fight against Fall. But so far, none of them have had any concrete ideas about how to track down the dream and prevent it from being passed. All they've been able to do is try, without much success, to run campaigns for tolerance and acceptance. Catherine Santos mounted a multicultural display at the library, which was poorly attended, and though she and Victoria have been handing out leaflets on Main Street condemning hate crimes, they haven't gotten much of a response.

Victoria stands, stumbling out of the room toward the bathroom. She passes by a closed door behind which Danny Correia sleeps—a precaution Kip had insisted on, fearful that Fall might try to take revenge on Danny for defying him and bolting from the congregation. They hold some concern for Catherine Santos as well; surely Fall must know that she alone has refused to accept the dream. But the feisty librarian has insisted she can manage on her own. "Tommy Keegan remembers me," she told them. "He knows he can't beat me. I'm stronger than he is."

That's the mantra Victoria keeps repeating to herself, too. *I'm stronger than whatever haunts me.* She steps into the shower, letting the spray invigorate her. She thinks about her life back in Boston. It seems such a world away now. Edna Danvers, her colleague in the history department, would be preparing for the new semester now, getting ready for the return of students next week, checking class lists, ordering texts. A pang of homesickness hits Victoria in the gut, but it doesn't last long. In truth, she's never felt more alive than she does right now. Finally, after all these years, she's confronting her past and the demons that have haunted her.

She steps out of the shower and wraps a towel around herself. With her fist she wipes off the steam on the mirror, making a squeaking sound against the glass.

She gasps.

In the mirror she sees Petey McKay standing behind her.

She spins around, certain that he'll be gone when she does. But he remains standing there, looking exactly the same as he did the last time she saw him. Dressed as a vampire, talcum powder all over his face, blond hair slicked down with an unruly cowlick in back.

"You promised you'd find me," Petey says sadly.

"Petey. Oh, Petey—"

"*Find me,* Victoria."

Just then, someone knocks on the bathroom door. "Victoria?" comes the slow voice of Danny Correia. "Are you in there? I gotta go real bad. Sorry."

Victoria's eyes are averted for just a moment. When she looks back, Petey's gone.

But she knows what she has to do today.

* * *

She walks past the deserted cottages on Lighthouse Beach. Gulls swoop overhead in circles, reminding her of vultures over a ghost town. It's the height of summer, a few days before Labor Day, and Falls Church is as quiet as it is in March.

Just what the locals have always claimed they wanted, Victoria thinks.

At Beach Road she takes a right, trudging up through the O'Keefes' backyard, within sight of the ruins of her old home. She takes a deep breath and enters the woods.

"I'll find you, Petey," she whispers. "I'll find you."

She's attempted this several times in the past but has always backed out. The last time had been with Nate. He'd suggested they spend the day together and she'd agreed, losing her heart to him in the process. It was a bad move, a distraction she didn't need. She couldn't fall in love with Nate Tuck, not if he remained on the side of the nonbelievers.

But she won't give in this time. She'd agreed to go with Nate because she'd been scared of these woods. It's as simple as that. She hasn't wanted to admit her fear to herself; she prefers the constant repetition of her mantra about being stronger than what haunts her. But scared she has been, and in these woods still lives the source of her fear. For it was here that her world first came unraveled. It was here where she first saw the evil that would destroy them all.

It's impossible to remember exactly where she and Petey were when they saw the ghost. It was autumn then; most of the leaves were off the trees. Now the woods are shadowed deep and green, with occasional, sudden bursts of sunlight through unexpected openings in the branches.

What do I hope to find? Why is finding Petey so important?

She doesn't know but trusts it is a step she must take to fight Father Fall. No matter what, she owes it to Petey. She ran away from him once. She won't do so again.

"Victoria!"

She turns with a start. It's a voice she recognizes. A man's voice.

Nate?

She looks around. She sees nothing but green. She can't see the yards or the beach anymore, though the surf remains in her ears. Twisted, gnarled trees grow all around, heavy ivy growing over them and cloaking off much of the sun.

"Victoria!"

"Who is there?" she calls.

Part of her hopes it's Nate. Her heart lifts. She's frightened, and seeing Nate would reassure her.

"Victoria!"

But no . . . It's not Nate. *Kip?*

"Victoria!"

It's impossible to tell from which direction the voice comes. She turns around and then around again, looking for whoever it is.

She hears the snap of a twig behind her.

"Victoria!"

She turns and sees who it is. She gasps.

It's her *father*.

"We've been looking for you," Bill Kennelly says. Behind him come her mother, Sylvia, and her sister, Wendy. "Where have you been?"

Victoria says nothing. She just watches them approach, getting nearer, looking exactly as they did when she was a girl. Her mouth goes dry.

"Why are you out here, Victoria?" her mother calls. "You could get lost."

"Victoria thinks she knows everything," Wendy says, her voice just as it was more than a decade ago. Taunting, scolding. "Victoria thinks she can *never* get lost."

"Oh, but she *can*," her mother says.

"Yes," agrees her father. He's no more than a couple of feet away from her now. "You're lost right now, aren't you, Victoria?"

"No," she says. "I'm not lost. And you're not my father."

Just then, the face of Bill Kennelly turns savage. Blood pours from his eyes and hideous fangs grow from his mouth. Victoria screams.

The woods are suddenly on fire.

She wakes up, sprawled out on the beach.

"Dear God," Victoria says, sitting up and holding her head.

She must have run out here. Her knees are scratched, her shorts torn. She looks behind her. The woods stand green. There is no fire.

"Petey, I'm sorry," Victoria whispers. "He won't let me find you. I'm not stronger than he is." Her voice catches in her throat. "I'm . . . *not* stronger."

She covers her face and cries into her hands.

Labor Day, September 2, 1:11 P.M.

Despite all the bad news, a few brave souls do drive into Falls Church for the holiday weekend, the traditional last blast of the summer. They're risk-takers, daredevils, the kind who would come to a place known for trouble just to say they did. For the first time since July, Dicky's is packed, and the Falls Church police force braces itself against trouble. But it's as if the locals are lying in wait, watching. Only a few minor disturbances end up on the police blotter. There are no reported cases of harassment. No fistfights. No hate crimes.

Officer Dean Sousa remains on guard, however. "Ah, yes," he assures himself while looking in the mirror at the station, adusting his hat and his holster. "No one need fear walking these streets when Dean Sousa is on duty."

Walking the boardwalk at the town beach, he keeps a trained eye on the sunbathers, fewer than usual but still enough to stir up some mischief if they chose. He's seen it happen all summer. Why should he trust in any truce now?

Just let one of them try something, Dean thinks, his hand on his gun. *I'm ready for 'em.*

A barefoot boy, nine or ten years old, runs by, chased by his even younger sister.

Dean grips his gun out of surprise. "Whoa!" he tells them. "No need to knock folks over!"

The kids slow down. Dean smiles with some satisfaction. *See? I've got things under control here.*

He doesn't even trust *kids* these days. Kids have been some of the leading troublemakers this summer, some even as young as those two here. Dean just doesn't understand the change that's come over this town. It's that Reverend Miller who's behind things, Dean's certain of that. The young minister has even managed to turn the heads of Dean's mother and sister, not to mention several of his aunts, uncles and cousins. They've all been fighting amongst themselves for weeks and holding grudges against their neighbors. Dean's never known his family to act this way. His sister, Diane, has accused his mother of all sorts of things—invading her privacy, stealing from her—and last week she moved out of the house. Now mother and daughter aren't speaking. It breaks Dean's heart. He blames Miller, but neither Mom nor Diane will hear anything against the minister when he brings it up.

Dean knows Nate's suspicious of Miller, too, but like so many folks these days, the chief won't hear anything bad said about the minister or his church—not even with all the bad press he's brought to Falls Church. Chief Hutchins has started coming back into the station a couple of days a week now and he's forbidden them from any further questioning of Miller. There's definitely tension between the chief and Nate, who's confided to Dean that he thinks Miller is dangerous. "Keep an eye on him," Nate said. "Let me know if he so much as runs a stop sign."

"You got it, Nate," Dean promised.

"Well, hello, Officer Sousa," comes a voice.

Dean is startled back to the present. There, approaching him on the boardwalk, her face disguised under large sunglasses and a sunbonnet, is Carolyn Prentiss.

"Oh, hey, h-hello," he stammers. He'd recognize her any-where, even if none of the clods on the beach know that the movies' biggest female star is just a few feet away. Dean's throat goes dry as it always does when he's around Carolyn Prentiss. She's wearing a tight-fitting blue one-piece bathing suit. She is staggeringly beautiful.

"Keeping our beaches safe, I see," Carolyn purrs.

Dean gulps. "Yes, ma'am. Can't let my guard down. Not with all that's been happening."

She pulls close to him. "Don't I know it. And me, all alone in that big house up on the cliff."

"Alone? Um, um, don't you have your . . . your manager with you?"

"He had to fly back to Hollywood on some business." She lowers her sunglasses so he can see her eyes. "I'm *all alone* up there, Dean. *All alone.*"

He thinks he might just pass out. He steadies himself. "Well, I'll do a couple drive-pasts on my patrol. Just to—just to reassure you."

"Oh, that *would* reassure me, Dean." She moves her sunglasses back up her nose. "And if you like, stop by and say hello."

He can't find an answer. She doesn't give him time, just puckers her lips quick and continues on down the boardwalk.

"Dean."

He doesn't hear the voice calling him. He's still dazed from Carolyn's words. He even sways a little as he stands there.

"Dean."

He blinks his eyes. He focuses. It's Mrs. Shanker. The wife of the Methodist minister in town. She doesn't look good.

"Mrs. Shanker," he says. "Something wrong?"

"Oh, Dean," the woman says. "Please. Can we find a place to sit down? I need to talk with you. Please."

He throws his shoulders back. "Of course, Mrs. Shanker. That's what I'm here for. To protect the citizens of Falls Church, to listen to their problems and help find their solutions."

Mildred Shanker smiles. Her soft blue eyes are bloodshot and swollen, as if she's been crying. "That's what I thought you'd say, Dean," she tells him.

He helps her sit down on a nearby bench. She's not an old woman, no more than fifty probably, but she's trembling, unsteady on her feet. Dean sits beside her.

"Now tell me, Mrs. Shanker," he says. "Tell me how I can help you."

She takes his hand. "Oh, Dean, last night I had a dream. . . ."

* * *

And so Dean Sousa, protector of Falls Church, has the dream himself that night. In it, he watches helplessly as the Falls Church office of Outer Cape Savings and Loan is robbed at gunpoint. He goes instinctively to draw his gun but finds he's forgotten to put it in his holster. Teenagers speed by him then in their cars, ignoring the speed limit—but Dean discovers he's riding a creaky old bicycle, unable to pursue them. Hopping off the bike on Main Street, he witnesses his mother and sister being mugged and assaulted by a pair of hooded felons. He tries to stop it from happening but finds he cannot move. He looks down. His feet are stuck in tar.

Chief Hutchins looms over him suddenly, firing his sorry ass—telling Dean he's no good as a cop, an embarrassment to Falls Church. The whole town gathers around to laugh at him.

And the one who laughs hardest is the man with the worms in his mouth.

Carolyn Prentiss sees the headlights swing up her driveway through the darkness. A police cruiser. *So he really does have the balls,* she thinks, a smile crossing her face.

She knows she was being naughty, flirting with the poor guy like she did earlier today. But she finds Dean cute, and the idea of maybe getting to know him a little better is appealing to her. Officer Dean Sousa is about as far away from Hollywood as she could get. And getting away from Hollywood remains her fondest wish.

When he knocks, she opens the door with nothing but a towel wrapped around herself.

"Oh, Dean," she purrs, smiling. "I was just getting ready to sit in the hot tub. Care to join me?"

He looks glassy-eyed. He steps inside and she closes the door.

"I'm so glad you came," she says softly, dropping her towel to the floor.

He barely reacts. His eyes move down the length of her naked body, then move back to her eyes.

"Miss Prentiss," he says, "may I tell you a dream I had?"

She smiles, pulling in close to him and kissing him on the lips. "Oh, please do, Dean," she says, licking his ear. "Tell me *all* about your dream."

"But what's the name of the film? What's the name?"

She must be eighty years old. *Ninety!* She catches a glimpse of herself on the video screen, the camera recording her movements live. She's done up in heavy powdered makeup and false breasts and looks like a gargoyle.

"The name of the film, Miss Prentiss," the director tells her, "is *The Space Beast Who Ate Cleveland.*"

"And I'm the star?"

"No, Miss Prentiss. Just a walk-on." The director guffaws. "Though you're certainly ugly enough to play the space beast!"

He and the whole crew—all of them dozens of years younger than she is—laugh at her. Right away, Carolyn knows what she's become: a pathetic old crone desperate to hang on to a long-forgotten stardom, appearing in low-budget pictures simply to keep her face in front of the cameras, unconcerned about quality, unable to leave Hollywood behind.

"Okay, Miss Prentiss, do your walk for the camera," the director instructs.

"No," she says. "I don't want to be here."

"Oh, yes, you do," the director says. He's dressed all in black, in a tall black hat. "You can never say good-bye to Hollywood. It will keep you ensnared forever!"

He laughs again. *Dear God,* Carolyn thinks. *In his mouth, there are—*

"Wake up, darling, wake up!"

She opens her eyes. Edmond, back from Hollywood, is shaking her awake.

"You must have been having a nightmare, darling," Edmond tells her in his pseudo-British accent. "You were screaming."

"Edmond," Carolyn says, pulling him down by his lapels. "You must listen to me. I had a dream. . . ."

Monday, September 9, 5:30 P.M.

So on it goes: Edmond Tyler runs through the woods to tell the dream to their closest neighbor, Tommy Winn, who tells his wife, Carol, who tells her best friend, Dee, who tells her husband, Greg, who tells their eldest son, Jake, who tells his sister, Emily, who tells her friend Karen, who tells postmistress Bessie Bowe. . . .

But the dream slips past those who are looking for it, those who want to stop it, to squelch it, to prevent it from spreading any further.

Falls Church is quiet. The season is over. A few of the businesses have hung out signs that say SEE YOU NEXT SPRING, with their proprietors offering a silent little prayer: *we hope.* A couple of shops have closed for good. Precious Moments is up for sale, and Cooper and Miranda Pierce remain undecided about what to do with Hornet. Some days they want to pack up and sell, move far away from Falls Church. Other days it's as if they're paralyzed, unable to move, and they just sit there in their house, not talking, not even to each other.

Duvalier's Restaurant is boarded up, its furniture and fixtures up for auction. Yvette and Paul don't even have the cash to fly south for the winter. They've become recluses in their house up on Cliff Heights, except for attending Sunday services at the old church.

Yesterday Bessie Bowe told her fiancé Noah Burt about a

terrible dream she had, and then last night he had a similar dream. So upset was Noah by the dream that even when Bessie called him this morning to break off their engagement—telling him she could never marry a *nigger*—he barely reacted, being far more focused on getting the dream passed on to Marcy Carboni, a young single mother living in his building on Cranberry Terrace. Only then did Noah feel the pain of Bessie's cruel and inexplicable rejection, and he's still sobbing into his pillow as the sun begins to sink below the horizon.

The heat of summer has finally given way to the first chill winds of winter. The leaves on the trees are starting to change, even beginning to fall in some places, a far earlier autumn than most folks can remember. Father Roche has recovered somewhat, taking walks around the block with his devoted Agnes Doolittle, but with the summer residents all having left, attendance at Sunday mass at St. Peter's has fallen to virtually zero, so the bishop has closed the church. Usually such a move prompts protest from the parish, but not a voice was raised in Falls Church.

The Methodist church, too, has closed its doors. Attendance there was down, and the Reverend Wilfred Shanker and his wife surprised many in town by becoming members of the old church. "We just feel Reverend Miller better represents the values we hold," Reverend Shanker told a reporter. "Finally here is a church unafraid to stand up for the light of truth and wisdom."

Throughout the area Mark Miller has become a name well known, and indeed there have been some newcomers to Falls Church, attracted by his fire and brimstone, to replace those who have left the town. The young minister has been profiled by most of the local media, on television and in print, and while most have condemned him as an extremist and a bigot, others have found in his words a calling. When Miller was shown on Channel 7 blaming current social ills on a whole array of people—gays, feminists, pagans, abortionists—he drew several dozen new followers to his church the following Sunday. What many didn't know until they got there was that Miller included many of *them* in his list of criminals. He added "Pope Catholics and Jews and Oriental heathens" to the list—though only a couple of the newcomers walked out in protest. Most simply nodded their heads and agreed.

This morning, just as Bessie Bowe was breaking up with Noah Burt, Marcella Stein awoke to find a giant swastika drawn on the side of her house. On her driveway was spray-painted in red: GET OUT OF TOWN, YOU FAT JEW BITCH.

And so the troubles in Falls Church began heating up again.

"We've got to say something," Miranda Pierce says quietly to her husband as they watch the news, images of Marcella Stein's house filling their television screen.

"And risk those dreams coming back? Do you *want* that, Miranda? Do you?"

"No," she says in a little voice.

Cooper watches the television, and listens as Marcella accuses the members of the old church. He listens to Reverend Miller's calm denial of any responsibility or knowledge of the vandalism, his expression one of sympathy for Marcella's pain.

"You *bastard*," Cooper says in a small voice.

And yet he dare not speak up. Dare not say how he feels. Because at night the man in black still haunts both him and his wife, tearing apart their rest. *He will destroy us if we say anything,* Cooper tells himself. *He will destroy us.*

As if he hasn't already done so. Cooper feels the outrage burn in his chest. *He's taken away our business, our sense of security, our home. He's taken away our pride.*

What more could he do if we spoke up?

He thinks of Claudio Sousa's guts ripped out of his body.

Perhaps much more, Cooper thinks fearfully. *Perhaps much, much more.*

That's why they remain silent. That's why they live like prisoners in their own home.

"Nate, may we speak with you?"

Nate looks up from his desk. He and one of the temporary cops are the only officers at the station, Chief Hutchins and Dean Sousa having gone off duty. In front of him now stand five Falls Church citizens, an odd assortment by the looks of them: Fire Chief Chipper Robin and his wife, Nancy, who's the town's licensing agent; with them are Smokey Buttons from the liquor store, Dandy Davis, former secretary to Martha Sturm, and Sam Drucker from the general store.

"Chipper," Nate says, "what's up?"

"We wanted to wait to speak with you until the chief and Dean were gone," Chipper says. "We feel you're the only one we can talk to about this."

"Close the door," Nate says. Smokey obliges. "So tell me what's up. What brings all of you together?"

"We're the only ones left," Sam says, his deformed hand trembling at his side. "And we're afraid we're going to be next, Nate."

Nate looks at him oddly, then at the faces of everyone there. Each of them is gripped by fear. "What do you mean," he asks, "the only ones left?"

"Admit it, Nate," Chipper says. "You've seen what's happening in town, what took place all summer. We tried to ignore it, pretend it wasn't happening. But with the season over, with the summer residents leaving, we couldn't avoid it anymore."

His wife chimes in her own thoughts. "Almost everybody has changed," she says. "Nate, you *have* to know what we're talking about."

"Yes," he acknowledges. "I—I know."

"They've all become members of that church," Dandy Davis says, shivering. "Everybody espousing such hateful, extremist views. What happened this morning at Marcella Stein's prompted us to come here. We're *frightened*, Nate."

"Believe me, I want to catch the culprits as much as you," Nate says.

"The culprit is over there at the church!" Smokey insists. "We've watched it creep through town, Nate. One by one, people have been falling under his spell. And pretty soon we've been able to recognize who's who—who's still thinking in his right mind and who's gone over to the other side."

"Nate, something *is* happening," Chipper says. "I see it with the guys who are volunteer firefighters. I see it on their faces down at the station. Brian Silva, Manny Duarte, Fred Pyle, Dave Carlson—all my guys. They're all caught in it. I can't explain it. But it's true, Nate. You *must* know it to be true. It got Rusty. It got Job. And now, Dean too.''

"Dean?'' Nate looks at him sharply. "Dean's fine. I just talked to him today.''

"I saw him go into the church yesterday,'' Nancy says. "Walking in with all the town officials. Alan Hitchcock, Mary Silva, Richard Longstaff—''

"Dean was probably just—just checking things out.'' Nate wishes he could be sure of that. Dean hasn't spoken much to him in a few days. He's been quiet. But people get quiet once in a while. Nate tries to smile. "I told Dean to keep an eye on Miller. I'm sure that's why he was there.''

"Whether he's one of them yet or not,'' Sam Drucker says, "he soon will be. We *all* will, unless we can stop it.''

Nate looks at him. "Don't you think that sounds a little paranoid?''

"You weren't here before, Nate,'' Sam tells him. "You weren't here when it happened before.''

Nate feels all of Victoria's theories rush back at him. *It's happened before.*

"So tell me what I need to know,'' he says.

"There was a woman,'' Sam says. "Her name was Grace West. My wife, Alice, and I joined a Bible study group with her.''

Nate nods. "I know about her. She led the charge to get those boys with AIDS kicked out of school.''

"She was evil,'' Chipper says. "I know, Nate. I was part of that group, too. It was as if Grace West's group became the most important thing in the whole world to me. I was just a high-school kid, but I was *dedicated* to her. I believed *everything* she said. The world was being threatened by sin, and sin was being manifested by those kids with AIDS. It was a *pervert's* disease, she said, and it was *perverting* our town.''

"I remember her, too,'' Smokey Buttons says. "But I had forgotten all about her—about all that nastiness, until Sam reminded me.''

It's exactly as Catherine Santos described it. As Nate listens to them, a cold chill creeps up his spine.

"We would meet at Grace's house,'' Sam says, "Alice and me and Florence Reich and Frank and Anne Winn and Chipper.

And others, too. One by one, people joined. Oh, it wasn't as bad as it is now. It never got so big. But just like now—you could tell then who was with you and who wasn't . . . just by looking in their eyes!''

Chipper places both hands down on Nate's desk and looks him forcefully in the eyes. ''I know this sounds far-out, Nate,'' he says. ''I can't explain it. None of us can. But it's happening. Something is happening and we don't like it.''

''I want to take our kids out of school,'' Nancy says. ''Move up Cape with my parents.''

''But there's one good sign,'' Sam Drucker tells him, shaking one of his remaining fingers. ''That girl, Victoria Kennelly, who came back to town this summer.''

''Why is Victoria a good sign?'' Nate asks.

''She was the one who made Grace go away before. Maybe she can do the same this time. That *must* be why she came back.''

Outside, a sudden wind kicks up, rattling the shutters of the station. It's a reminder that winter is fast on its approach, and Nate feels its chill, even here, inside his office, surrounded by these people, among the last free souls of Falls Church.

He thanks them for their caution, promises them he will take their words to heart. He considers telling them to beware the bearers of dreams, but he decides against it. Things are hysterical enough as they are.

Sunday, September 15, 11:55 A.M.

Nate lifts his eyes to the newly repaired steeple. Once more, the spire proudly points to the sky. Church bells ring, calling the faithful. Nate watches as they arrive. Pidge and Alan Hitchcock. Betty and Hiram Silva. Gladys McDaniel and the kids. Isabella Sousa Cook. Bessie Bowe, without Noah Burt. The Carlsons. The Garafolos. Roger and Laura Millay.

No one talking. No one commenting on the weather, on the baseball standings, on the new fall television season. They all simply pause to look up at the steeple and listen to the bells. Then they climb the steps into the church and take their seats in the pews.

"Good morning, Nate."

He turns. It's Dean Sousa. And with him, Nate realizes, his eyes growing large, is movie star Carolyn Prentiss and her manager.

"Dean," Nate says, though he can't keep his eyes off Carolyn. She's not trying to disguise herself or anything, though no one except Nate seems to notice her. "Good morning."

Dean's aware of Nate's surprise. "This is Carolyn Prentiss," he says.

"Yes," Nate says, beaming. "I know."

He shakes hands with the movie star. She gives him a small smile.

"And Edmond Tyler," Dean says. The manager moves forward and pumps Nate's hand heartily.

"I'll meet you in the church in a moment," Dean tells the pair. "I'd like to talk with Nate first."

They nod and head up the steps. Nate watches Carolyn until she's inside the church.

"I didn't know you and Carolyn were buddies," Nate says.

"She's very nice," Dean tells him.

Nate grins. "I'll say. Very nice indeed."

There's a moment of awkwardness. Ever since Chipper Robin accused Dean of being part of Miller's flock, Nate has watched the officer closely. He hasn't wanted to believe it, but he has to admit Dean has changed. Not in the way others in town have—he hasn't been angry or belligerent or hostile—but his spirit seems dampened, his boyish enthusiasm sapped, his nervous energy drained.

"Dean," Nate asks, "are you here to keep an eye on Reverend Miller?"

"Of course," he says. "And you?"

Nate nods. "I figured I ought to hear one of his sermons. Especially after the vandalism at Marcella Stein's. See if there's anything I can pinpoint that might be called incitement."

"Of course," Dean says. "Well, I've got to join Carolyn."

"Sure," Nate says.

He watches Dean walk into the church. *He's here because of Carolyn. That's got to be the reason. Dean has had a crush on her ever since she moved to town. So I'll bet that's why he keeps coming. Carolyn Prentiss is here. He gets to sit next to her. That's the only reason Dean keeps coming to these Sunday services.*

The bells ring above him. Nate hurries up the steps and slips quietly into a back pew.

"And I say to you, my people," Reverend Mark Miller intones from his pulpit, "I know you are hurting. I know you are suffering. For many of you, your livelihoods have taken a thrashing this year. The economy of Falls Church is in a tailspin."

"Help us, Reverend!" calls Yvette Duvalier.

"Help you?" His eyes bear down upon his flock. "But can you not see that only *you* help yourselves? Your suffering is the result of *sin*. Ever since Eve betrayed Adam and they were cast out of paradise, pain and suffering have been the result of sin. Look around you, my people. God is angry. God is angry that you have given your town to foreigners and summer people who come here with no understanding, no appreciation of our values, who take our town further into a secular world where God's Word does not matter."

"We have cast them out!" calls Mary Silva.

"Amen!" cheers Dicky Sikorski.

"But I say to you," Miller says, grabbing his lectern with both hands and leaning his face in toward the congregation, "where *else* does sin live? So long as sin lives in this world, none of us are safe. Suffering will endure. We must cleanse our town of sin and vice. Look around you, my people. *Where does sin live?*"

"Well," Mark Miller says, "I must say I was pleased to look out and see you sitting among our congregation, Detective Tuck."

They're walking downstairs into the nearly renovated church hall. A few church members are still lingering about after the service. Kathy McKenzie eyes Nate suspiciously. Reverend Miller gestures for Nate to follow him into his private office.

The little room is austere, with only a desk, two chairs and a few books on a shelf. On the desk rests a Bible. "Please," Miller says, "have a seat."

"Thanks," Nate says.

Miller sits behind the desk. "So tell me. How can I help you?"

"I just wanted to ask you a few questions."

The minister smiles indulgently. "More questions? Well, at least you didn't call me down to your office. What do you suspect me of this time?"

"I just wanted to talk with you after hearing your sermon." Nate tries to see into the man's eyes. See *something*. Anything. Guilt? Fear? Anger? He can detect nothing. "I couldn't help but feel there was some contradiction. I recall when you first came to town, you talked about community building You wanted this place to be a community center more than a church. A place where kids could come. A place where people could maybe have craft fairs, sell their products—''

"I think we have enough outlets for capitalism in this town, don't you, Detective?" Miller folds his hands placidly on top of his desk. "And hasn't that pursuit of the almighty dollar been at the heart of so much of this town's suffering?"

"Maybe so," Nate says. "It's just that I noticed the contradiction between what you said then and what you offer now."

"I simply responded to what the members wanted. That's what any good minister does. It quickly became obvious to me that there was a yearning—a *need*—in this town for a return to simple, old-fashioned, religious values. I simply went where the congregation wanted to go."

Nate laughs sarcastically. "They wanted to find scapegoats? They wanted to be lectured about sin?"

Reverend Miller smiles. "This is their truth, their wisdom. This is what is in their hearts."

Nate leans in toward him. "I don't believe this is what's in their hearts. I *know* these people. They would never have turned on Job and Berniece, or Cooper and Miranda, or Clem Flagg, or anyone else. They weren't looking for scapegoats. But you've given them some."

"All I have done is warn them against sin. If you're suggesting that it was my idea to excommunicate those people you've just named, you're wrong. It was entirely the decision of the congregation. It broke my heart to see them go. But I need to follow my members' wishes."

Nate stands. "Reverend Miller, there is a fine line between what you preach and the actions taken by your members."

The young minister lifts his eyebrows as he looks up at Nate. "Are you charging me with any crime?"

"Not yet." Nate looks back at him hard. "But I'm watching you. Remember that. No matter what kinds of protections you think you have, I'm watching you. Don't for a minute ever think I'm not."

Miller says nothing. He just holds Nate's glare.

"And another thing," Nate says, turning around as he's about to leave. "You say that you're only giving these people what's already in their hearts. I agree, Reverend. The capacity to hate is in all of us, and it's easy to scratch the surface and find it. But more important, we also all have the capacity to love. And that's going to prove stronger. I promise you that.''

He knocks back the last of the scotch, watching the waves from his door. The fog is rolling in. The lighthouse sweeps its beacon around and around, illuminating Nate's small cottage for the briefest of seconds before it disappears again. The low, mournful call of the foghorn unnerves him. *It's a warning,* Nate thinks. *A warning for me.*

Ever since he confronted Reverend Miller this afternoon, he's been uneasy. He'd watched as Dean drove away with Carolyn Prentiss. He'd watched all the church members disperse, go back to their lives. *He has their souls,* Nate couldn't help thinking. *He has them all.*

All of the crazy theories Victoria and Kip Hobart believe have come crashing back at him. Theories that, in the haze of the alcohol, don't seem so crazy anymore. Nate remembers the papers that burned to the touch. And yes, there *had* been a scream that night in the church. Father Roche *had* seen something. And that was no loose beam that collapsed the floor, killing Alexis. It was the vengeful ghost of Father John Fall.

Nate closes his eyes. He sees the horribly mangled body of Claudio Sousa. He hears Monica Paul's voice calling for him. He pictures Rusty McDaniel laughing as he shoots that innocent kid.

Dear God, help me. I'm going crazy myself.

From here, he can barely make out the beach. He thinks he sees someone there, a figure moving up from the water toward him. He strains through the fog to make out who it is.

It's a man.

In a tall black hat.

Nate feels cold. His scrotum tightens and his cheeks flush. *It's the dream. Dear God, am I having the dream?*

The man continues to walk closer.

"Nathaniel Tuck."

Nate wants to pull away from the door, slam it closed, cover his ears. But he can't move. He watches the man walk closer, calling his name.

"Nathaniel Tuck."

Victoria said he had worms in his teeth. Nate feels frightened, like a little boy. *Please don't let him open his mouth. Please don't let me see!*

The man in black is now just on the other side of Nate's screen door. He can see the bloodshot eyes, the sallow skin. He can smell the stink of him: rancid breath and decaying flesh. His clothes are old. On the hat a silver buckle rusts in the sea air.

"Nathaniel Tuck," the thing speaks, and yes indeed, worms burrow through his gums. "I am watching you. Don't for a minute ever think I'm not."

Hideous bony hands claw into the screen door. Nate jumps back.

"I'm saving you for last, Detective. The last to go sees all the rest go before him." The thing grins. Worms fall from his mouth. "Especially your beloved Victoria. She will be mine soon. *Mine.*"

The phone rings behind him. Nate screams. He breaks free from whatever force held him there, stumbling backward. When he looks back, the man in black is gone.

I'm drunk. I'm drunk and hallucinating.

Nate picks up the phone. No one's there. He slams it back down, dizzy now. He sits down, trying to steady himself.

He looks back at the door. The fog rolls in ever thicker, seeping into his cottage. The foghorn wails.

Nate stands again, approaching the door. *A hallucination,* he thinks, even as he fingers the tears on the screen. *It's an old screen. These tears were here before. Weren't they?*

He looks out into the fog.

The last to go sees all the rest go before him.

Saturday, October 5, 10:10 A.M.

The town is abuzz with the news: Rusty McDaniel is back. His father, old Will McDaniel, dropped dead from a brain hemorrhage last Wednesday, so the state police have allowed Rusty to return for the funeral, shackled at his hands and his feet. His trial starts in a few weeks. Folks call out words of support to him as Rusty staggers across the cemetery grounds, a state cop and Dean Sousa each at his side.

But the final prayers over Will McDaniel's coffin are not intoned by the family's longtime priest, Father James Roche. Rather, it's the Reverend Mark Miller who holds up his hands as if imploring the sky.

"We give our departed brother, William McDaniel, a proper, holy burial. It is the last act of mercy we can show him. It is the final request any of us can wish for, to be buried with blessings and the hope for a new life."

Rusty stands with his wife and children, looking down into the hole where his father's body will rot, where the worms will eat through his face. His eyes, his mouth.

"Our Father in heaven, we trust the soul of our brother William to You. Whether You take him in your eternal embrace or cast him into the miseries of hell, we cannot know. But we bury him in accordance with Your wishes and send his soul to You."

"Not exactly the most comforting words for the family,"

Catherine Santos whispers to Kip Hobart, standing a few yards back from the mourners.

"But it's what he preaches," Kip replies. "It's the same Puritan theology that Father Fall would have believed. That salvation is predestined, that no amount of good deeds in this life can guarantee entrance into heaven."

Catherine shivers, looking around. "Practically the whole town's here, Kip. He's got them all. He's succeeded far more completely than Tommy Keegan or Grace West ever did."

Kip sighs. "I've talked with everyone I could, tried to gather whatever clues are out there. But still I have no idea where the dream is, who's in line to pass it on next."

"He's gone after everyone who lives here. Out-of-towners who work here haven't been affected. They just carry back to their homes strange tales of what's happened in Falls Church."

Kip nods. "It's clear he wants control of his old congregation back."

"I've been making a list," Catherine says. "Names of those few in town I believe still to be *uninfected,* as you say. Free of his mind control. I think we need to gather them together, warn them against listening to any dreams, the way Nate warned me."

Kip sighs. "We risk having him take us on directly if we do that, but we may have no other choice."

Catherine begins counting on her fingers. "There's Chipper Robin, the fire chief," she itemizes. "Sam Drucker. Smokey Buttons. Georgia McHale. June McKay. Stan Piatrowski. Dandy Davis. . . ."

"I suppose if we can get them to listen to us and not call us crazy," Kip says, "we *could* ask that they call us and let us know if anyone tries to pass the dream on to them. We could then go to that person and . . ." Kip's voice falls off.

Catherine looks at him closely. "Yes, Kip. Continue. We go to them and . . . ?"

He smiles ruefully. "And *what*? Kidnap them? Tie them up and gag them? You see, that's our dilemma, Catherine. If Nate was still on board, maybe *he* could detain them, keep them quiet, as he tried to do with Danny Correia. But even still, we know what torture people would go through until they could pass the dream on, get it out of their system. How could we subject someone to that?"

"Shh," Catherine tells him. "The crowd's coming this way."

The services are complete. The mourners walk solemnly from the grave site. Kip and Catherine nod to Gyp Nunez, Brian Silva, Cliff Claussen, Sandy Hooker. They look up. Mark Miller is heading directly toward them.

"Hello, Miss Santos," the minister says. "Dr. Hobart."

"Hello," Catherine replies.

"How nice of you to come," Miller says. "I wasn't aware you were friends of Mr. McDaniel."

Catherine stands defiant. She recognizes his eyes. They're Tommy Keegan's eyes. "I've known Will and Rusty for years. I've been in town a long time." She pauses. "And I have a very good memory."

He smiles, turning to Kip. "Dr. Hobart, I must say that I'm *fascinated* by the work you do. *Past-life regressions*, I think I read in your advertisements."

Kip smiles tightly. "I would think you'd consider it a pagan practice."

"I suppose it is. Or Buddhist, possibly."

Kip studies him, wishing Alexis were here to look into his eyes. *This man killed Alexis,* Kip thinks. *He killed her because he was scared of her. Scared of what she might see and reveal about him.*

"I'd be glad to do a regression for you, Reverend," Kip tells him. "Free of charge. See who you were in past lives. I'd be *very* curious about that."

Mark Miller smiles. "You seem like a very curious man."

"I am."

"Well, remember what curiosity did to the cat." Reverend Miller smiles. "Good afternoon to both of you."

He moves off, joining Kathy McKenzie, who'd been waiting for him.

Up ahead, Dean Sousa and the state cop are walking with Rusty McDaniel back to the waiting police car. "You're going to let me go back to my father's house, aren't you?" Rusty asks. "Please."

The state cop rolls his eyes. "Listen, buddy, I'm tired of

hanging out with all these hicks. We've got to get you back to jail."

Rusty's eyes flash. "Come on, man. I'm a cop, just like you. You know I didn't kill that kid without reason. You know I'm being framed. Come *on*, man. Let me go back to my father's house with the rest of the mourners. It's only decent."

"Look, Todd," Dean Sousa says, looking over at the state cop. "Go on and have a cup of coffee at the diner. I'll take Rusty over to the house, let him make an appearance for ten minutes and then meet you back at the station."

The state cop seems unsure.

"Come *on*, man," Rusty pleads. "It's my *dad*. I *lived* for that man. He was my whole *life*. Give me just ten minutes. *Please*."

"All right," the state cop says. "I'll meet you back at the station."

A small, almost imperceptible look passes between Rusty and Dean.

Dean pulls over on Beach Road, a lonely stretch where the only witnesses are boarded-up summer cottages. He gets out of the car, opens the back door and motions for Rusty to get out. He quickly unlocks the shackles around his wrists and ankles.

"How are you going to explain this, Dean?"

Dean Sousa looks up at him. "It won't be hard. Everyone expects me to fuck up, don't they? They call me Barney Fife. Dopey Dean. Why *wouldn't* they believe you were able to overpower me and run off?"

He hands Rusty the keys.

"Now hit me," Dean says. "Hit me hard."

"You sure?"

Dean smiles. "What's a broken nose for the glory of God?"

Rusty smiles back. He folds up his fingers into a fist and punches Dean straight in his thin, fragile little face. He hears the crack of a bone or two. Blood spurts from Dean's mouth. He thinks even a tooth goes flying.

Dean crumples onto the ground. Rusty heads off into the woods.

Sunday, October 6, 11:45 A.M.

Rusty McDaniel's escape makes the front page of all the newspapers from the Cape up to Boston. A dragnet of state police officers descends onto Falls Church, fanning out across the beaches, through the woods, into the marshlands. Roadblocks are set up in Chatham and Orleans and at the two bridges over the canal.

"*You* let him go," Nate charges, facing Dean.

The door to Nate's office is closed while the chief deals with the state police. Dean's face is swollen purple and bandaged.

"If I let him go," Dean says calmly, "why would my face be like this?"

"Because you had it planned that way." Nate eyes him coldly. "Dean, do you remember when you complained to me that your mother and sister had changed? *You've* changed, too, Dean. And it's partly my fault. Because I didn't warn you against the dream."

Dean holds his gaze. "You're talking crazy, Nate. Chief won't like to hear you talking such craziness."

"You going to tell him?" Nate dares.

"Maybe."

"Why hasn't *Chief* had the dream yet, Dean? What's holding the reverend back? Why's he had to win the chief over through old-fashioned brainwashing and not the hocus-pocus he works through his nightmares?"

Dean holds his gaze. "Are you finished questioning me, Nate? If so, I need to go take another painkiller."

Nate says nothing. He just glares at Dean. The younger man stands and walks out of Nate's office, closing the door behind him.

Nate punches a series of numbers on his phone. Victoria's cell phone. As usual, he gets her voice mail. "Victoria," he says. "I've left three messages. Please call me back." He hangs up the phone and sits back in his chair.

Does he believe? She'll ask him that. She'll ask him if he believes, and if he tells her yes, she'll talk with him. If he tells her no, she won't.

Nate lets out a long sigh. How can he *not* believe? Dean can deny it all he wants, but it's just too perfect. Rusty is now on the loose, just what they all wanted, and Dean was the one who let him get away.

But the chief will never buy Nate's theory. Dean is the shakiest gun in the East, the biggest klutz on the force. It's very believable he might've screwed up. Rusty was bigger, stronger, more clever. What a perfect setup.

Now who's sounding paranoid? Nate shakes his head. *Now I'm the one thinking conspiracy theories.*

He wishes desperately that Victoria would return his call.

Tuesday, October 8, 2:30 P.M.

"How are you feeling today, Father?" Victoria asks.

Father Roche smiles. He's raking leaves on the grounds of the rectory. The giant oak, resplendent in bright yellow, has begun to drop its leaves. The day is bright, the air crackling with the crispness of autumn.

"Today is a good day," the old priest tells her. "I'm thinking the bishop will let me stay on here at the rectory, even if the church remains closed."

Inside her purse Victoria's cell phone rings. She takes it out, checks the caller identification and replaces it in her purse.

Father Roche looks at her sadly. "Is that Nate again?"

She nods. "I can't talk with him."

"Maybe he's come around."

Victoria shakes her head. "I left him a message finally, telling him I only wanted to hear from him that he was rejoining our fight. He left a message back saying he wasn't sure what he believed anymore." She pauses. "That's just not good enough for me."

Father Roche raises his eyebrows. "But there's movement, my dear. He's coming around."

She sighs. "Maybe. But he'll have to come around on his own then. I can't set myself up, Father. For too long I've surrounded myself with people who didn't believe in me. When

Nate can honestly say he believes—and believes fully—*then* I'll speak with him."

He smiles at her. "You are one very stubborn lady."

She looks at him kindly. "And what about you? Are you ready to rejoin our fight?"

He looks off at the sky, unable to answer.

"We *need* you, Father. Your word is respected in town. We've started going around to people, those we think haven't been told the dream yet. Those whose minds are still free. We've talked to a few, and a few responded well, but most thought we were crazy."

"And you want me to convince them you're not?"

"They'd listen to you, over Kip or me."

He shakes his head. "I'm not so sure. I've heard the talk myself. *Poor old Father Roche, gone mad with despair over the loss of his church.* I'm not sure I would be very convincing."

"Still, you could try."

His old face creases in a sympathetic frown. "I'm sorry to always sound so hopeless. But I'm not sure what any of us can really do. I've been praying—praying so hard—but the evil keeps happening. It manifests all over town. Did you hear Marcella Stein resigned from the Board of Selectmen due to their lack of support for her? So has Cooper Pierce."

"Yes," Victoria says. "Which is exactly what Fall wanted. And he's not going to stop there, Father. Gays, Jews, Muslims, African Americans—these were just the first, obvious targets. The way Miller turned his congregation against overweight folks shows where he's going next. He needs constant turmoil and unrest. All sorts of petty hostilities and animosities are brewing."

"Yes, I am very fearful," Father Roche says. "Not only about where all this is leading, but fearful for myself. I'm not proud of that fact, Victoria. But it was *hell* what I went through in those weeks after the exorcism. Plain and simple. *Hell.* I saw the face of the Beast every time I closed my eyes. I can't go back there. I can't let that happen again. I'm not strong enough to survive it twice."

She takes his hand. "I understand, Father. But you're stronger than you think. We all are."

"I'm sorry, Victoria. But I think all I can offer you are my prayers. That's all I can do. I'm an old man. A priest, but still a man. Please try to understand. All I can do is pray."

She smiles tightly. "Well, that's something." She sighs, clearly disappointed. If she'd hoped he might go about the town with them, or request permission for a traditional Catholic exorcism, she knows none of it will happen now. "Keep saying your prayers, then, Father. We're going to need all of them that we can get."

Wednesday, October 9, 4:30 A.M.

The woman has enormous blue eyes. A beautiful woman. Blond hair. And she's consoling Ellen Hutchins, the police chief's wife.

"Why is Ellen crying?" asks Sargent Crawford, approaching them on the road that leads into Falls Church.

"Because she can't get through," the woman with the stunning eyes tells him. "She can't get into town."

"Neither can I," Sargent says. "I keep trying, but I can't get home."

Ellen looks up at him through her tears. "But that's because you aren't dead yet, Sargent. I am. I should be able to get there and say good-bye to Phil."

The blond woman wipes away Ellen's tears. "Come with me. I'll take you there."

"But why will you be successful getting into town if she's failed?" Sargent asks.

"I know what's down there," the blond woman tells him. "I've looked it in the eyes. I know what to expect."

"All these riddles," Sargent laments. "Am I never going to understand what's going on?"

The woman's eyes seem to see right into Sargent's soul. She takes a step toward him. She reaches out with her hand and touches Sargent's face. "Yes, my good man," she tells him. "You *will* know. But tell me what you know now."

He thinks and then speaks. "Well, I know that I was consumed by my own petty problems and was really much too greedy. I was awfully judgmental of people, so quick to make assumptions. I was working myself too hard, and for what? So I could have a heart attack. So I could stand here and watch my whole community fall apart."

"Good," the woman says. "You've learned a little about how to see."

"Please," Ellen calls from behind her. "Take me into Falls Church so I can say good-bye to Phil. He needs me. Until I can say good-bye to him, he'll remain with that man, that horrible creature. Please take me now!"

"What horrible creature?" Sargent asks. "What does she mean?"

"Go back," the woman tells Sargent. "I must take Ellen now. Go back and wait. You will know more answers soon."

He watches them move down the road toward town.

Sargent turns around. Of course, the burned woman is there. "In the church," she reminds him. "He's in the basement of the church."

"Yes, yes," he says wearily. "I know."

"What's that you say, Sargent?"

Now who's talking to him?

"Who's there?" he asks.

"It's Dr. Kendall, Sargent. Can you hear me?"

"Dr. Kendall?"

Sargent opens his eyes. He's in bed. In a hospital. His doctor is looking down at him.

"What am I doing here?" Sargent asks, trying to sit up.

"Good Lord," Dr. Kendall exclaims as nurses restrain the patient. "It's a miracle!"

Friday, October 18, 4:30 P.M.

"It's as if he vanished into thin air," the chief laments over the phone to state police headquarters. "Your men, my men—nobody's turned up so much as a footprint on Rusty."

He sighs, nodding his head, listening to them rant. "Yes, yes. Of course. We'll talk later." He hangs up the phone.

Rusty's been on the lam for nearly three weeks now and everybody's feeling the heat. *What a way to end my career,* the chief thinks, pulling open his desk drawer and chugging down a shot of Maalox. *The town's falling apart; it's become a haven for right-wing extremists, and now I've lost a prisoner charged with first-degree murder. One of my own men, to boot.*

His heartburn scalds its way up his esophagus and into his ear canals.

"Oh, man alive," he groans. "Ellen, I need you so much."

Once upon a time Chief Phil Hutchins loved this job. Once, he imagined retiring happily with Ellen. Once, he had felt confident turning over his office to Nate Tuck. He believed he'd be leaving the force in the hands of good men. Rusty would have been Nate's number two officer. Job would've been promoted, too, and even Dean showed potential. What Dean lacked in skill he made up in determination and commitment, and it had been the chief's firm opinion that Dean would turn out all right.

That was sure a laugh now.

In the weeks after Ellen's death, the chief had taken some solace from the community of church members who flocked around him, but in the wake of Rusty going missing, even that made little difference now. The chief had personally led many of the searches through the woods and up by the lighthouse. He checked out every locked shop, every boarded-up cottage. Who knew this town better than he did?

No one.

Which is why Chief Hutchins is frightened.

This is not the same town I've lived in all these years. These are not the same people.

Even more than Rusty's disappearance, it was the vandalism at Marcella Stein's house that got to Chief Hutchins. The lack of outrage among the people who still brought him chicken soup and tuna casseroles every night began to gall him. Yes, if he pressed, he could get Betty Silva or Tess Woodward to say it was a shame. But they didn't *feel* it. No—they were *glad* of it, the chief has come to realize. They were *glad* when Marcella resigned. They were glad that Clem Flagg has turned the diner over to Marge Duarte. They were glad that Mary Silva and Joe Sousa were at each other's throats. They were glad that Rusty had escaped—not because they thought him innocent, but because it meant more problems for the town.

It's as if they want this town to simply collapse under its own dead weight, the chief thinks. *As if they're rooting for things to get worse.*

It's a crazy thought, but it's occupied the chief's mind for the last few days. He can't shake it. He feels as if he's merely acting out a charade, presiding over the destruction of the place he and Ellen once called home.

He covers his face with his hands. He can feel the tears coming on again.

I mustn't, he thinks. *I'm Chief of Police and this town is in crisis. I can't sit here at my desk and bawl like a little baby.*

"Why can't you, Phil?"

He looks up.

He makes a little sound.

Ellen stands in front of his desk.

"Oh, darling. I've been trying to get to you, to say good-bye, but he hasn't let me."

"Dear God," he gasps. "Ellen?"

"Phil, you've got to fight him. I've done my best, keeping him out of your head at night, but I can only do so much. I've got to move on. We've got to say good-bye and you've got to let me go."

I must truly be going crazy, the chief thinks. He stands anyway, trying to embrace Ellen, but when he looks at her directly, she fades from his sight.

"Oh, my dear, I know how hard it is," she tells him. "You have a right to cry. I've been crying ever since I left you. You know I didn't want to, Phil, and you know I wish I could stay at your side. But I can't. I've got to move on, Phil."

"Ellen, is that really you?"

He feels her hand on his face. For a moment he can feel her warmth. For the slenderest of seconds they embrace and he feels her lips upon his.

"You've got to fight him, Phil," Ellen whispers in his ear. "Trust in your heart. You know the truth. He *lies*, Phil. You've got to fight."

"Who lies, Ellen? Mark Miller? Is it he who lies?"

He can't feel her anymore. He rushes about the room, calling her name.

"Here, Phil," she says. "Here I am."

Their eyes hold once more.

"I came to say good-bye, Phil. I need to move on. As do you. But know that I will never be too far away, and that I will love you forever. We will be together again, Phil. But for now, I must go."

"Ellen, don't—"

"Good-bye, my darling husband."

The room is silent. The chief staggers back a bit, then sits down in a chair.

"She came to say good-bye," he tells himself.

He's all right. Suddenly the heartburn that so oppressed him is gone, dissipated—and even more, the grief that had gripped him for all these weeks no longer paralyzes his thoughts. It no longer clouds his judgment, warps his perspective.

He knows Ellen is right.

"I've got to fight him," Chief Hutchins says aloud. "He *lies*. And he's got to be stopped."

Tuesday, October 22, 3:15 P.M.

Where could Rusty be? Nate's looked everywhere in town. Unlike the state cops, who are convinced that he fled Falls Church—even the Cape and possibly the state—Nate knows Rusty is still here.

He's part of this thing that's happening. He's part of Miller's flock. He's not going to run away from that. He's here, somewhere.

The whereabouts of the Emersons are just as perplexing. Job and Berniece took Jamal from Miller and ran off. Jamal hasn't been seen in school since. Might *they* have left, found safety someplace far away? It's more likely, perhaps, given that they had defied Miller and Rusty hadn't. But Nate doubts it. He believes the Emersons are still here, too. *If Job was completely free of Miller's control, he would have contacted me. He would have let me know where he is.* Nate feels certain that the Emersons are in the same kind of anguished netherworld the Pierces and the Khans and Clem Flagg have found themselves in. Excommunicated by their master, they nonetheless long for reconciliation. They might have doubts, but they still fear his power enough to keep quiet. Nate remembers the frightened looks on the Pierces' faces, the terror in Sandipa Khan's eyes as her husband braved a few words about the coming jihad. No, these people were not free.

Nate parks his car in front of the general store. He can't

bear to stop in the diner anymore for his coffee. Not since they barred Clem from entering. He'll get his java from Sam Drucker instead, and check in with him about anything he's seen.

"Thanks, Sam," Nate says, taking the Styrofoam cup from Sam's three-fingered hand and securing a plastic lid on top. "How are things going?"

"I can't complain," the store owner says.

Nate looks at him. "I've been keeping my eye on Miller. I promise you. The moment he so much as jaywalks—"

"The Reverend Miller is a godly man," Sam says, interrupting him. "He would never transgress the law."

Nate starts to smile, thinking Sam is being sarcastic. But in seconds he realizes the complete sincerity of his words, and Nate's blood runs cold.

"Sam," he says. "Sam, please. You haven't—"

"I haven't what?"

"Dear God. You're part of his church now, aren't you?"

"I went last Sunday for the first time." Sam gives him a creepy little smile. "You should try it, Nate. All my cares, all my concerns, were suddenly gone. I found the light of truth and wisdom."

Nate feels sick to his stomach. "It's my fault," he murmurs to himself. "Just like it was with Dean. I'm sorry, Sam. I didn't warn you about the dream. I was too caught up with my own bullshit, not wanting to believe—"

"I don't know what you're talking about, Nate," Sam says simply.

"Chipper," Nate says all at once. "I've got to get to Chipper."

He races over to the fire station in his cruiser, the red light flashing. But he finds Chipper Robin the same as he found Sam Drucker.

"No, Nate," Chipper says. "I don't recall coming into your office with any concerns. Things are *fine.*" He offers him the same grin Drucker had given. "I hope Nancy and I will soon see you at Sunday services."

"It's my fault," Nate keeps repeating, over and over, as he speeds up Main Street toward Smokey's Liquors. He rushes in, nearly upsetting a display of Absolut vodka.

"Whoa, doggies," old Smokey says, his big mustache quivering under his nose. "What's got you in such a state, Tucky?"

Nate comes face-to-face with Smokey. "Have you been going to the old church? Have you started attending services there?"

"I should say *not*." Smokey is in a huff. "Not with the way them church members have been coming by here, telling me alcohol is the Devil's tool, threatening to shut me down."

"Thank God I got to you in time," Nate says, letting out a long breath. "At least you."

"What are you talking about, Tucky?"

"You haven't had any dreams, have you, Smokey? Bad dreams."

Smokey scratches his head through his unkempt hair. "I never remember my dreams."

"You'd have remembered this one." Nate looks at him in all seriousness. "Listen carefully. I should have told you this before. It's how that church passes on its control. Through *dreams*, Smokey. Don't let anyone tell you their dreams."

Smokey listens. He doesn't call Nate crazy. "Yeah," he says. "Miss Santos and that Dr. Hobart were by to tell me the same thing."

"Thank God for them," Nate says.

"I've seen enough in Falls Church these past several months that I believe," Smokey says. "If anybody tries to tell me anything, I'll punch him in the face."

"No more violence, Smokey," Nate pleads. "Just make sure you tell anyone who hasn't been snared yet. We've got to put an end to this."

Thankfully, Dandy Davis hasn't been infected yet, either. Nate pauses to think who else might still need to be told.

The chief.

But he can't find Chief. He's not at the station, and not at his house, either.

Tuesday, October 22, 9:35 P.M.

*I've still got it. I'm not so old, ready to be put out to pasture.
I can still be a detective if need be.*

Chief Hutchins is downstairs in the hall of the old church.
The flock has fixed it up quite nicely, he thinks. *You'd never
know this place was crawling with rats only a few months ago.*

He swings his flashlight beam in a semicircle. It's a large
room with several tables and chairs. *They meet here for Bible
studies and to plot taking over the world,* Hutchins thinks, a
small smile playing on his lips. *Oh, yes, I'm on to you now. I
know what you're doing.*

He also knows it was very dangerous to come here tonight.
That's why he didn't tell anyone, not even Nate. He waited
until he was sure that Miller was at his apartment down near
the wharf. He'd watched as Miller got out of his Porsche and
walked with Kathy McKenzie and her son into the building.
Then the chief snuck back up to the church and let himself in.

He remembers with repugnance the kind of talk that went
on in this hall. He'd been to enough of their gatherings to know
how they talked, the hateful gossip, the accusations, the bigotry.
How they scapegoated the world for the problems of their
lives—problems that, before Mark Miller had arrived, had
seemed simple, manageable, ordinary.

This afternoon Chief Hutchins had paid a visit to Catherine
Santos. Thankfully, she had no tolerance for Miller and his

church, and the chief found her a willing ally. She produced old blueprints of the church before its most recent renovation. It was just as Chief suspected: Beneath this hall there was another level. And below that, the original foundation of the very first church on this site. The church of Father John Fall.

Somewhere there had to be a way down to that level. Miller wouldn't have closed off access completely. Chief suspects there are secrets to be learned down there. Maybe even people to find. Rusty McDaniel, perhaps?

With his flashlight he illuminates every corner, every crevice of the hall. He can see nothing.

"Ellen," he whispers. "Help me."

He hears a footstep. A light sound in the dark, just a tap, and then another, against the hardwood floor.

He turns in the direction of the sound, swinging the beam of his flashlight. If it's a church member, he'll have to face them. He has no search warrant, but he is, after all, the chief of police.

But he has a feeling it's not a church member. No, nothing as simple as that. Yet his flashlight fails to illuminate whoever it is that now very clearly walks toward him in the dark. Rather, instead of seeing who it is, Chief *smells* the presence.

It's the odor of rotting flesh.

"Who is there?" he demands, the fear obvious in his voice.

Finally, not two feet in front of him, grinning into the glare of his flashlight, comes the bloody, decomposing face of Priscilla Googins.

The chief screams and his flashlight goes dark.

Halloween, 7:45 P.M.

This is the night it happened, Victoria thinks. *This is the night Petey disappeared and my family was killed.*

This is the night I go back into the woods.

Maybe she's being a fool. But she has not forgotten her promise to find Petey, nor the conviction that somewhere she needs to take this step to fight the power of John Fall. Somehow the fear is not nearly as overpowering as it was the last time she ventured in here. And she survived that ordeal; she's confident she'll survive this one.

But will she find what she's come here to find? Will she find Petey McKay?

In town the streets are dark and quiet. No costumed witches or pirates roam the neighborhoods, ringing doorbells asking for handouts of candy. The Reverend Miller had declared Halloween a pagan holiday, forbidding his church members from participating. Once again newspaper articles denounced Falls Church for its "repressive, puritanical ways." But few in town even know—or care—what the outside press says anymore.

It is the time of year when Falls Church always closes in on itself, retreating into its remoteness from the rest of the Cape, indeed from the rest of the world. But this year the isolation has come with an unimaginable starkness. Few even watch TV these days. Miller had declared television a tool of the Devil, and Musty Moore had been only too glad to pick up dozens of sets, along with many VCRs, computers and CD players, as he made his morning rounds for trash.

"You have not won," Victoria whispers into the night. "You have not won, no matter what you think."

She told no one what she was doing tonight. Kip would've tried to stop her, or at least insisted that he come along. But she knew she had to do this on her own.

This is why I came back to Falls Church.

The woods are dark, with only a pale golden moonglow to guide her way. It's a cold night, chilly and damp, and the crickets keep up a loud and edgy chorus. She tries to retrace the steps she would have taken that night with Petey. She can hear the surf. Every few minutes the foghorn wails. She tries her best to stay on the path but, just as it was that night, the path is obscured by a blanket of fallen leaves, and eventually Victoria knows she's strayed. The trees are different.

And she hears a snap of twig, a crunch of leaves underfoot, behind her.

She turns. It is too dark to make out much of anything. She's ready this time. Would she have a vision of her parents again? Or did Fall have something else in mind for her?

The trees around her have been twisted by the sea winds, misshapen husks that cast contorted shadows in the moonlight. Victoria braces herself. She sees nothing in the shadows, and the sound is gone. Just the foghorn, low and wailing.

She keeps on walking. She stops at a small clearing, where the moon can be seen through an opening in the trees. *This is it,* she tells herself. *This is where Petey disappeared.*

Ahead of her, another crunch of leaves. She looks in the direction of the sound.

She gasps.

It's the ghost. The kid with the sheet over his head. Standing there, not moving, just waiting for her, in exactly the same place he was all those years ago.

I know what's under that sheet, Victoria thinks, her heart suddenly pounding in her ears. *I know what I'll see if I pull it away.*

She takes a deep breath and begins to approach the figure. *I won't run away this time, Petey. I won't leave you alone.*

The ghost doesn't move. It just stands there, waiting. The world around Victoria changes, just as it did that night. The way she walks, the way she thinks. Her steps feel heavier, as if the pull of gravity has been ratcheted up tenfold. Her thoughts become thick and muddled. She just moves on ever closer to the demon waiting for her.

She stands before it at last.

"I do not like thee, Father Fall," she whispers.

A crow calls, somewhere in the dark.

"The reason why I can't recall. But this I know, for one and all—"

Her voice catches in her throat.

"I do not like thee, Father Fall."

She reaches up and pulls the sheet away.

Father John Fall laughs, worms in his mouth. His bony hands reach out for her. Victoria screams.

Nate hears the scream.

"Victoria!"

He runs through the dark, hoping to God he's not too late.

Chief was right. Chief was right. She's in here.

With him!

"We've got to get to the woods, Nate," the chief had insisted to him at the station. "Victoria's there, and she's in danger."

"Victoria?"

"Yes. Don't ask me how I know. Let's just hurry. Father Fall is there, too. He wants her, Nate. He's wanted her all along, more than anyone else!"

Nate took a moment to grip the chief's shoulder. "Fall?" He bore down on him. "Then you *do* believe. You *do* know."

"Yes. For God's sake, Nate, we can't delay."

Nate's not sure if the chief has heard Victoria's scream, too. He's off searching in another part of the woods. But Nate has no time to call to him. He just runs in the direction he thinks Victoria's scream came from.

Please, dear God, Nate prays. *Don't let me lose her, too!*

* * *

"You're mine, Victoria. At last! All those years ago, you alone stood up against me. You alone!"

She trembles before him. He stands tall, seemingly a giant, seeming to tower ten or more feet into the night air.

"You alone sent me back to the coldness, to the unholiness I have been forced to endure. Ever since, I have wanted you—wanted your warmth, your belief, your love! And now you are mine!"

"No!" Victoria screams. She lunges at the creature, throwing her arms around it, feeling its fragile bones crack under her grip. It shrinks in her hands, loses its effect on her. She gets her hands around its neck and begins to choke it. Worms rush from the snapping skeletal jaw. "I will never be yours! *I am stronger than you!*"

The demon is surprisingly easy to subdue. It thrashes a bit under her grip, but it soon falls still. She lowers the thing to the ground. Only its jaws continue to snap, the rest of its bones ceasing any movement under its rotting black coat. Victoria stands up, looking down at the creature in the moonlight.

"Victoria!"

She doesn't stop to wonder how Nate knew she was here. As he runs up behind her, she just keeps staring down at the figure of the man in black. The last of the worms slithers from its lips, but its mouth still opens and closes, as if struggling to speak.

"Victoria," Nate says breathily, looking down with her. "What is it?"

"Listen," she commands.

It is speaking. Low, hollow words.

"You will be mine, you will be mine," it says, wisps of sound, caught in the salty sea breeze.

Then it falls completely still.

Both Nate and Victoria keep their eyes glued on the thing. Its decaying skin begins to shrivel up and flake away. Its clothes disintegrate in front of their eyes. All that is left are bones, and the breeze suddenly whips itself into a powerful wind, scattering leaves and earth and twigs across the skeleton. As they watch, it becomes the remnants not of a terrible man but of an innocent little boy, bones exposed at long last from the soil.

"Petey," Victoria cries.

She falls to her knees.

"I've found you, Petey." The tears run down her cheeks. "I've found you at last."

Friday, November 1, 4:30 P.M.

The news makes headlines the next day: REMAINS OF LONG-LOST BOY FINALLY FOUND. Chief Hutchins tells reporters that his department, never having given up on solving the crime, had been searching the area and had come across the bones. He speculated that the rains earlier in the year must have dislodged enough accumulated soil and debris to expose the skeleton.

"Now, at long last," the chief told reporters, "little Petey can have a proper burial."

The boy's mother, June McKay, immediately requested a service at St. Peter's Church. Father Roche received permission from the bishop to open the church for the purpose, and he consented to say Petey's funeral mass.

Kip and Victoria have come to the police station to meet with the chief and Nate. "Curious that Fall never took Mrs. McKay under his control," Kip says. "Not yet, at least. If he had, surely she would have wanted *Miller* to conduct the service."

"Perhaps she would have been more difficult to subdue," Victoria speculates, "since she was the mother of one of his victims from last time."

At the station the chief and Nate sit opposite them, listening to their theories. Nate keeps looking over at Chief, wondering what his reaction will be to all this supernatural talk. But the older man's face remains solemn. He listens respectfully, nodding his head.

"Tell me, Hobart," Chief Hutchins says. "Do you believe Mark Miller is the same person as Grace West? The same as Tommy Keegan? The same as all of these characters Catherine Santos has discovered over the last two centuries coming into town and stirring up trouble?"

Kip looks at him. "Yes, I do. They're all the same. They're all John Fall."

"Father Fall," the chief murmurs.

Nate watches him. Chief stands, walks across the width of the station, then back again, rolling something over in his mind.

"I do not like thee, Father Fall," he recites. *"The reason why, I can't recall. But this I know, for one and all—"*

"I do not like thee, Father Fall," Victoria finishes.

"A kids' rhyme," the Chief says. "I've heard it sung at the playground many times over the years."

Kip nods. "A little bit of oral history passed down from generation to generation, I suspect. Originating with those first citizens three hundred years ago who rose up against him."

"There's a similar rhyme about Prissy Goo," the chief says. He looks at them all. "I've *seen* her, you know."

Nate's mouth drops open. "You've *seen* her?"

The chief smiles. "Yes, I've seen her. She tried to show me a way into the basement of the old church, but then I heard someone upstairs. It was Miller. I had to get out of there before I could investigate further." He nods over at Victoria. "But just as you reported seeing her once, I believe Priscilla—and maybe Petey and others of his victims—are trying to help us."

Kip cocks his head, looking at the chief. "So what were you looking for in the basement of the church?"

"Rusty McDaniel, maybe. Who knows what else."

"Wait a minute," Nate says. "You say Priscilla Googins tried to show you how to get in there? Chief, forgive me, but it's just difficult shifting gears here. A few days ago you would've thrown us all out of your office if we suggested we were talking to ghosts."

The chief smiles. "That's before I got to know a few. Not just Prissy, but my wife as well. That's right. Ellen. I figure you three might be the only ones to believe me. Ellen helped me to see how I was being hoodwinked by Miller and his crew. She's also the one who told me *you* were in danger, Victoria. That's how I knew you were in the woods."

"Then we *do* have some important allies against him," Victoria says.

Nate sighs. "It's all so fantastic."

Victoria levels her eyes at him. "Don't tell me you *still* don't believe after what you witnessed last night in the woods."

"I believe," Nate says. "I believe it all. It's just that it's all so fantastic to comprehend."

"That it is," the chief says. "But our strategy now has to be to get Miller. If we can take him, we break his hold over town."

"We've thought of that," Kip says. "Nate here wanted to throw him in jail months ago, but he's broken no law that we can pin on him. And we've seen how he can mobilize people. If you take him in, there will be riots in the street."

"So what do you propose, then?"

Kip sighs. "We need to start going after his flock. Victoria and I have been trying, but with limited success. First we need to secure people against the dream."

"I've—I've already been doing that," Nate says.

Victoria gives him an appreciative glance.

"The second step," Kip says, "is to step up our campaign for the hearts and minds of his followers. Win them back away from him."

The chief nods. "How do we do that?"

Victoria stands. "I think we've already started. This town grieved for Petey McKay for a long, long time. Did you see how many people showed up at his mother's house today? They were there to offer sympathy, to be supportive. Down deep, they *must* know their good reverend is responsible for that boy's death. We've got to get that message out, person to person. We've got to jump-start their consciences."

Nate makes a face. "I'm not sure I trust the expressions of sympathy in this town. They took Chief here to their bosom, too, when Ellen died. But it was a sham. A way of sucking him in, neutralizing him so he wouldn't take action against their leader."

"I'm not sure it was fully a sham, Nate," the chief says.

"With Miller, yes. But not with the others. Maybe I just don't want to believe it, but I think their sympathy, their support, was genuine."

"I do, too," Kip says. "I believe the human soul is not so easily corrupted. I believe that in their complex humanity, people can rise above Fall's control. That's why I think we can win. But it has to be an all-out effort, and we have to start now."

So they plan: Chief Hutchins will call a special Town Meeting to talk about the problems facing the town. He'll get the press to endorse the idea, so Town Manager Alan Hitchcock can't squash it. They'll get people to talk at the meeting: Mrs. McKay, hopefully, about how finding Petey's remains can help them all heal. Marcella Stein and Clem Flagg, about how the hatred expressed against them was hurtful and wrong. Father Roche could speak; as could Catherine Santos, Cooper Pierce, Sandipa Khan. Maybe even Danny Correia, standing up to offer them one of his heartfelt sayings of goodwill. Peoples' hearts will melt. None of Miller's fiery rhetoric will be able to match that.

"It worked before," Victoria says to Nate after the others have left. "It took a little time, but it worked. When I spoke out at Town Meeting as a girl, my words had a domino effect. The papers the next day all said I alone had had the courage to speak the truth, and suddenly minds began changing all over town. That's why Grace West was so furious. That's why Fall, realizing he was defeated, took his revenge against me. I'm convinced it was *me* he wanted in the woods, not Petey, and when he couldn't get me, he burned my house down and killed my family."

Nate takes her in his arms. "We're going to put an end to your nightmare, Victoria. I promise you."

"Nate," she says, looking up at him. "Thank God you believe."

Their lips are about to meet when a horrible bang in the outer office rips through the stillness. "Kevin?" Nate calls to the temporary cop at the front desk. There's no response. He tells Victoria to stay behind and advances into the hallway. He makes a sound in horror.

Kevin is slumped over his desk in a pool of blood, which is already dripping onto the floor. Gray brain matter is splattered across the wall behind him.

"Dear God," Nate gasps, his hand on his gun.

From behind him he hears Victoria start to scream, a sound quickly silenced. Nate spins around, rushing back into the main office. There Rusty McDaniel stands, Victoria held in front of him. With one hand he covers her mouth. With the other he holds a gun to her head.

"You don't want her to meet the same fate as that poor pathetic slob out there, do you, Nate, good buddy?" Rusty grins. "Really, Tucky. Did you think that loser could fill in for *me*?"

"Rusty," Nate says, his voice even, "you don't want to do this. You're a good man, a good cop."

Rusty sneers. "You didn't think so when you had me taken off to jail."

"It's not you who's doing this, Rusty. It's Miller. He's making you do things—"

"Things that maybe I should've done a long time ago!" Rusty shouts. "What did I have to hope for, Nate? Of maybe someday getting promoted to your number two man? No thanks. I'm going to be the chief when the old man retires. Understand that, Nate? *Chief!*"

Nate keeps eye contact with Rusty. "Okay, then, so your issue's with me, Rusty. Not her. Let Victoria go."

"Her life for yours, Nate," Rusty says.

"Fine," Nate says.

"Actually, I should off both of you. But he wants her alive, though. Says he has plans for her."

Victoria makes a sound behind Rusty's hand.

"You like that idea, Tucky? Reverend Miller getting his way with the little lady here? Oh, he wants her bad, Tucky. He wants her so—"

Victoria suddenly swings up with her elbow, knocking Rusty's gun away from her head. In that instant she breaks free, giving Nate enough time to withdraw his gun and aim it at Rusty. But the rogue cop, enraged, has recovered his stance enough to draw down his gun and level it at Victoria. "I don't care if he wants you, bitch, you die for that!"

"Oh, no, she doesn't," Nate shouts, pulling his trigger.

His bullet hits Rusty in the side. He goes down in a shrill howl, his gun flying across the room. Nate's quickly on him, barking to Victoria to call 911.

"No," Rusty gasps, clutching his side. Blood oozes through his fingers. "Don't call anyone. Let me die."

"You can't die, buddy," Nate says, rushing to him, holding him in his arms. "You've got to live to fight this madman. You've got to help put a stop to all this."

"I can't, Nate," Rusty says, struggling to breathe. "I'm not strong enough. I can't fight him."

"Yes, you can. Hang on, Rusty."

Victoria's got the emergency service on the phone, telling them to get to the Falls Church police station immediately. But Rusty's face is already turning blue.

"Take care of my family, Nate," Rusty says, his words difficult. "Don't let that monster keep them in his power. Save them, Nate."

"Hang on, Rusty," Nate pleads.

But by the time the paramedics arrive, Rusty's dead. He was a wanted fugitive, so in some places Nate will be hailed, once again, as a hero. But as he watches Rusty's body taken away, he feels anything but. Later, behind the closed door of his office, Nate breaks down and cries, and Victoria takes him in her arms.

Friday, November 8, 2:30 P.M.

That November is the coldest on record, but it's the dampness that's even worse, the raw, wet chill that grips the town and refuses to let go. The sea is so fierce and choppy that Manny Duarte's fishing boat tips over in the waves. He loses thousands of dollars' worth of equipment, barely making it back to shore with his life.

Hanging over the town is a damp, gray despair. Rusty Mc-Daniel's funeral was a somber, mournful affair, with the town expressing not the outrage Nate and the chief had feared but rather a deep, despondent gloom. It's as if people are suddenly resigned to their regrettable fate. Nothing seems left of the old Falls Church. In the window of Wong's Chinese, a town fixture for two decades, a For Sale sign now hangs. Inside, the tables and chairs and smiling Buddha are gone. Sam and Margaret have left town, driven out by people they've known for years.

It's the same at Dicky's, where Dicky's fellow church members one day turned out in force to protest his serving of alcohol. They frightened him enough to close his doors. The next day the Board of Selectmen unanimously passed an ordinance making Falls Church officially dry. Brokenhearted over his comrades' betrayal, Dicky went on a massive bender and now sits sulking in a holding cell at the police station. Smokey's Liquors, too, is closed, with its proprietor hiding out in fear in his apartment out back, refusing to see anyone, lest they try to tell him their dreams.

More than one stray tourist, wandering off Route 6 and finding Falls Church at the end of the causeway, has called it a ghost town. With nowhere to stop except the diner—where a sign in the window declares LOCALS ONLY PLEASE—few linger in the town very long. The only sound heard now along Main Street is the low occasional wail of the foghorn.

Three days ago Catherine Santos was fired by the library's Board of Directors, chaired by Mary Silva, who cited Catherine's "immoral and improper support" of multicultural exhibits, like Gay History Month. A growing hostility had been obvious between Catherine and her board all summer and fall, but the final straw came when she tried to mount an observance of Ramadan, the Muslim holy month. No one attended the event, not even the Khans, and the board met to consider Catherine's dismissal. Helen Twelvetrees was immediately appointed to take her place, and Helen presided the next day over a huge book burning on the Town Green. Despite the presence of some very vocal protesters drawn in from Boston and other parts of the Cape, the board seemed unfazed by any criticism.

"We're simply creating the kind of community many of us have wanted for a long, long time," Helen Twelvetrees told a reporter as copies of *Catcher in the Rye, Madame Bovary* and *Heather Has Two Mommies* snapped and shriveled in the blaze.

So it was that, flush with these victories, many of Falls Church's citizens stayed away from Chief Philip Hutchins's Town Meeting. They had, in fact, been urged to boycott it by Reverend Miller, who declared that the meeting was merely an attempt to "secularize" the town, to deny his followers their faith. To attend the Town Meeting, Miller declared, would be a "sin." Still, a few hardy souls ventured out on that cold, rainy night, and their presence encouraged Hutchins.

"You see?" he whispered to Nate and Kip. "Not everyone is completely in his thrall."

But looking out at the hall, with only forty or fifty chairs filled out of a total of seven hundred, Nate couldn't help but feel downcast. They hadn't even been able to convince folks like Clem Flagg or Cooper Pierce to speak, so frightened were they of Miller. Such fear wasn't difficult to understand; Danny Correia awoke every night with terrible dreams, thrashing about in his bed, fighting off images of Father Fall. He would be so agitated that it took Victoria and Kip several hours to calm him down.

But Danny at least found the courage to speak at Town Meeting, while the others hadn't. "An apple a day keeps the bad man away," he said from the podium. The scattered few smiled. They knew what he meant. The truth was as plain as an apple, and theirs for the asking.

"We made some inroads," the chief insisted optimistically, reporting that Joe and Angela Sousa thanked him for organizing the event. So did Marge Duarte and the Reich sisters, who were seen embracing Danny Correia afterward. "All's not lost," Chief declared. "We'll reach people if we have to go door-to-door. We'll get through to their minds and hearts."

Sitting in his office now, Nate wishes he could be as optimistic. Sure, maybe they had reached the Sousas and the Reich sisters and a handful of others, but how about the hundreds of citizens who refused to attend? How about all those who slammed their doors when they recognized Nate and Kip and Victoria, standing on their doorstep like a trio of unwanted Jehovah's Witnesses?

And how long would Fall allow them this counterrevolution? What would he do to put an end to things? Nate had no doubt that he would do something.

"Excuse me," a man says, sticking his head into Nate's office. "Are you the chief?"

"No, he's in the next office. Can I help you?"

The man seems a little timid. He's in his fifties or early sixties, with snow white hair and pink cheeks. "I was told at the front desk I could find the chief back here. I'm Eddie McKenzie, and I want to talk about my daughter."

"Kathy's father?" Nate stands, walking out of his office and escorting the man down to the chief. "Is there a problem?"

"That's what I'd like to find out," Eddie McKenzie says.

Nate taps lightly on the chief's door, which is open, then makes the introductions. Eddie McKenzie sits in the chair opposite the chief, and Nate stands against the sidewall.

"I'm worried about my daughter," McKenzie explains. "I think she's in trouble."

"How so, sir?" Chief asks.

"Well, I live up Cape, and she used to drive up with my grandson at least once a week to see me. She never does that anymore. I've had to come down here to see them. And she's not herself. She's living with that reverend, the kook who's been in the news all the time."

"Mark Miller," Chief says.

"That's the one. I tell you, he's *done* something to her. And I think—I think he hits her."

"Do you have any evidence?"

"She's got a black eye. I just came from seeing her. She claimed she hit her head moving some boxes over at the church. But I know my daughter. She's been through this before. Josh's father used to hit her, and she swore she'd never let herself get into such a situation again." The man's voice chokes up. "But she *has*. This monster's done something to Kathy's will. She's gone back to being the frightened, abused little girl Sly turned her into. That was her worst fear, and Miller's made it happen again."

The chief turns to Nate. "Go over there and pick Miller up on suspicion of domestic violence."

"Gladly," Nate says.

"But be careful," Chief warns.

Nate just nods, and he's out the door.

Miller agrees without a struggle to accompany Nate back to the station. He actually seems amused by the whole situation; in fact, a tight little grin remains fixed to his lips even as Nate reads him his rights and puts him into the back of the cruiser. It's Kathy McKenzie who reacts to the arrest with outrage and vitriol, screaming that Nate has no right to do this, that he's a "fucking bastard" and a "motherfucking asshole." No such violence has occurred, she insists, promising Miller she'll call Cliff Claussen immediately.

Nate says nothing as they drive back to the station, but he can't deny feeling spooked with Miller's eyes on the back of his neck.

What are handcuffs? Nate thinks. *What are guns and laws and jails when this man can rip Claudio Sousa's guts out with one hand? When he can get into our dreams and into our souls?*

But then he remembers Victoria's mantra.

I'm stronger than he is, Nate tells himself. *I'm stronger.*

Indeed, Claussen is already at the station when they arrive. "You can't hold him," the attorney rasps. "You have no evidence."

"Kathy McKenzie's black eye is all the evidence we need for now," Nate tells him.

"Thank you for coming, Cliff," Miller says calmly as Nate takes him downstairs to the lockup.

"I'll have you out of here in no time," the attorney promises. He turns to the chief. "You've overstepped your bounds, Hutchins. I'll have the ACLU down here."

"Go right ahead," the chief says. "I've got a sworn statement from a citizen saying she witnessed Miller strike Kathy McKenzie."

"Who?" Claussen demands.

"Victoria Kennelly," he says.

"She lies! She's a crazy woman!"

Kathy McKenzie has come into the station now, Josh tagging behind her, his little legs trying to keep up. "I'll post bail," she cries.

"Even if you were the queen of England, you wouldn't have enough money to get him out," the chief informs her.

"He never hit me!" Kathy shouts, even as her father tries to console her. "I bumped into a door! That's how I got this black eye. He never hit me!"

"Yes, he did, Mommy," Josh calls out. "He hits you all the time!"

The little boy starts to cry, turning his face into his grandfather's chest. Eddie McKenzie pulls Josh close.

A silence falls over the group. Kathy makes a small sound in defeat, wrapping her arms around herself and turning on her heel, walking away. Claussen lets out a long sigh. The chief looks over at Nate, who's just come back upstairs.

"The prisoner is secured," Nate tells them. Claussen stews but makes no further effort.

"Why don't you take Kathy and Josh back to your place?"

Chief Hutchins suggests to Eddie McKenzie. "Keep them out of Falls Church for a while."

"I'll do that," Eddie says.

"I won't go," Kathy says, crying now. "I can't leave him here."

"Listen to me, Kathy," Nate tells her. "You've *got* to leave him. Josh already has. If *he* can break free, so can you."

She looks at him with big eyes.

"You know what I'm talking about," Nate says. "So do you, Cliff. You can break free from him. You know as well as I do that no jail cell will hold him for long. But we can keep him in his prison if you break out of yours. He can only be stopped if you rise up and stop him."

Claussen won't look at anyone. But Kathy's eyes have remained fixed on Nate as he speaks. She looks from him over to her father, then down at her son. She suddenly leans down and takes Josh in her arms.

"I promised once I'd never let anything happen to you, baby," she says softly to the boy. She kisses his hair, tears falling down her cheeks. "And I'm going to keep that promise." She looks up at Eddie. "Take us out of here, Daddy. Take us far away."

They all watch as the McKenzies leave the station. Then Cliff huffs. "Well," he says in a clipped voice. "I suppose you'll be hearing from me in court."

"Think about what I said, Cliff," Nate tells him.

Cliff says nothing, just walks out of the station, trying to hold his head high.

Meanwhile, downstairs, Mark Miller sits patiently in his cell.

Saturday, November 9, 1:43 A.M.

Do you think these puny bars can hold me?

Danny Correia tosses in his sleep. The bad man is back in his head again. He's in a cage, rattling the bars with his skeletal hands.

I'm coming for you, Danny. I'm coming for you.

"Noooooooo," Danny moans.

Across town Cooper Pierce is having the same dream, his pillow suddenly drenched in his cold sweat.

The time draws close, the man in black warns him. *Soon it will be time.*

"Time for what?" Cooper murmurs in his sleep.

Time for you to die.

Cooper sits up and screams himself awake. His wife tries to console him, but she knows it's impossible. Miranda has had similar dreams for weeks. There's no escape from the evil.

Clem Flagg has also been scared awake. He sits staring out his window now at the moonlit steeple of the old church. He's been trying to diet, eating nothing but carrots and celery and a little yogurt, hoping to win back Reverend Miller's affection. But still he comes to taunt Clem in his dreams.

As soon as she drifts off to sleep, Sandipa Khan sees the man with the worms in his teeth. He's in jail, and he's angry.

No prison can hold me, he tells Sandipa. *How dare they think they can keep me here?*

"They've just made him angrier, more determined," Sandipa tells her husband, but in her dream he doesn't hear her. He just sits dejected, as he does in life, with his face in his hands.

To Joe Sousa, tossing fitfully beside his wife, Mark Miller reveals that the end is coming soon. *You know what is coming, don't you, Joseph? You know the time draws near.*

"No," Joe says. "Please. Leave us alone!"

Mark Miller, standing in jail, just laughs.

Father Roche sees the face of the Beast. Its red eyes hover over his bed, its snaky tongue darting toward him.

Why has your God abandoned you, James Roche? the Devil asks him. *Why has he left you here for me to destroy, to take back with me to the fires of hell?*

"No," Father Roche gasps. "You cannot take my soul. You might destroy me, but my soul will never be yours."

The thing laughs, a horrible sound, like iron bars rattling.

The time draws near, priest. The time draws near.

Its foul-smelling breath consumes him, its talons gripping him by the shoulders as if to tear him apart.

Father Roche awakes screaming. Agnes Doolittle rushes into his room, taking him in her arms. He cries like a small boy on her shoulder, unable to speak.

A few blocks away, Catherine Santos is startled awake. A sound. Someone is in her room. She quickly flicks on the lamp beside her and squints into the soft amber glow.

A footstep. Just outside her door.

She stands, grabbing her robe and pulling it around her. *I am stronger than whatever it is that haunts us,* Catherine tells herself, repeating the mantra taught by Victoria. *I fought you off before. I'll fight you off again.*

There it is. The footstep once more. Someone is directly outside her door. Catherine snatches the cross hanging on the wall and holds it out in front of her. She pulls the door open and gasps.

Tommy Keegan stands there, grinning.

"Hello, Catherine," he says. "Long time no see."

He looks just as he did nearly forty years ago. His bright orange Afro, the wispy beard on his chin. He wears a tie-dyed shirt and a peace sign pendant, patched jeans and sandals.

"Aren't you happy to see me, Catherine?" Tommy asks.

"I am stronger than you," she tells him, thrusting the cross at him.

He knocks it out of her hand and takes a step forward. Catherine backs up. He comes after her.

"I'm stronger than you," she says again, terrified. "Stronger than you!"

He laughs at her, worms in his teeth. "The time is drawing very near, Catherine. Very near." He raises his hands as if to strangle her.

Catherine Santos screams.

In the east end of town, Victoria Kennelly sits bolt upright in her bed. She had just fallen back to sleep, having spent the better part of an hour comforting Danny Correia over his nightmares. A scream awakened her just now, but there's nothing, no sound, when she gets up out of bed and listens at her door. A terrible stillness hangs over the house. She tiptoes down the hall and looks in on Danny. He's sleeping peacefully finally. She closes his door.

She's sure she heard a scream.

Her eyes follow the length of the hall. There, at the far end, there's movement. In the shadows Victoria sees something white. She walks slowly toward it, the moonlight gradually revealing a figure with which she's all too familiar.

The ghost.

"I am no longer afraid of you," she says out loud. "You're nothing more than a pathetic man with a sheet over your head."

She approaches it just as she had in the woods, taking ahold of the sheet and whisking it away. But instead of the man with worms in his mouth, Victoria looks upon the face of someone else. Someone she hadn't braced herself to see.

It's Grace West.

"Hello, Victoria," Grace says, her black eyes searing into her just as they had all those years ago, turning around to glare at her at Town Meeting. Her gray hair catches the moonlight, seeming to pulse with a hideous glow. "Still the same little troublemaker as always, aren't you?"

Victoria takes a step backward. Grace West approaches.

"The time has come, Victoria," the old crone tells her, raising her hands. "It's time."

Grace West's cold hands grip Victoria around the neck and begin to choke.

Monday, November 11, 8:55 A.M.

For the first time in many weeks, the bells of the old church do not ring on Sunday morning welcoming the flock. In their place newspaper headlines blare: CONTROVERSIAL MINISTER ARRESTED ON DOMESTIC VIOLENCE CHARGE. Word spreads quickly throughout Falls Church that Kathy McKenzie has decided to bring charges against Reverend Miller. It's all anyone can talk about at the True Value and the diner, with opinion seeming to split folks right down the middle.

"You know," Marge Duarte confides to Sandy Hooker as she serves his bacon and eggs, "I was always a little worried about Kathy living there with him. It didn't seem right."

"Don't you start judging the reverend, Marge," Sandy snarls. "It's not your place."

"I don't know," says Musty Moore, overhearing. "This ain't the first time I'd seen Kathy with a shiner. I was starting to wonder about our good reverend, if maybe he was really as good as he liked to make out."

"Now, all of you, stop your speculating," Betty Silva scolds, coming up behind them. "Reverend Miller is a good and decent man. He'd never lift a hand against a woman. He knows that God would strike him down if he tried!"

As much as the chief would have liked to, however, he can't hold Mark Miller forever. He's arraigned in a Barnstable court, and that afternoon is finally released into the custody of his lawyer. The judge makes him promise he won't try to flee, that he won't leave Falls Church.

"Oh, you have my word on that," Miller replies, calm and collected, that little grin still playing on his lips.

When he passes Chief Hutchins, he stops, offering him a smile. "I'm just sorry that we've had such a rift grow between us, Philip."

The chief says nothing, just glares at him.

"We were very close once. I hope we can be close again."

"I see through you, Miller," Chief snarls. "I know what you are."

Miller smiles. "You will see much more of me, Chief. I promise you that."

From the window at the police station, the chief watches Miller get out of Classen's car and walk along the sidewalk on Pearl Street. A group of the faithful have gathered to collect around him: Laura Millay, Betty and Hiram Silva, Pidge Hitchcock, Manny Duarte. But that's all: there's no riot in the street the way there was when Rusty was sent away, and there have been no protests all weekend while Miller was held in jail.

"We've made a dent in his armor," the chief tells Nate, who's come up behind him. "We've got folks on the fence. Some are moving over to our side. You just watch."

"And it's made him very angry," Nate says. "Both Victoria and Catherine Santos report having encounters with some of Fall's various guises. Victoria saw Grace West; Catherine saw Tommy Keegan. Ultimately Fall wasn't able to do anything to them but scare them half to death. But he kept repeating that the time was drawing near."

"Time for what?" Chief asks.

Nate shrugs. "Your guess is as good as mine."

Suddenly they hear the back door to the station open, and Job Emerson walks inside.

"Job!" Nate shouts.

"Good Lord," the chief responds.

Job staggers to his old desk and sits down. He's in uniform, but the way it hangs on him attests to the considerable weight he's lost in the last several weeks. He looks years older, horribly gaunt, and his hands shake as Nate and the chief grab them.

"Where have you been?" Nate asks his friend. "Are you all right?"

"And Berniece?" the chief adds. "And Jamal?"

"I had to come back," Job tells them, his voice weak and raspy. "I had to come back and try to fight him."

"We know," Nate says. "We know what he's been doing."

"He got in our heads," Job says. "He took Jamal from us. He tried to keep us apart."

"Where have you been?" Nate asks again.

"Up in one of the old shacks in the marshlands," Job says. "We moved from place to place so no one would find us. That's what he told us to do. To hide, to stay out of sight, but to remain close by in case he needed us."

"But he kept Jamal," Nate says.

Job nods. "Until we came back and got him. But he's not free, Nate. Miller haunts Jamal every night in his dreams. It's tormenting him, driving him mad. I had to come back. I had to try and fight Fall to save my son."

"We're going to win," Chief tells him.

Job reaches up and grabs ahold of Nate's shirt. "That girl, Nate. The reporter."

"Monica? What about Monica?"

"He had me get rid of her body," Job says, starting to cry.

Nate's silent for a moment. "So she *is* dead, then," he says. "I've known it, but I still hoped that maybe—"

"Where is her body?" the chief asks.

"Out in the marshes. Not much left of her."

Nate feels sick to his stomach. How pretty, how spunky, Monica Paul had been. He can see her standing right here, winking at him, flirting with him. He has to walk away, overcome with emotion.

"Well, this gives us a reason to go get him," the chief says. "We can charge him with murder. We can—"

"No," Job says, his eyes pleading. "He'll kill Jamal if we do that. I just know he will. Jamal won't wake up. He'll kill him in his dreams and he won't wake up."

Nate composes himself. "We already know he's mad enough as it is," he says from across the room. "I suggest we wait."

The chief nods. "But he says the time draws near. He's planning something. We have to stop whatever it is."

"First thing we do," Nate says, rejoining them, "is get Berniece and Jamal over to Kip Hobart's house. They can't be sleeping out in the marshes anymore. They may need some medical attention, too."

Job nods. "Just being here, just talking with you, I feel stronger. As if fighting off his control might really be possible."

"That's what has got him so pissed off, I think," Nate says. "We're breaking his hold. People are slowly coming around. And he doesn't like it." He looks at Job and then at the chief. "He doesn't like it at all."

Tuesday, November 19, 11:00 A.M.

"Under no circumstances are you to inform my family that I'm coming home."

Dr. Kendall crosses his arms over his chest. "Sargent, I'm sure your wife will *want* to know."

The patient sniffs. "You called her when I woke from my coma, didn't you? And did she come see me then? No. Did she come at all over the last several months?"

The doctor shakes his head. "I don't know what's going on, Sargent. But, no, she stopped coming a few days after you were admitted. And when I spoke to her on the phone, she seemed distant."

"As if she didn't *care*." Sargent Crawford narrows his eyes. "That's why I'm insistent. *Do not tell Pat or anyone* back in Falls Church when I'm released." He pauses. A little grin flickers across his face. "I want to surprise them."

"Okay." Dr. Kendall sighs. "It's your decision."

"Now," Sargent says, "what about *your* decision? When do I get out of here?"

"Well, I just want to make sure you're really as okay as you seem to be."

"All the tests have come back fine, haven't they?"

The doctor nods. "Yes. But, Sargent, you had a major heart attack and quadruple bypass surgery, after which you fell into a coma for several months. Now you're awake and fully functioning. Your case is extraordinary."

"So you're keeping me here to study me? Look, Doctor, I'll sign myself out if I have to."

"Just give us a few more days, Sargent. Just to make sure you don't have a relapse."

Sargent sits back against his pillows. "I'm very anxious to get home. I have a business to run." He pauses. "And a few other things that need tending to."

"Just a few more days," his doctor says. "A week at most, if all continues to go well."

Sargent darts his eyes quickly at the doctor. "And no word of my condition to Pat. To *anyone*."

Dr. Kendall nods. "Yes, Sargent. I'll respect your decision."

"I want to surprise them," Sargent says again, quieter this time, more to himself than to the doctor. "Oh, yes. I want to surprise them all."

Thursday, November 21, 1:25 P.M.

"Pagans out of Falls Church! Pagans out of Falls Church!"

Kip pulls back the curtains on his second-story bedroom window and looks down at the ragtag group of protesters below. Among the crowd of about two dozen he recognizes Pidge Hitchcock, Mary Silva, Diane Sousa, Dave Carlson and—wonder of wonders—movie star Carolyn Prentiss, whose presence has guaranteed that the TV cameras are there, too.

"We should have expected this," Kip says, looking back at Victoria and Berniece Emerson. "He knows we're all in here. All of his enemies now in one place."

Indeed, now that the Emersons have moved in, Kip's house has become "Ghostbusters Central," as Catherine Santos dubbed it. She's here most of the time, too, reading through old manuscripts. At the kitchen table Nate, Job and the chief plot strategy. Victoria spends hours comforting Danny Correia in his room. The poor guy is too terrified these days to even step foot outside Kip's door.

"I knew they'd target me soon enough," Kip says, looking back down at the crowd below. "I heard Mary Silva once at the True Value describing the stars and the moons on my logo as 'satanic.' "

"Considerable irony in that remark, no?" Victoria asks, looking down herself.

"I'm frightened," Berniece says. "When I close my eyes, I can still see him. He's still there, in my head."

Victoria takes her hand. "We're going to win."

"But how?" Berniece asks, near tears. "He has the whole town under his thumb."

"He's losing his control," Kip assures her. "And he loses power every time someone else defects from him."

"He thrives on dissent, like the protest down below," Victoria says. "But look how few there are. He can't mobilize people in the same way he once did."

"But he's got something planned," Berniece says. "He's told me so in my dreams."

"That's why Nate and the chief plan to take him in again sometime early next week, charge him with the murder of Monica Paul."

"But he'll hurt Jamal!" Berniece protests. "And others. Like Danny. Like Father Roche. Anyone he can still terrify."

"We believe that by then even more will have defected, and he'll no longer have the power to hurt people." Kip looks at Berniece sympathetically. "Please try to trust us. Nate said he's been talking to people in town, encouraging them to drop out of the church. Marge Duarte at the diner has agreed, and she's been convincing others. Joe and Angie Sousa have dropped out. Selectman Richard Longstaff has dropped out. And they think Town Clerk Isabella Sousa Cook is near to dropping out—"

"But he won't just *let* you do this." Berniece's eyes are wide with fear. "He won't just stand back and be defeated that easily."

"He may have no choice, if we weaken his power enough." Kip hopes he's being persuasive enough to calm Berniece's fears, because—in all honesty—he's not fully convinced himself. Their plan makes sense, but so do Berniece's arguments. Fall hasn't come this far to surrender his gains so easily. He won't go down without a fight.

Maybe that's what he means when he warns that the time has come.

When reporters ask Kip for a comment on the protests, he fires a salvo that he hopes wins more converts away from Miller's cause. "This is not what Falls Church is about, indeed not what America is about," he says. Those few left in town who still own television sets see him on the evening news and shake their head in silent agreement. Isabella Sousa Cook makes a decision then and there to back out of her church membership—what had she been *thinking?*—and calls Bessie Bowe and convinces her to do the same. "And call Noah while you're at it," the town clerk tells her. "You had a good thing going there. Get him back while you still can."

But others merely dig in their heels. Mary Silva gets a visitor late that night. She welcomes Mark Miller inside. He's followed by Alan Hitchcock, Pat Crawford and Manny Duarte. "We need to take action against the infidel," the young minister tells them, his eyes blazing. None of his flock says a word when the worms begin falling from his mouth. They just listen to his instructions, then do what he says.

Danny awakes first. There's smoke in his room. He sits up in bed. He starts to scream for Victoria.

The fire spreads quickly. Victoria sees it jumping up the stairs like a thousand malicious little imps. She runs down the hall and pulls Danny from his bed, calling for Kip. He stumbles out of his room, rushing to the end of the hall, breaking a window with a chair. "Here!" he shouts. "Get out onto the roof. We can get down by grabbing onto the pine tree."

Victoria looks down the stairwell into the blazing inferno below. "Berniece! Job!" she screams. The Emersons sleep in a room on the first floor. But there's no way to get down there. A wall of flame burns at the foot of the stairs.

There's also no way to save all the documents piled on the dining-room table, documents detailing Fall's crimes throughout the decades. The papers are consumed rapidly by the ferocious, hungry flames. By the time Kip, Victoria and Danny drop to safety on the front lawn, the first floor is burning out of control.

"Dear God," Victoria cries. "Berniece! Job! Jamal!"

"There they are," Danny calls, pointing.

On the side of the house, Job staggers with his son in his arms. They're both coughing. Victoria takes Jamal from him and Job prepares to go back into the house. Kip stops him. "You can't, Job! You'd never make it back out!"

"Berniece is still in there! I have to save Berniece!"

Just then, the second floor of the house collapses in on the first. Balls of flame shoot out at them. Job screams, covering his head and falling to the ground.

"Where's the fire department?" Kip shouts. "*Where is the goddamn fire department?*"

"Chipper Robin," Victoria says in horror. "He's still under Fall's control."

Kip watches his house burn. A few neighbors have gathered to watch impassively as well.

Finally a lone siren in the distance. In seconds a fire truck has appeared, driven by a single firefighter. Hickey Hix. He's quickly off the truck and unraveling the hose.

"I couldn't just sit there," he shouts to Kip. "I couldn't just let a house burn, even if he wanted me to! I just couldn't!"

He aims a gush of water at the blaze. But it's too late. In minutes Kip's house is a smoldering, snapping heap. Somewhere in the ruins lies the body of Berniece Emerson.

She was right.

He won't just stand back and be defeated that easily.

Kip Hobart falls to his knees and cries.

Friday, November 22, 9:01 A.M.

They know they have to act quickly. Early the next morning Job Emerson—fired with revenge over his wife's death—swears to a statement that the Reverend Mark Miller called him to the old church early on the morning of June 29 to retrieve the badly decomposed body of Monica Paul from a secret room in the subbasement. Job then buried her in a shallow grave in the marshlands. Her body has now been positively identified by the coroner in Bourne, and a warrant is issued for the arrest of Mark Miller.

The chief makes sure the media is there when the three police cruisers pull up to the Grand Avenue Apartments. When Nate bangs on the door to Miller's apartment, it's opened by Laura Millay. When she hurries down the stairs past the waiting reporters and townspeople, many of those gathered are shocked. Pidge Hitchcock is horrified by the implications, and wastes no time in calling Laura a whore. When she sees the Reverend Miller led out in handcuffs, she turns away, sick to her stomach. She wants out of this town, she tells anyone who'll listen. She's always despised Falls Church and now, more than ever, she wants to leave these undesirables behind.

Especially that hypocrite Mark Miller!

Nate's glad the townsfolk are here to see their savior once again hauled off in handcuffs, once more charged with a crime and taken away in a police car. Word has quickly spread that someone else has stood up to him: Job Emerson, who lost his wife tragically the night before. *So many tragedies,* many people are thinking. *When will it end?*

"You know this is the final act of our little play," Miller says to Nate and the chief from the backseat of the cruiser.

They say nothing. Once again, Miller had accompanied them without a struggle. He offered no reaction when the charges were read to him. But now, he speaks. Nate wonders if he's tired of pretending. Maybe, in fact, he's ready to admit who he really is.

"So tell us," Nate says. "What kind of final act do you have planned?"

Mark Miller smiles. "And give away the ending? Never."

He says nothing more. Not until they've reached the station does he speak again.

"Looks like snow," the minister says, looking out the window. "Could be that a major storm is headed this way." He looks at Nate. "Do you think?"

Reporters snap pictures as Miller is led into the station. Nate secures him in the cell he'd only recently vacated. Even as he locks him in, Nate knows Miller has the power to escape if he chooses to. *The last act of our little play.*

But Miller sits quietly in his cell. He doesn't ask to call his lawyer. Neither does Cliff Claussen show up to argue on his behalf. The chief is on the phone, making plans for Miller's transfer. He recommends the minister be held without bail.

Nate knows Kip is on his way. He's going to try to persuade Father Roche to come as well. Another exorcism will be attempted, with Miller present this time. He hasn't nearly the power he had months ago, when the exorcism failed so miserably. Now they will attempt it while they have him in custody.

"Is there something wrong with the heat?" one of the temporary cops asks. "It's awfully hot in here."

Nate realizes he's right. He glances at the thermometer on the wall. It's over 80 degrees, even though the thing is set at 70. He touches the radiator. He pulls back his hand from the heat.

"Yeah," Nate says. "Maybe you ought to call a repairman."

But he knows no repairman can fix this. This is Father Fall's anger he feels: white hot, raging, boiling.

Where is Kip? Nate looks out the front window.

The thermometer on the wall now reads 88. Nate steps outside to cool off. On the front steps of the station the air is dramatically different: a frosty chill has taken hold since they came inside. The sky is ominously gray. Slivers of snow dance in the air.

"Come on, Kip," Nate whispers. "Come on."

"But I can't," Father Roche protests. "It's hopeless."

"Please, Father, please come with us and try," Victoria begs.

The old priest stands. "He's too powerful. He'll destroy us all."

Kip takes him by the shoulders. "If both of us attempt the exorcism, we can overpower him."

"I'm an old coward." Father Roche cries. "I'm sorry."

"You must believe in yourself," Victoria tells him.

"And why should he?"

They all turn. Father Roche's housekeeper Agnes Doolittle stands in the doorway. She looks different. Her eyes are hard. Her face, usually so compassionate, is tight.

"He's no man of God," Agnes says. "He sits here, shaking with fear. He's lost his faith. That's what I've been telling him. Haven't I, James?"

He nods, his hands trembling.

Victoria glares at the housekeeper. "He was getting stronger. But you—"

Agnes Doolittle approaches Father Roche. "You have no power over the Beast. You are nothing but an old man. A man with no faith."

Father Roche collapses into his chair, sobbing.

"You've had the dream!" Victoria shouts at Agnes. "Fall's gotten into your mind."

The housekeeper ignores her. She just keeps looking down at Father Roche.

"No faith," she repeats. "A man of no faith."

"Don't listen to her, Father!" Victoria says. "She's with him—she's with Fall!"

"It's useless, Victoria," Kip says. "It's our fault. Our fault for not warning her."

"But we need Father Roche," Victoria says. "We need him!"

The old priest just continues sobbing into his hands.

Nate's gone out in his cruiser to find Kip. He's heading down Main Street toward St. Peter's when an old Mustang speeds past him, going about seventy miles an hour. "Jesus," Nate grumbles, just as the car skids and hits a parking meter in front of the boarded-up Hornet.

"Just what I need," Nate grouses. "I'm trying to save the world and I have to stop and give a speeding ticket."

He pulls the cruiser over and hops out. He approaches the Mustang. The driver has gotten out to survey the damage. He's a young guy, twenty or so. His hands are in his hair. He's clearly distraught.

"What's the hurry, buddy?" Nate asks.

The man turns to face him. His eyes are wide, bloodshot and terrified. "I have to get home," he says. "I have to get back to Hyannis."

"Well, first you're going to have to pay for that meter," Nate says.

"Please, you have to let me go," the man says. "I've got to see my girlfriend."

"What's so pressing?"

"Look, I just got to go—"

Nate shakes his head. "Not until I write you a ticket, buddy."

"Please!" the guy screams. "You don't understand. I've got to tell her my dream!"

Nate feels an icy cold hand at the back of his neck. "What do you mean, dream?"

"I just got to tell her. Please!"

Nate grabs the guy by his shirt. "What were you doing in Falls Church?"

The guy trembles. "I was just fishing. I slept out at the beach."

"And you had a dream," Nate says.

"Yeah, yeah. I had a dream. Please let me go."

Nate just twists his shirt harder. "Who told you this dream? The dream that you yourself had?"

"I don't know Some lady She just came up to me and told me. I thought she was crazy. But then I had the same dream myself last night."

Nate looks him deep in the eyes. "And now you feel compelled to tell your girlfriend." He pauses as the full implication hits him. *"Your girlfriend back in Hyannis."*

"Yes. Please let me go. I'll go crazy if I don't tell her. It feels like my head is going to bust open."

Dear God, Nate thinks. *He's going beyond Falls Church. The last act of our little play.*

"I can't let that happen," Nate tells the guy.

"Please!" he begs, crying now. "It's killing me!"

"Tell the dream to me," Nate says. "I know you feel compelled to tell your girlfriend, but if you love her, tell me."

The man struggles in Nate's grip.

"Tell me the dream!" Nate shouts.

So he does. "There was this man ... dressed all in black. . . ."

Friday, November 22, 10:59 A.M.

Just as the chief decides they can no longer bear the heat, the furnace of the police station explodes.

"Get out!" he calls to his temporary officers as he hurries downstairs. The holding cell is in flames. There's no sign of Miller.

This time the fire department is on the scene within minutes. The blaze is contained in the basement, and damage, surprisingly, is minimal. But Miller is gone. A search reveals no body in the cell. The door had been blown off its hinges by the blast from the furnace. The prisoner must have escaped.

An all-points bulletin is released. The chief tells neighboring police departments and the state police that Miller should be considered at large and dangerous.

"Keep a watch at the old church around the clock," the chief instructs his officers. Then he heads over to search Miller's apartment.

It's a cold, drab, spartan place. He never bothered to furnish it with more than a chair, a desk and two cots. There is no television, no radio, no stereo. The refrigerator is empty except for a spoiled carton of milk. There's a smell in the place, however, that no amount of rotten milk can explain. It's the dank smell of death.

Under one of the cots the chief finds photographs of Kathy McKenzie and Laura Millay in various stages of undress, some completely nude. He sets a match to them in the bathroom sink. The poor women deserve that much, so no one else will ever see these pictures.

The chief watches them curl and sizzle. Standing over the sink, he opens the medicine cabinet. It's empty. Stark empty. Holding nothing that might reveal anything about Mark Miller. But then the chief considers that clues are sometimes gotten by what's *not* there as well as what is. No razor. No shaving cream. No toothbrush or toothpaste. No deodorant.

"As if he never had to do any of those things," the chief says to himself. "None of those human things . . ."

When he heads back to his car, he's stopped by Dean Sousa, still on suspension. "Find him, Chief," Dean tells him. "You've got to find him."

"I will, Dean. And the more you and others can pull away from him, the better chance I have."

Friday, November 22, 1:45 P.M.

"I won't go to sleep," Nate tells them. "It's as simple as that. Not until we've found Father Fall and defeated him."

No one can manage a response. They're still stunned by the account Nate has just shared with them. That he was actually *told the dream*. That he's become the next link in the chain of horror. That Father Fall waits for him the next time he closes his eyes.

They've gathered at Catherine Santos's house. Kip and the rest have been staying here since the fire. When Nate told his story, the chief's face had gone pale. Victoria had gotten up and taken Nate's hand. Job had cursed, banging his fist against the wall.

"I can stay awake," Nate insists. "I've gone five days without sleep before. I went out and bought all the No Doz on the shelf at Woodward's Pharmacy. I'll drink coffee until it's coming out my pores. I'll be a jangle of nerves, but I'll be awake."

"Nate," Victoria says. "You're taking such a risk—"

"What was I going to do? Let that guy pass the dream on to yet another unsuspecting community? Don't you all see? That was Fall's plan. To take his power beyond Falls Church. To get those congregations he left behind three hundred years ago."

"Possibly," Kip says. "Or he was simply cunning enough

to pass it on to you in the one way he knew would force you to listen."

Nate falls silent. No one says anything. Kip's right. This could be *exactly* Fall's plan. Which of them, out of compassion, will listen to Nate tell them the dream—and then how long will it be before all of them have fallen under Fall's power?

"Regardless," Nate says. "I can stay awake."

"Not forever," Kip says plainly. "There's no guarantee we can defeat him in five days, Nate."

"I've thought of that," Nate says. He looks at the Chief. "In the event I *do* fall asleep and have the dream, you need to drug me. Keep me unconscious. Keep me locked up. Don't allow me to pass the dream on."

"But there's no telling what that could do to your mind," the chief protests.

"That's right, Nate," Victoria says. "It could drive you mad."

"What other option is there?" He looks around at all of them.

"If we find Miller," Job says, "I think we should shoot him on the spot. I don't care if the outside world sees it as murder. I'll take the rap. I'll go to prison."

"It wouldn't do any good," Kip says. "He's already dead, Job. The fact that he survived that explosion proves he's not human. I once thought Mark Miller might be just an innocent host for Fall's malevolent spirit. But what the chief saw in his apartment convinces me that Mark Miller—like Tommy Keegan and Grace West before him—is merely a manifestation of evil, not a human being that can be hurt by fire or bullets."

"So how about those letters of reference?" Chief asks. "The academic transcripts? The yearbook entries?"

Kip smiles. "Do you think conjuring up pieces of paper is a difficult task for a being who materializes human form, who has defied the grave for three centuries?"

Catherine Santos stands. "So all we can do for the present is keep trying to win his followers back to our side." She looks with sympathy at Nate. "And keep this young man awake. I'm going to make some coffee."

Victoria grips Nate's hands. "You're stronger than he is, Nate," she whispers.

He just looks at her.

He can't deny how tired he feels. How much he wants to close his eyes. How his body seems to crave sleep while his mind rebels from the thought.

This is what they all went through, he thinks. *People I care about in this town. Marge and Betty and Hiram and Clem . . . and others, too. People I've never really liked, people like Mary Silva and Max Winn and Yvette Duvalier. They're all with me now. All of us, in this together . . .* in a way none of his comrades surrounding him now can understand. Not even Victoria.

The dream is inside me, Nate thinks. *No matter how hard I try to stay awake, it will find me. I will have the dream.*

Saturday, November 23, 12:22 P.M.

Sargent Crawford pays the cabdriver and watches him drive off down the street, heading back to Route 6, away from Falls Church.

It's started to snow. *It was snowing in my visions,* Sargent remembers. *It was always snowing when I dreamed of coming back here. It was snowing when I saw the burned woman, when she told me the secret I had to remember.*

Sargent had deliberately asked the driver to let him out on the outskirts of town. He wanted to walk into Falls Church, to succeed where in his visions he had always failed. Ellen Hutchins had made it into town finally. He was sure of that. And the woman with the enormous eyes had promised him that he'd make it, too.

He passes by the spot where he knows months ago a body lay, bleeding in the rain. Rusty McDaniel killed a college kid. Sargent knows it shouldn't be possible for him to know that, but know it he does. He knows, too, that Claudio Sousa is dead, and Berniece Emerson, and even Rusty now, too. And there will be more deaths if he doesn't get home and let everyone know what the burned woman told him to remember.

He's in the basement of the church.

The snow is whipping pretty fierce. An early squall, icy and wet, sticking to his hair. His cheeks burn from the cold, but he trudges on, down Main Street, past Cranberry Terrace, past

Dave's Sunoco. Across from the firehouse he turns left onto Cliff Heights. He can see his castle perched up on the cliff, overlooking the town and the harbor. How the townsfolk resent these trophy homes looking down at them. For the first time Sargent understands their vantage point. Usually he glides up this road effortlessly in his Jaguar. Now he huffs and puffs through the stinging snowstorm, out of breath as he climbs the hill, fearing his heart might give out again.

No, it's strong enough to do what I have to do.

He has to relay the message given him by the burned woman.

He's in the church. In the basement.

We're all in this together, he thinks as he looks out over the somber little village being blanketed by snow. *Newcomers and native, summer people and year-rounders, tourists and locals. Why did I spend so much of life creating divisions between people?*

He arrives at his house. He pauses at the foot of his driveway, catching his breath. Then he walks up to his front door, his footprints behind him in the snow. He rings the bell.

His wife opens the door and stares up in shock at Sargent.

"Hello, Pat," he says. "I'm home."

Thanksgiving Day, November 28, 2:05 P.M.

Catherine has made a turkey with stuffing and some sweet potatoes. Their celebration might be low-key, but it's important to have, she insists. "We're winning," she tells them. "I got the Khans to speak out, file a complaint of discrimination against Miller and his church."

The congregation, what's left of it, had gathered last Sunday, struck by how many of their comrades had fallen from grace. Reverend Shanker, late of the Methodist persuasion, took the pulpit in place of their missing minister and condemned those who had dropped out due to fear. "Their faith is weak," he charged. "Our mission remains unchanged. We seek the light of truth and wisdom!"

The chief was there, watching it all. He reported that Alan Hitchcock rose from his pew—his wife noticeably absent—and seconded Shanker's remarks, imploring Miller "wherever he is" to remain steadfast and assured by their belief in him.

"It's almost as if he thought Miller could hear him," the chief says now, accepting a platter of sliced turkey and sliding some onto his plate. "As if Miller was there."

"You believe he is, don't you, Chief?" Kip asks. "You think he's down in the level below the church hall."

The chief nods. "The ghost of Priscilla Googins tried to lead me to it, but I wasn't able to find the entrance. And despite how often I've tried to find it since, I can't."

"We need to take possession of the church," Job says, his son, Jamal, sitting beside him. Neither eats much. Jamal's eyes have a lost, wounded look. His tormenting dreams have stopped, but now he lives in constant grief over the loss of his mother. "We need to get into the church, tear up those floorboards," Job says.

"I'm pretty certain we can do that tomorrow or the next day," Chief Hutchins says. "The few die-hard supporters will give us holy hell, but we'll move in and take the church. By the time Cliff Claussen tries to bring in an outside force to stop us, we'll have hopefully gotten to where we need to go."

Across the room, in a straight-backed chair by the window, Nate sits bleary eyed, staring at them. Victoria is with him, holding his hand.

"Whatever you do," Victoria tells them, "you've got to do it fast."

"Nate," Catherine says, approaching him. "You should eat something."

He shakes his head slowly. "Turkey always makes me sleepy," he tells her, managing a smile.

He's been awake now for nearly seven days straight. Victoria and the rest have taken turns sitting with him, constantly talking to him, nudging him when his eyelids start to flutter. They've all been all over town, searching for Miller or some sign that he's gone. But while every day more people seem to be defecting, breaking free from his power, the very fact that *some* remain in his thrall is evidence he's still around.

Still around—and waiting for Nate to fall asleep so he can claim his soul.

"I can't last much longer," Nate whispers to Victoria.

"You've got to, baby." She leans in close to him. "I'm going back out there tonight. I'm going into the church. I'm not waiting until tomorrow or the next day. They won't approve, but I'm going anyway."

He's too light-headed to argue with her, even if he thinks it's dangerous. At first, staying awake had been relatively easy. The second night had been difficult, but then he seemed to get a burst of energy and managed okay. But yesterday afternoon he had fallen, overcome with dizziness, and since then he's felt immobilized. Even lifting his hand has become difficult. Talking is next to impossible. He listens but can't contribute as Chief Hutchins plans how they will search for Miller in the church. Kip is planning to conduct an exorcism in the church hall. They're optimistic that Fall's defeat is imminent.

Then I might as well fall asleep, Nate thinks. *By the time he tries to take control of me, he'll be vanquished and I'll be free.*

Or they can drug me. . . . Yes, that's the way. Let them drug me. At least I'll be asleep. . . .

"Nate."

Victoria is in front of him. "Catherine's going to sit with you. I'm . . . taking a walk."

"No," he mumbles. "Don't go to the church—"

But she's moving away. He tries to move to stop her but can't. Catherine settles down next to him, taking his hand.

"Okay, Nate, what shall we talk about? We're just going to keep talking, keep you awake. Let's see. It's getting cold out there, Nate. Winter seems in a real hurry to get here. Every day there's been snow. Melts pretty quickly, but some days there's enough that I've had to brush off my windshield. I hope it doesn't mean we're in for a bad winter. You know, Nate, the worst winter I ever remember in Falls Church was back in 1974. Oh, my, that year . . ."

But her voice has become so much white noise to Nate. In his mind he follows Victoria. Somehow he sees her walking down the stairs, out Catherine's front door. The sun is setting, casting the town in a soft amber light. A cold wind whips in from the sea. A few flakes of snow swirl here and there. Victoria hurries across Lighthouse Road to Grand Avenue, then down the length of the street to the old church. Nate can see her clearly. He watches as she sneaks in through the side door, flicking on her flashlight to guide her way.

"No," Nate murmurs. "Don't go in there. . . ."

He loses Victoria in the darkness. He sees the light of her flashlight up ahead of him, shining motionlessly from the floor. He reaches for it, takes it in his hand, shines its light around. He sees a body crumpled on the floor.

It's Victoria. In a pool of blood.

"Noooo!!!!"

But when he turns her over, it's Monica Paul.

No!

It's Jesus Ramos.

No!

It's Siobhan, and her eyes are open.

"You killed me, Nate," she says, her face blue.

"No!" Nate screams. He backs up. There's someone behind him. He spins around, shining the flashlight up into the face of his father, looming over him in an Oakland police force uniform.

"You are nothing but a failure as a police officer, Nathaniel," his father says. "Look at all the blood on your hands."

Nate looks down. His hands are indeed dripping with blood. He drops the flashlight. It clatters to the floor, snuffed out.

There is quiet.

Dear God, Nate realizes. *I'm having the dream. Somehow I'm having the dream!*

Footsteps approach him in the dark. Nate knows who it is.

Wake up! he commands himself. *Wake up!*

"Nate!"

A voice. Who is it?

"Not so fast," comes another voice. The voice of the man approaching him. A voice Nate recognizes.

Suddenly the flashlight pops back into life. But now it's held by the man standing in front of Nate. He points it upward so it illuminates his own face.

It's the man in black. The man who had come to the door of Nate's cottage.

It's Father John Fall.

"Finally, Nate Tuck," the creature says. "Finally you're mine."

"No," Nate groans.

"Nate!"

It's Catherine's voice. And now Kip's voice, too. And Chief's. And Job's.

They're trying to wake me up.

"I'll never be yours," Nate tells Father Fall. "Never!"

"We'll see about that," the demon says, grinning.

Nate tries not to look. But just before he forces his eyes to open, he sees the worms slithering in the creature's mouth. Except it's not Fall's mouth anymore. It's Siobhan's—and Nate realizes he's had a glimpse into her grave.

He screams, opening his eyes.

"Siobhan! Siobhan! I killed Siobhan!"

"Dear Lord," the chief says. "He fell asleep right in front of us! He's had the dream."

Nate breaks down sobbing. There's nothing to do now. He belongs to John Fall.

Friday, November 29, 9:01 A.M.

Father Roche sits alone in the rectory, having been abandoned by Agnes Doolittle. Catherine has been bringing him food and has encouraged him to join them at her house, but he's preferred to remain here.

"Are you praying at least?" Victoria asks, kneeling before him, taking his hand in hers.

He looks at her sadly. "I can't even find the will to do that."

"Father, you've got to try to help us. We need you." She pauses. "*I* need you. When I was a girl, you were the first one to give me hope after my family was killed. *Please*. I need you again."

"What can I possibly do? The Devil has won."

Victoria stands. "You have allowed him to sway your mind, that's all. He hasn't won. Every day more people are deserting him."

"But you say Nate has had the dream now. He has taken Nate. Who's to say the rest of us aren't next?"

Victoria walks over to the old priest's bookshelves. She runs a hand along the spines of the volumes stacked there. She remembers being in this room when she was a girl, a frightened child still in shock over the horror that had claimed her family. This room gave her comfort then, a feeling of safety being surrounded by these old books, the crucifix upon the wall.

"Look, Father, I want you to listen to me." She turns back

to face him. "Last night I made it into the old church. I felt something—or rather, I felt the *lack* of something. The last time I was there Father Fall's power and authority was awesome. It was almost a physical thing—it was so strong. But last night it wasn't there. So many people have now deserted him. He's *losing*, Father, and he knows it."

"I want to believe that," Father Roche tells her.

She walks back to him, taking his shoulders in her hands. "Then *believe!* Come with me now! We need you."

"I'm frightened," he says. "I'm an old man."

"We're all frightened, Father."

He looks at her. Victoria falls to her knees again, gripping his hands.

"Please, Father," she says.

Their eyes hold.

Friday, November 29, 11:15 A.M.

He listens, but he doesn't believe. Kip Hobart is talking with such passion. His hands are expressive, his eyes wild. Father Roche looks over at Chief Hutchins and Job Emerson, who are nodding their heads in agreement. Catherine Santos is offering historical commentary, explaining how Father Fall has been beaten in the past. But Father Roche just listens. Listens, but he doesn't believe.

They want him to perform an exorcism. He agreed to come here with Victoria, but he knows he doesn't have the power— the faith—they expect from him. They want him to recite the ancient ritual without permission from the bishop. But words are just words. James Roche knows that his words would be meaningless without faith behind them.

"Tonight," Kip is saying. "We must do it tonight."

"Yes," Catherine agrees. "Nate can't take much more."

"We're going to have to drug him," the chief says. "Poor kid's going up the walls."

Father Roche can hear Nate in the other room, pacing back and forth. Victoria comes out of the room now, carefully locking the door behind her.

"How is he?" Job asks.

"He's so incredibly strong," Victoria says. "It's eating him up, but he keeps trying to beat it back down."

"Has he asked for any drugs yet?" the chief inquires.

"No, not yet. But if we aren't successful in defeating Fall quickly, he'll need them." She pauses. "Though I'm still frightened of what that might do to his mind, for the dream is inside him. It's like a cancer, eating away at him until it can be cut out and passed on."

"The poor soul," Father Roche says. "But aren't you afraid he'll try to tell the dream to you while you're in there with him?"

Victoria looks at him. "No. Because he's not being compelled to tell it to me."

"Someone else, then," Father Roche says. "Do we know who?"

"Yes," Victoria says.

"Who, may I ask?"

Victoria levels her gaze at him. "You, Father. He feels compelled to tell it to you."

The old priest falls silent.

"You see?" Kip asks. "John Fall knows exactly who his enemies are. He's aware that we're trying to stop him. He's aware that you're taking this next step with us, Father. That's why we must act swiftly."

Father Roche just looks blankly from Kip back to Victoria. Behind the locked door he hears Nate scream in agony, thudding the wall with his fist.

"That poor, poor man," Father Roche says, overcome by the horror.

"I'm going to start preparing for the ritual," Kip announces. "Since all my papers were burned in the fire, I requested materials from a colleague in New York. They arrived at the post office this morning. I'm going over to pick them up. But I already know a few things that I'll need. A forked stick, a sprig of hemlock—Catherine, do you have them written down?"

"I do. And I'm on my way to gather them."

They head out to begin their preparations. Everyone's taken for granted that Father Roche will assist them. They assume he knows all the words to the Catholic rite of exorcism by heart. Father Roche sighs. Even if he possessed the faith to back up the words, he'd have to find the specific books of ritual to tell him what to do. He isn't even sure he has such books.

But it doesn't matter. He won't be performing any exorcism. He can't help them there.

But he may be able to help them in another way. . . .

He sits quietly, saying nothing, watching the group disband. Job has taken Jamal to visit his mother's grave. They will pray for her help in the task ahead of them. Chief Hutchins heads back to the station to check in with his officers on whether there's been any sighting of Miller. Now it's just Victoria left, and she looks down at Father Roche with gratitude in her eyes.

"I knew you wouldn't let us down," she says.

He doesn't reply.

"I'm heading over to the general store and then to the fire-house. Both Sam Drucker and Chipper Robin are wavering in their support for Fall. I think I can convince them—bring them back to themselves. Will you come with me, Father? They'll be more apt to listen to you. If we can take even a *couple* more away from him, we can reduce his power even more so that when we attempt the ritual tonight, we'll be sure to succeed."

He looks into her eyes. What help could he possibly be? How could he persuade others to fight the Devil when he himself can't do it?

"I need to stay here," Father Roche tells her. "I need to . . . prepare."

She nods. "All right, Father."

"Victoria," he says.

She looks back at him.

"The key to Nate's room. You ought to leave it."

"No," she says. "You're *not* to go in there, Father. Understand? It's too dangerous for you."

He tries to smile. "I'm simply concerned about an emergency. What if Fall were to set fire to *this* house, too? Nate would die in there."

She considers this. "Well, Catherine will be right back. She's only gone into the woods to gather a few things."

"Still," the old priest says. "Things happen very quickly."

Victoria sighs. She withdraws the key from her pocket and places it on the table. "All right. But please don't go in there, Father. If Nate should need anything, just tell him through the door Catherine will return any minute." She hesitates. "Maybe I ought to wait—"

"No, no, go, Victoria. It's good what you're doing. Talk to Sam and Chipper. I'll be fine here. So will Nate."

She thinks of something else. "And don't let him know it's you out here, Father. Don't let him hear your voice. He'll try to fight it, but remember, you're the one to whom he's supposed to pass the dream."

It's the only way, thinks Father Roche after she's gone. *The only way I can help them.*

The only way I can fight the beast.

He stands at the window and waits until he sees Victoria hurrying down the beach toward Main Street. Then he walks over to the table. He takes the key in his hand.

Catherine will return any minute.

"I don't have much time," Father Roche whispers to himself.

He slips the key into the lock and turns it.

The first thing he sees is Nate's face, panting at the door like a crazed dog. Father Roche pulls back instinctively, as if Nate is ready to pounce at him.

"No!" Nate shouts, suddenly withdrawing. "Who let you in here? Get the fuck out of here! You cocksucking fool! Get the fuck out of here!"

The language. Yes, it's a sign of the dream. A sign the Devil is trying to take control of Nate's mind.

"Get out!" Nate screams. "You're the one person who can't ever come in here! *Victoria!* Get this asshole out of here!"

"There remains enough of your soul to still rebel against what you feel compelled to do," Father Roche says. "Nate, you are a brave man."

"Get out!" Sweat drips off Nate's cheeks. "Don't you know how it's eating me up?"

"I *do* know, Nate. That's why I'm here."

Father Roche looks at the poor man. Nate's eyes are wide and bloodshot. His hair is tangled, matted down with sweat. He wears nothing but a ratty old tank top and sweatpants. He's been clawing his arms with his fingernails. Scraped skin and little tracks of dried blood stand out on his biceps and forearms.

"Get out," he cries pitifully. "Get out, get out, get out!"

Nate collapses into a chair, his hands on his head. He starts to heave with sobs.

Father Roche sits beside him, draping an arm over his shoulder. "It's all right, Nate. It's all right."

"No," Nate cries. "It's not all right."

"Go ahead, my good man. Tell me the dream."

"No . . ."

"It is burning inside you, needing to be released. I can't watch your torment, knowing he's using you to get to me. Let me take it from you."

Nate looks at him with wide, wild eyes. "Get out," he says in a little voice.

"Tell me the dream, Nate."

"Victoria!" he shouts, standing. "Victoria!"

"No one's here, Nate. Just you and me. Tell me the dream!"

Nate grabs him roughly by the shirt, lifting him up and pushing him against the wall. "Do you have any idea what you're asking for? The kind of *hell* you're asking to get?"

"Yes, Nate, I do," the priest insists. "Tell me the dream!"

"Fine! Goddamn it all to hell! I'll tell you the fucking dream!"

So Nate does. He tells him about the dead bodies, Siobhan in her grave, the man in black who is really John Fall. The Beast. The Devil, who will own them all.

When he's through, Nate collapses against the wall in a torrent of tears. Father Roche backs away, overcome. At that moment, Catherine Santos appears in the doorway, surmising what has just transpired. "Dear God, no."

"It's all right, Catherine," Father Roche assures her. He kneels down beside Nate and makes the sign of the cross over him. "You will be all right now, Nate Tuck. You have given me a great gift. You have given me back my faith."

He turns to leave. Catherine tries to stop him. "You can't go," she says. "We need to keep you here, keep you from falling asleep—"

"It's all right, Catherine," he says. "It's going to be all right."

He walks out of the room and down the stairs. He leaves Catherine's house, crossing the beach toward the town pier. Catherine picks up the phone and calls the chief.

* * *

"You thought you could claim my soul," Father Roche says into the cold, damp wind that howls in off Nantucket Sound. "But I'm stronger than you. I'm stronger than you because I have *faith*."

He stands at the very end of the pier. The fishing boats have all gone out for the day, and there are no tourists wandering about taking photographs of seals. Not anymore. Tourists no longer come to Falls Church.

Father Roche considers the twisted irony of the town's name. "Very soon, this town will no longer be yours," he promises the wind. "Soon you will have no one—no one at all—in your perverted church."

His voice sounds shrill in the cold rush of air that slaps his cheeks.

"Listen to me, John Fall! The god you claim is no god at all! The God of my faith is compassionate and tolerant and forgiving and accepting. Your god is one of hatred and greed and power and control. And your god no longer has power here!"

He looks down into the cold, roiling waters beneath the pier.

He knows the taking of one's own life is considered a sin in the Catholic religion. But he also knows that God—no matter what John Fall believes—does not set rules in strict black and white.

"I do this so that others might live," James Roche says into the wind. "I do this so that the horror might be ended, so that the power of the Beast is cast back to hell."

He takes one last breath.

"I do this with faith in the Lord my God."

Father Roche jumps.

Later, when his body is washed up onto the beach, a crowd gathers around it. Chief Hutchins finds them on their knees in the sand, praying silently. Manny Sousa, Tess Woodward, Fred and Lucille Pyle, the Reverend Wilfred Shanker and his wife, Mildred. And Agnes Doolittle, holding the dead man's hand to her lips and crying silently.

The chief joins them in prayer. "We will win," he whispers as he falls to his knees.

Father Roche's body is not bloated or blue. He seems merely asleep.

He has found peace at last.

Sunday, December 1, 12:00 P.M.

Alan Hitchcock and Cliff Claussen stand guard in front of the doors of the old church. "You can't come in here," Cliff barks. He thrusts a piece of paper at them. "The judge's order!"

The chief and Nate stand on the steps, looking up at them. "We know that, Cliff," the chief says. "We just hoped you might have come around. Changed your mind, like so many other folks."

"Never!" Claussen insists.

"Never!" Hitchcock echoes.

Father Roche's bravery has given them some time. The dream has been stopped dead. No further recruits will be brought over to Fall's side, and the number of his followers continues to dwindle. As word of the old priest's sacrifice spreads through town, a dozen more people have pulled away from Mark Miller's church. But some remain steadfast in their loyalty. The day after Roche's death, Cliff Claussen presented the chief with an order from a county court judge forbidding any further police action at the church. A hearing has been scheduled for two weeks from now. There the chief can make his case that he believes the church to be a crime scene and therefore his force needs access to it. But it's a claim refuted by much of the town government—Town Manager Alan Hitchcock and Selectwoman Mary Silva, especially, who remain fiercely devoted to Miller and who use their considerable influence with the courts to press for delays. They've vowed to keep the church as a holy sanctuary until which time the reverend is found and cleared of all charges.

That means Kip's exorcism is off for now—and with Father Roche freeing Nate from his agony, the ritual, in truth, has become less immediately urgent. Perhaps even unnecessary, Kip thinks, if they can continue to pull more townsfolk from Fall's control.

"Cliff, listen to me," Nate says now, standing on the church steps. "I had the dream, too. There are times I can see him still. I close my eyes and he's there. Grinning that horrible smile—the worms in his teeth! But, Cliff, I push him away when I see him—and others have, too. All over town people are pushing him away. Help us! Push him away! You too, Alan!"

They remain silently defiant.

"Come on, Nate," the chief says. "Let's go. They're lost causes. Even his wife leaving him hasn't moved Hitchcock."

They head back down the stairs. Nate looks across the church-yard. There's a woman approaching them. A woman he recognizes . . .

"No!" he shouts.

"What is it?" the chief asks.

"No!" Nate covers his eyes but can still see her. It's Monica Paul, covered in blood, walking through the old broken stones of the churchyard.

"It's another vision," the chief tells him, grabbing his hands away from his eyes. "He's doing this to you. Look again, Nate. Whatever you think you saw, it's not there."

Nate looks. The chief's right, of course. Monica Paul is dead and buried. But not in his mind. Father Fall can still get inside Nate's mind, tearing at his thoughts, playing havoc with his fears and memories. Even though Nate's fought off his control, he understands now the torment others who have had the dream have suffered. Jamal Emerson. Danny Correia. Clem Flagg. Cooper Pierce. Habib Khan.

It's given him more compassion toward the citizenry of Falls Church. *He plays with their secret fears, their worst nightmares,* Nate realizes. No wonder he has such a hold over them. And everybody who breaks free is actually triumphing over their own dread, their own fears and doubts about themselves.

We are stronger than what haunts us, he reminds himself. He prays that he won't forget that. Ever.

Thursday, December 5, 5:45 P.M.

"But we *always* put up our tree the first week of December," the child pleads. "Please, Daddy? Please, Mom?"

Laura Millay looks down at her youngest daughter, Nora. She breathes a silent prayer of gratitude that her children at least have been spared the dream. For some reason she thinks they're safe now, that the dream has been stopped, that the old priest's death meant that it won't come around to grab her children as she's feared. She prays desperately that she's right.

As if God can even hear my prayers anymore, Laura thinks bitterly.

"We will no longer be putting up a Christmas tree, not ever again," her husband, Roger, tells the children. "It is a pagan tradition. I won't allow it in my house."

The children beg and cry, but their father is unmoving. Their mother retreats to the large picture window, looking down the cliffs over the village. Laura can see the pier, the spire of Town Hall, the steeple of the old church. The sun has set. Falls Church is bathed only in moonlight, obscured by shadows.

"It *is* peculiar," she muses aloud, "looking down at the town this time of year without all its holiday lights. By now, it's usually so festive, so full of color."

"A blasphemy, and you know it," Roger scolds. "Alan Hitchcock and the selectmen were right to forbid it. It's what Reverend Miller would have wanted."

She looks at him. Roger's eyes are hard, cold—the way they've been ever since he had the dream. The way hers look when she studies them in the mirror. Laura turns away from her husband, looking back down over the sorry little village. Why can't they break free? Others have. Kathy McKenzie. Pidge Hitchcock. Right next door, Pat Crawford has told Laura that ever since Sargent came home she no longer wants to go down to the church. "It's not right," Pat said. "We have to take back our town." Yvette Duvalier has said the same thing. "Reverend Miller has done some bad, bad things, Laura," Yvette insisted. "I'm glad he's gone."

But he's *not*. Even those who claim to have broken free of him aren't really free. Laura has heard Pat Crawford's screams in the night. She sees how Yvette and Paul stay hidden in their house, afraid to venture outside. And Claudio—Claudio had tried to break free, hadn't he? Look at what happened to him.

Poor Claudio, she thinks. *Poor Claudio.*

"There's an evil in this town," Sargent Crawford told her a few days ago as he closed the office. He had to. Business had declined so much that Seaside Realty may be forced into bankruptcy. "I've seen it, Laura. I saw it while I was in my coma. I saw the evil that has taken hold here. An evil that has gripped people's minds."

"It's not evil, Sargent," Laura told him. "We have simply seen the light of truth and—"

"Cut the bullshit, Laura. Pat tried that with me at first, too. But you can break free. Both you and Roger! You must break free."

Must break free . . .

She looks back over at her children, sitting dejectedly, turning Christmas ornaments over and over in their hands. Ornaments that won't hang from any tree this year.

My children . . .

Must break free . . .

What would happen if she just left? Kathy McKenzie had left. Taken her boy and left town. Nothing's happened to her—not as far as Laura knows. If Kathy McKenzie can do it, why can't she?

She waits throughout the night. She watches as the children totter off to bed, sniffling a little. She watches as Roger falls dead asleep on the couch in the den, the way he's done ever since having the dream. He's come to view sleeping with a woman—even his own wife—as immoral. Laura waits, unmoving by the door, listening to the steady rise and fall of his buzz saw snoring.

Then she hurries into the children's rooms, wakes them up, tells them to put on their sneakers and coats. "No time to get dressed," she whispers. "We're going to a party. A Christmas party! And it can't wait."

"Daddy too?" Nora asks, rubbing her eyes.

"No, dear. Daddy's sleeping. You mustn't wake him."

She hustles them out to the car. The two older ones slip into the backseat; Nora sits up front. Laura walks around the car and carefully lifts the garage door, fearful at any moment that Roger might awaken. She notices it's started to snow lightly. She's always fearful of driving in the snow.

"Where are you going?"

She gasps. Roger is standing outside. He's dressed in a coat and boots. Snow has collected on his shoulders and his hair. It's as if—as if he was waiting for her to do this!

"What are you doing out here?" she asks her husband.

"I asked you first," he says calmly.

"Mommy, are we going to the party?" Nora calls from the passenger window.

"A party?" Roger asks. "At this time of night?"

Laura grabs him by his coat. "If you love your children, you'll let me take them away from here!"

"You know parties are immoral," Roger says dispassionately. "Were you planning on corrupting our children?"

"Let us go, Roger."

"Oh, no. I couldn't allow you to corrupt our children the way you've corrupted yourself." He reaches into his coat pocket and removes some photographs. Laura recognizes them. They're the ones she's seen in her dream. She and Claudio in various stages of fornication. "Shall I show the children what a whore their mother is?"

"No!" She grabs his arm. The photographs flutter down into the snow. Roger laughs at her.

"I'll take the children away," he tells her. "Though not to a party, of course."

He snatches the keys from her hand.

"Roger, no! Don't hurt them. Don't let him get to them! You've got to protect them. You're their father!"

He looks at her with contempt. "*Am* I?"

She grabs his arm. "Where are you taking them?"

"Go inside, Laura. There's someone waiting to see you."

"No," she moans.

Roger smiles. "I've made a deal with him. I get to take the children away, but he gets to have you."

She looks up at the door into the house.

"Go on, Laura," he tells her. "He's waiting."

Roger walks around to the driver's side and slides in behind the wheel. Laura hears the children ask if they're still going to the party, if Mommy is coming, too. She doesn't hear Roger's answer. He turns the ignition and backs down the driveway. Laura watches them drive away through the snow, Nora's little hand waving good-bye.

I'll run. I'll run down into the town. I'll go to the chief of police. I'll go to Catherine Santos's house . . .

But she can't. Without the maternal instinct to drive her, Laura no longer has the strength to flee. She turns and walks back into the house.

Mark Miller is waiting there for her. But he looks different. He's aged—the bright, youthful gleam in his eyes is gone. His face is sallow and lined. When he reaches out his hands toward her, she sees he is trembling.

"I knew *you* wouldn't desert me, Laura," he says. "Not after all we've shared together."

He draws her to him, fondling her breasts, moving his face close to her neck.

She steels herself in his grip, summoning the last reserves of her will. "And each time you had sex with me," she says, "each time you had sex with Kathy McKenzie or any of the others, you hated yourself for it."

He releases her, pulling back to glare at her, arching his eyebrows in surprise. "You speak nonsense," he growls.

"No. I speak the truth." She tears open her blouse, revealing her breasts. "There. This is what you want, isn't it? This is what drives your lustful desires. Your need for flesh. Your *sin*!"

"How dare you!"

"I *dare*—in the name of all those who have been victimized, John Fall! How many have there been over the centuries since you killed your wife?"

His face goes white and he bares his teeth. "Do not mention Abigail!"

"I will! I will mention Abigail—who you pushed down the stairs! You killed her, John Fall! I know! I have seen! Through you, I have been permitted to see so much."

He growls at her. "Say no more."

"What was it that turned you into a monster, John Fall? Who taught you to hate? Who taught you to fear your humanity?"

"Stop it!" he cries, covering his ears.

"How many have suffered because of your pain, John Fall? How many more—how many more like poor Constance Ward—on whom you blamed your own sin, trying to burn her at the stake as a witch?"

He backhands her hard across the face. She falls into a table, knocking it over, smashing a lamp. He looms over her. "You filthy tramp!" he rasps, and his face changes as he looks down at her. All trace of the young man who came to Falls Church dissolves. He becomes a grotesque walking corpse, his flesh stinking, rotting off. His eyes protrude from his skull. Maggots eat through his skin.

"Constance Ward *was* a witch! She bewitched me! Just as Abigail did! Just as you have! If I commit sin, it is because of you! You witch! You whore! You temptress! It's the only explanation for what I have done—"

"Stay away from me," Laura begs.

"I cannot help . . . my sin—"

The filthy creature bears down upon her, its cold hands grabbing her breasts.

Outside, the falling snow grows heavier by the minute. It muffles but does not completely obscure the pitiful last scream of Laura Millay.

Thursday, December 5, 10:45 P.M.

It's begun, the voice tells her.

Victoria is asleep. She knows that voice. She struggles to see, but something's in her way, something enormous, something white.

It's snow, she realizes. *I'm walking in a snowstorm.*

"Over here," comes the voice.

Victoria trudges through the snow. Where is she? She's on a road. But she can't make out the place. Several yards ahead of her there's a figure beckoning to her. She doesn't feel frightened, just confused, as she strains her eyes through the blowing blizzard to make out the person's face.

It's the lay of the land that she finally recognizes, not the snow-covered structures along the side of the road.

I'm in Falls Church, Victoria thinks. *There, behind me, are the cliffs—but no trophy homes line their ridge. There, in front of me, is the pier—but where is the bait shop? Sousa's fish market? The boat excursion kiosks?*

"Victoria, you must hurry," the figure calls again.

It's a woman. Victoria can see her more clearly now—and suddenly realizes she's in Falls Church as it existed more than *three hundred years ago.*

When John Fall was very much alive.

"Who are you?" she calls to the woman.

The figure just points. Victoria follows the direction of her finger through the blustery snow. She points to a small building surrounded by farmland. It's not a building Victoria recognizes, but she knows what it is. It's Father Fall's original church. The churchyard beside it is new, with only a few stones erected.

"Why?" Victoria asks. "Why am I here?"

Suddenly she's aware that the woman is standing behind her. Victoria turns quickly.

It's Alexis. Her enormous eyes seem to burn holes through the heavy falling snow.

"Look inside the church, Victoria," Alexis tells her.

She turns to look back at the structure. Time and space and logic have no bearing on dreams, and Victoria now stands inside, the front doors flung open, snow whipping into the nave and the wind howling through the eaves. There are people pushing all around her. Men in colonial costume, with their high black buckled hats and frock coats. They're angry. They call out, "Fall!" From below, there comes a horrifying scream. The men hurry down the stairs, their boots tracking snow everywhere.

Victoria follows. There, in the earthen basement of the church, smelling of soil and fruit and great stacks of hay, she sees John Fall, a torch held aloft in his right hand. He is dressed all in black. His eyes are wild. In front of him he holds a woman, his left arm crooked around her neck, as if using her as a shield from the marauders.

"Give her unto us, Fall!" the leader of the men demands. "Give Constance to us!"

"She is a witch!" Fall shrills. "She is touched by Satan! She must die!"

"You are the only devil here!" another man shouts. "Give us the woman."

"She must die, if I must set the torch myself!"

Victoria screams, "No!" But she is not really there—just a witness to the horror. She watches as Fall puts the torch to Constance's dress. The flames quickly lap up her skirts. The poor woman screams in terror and pain. Victoria watches as the men descend upon her, trying to stamp out the flames, but Fall uses his torch to set fire to first one man and then another, and then finally to himself. It takes only seconds for the flames to jump to the stacks of hay and from there to the timbers of the church floor above. Victoria watches as the burning figures writhe in the flames, a terrible and yet graceful dance of death.

She sits up in bed.

"Dear God," she says. "The end is here."

She hurries from her room to Kip's, waking him up roughly. "We've got to assemble the others. It's time!"

He looks at her with uncomprehending eyes.

"It's time!" Victoria says again. "We've got to get down to the old church."

Friday, December 6, 6:03 A.M.

The sun isn't quite up yet when they all gather at Catherine's. The snow has continued to build through the night. At least three feet are on the ground and the forecast calls for another seven.

"It's a nor'easter," Catherine says, pouring them all coffee. "Never seen it so bad this early in December."

Nate takes his cup, allowing the brew to invigorate him. He's spent the past few days catching up on sleep, but he still has a hard time waking up. "Why do you think this is the end?" he asks Victoria. "Look, I want it to be over as much as anyone, but why now? Why is today Fall's last stand?"

"Alexis wouldn't have shown me that vision for no reason," Victoria says.

Kip smiles. "And if there's one thing we've learned, it's to pay attention to our dreams."

Catherine nods. "There's another reason to think this is it. Although the documents were burned in the fire, I remember very clearly that it was on December sixth that Fall killed Constance Ward and burned down his church in the process. So it all makes sense."

They all agree. "Put two and two together," Danny Correia says, nodding his head, "and you get four."

Victoria reaches over and squeezes his hand, giving him a smile.

"Well, the first thing is to stake out the old church," the chief says, looking at his two officers.

"But what about that judge's order?" Job asks.

The chief shrugs. "We'll just have to defy it. Besides, with the storm so bad, there's no way they can send in any sheriffs to stop us. If this is indeed the end, by the time they come to serve us any papers, our job will be done."

Nate sighs. "So what is it we're expecting him to do? Appear at the church and make one final pitch to his followers?"

Kip shakes his head. "Remember what it is he *really* wants. Unrest. Turmoil. Violence. Hatred." He looks around at each of them. "He can only succeed if he gets people riled up again against each other. Our job is to keep that from happening. I think Victoria's right. If we can prevent him from stirring up trouble today, I think we've finally won."

Just then, there's a loud rapping at the door. They all look at each other. "Who could be here so early?" Nates asks. Outside the window, daylight is still very new, only weakly claiming the sky through the blowing snow.

Catherine opens the door.

"Miss Santos, is Chief here?"

It's Sargent Crawford. The realtor just back from a long stay in the hospital. Catherine nods, stepping aside so he can enter.

Sargent doesn't act surprised to see them all gathered together around the table. He greets each of them in turn, then faces the chief.

"How did you know I was here?" the chief asks.

"I know a lot of things I can't explain," Sargent says. "While I was in my coma, I saw many things. I've waited to contact you because I wanted to make certain my family was safe. I think they are—but the same can't be said about others."

Nate eyes him with some suspicion. "How do we know we can trust you?"

Sargent doesn't respond. Instead, he keeps his eyes on the chief. "Tell me, Chief Hutchins, did your wife make it back to say good-bye to you? To warn you of what was happening?"

"Hey, now," Nate says, defensive of the chief's emotions. "Why are you bringing up Ellen?"

"It's okay, Nate," Chief says. "Yes, Sargent, she did. How do you know?"

"I saw her. I saw many things when I was asleep."

"We trust our dreams," Kip reminds the group.

"What is it you want to tell us, Sargent?" Job asks.

He looks around at all of them again. "I just came to give you all a message. I have no idea what it means, except that I'm supposed to give it to you. I saw a woman in my dream, horribly burned. Does that mean anything to you?"

"Constance Ward," Catherine says.

"She was insistent that I remember what she said. *He's in the basement of the church.* I don't know who *he* is, but I imagine it's that minister. Reverend Miller. The cause of all this."

The chief nods. "She means John Fall, but it's the same thing." He sighs. "I thank you for the information, Sargent, but we already knew that. What we need to do is get into that subbasement somehow. That's where we'll find him. Now I'm sure of it."

"There's one other thing," Sargent says sadly. "Laura Millay is dead. I heard a scream in the night and went next door to check. I'm sure he killed her. Miller—Fall—whoever. Nothing human could destroy a person in that way."

"Then it's already started," Victoria says. "Just as we feared."

Chief Hutchins calls the station and has a couple of his new officers—hired now as permanent, given the loss of Rusty and Dean—attend to the Millay crime scene. There's no need for him—or Nate or Job, for that matter—to see it yet. They already know who Laura's killer is. They also already know *where* he is. Their job now is to make sure he doesn't kill again.

Friday, December 6, 12:02 P.M.

Shortly after the noon hour, the snow turns to ice. And as it does several times each winter in storms like these, Falls Church becomes an island, cut off from the rest of the Cape—from the rest of the world, in fact. The one road leading into town is iced over. The sea is too choppy for any boat to navigate safely. A tree falls across Main Street up near Dave's Sunoco, bringing down power lines and cutting off electricity and telephones to the town.

Few islands are even as isolated as this.

Hail the size of golf balls hammers the roofs of the village. Fierce winds blow drifts of snow ten and eleven feet high. People stay inside their homes, huddled close to their fireplaces.

Town Manager Alan Hitchcock sits, brooding alone, in his house on Center Street, despondent over his wife's leaving him. He's been up all night, in fact, watching the snow come down. He sits in his chair, wringing his hands over the split in the church, the defections of so many. "I'm left with nothing," he mumbles. "If the reverend doesn't come back, they'll all find out how I embezzled money from the town. I'm all alone. The church is gone. The church is gone."

He closes his eyes. He sees Reverend Miller.

"And who can be blamed for that, Alan?" the reverend asks. "Come, Alan, you know who's to blame. See the light of truth and wisdom!"

Alan thinks. He ponders. *Who is to blame?*

Suddenly he knows!

It's the damned Portuguese who are to blame!

Alan stands up, fired by the idea.

The damned Portuguese—all the Sousas and Silvas and Duartes—all related to each other, convincing each other to drop out of the church. They're the real reason the reverend lost his power. Oh, how I've hated them—with their little cliques, their secret family deals. Oh, yes, it's the Portuguese— I hate the Portuguese!

He grabs his gun from his top desk drawer.

"And I hate Mary Silva most of all." He spits.

Of course, Mary Silva hadn't dropped out of the church— she remained devoted to the reverend—but that's not important. Alan decides she has to die. He trudges out into the snow, not even bothering to put on a coat, making his way across the street, leaving three-foot-deep footprints as he walks. He bangs on Helen Twelvetrees's door and persuades her it's all the fault of the Portuguese. "Everything!" he exclaims. "Everything's their fault! Even this blizzard!"

She agrees—she never did like that liberal bitch Catherine Santos—so, after watching Alan trudge off down the street, heading God know's where, Helen hurries over to Sam Drucker's to convince him, too, of the Portuguese guilt. But Sam isn't so sure, telling Helen that she ought to join him in rejecting Miller's power. "His time is up," Sam says. "The handwriting's on the wall."

"How dare you!" Helen shouts. "You—you deformed freak! From that hand I should have known you were a traitor."

She lunges at him. Neither is very spry anymore, but each puts up a good fight, scratching and punching and rolling through the snow.

Off by the woods, watching it all, a figure in black has a good laugh.

Several shots ring out down by the wharf, and when Joe and Angie Sousa rush outside their house to investigate, they see Alan Hitchcock running out of Mary Silva's house next door.

"You damned Portuguese!" the town manager yells. "You're next!"

He takes several shots at them but misses, the snow blinding him.

"Jesus Christ!" Joe shouts, telling his wife to stay down. He watches as Alan runs off down the street, then lets himself into Mary's house. The old woman is dead in a pool of blood on her kitchen floor.

"You did this!" comes a shout behind him.

Joe spins around. It's Mary's brother, Hiram.

"No," Joe says. "It wasn't me—"

"You've been fighting her for months. You hated her!"

"No," Joe says. "It was Alan Hitchcock—"

But Hiram isn't listening. He leaps at Joe, throttling him around the neck. Joe tries to pull him off but can't. And to his horror, he sees Mark Miller, standing in Mary's doorway, arms folded across his chest, laughing.

"Nate," the chief's voice crackles over the car phone, "tell Kip and the others to get to the church. It's starting. I just got a call that both Mary Silva and Joe Sousa have been found dead."

"Christ," Nate says. He's just back from responding to a call of a disturbance at Sam Drucker's house. Helen Twelvetrees—the fiftysomething old maid librarian—had *attacked* him. Jumped at him, scratched up his face. Nate had pulled them apart but issued no arrest. The woman isn't in her right mind. He simply ordered her back to her house, telling her if she dared step foot outside again today, he'd throw her in jail. That seemed to scare her, and she retreated.

He calls Kip now on his cell phone. The reception is bad, but he gets through, telling him to head over to the church and he'll join them there. "But be prepared," he warns. "Some of these folks are going to defend Fall to the death if need be."

Driving isn't easy in this storm. Nate's wipers barely keep his windshield free of snow. His tires slip and slide. Public Works Director Adam Carver clearly hadn't ordered any plows out onto the road today. No, that would defeat their goals. Carver's under Fall's control, too. They want to make this as difficult as possible. What better way to let chaos reign than to cut off the town's electricity during an ice storm and keep the roads unsanded and unplowed?

Finally Nate can travel no more. The drifts are too high as he tries to turn onto Main Street. He gets out of his car to walk the rest of the way.

The icy rain slaps his face. He pulls his coat tighter around him, raising the collar to shield his face as best as he can. As he passes Woodward's Pharmacy, he witnesses a shouting match between Tess Woodward and Max Winn. "Hey," Nate snarls. "Stop acting like children."

Max grabs him by the coat. "You're with us now, aren't you, Nate? You've had the dream, haven't you?"

Nate nods slowly, deciding to play along. "Yes, Max. I've had the dream."

"Just as I thought. So you've got to join us. Tess won't listen anymore. Too many are dropping out, and we need all the support we can get. Nate, you've got to join us!"

"Join you in what?"

Max looks around, then speaks again. "Alan Hitchcock is right. It's the Portuguese who are to blame. If we can defeat the Portguese, everything will be better again in Falls Church. All of this bad luck will end, and the reverend will come back."

Nate eyes him craftily. "So what do we need to do?"

Malice dances in the beady little eyes of the wizened old tax assessor. "We have to kill them. Kill them all."

Nate nods. "Come with me to the station, Max. I'll give you a gun."

"Yes!" Max Winn claps his hands. "Oh, yes! I can shoot those swine! Put bullets right between their eyes! Oh, I've always hated them!"

But at the station Nate merely locks Max in one of the holding cells not damaged in the explosion. He says nothing as he does so, paying no attention to the old man's crazed rantings. He has to hurry. The town is coming apart.

"You cannot enter here," Cliff Claussen tells Kip and Victoria, standing in front of the doors to the old church.

"Oh, yes, they can," Job tells him, coming around from the

side of the church. He has his pistol aimed at Claussen. "Step aside, Cliff."

"You're defying a judge's orders! Pulling a gun on me, abusing your power!"

"You can file charges on Monday," Job says, coming up the stairs and nudging the attorney aside. He opens the doors, gun held out in front of him as he quickly makes sure it's safe to enter. Then he motions for Kip and Victoria to follow.

It's getting close to three o'clock and the ice and drifting are getting worse, if that's possible. *The whole Cape must be shut down by now,* Victoria thinks as she steps inside the church. She shudders. *We're all alone. It's just him and us now.*

"What's taking the chief and Nate so long?" Kip asks.

Job shakes his head. "Situations are springing up all over town. They've got their hands full."

"We'll have to start without them then," Victoria says.

"But not here. We need to go downstairs. We need to find a way into the basement beneath the church hall."

"I'll be back!" Cliff Claussen warns. "And I'll bring others with me! We won't let you do anything to harm our church!"

"I'd better call for some backup," Job says, taking out his phone. "Whether anybody's available to come, however, remains to be seen."

The three of them start down the stairs.

"Listen to me," Hiram Silva says. "They're after us. That traitor Joe Sousa killed my sister. Of course I had to kill him for it. But they made Joe do it. They made him turn against his own."

"Who?" asks Hiram's cousin Manny Duarte. "Who made him kill Mary?"

"All them rich folk, all them out-of-towners who've come and destroyed our town."

Hiram's face is flushed from the cold. He ran all the way across town, pushing through ice and snow, to get to his nephew Brian Silva's house, where he knew an emergency meeting of the faithful was being held.

"I can see the reverend in my head," Hiram continues. "He's telling me who's to blame. It's those snot noses up on the cliffs. Cooper Pierce. Sargent Crawford. The Duvaliers. Roger Millay. And especially Richie Rostocki, that damned developer.''

"But Richie—and Roger and Pat Crawford and even Yvette—have all been good members of the church, followers of the reverend," objects another of Hiram's cousins, Connie Sousa, mother of Dean. "My son says we're all just being suckered in—that we're just being given scapegoats—"

"Is that what you believe, Connie?" Hiram demands, getting up close in her face.

She starts to cry. "I—I just don't know anymore. I want to believe; I really want to believe that the reverend will come back, that everything will be good again—"

"It *will* be good," Hiram says. "The reverend promised me it would, so long as we all stay faithful. Too many have been dropping out, like your son and your sister, Marge!"

"Traitors," says another cousin, Sammy Sousa.

In all, there are nine of them there. Nine angry, frightened people. "We can bring the reverend back, and we can restore Falls Church to its glory," Hiram assures them. "The reverend told me we could."

"How?" asks Brian Silva.

"Those people on the cliffs," Hiram says, his eyes growing wide. "They—and their trophy homes—have to be destroyed."

"I think this is where the chief said he saw the ghost of Priscilla Googins," Kip says, standing in the easternmost corner of the church hall. "So there must be an entrance near here to the floor below."

Victoria looks around. There's no door, no panel. Just white-washed walls and an unbroken hardwood floor. "But where?" she asks.

"You're standing on it," comes a voice.

They spin around. Richie Rostocki has just come down the stairs. "I helped Miller draw up these plans," the developer tells them. "I had to come here and try to help you when Cliff called me, trying to rally the forces to protest."

"So you've pulled out from Miller's control," Victoria says.

Rostocki looks at her. "I'm trying. I think most of us are. Only a few are still diehards like Cliff."

"Well, there are enough of those diehards to keep the police force busy today," Job says.

"There's a trapdoor right below here," Rostocki tells them, bending down. Sure enough, when they examine the floor, there's a very faint square outline. The developer pounds on it with his switch. Something unlatches below and the square moves up a quarter of an inch.

"If you lift this," he explains, gripping it by the edge, "you'll find it reveals a ladder going down."

Rostocki steps backward.

"Why didn't you open it?" Kip asks.

"Because I can't. Because he's still inside my head." He closes his eyes. "I can't do any more than that."

Job looks from him to the others. "I'll go down. I'm not sure if I trust this guy."

"Shouldn't we wait then?" Victoria asks. "If this is a trap—"

But Job has managed to lift the panel on its hinges. A ladder leading down into the darkness below is revealed.

"Well, so far he's telling the truth," Job observes.

"That's the last truth he'll ever tell!"

It's the voice of Cliff Claussen. Without any other warning he fires a gun he holds in his hands. Richie Rostocki clutches his chest and drops to the floor. It all happens in an instant. Just as Cliff turns the gun on them, Job fires back at him, hitting him in the shoulder, sending the attorney sprawling into the wall.

But there are others arriving now behind him. Paul Stoddard. Edmond Tyler. Carolyn Prentiss. Dicky Sikorski. Tim Lipnicki. A handful of others.

"We won't let you harm our church!" Carolyn Prentiss shouts.

If it all has seemed like a movie so far, the presence of the famous film actress only makes the situation more unreal. These newcomers are glazed-over zombies—crazed and vicious. Yet none of them are armed, Victoria sees, and since she's managed to retrieve Cliff's gun for herself, there's little they can do.

"We're going down," Kip tells Job. "You'll have to stay here and keep this mob from following us."

"I can't let you go alone, " Job says. "You don't know what's down there."

"Oh, we know," Kip says. "We know all too well what's down there."

He takes the first step of the ladder, armed with nothing more than a forked stick and some herbs. Victoria follows, with the gun.

As the sun sets, the wind has stopped. The snow and ice have ceased falling. A cold stillness descends over Falls Church. This night, most of the town will live by candlelight. But up on Cliff Heights, the windows of the homes burn as gaily as ever with generator-powered light.

Hiram Silva chuckles.

"That's not all they'll burn with," he says.

He whispers the command. "Now!" Two accomplices splatter gasoline all along the walls of the first home on the ridge. Only two of his cousins have had the balls to accompany him, the others suddenly turning chicken, renouncing their ties to Miller and his church, claiming it has all gone too far now.

Hiram will deal with them later.

"Torch it!" Brian Silva says, and a blowtorch sets the wooden shingles ablaze.

They hurry through the snow to the next yard, covered by darkness. Once more, gasoline is thrown, this time at Sargent Crawford's house. Once more, the flame is set, and once more, the band of arsonists trudges through snowbanks to reach the next house.

They do not fear apprehension by the police. Their only motivation to avoid being caught is because it would mean their task would remain incomplete. In all, they set fire to four homes that night, the Duvaliers' house across the street and finally the deserted home of Roger Millay. By the time they try torching their fifth, sirens are sounding in the night, and Pat Crawford and her children have run out of their house to safety. The owner of the fifth house, too, has come outside, and he has spotted the culprits just as they are about to finish their task.

"Hiram Silva!" shouts Cooper Pierce. "What is going on?"

"We're taking back our town," Hiram tells him, his face made hideous by the red glow of the fires along the street.

"You've gone mad," Cooper says.

His wife, Miranda, is behind him, trying to tear him away. "Cooper, let's just go! We should've left weeks ago! Let's just go before it's too late!"

"No," Cooper tells her. "I've run away from conflict for too long. It's time I stood up for myself." He takes a step forward. "This is my home! I have every much of a right to be here as anyone. I've worked hard. I've paid my dues!" He looks in horror at the flames leaping into the night sky. "You're going to pay for this, Hiram Silva!"

He makes a charge for the three arsonists. They scatter, suddenly terrified by Cooper's fury. He pursues Hiram, who's too old to run very fast. At the edge of Cliff Heights, Hiram stumbles, and Cooper is on him.

"Listen to me, Hiram," Cooper demands, pinning the old man down by his shoulders. "Fight him off! Fight the monster in your mind! You can win!"

"No!" Hiram cries. "He promised everything would get better! He said I'd be a man again! He said my daughter, Rose, would live again!"

"He lies!" Cooper shouts. "He lies!"

"No!" Hiram screams with all his might, and shoves Cooper hard. Cooper falls backward but manages to grab ahold of Hiram's leg. They lose their balance. The snow under them gives way. From the top of Cliff Heights, they both plunge into the freezing waters of the harbor, some two hundred feet below. Their screams echo all through the town.

And on the icy, windswept beach, looking up at the fires rending the night sky, Father Fall watches it all and laughs.

Nate gets to Betty Silva's house just in time. She had remembered his cell phone number, thank God, and called to say that someone was trying to break into her house.

"Drop your gun, Hitchcock!" Nate shouts, coming into Bet-

ty's house just as the town manager levels his weapon at the
terrified woman's head. "Drop it now or you're a dead man."

Alan Hitchcock obeys. Betty runs to Nate, who motions her
into the living room, out of harm's way.

"He w-wanted to kill me!" Betty stammers. "He said he
was killing all the Portuguese! He—he said he'd already killed
Mary Silva!"

"Is that true, Mr. Town Manager?"

Alan looks at him as if he doesn't understand the question.

"Turn around," Nate orders. "Look out that window. Look
up on the hill. Up on Cliff Heights. Do you see, Alan? It's all
ablaze. This whole town is burning up, destroying itself. You
want to be a part of that?"

Indeed, outside the window, red and orange flames light up
the night sky. Betty Silva is crying. Alan Hitchcock watches
the fire for several moments, then sinks to his knees, sobbing
himself.

"What's happened to me?" he wails, covering his head with
his arms. *"What's happened to me?"*

Nate secures the town manager's hands behind him in handcuffs. "You're going to have to walk with me, Alan. The roads
aren't passable to drive. I'm going to take you to the station."
He helps the sobbing man to his feet.

"Nate," Betty says, grasping his arm. "Hiram's out there
somewhere. He's not right in his mind. None of us are."

He looks at her with compassion.

"I am so sorry, Nate," she says in a tiny voice. "I have
become something I loathe."

"Not anymore," Nate tells her. "You'll see, Betty. Tomorrow everyone will be back to normal."

That is, if anyone's still left alive after this night is over, he
thinks, leading Alan Hitchcock out into the snow. *And will*
normal *ever mean the same thing again—once the people of*
Falls Church look around and see what they've done?

"Yes," Victoria says, peering through the dark with her
flashlight. "This is the place."

They're in the original basement, the old fruit cellar, of the old church. It's cold and wet down here, with earthen walls and rotting timbers.

"This is the place I saw in my dream. This is where John Fall died."

Kip lets out a cold breath. "Then this is where we need to conduct the exorcism."

"You believe it will work this time?"

He nods. "Fall is so much weaker now than he was when we tried last time. There's only a handful of people upstairs trying to defend him. Everyone else has turned away from him."

"Shouldn't we wait for Nate and the chief, though? If anything happens, Job is alone up there with them."

Kip considers it. "We can't wait long. It's getting late now. What time is it?"

Victoria moves the flashlight to illuminate her watch. "Almost eleven."

"Why are they so late? What's going on in town that we don't know about?"

That's when they hear the laughter. Low at first, the sound of mice scurrying along the timbers. But it becomes louder and more pronounced: the laughter of a madman.

Victoria swings the flashlight beam through the darkness. It reveals the rotting corpse of John Fall, sitting against the far wall in his tall black hat. He's laughing at them.

Saturday, December 7, 12:01 A.M.

On Cliff Heights all of the homes except Cooper Pierce's have been severely damaged by fire. It took more than thirty minutes for the first fire engine to reach the blaze, struggling up the steep icy hill. By then, most of the damage had already been done. Although Sargent Crawford got his family out in time and no one was home at the Millays', others weren't so lucky. Yvette and Paul Duvalier burned in their beds, Linda Rostocki died of smoke inhalation, and a frantic Miranda Pierce told the chief that she watched in horror as her husband and Hiram Silva fell over the cliff. They're presumed dead as well.

It has been a night of madness. At the station, the holding cell is full: Max Winn, Alan Hitchcock, Manny Duarte, Brian Silva, each to be booked on charges ranging from intent to do bodily harm to arson and murder. In the back room, a makeshift morgue has been set up, where the bodies of Mary Silva, Joe Sousa, Linda Rostocki and Laura Millay await removal to Bourne once the roads are cleared.

The winds have died down now. The snow has ceased its terrible blowing. An eerie quiet settles over the town. Finally Nate and Chief Hutchins make their way to the old church.

"I'm glad you're here," Job tells them as they enter the hall. "This crowd is getting ugly."

Fall's ragtag group of supporters mutter among themselves.

"Dear Lord," the chief groans upon seeing the dead body

of Richie Rostocki sprawled out on the floor. "How much more can we take?"

"As much as he will give!" shouts the wounded Cliff Claussen, cradling his shoulder. Someone's knotted a tourniquet around his upper arm. "Our master will return and deal with you all!"

The mob of people push forward. Nate keeps them back with his gun. He scans their faces. All as glassy-eyed as Alan Hitchock. Among them there's the kindly repairman Paul Stoddard. Everybody's favorite bartender, Dicky Sikorski. Baby-faced Tim Lipnicki. And—Nate's eyebrows rise—Carolyn Prentiss, world-famous movie star.

"If one of you even makes the slightest move, you're going down," Nate tells them. "You have my word on that. I've been through just about enough tonight."

The chief has stooped down to call through the trapdoor in the floor. "Have you started?" he asks.

"We're just about to begin," Kip answers. "We're looking at him, face-to-face."

Nate's blood runs cold. *He's down there. Father Fall is down there with Victoria.*

"You can't let them do this," Carolyn Prentiss begs. "Please. It will only make things worse."

Nate throws her a look. "Half the town's burned down; I've got dead bodies left and right. Lady, even a Hollywood movie can't make it worse than that."

He hears Kip beginning the incantation below.

"John Fall!"

Kip's voice rises up through the floorboards.

"Your time has come! You must face the reckoning of the living!"

Fall's followers begin to tremble and moan.

"I abjure thee; I repudiate your power!" Kip's voice is loud and strong. "Your hold over this place is ended!"

"Make him stop," Carolyn begs. "Oh, *please*, make him stop!"

Nate keeps his gun trained on them.

"Odious and contemptuous spirit, I command you to depart! By the judge of the quick and the dead, by your Maker and the

Maker of all things, depart this place in haste! Your restless, hostile spirit shall no longer hold power here!''

There's laughter. Hideous laughter from below. Suddenly the church shakes, as if hit by a tremendous gust of wind. *Just like last time,* Nate thinks, his heart beating high in his ears. A scream cuts through the night. *Not a scream of the living,* he remembers Alexis telling him. *It is an echo of one of the screams of the many who have died in this place.*

It's quiet now below. Nate turns, gesturing to the chief, who stands at the trapdoor. "Call down to Victoria," he says. "Are they okay down there?"

The chief peers down through the door. It's dark. Victoria's flashlight no longer cuts a swath through the blackness.

"Kip?" the chief calls. "Victoria?"

"Can you see them?" Nate shouts anxiously. "Are they all right?"

"I can't see anything," the chief says, moving his flashlight into the panel.

"Victoria!" Nate calls at the top of his lungs, ready to run down the ladder.

But just then, a hideous skeletal hand suddenly thrusts itself up from the trapdoor and grasps the chief by the throat. The chief calls out, trying to tear the hand from his neck, but the thing is too strong. It drags him down into the darkness.

"Chief!" Nate screams.

"I told you it would be worse," Carolyn Prentiss says.

Nate is halfway down the ladder when he hears Kip's voice resume. *"Release him, John Fall! By your Maker be cast back into the outer darkness!"*

Nate swings his flashlight beam to see Fall, a monster of strength, holding Chief Hutchins off the floor by one hand at his throat.

"Begone, John Fall!" Kip shouts, thrusting his forked stick at the creature. "You have no power here any longer! Your followers have deserted you! They no longer believe in you!"

The thing growls, shaking the chief's body as if he were a rag doll.

"Your sins have caught up with you, John Fall!" Kip cries. "The spirits of Monica Paul, Rusty McDaniel, Claudio Sousa, Berniece Emerson, James Roche, and''—his voice cracks—

"Alexis Stokes. They all command you to stop! And Constance Ward! And your wife, Abigail!"

John Fall lets out a terrible scream. He drops the police chief, who hits the earthen floor with a horrible thud. Then the thing in the black hat disappears.

Nate hurries to Chief. He checks his pulse. He's alive, thank God.

"Is it done then?" he asks, looking over at Kip. "Is he gone?"

Kip moves into the beam of the flashlight. "I don't know. He was stronger than I expected."

"Where's Victoria?"

"Here," she says, moving into the light herself. "He knocked us out. It was like the air was just sucked out of us."

"Let's get out of here," Nate says.

Outside the church, those whom Fall has sinned against gather.

"This is the home of the Beast," Clem Flagg tells the rest. "This is where the evil lives."

They have watched their friends and loved ones die. They have seen their beloved community shattered. On the cliffs the homes still smolder in the still, clear night. How many more bodies will be found in the homes of Falls Church once the sun comes up?

"He burned our homes," Sargent Crawford says. "Now let us burn his."

Gasoline is thrown against the shingles of the old church. A blowtorch is ignited.

"Die, you creature from hell! Die!"

The crowd of thirty cheers as Clem sets the flame against the church. Marge Duarte claps her hands. Pat Crawford hugs her husband. Sam Drucker cries.

The fire catches, spreading quickly up the side of the church.

Nate and Kip lift the unconscious Chief by his armpits and manage to get him up the ladder. Job waits there for them, still holding the mob at gunpoint. They seem less threatening now. A couple of them are shivering. Carolyn Prentiss is crying.

"Is he gone?" Job asks them. "Was it successful?"

"I don't know," Nate tells him. "Let's hope so."

But his hope is a hollow thing. Even as he speaks it, Nate knows it's not true.

And it doesn't take long to discover he's right.

Behind Job there comes a shadow.

"Watch out!" Nate calls, but it's too late. With one blow, John Fall knocks Job to the ground, his gun flying across the room. Fall's followers gasp in their master's presence.

"You thought me weak!" Fall bellows, arms spread wide. "You thought I could be defeated!"

The dead man stands before them in all his decaying flesh. His bony hands come to rest on his hips. He leans back and laughs, a horrible sound that echoes through the room. Nate levels his gun at him, preparing to shoot, but suddenly the weapon becomes white hot in his hands. Nate yelps, dropping the gun to the floor, where it skids toward Fall. The corpse stops it with his foot.

"After all I have accomplished tonight," Fall says, leering at them with his hideous grin, "after all the death and destruction, you think me *weak*? You think I can so easily be defeated by your pathetic little spells?"

"Yes," Victoria says, advancing toward him. "Yes, I *do* think you weak. I am stronger than you, John Fall, and I will defeat you as I did before!"

His eyes burn with a desire for her. "Ohhhh," he purrs, "this night you shall be with me in hell, Victoria. You will at last be mine."

"No," she says, her voice calm and strong. "You may be going to hell, but you're going there alone. Look. Even now, your followers desert you."

Indeed, several of the group have withdrawn in horror at the sight of him and are cowering at the far end of the room.

Fall laughs. "You think they have deserted me? You are *wrong!* Let me prove my point."

From his black coat he withdraws a long knife. It catches a glint of moonlight, sparkling as he moves it through the air.

"Here, Edmond Tyler. Kill Carolyn Prentiss. Show these fools you have not abandoned me."

He holds out the knife. Tyler's eyes seem dazzled by it.

"No," Carolyn says in a tiny, terrified voice.

Tyler hesitates for a moment, then begins to walk toward Fall.

"Don't do it, man!" Nate shouts. "Fight him!"

But Tyler acts as if he cannot hear. He takes the knife from Fall's hand and turns back around, walking toward Carolyn.

"No!" Kip cries out.

"If we rush him," Nate says, "we can stop him."

"Fall will kill you," Victoria says.

"We can't just let him kill her!"

The rest of the group has parted, pulling back in fear of Tyler and his outstretched knife. Carolyn cowers in the corner, crying hysterically. Tyler raises his weapon.

"Now," Nate says.

But suddenly there's no need to act. A shot cuts across the room, catching Tyler in the shoulder and sending him sprawling back against the floor. All eyes turn to the stairway.

Dean Sousa stands there, gun in hand.

"Damn you!" Fall rages.

"No," Dean says, "damn *you*."

He turns and fires at the dead man. The bullet hits him, but it serves only to infuriate the Beast more.

"Damn you! Damn you! Damn you!"

"Listen to me, people," Nate shouts. "You can break free from him! He has killed your friends, your families, your neighbors! He has taken possession of your homes, your jobs, your children—your souls! But we can defeat him! Together we can defeat his hatred and his evil!"

Fall gnashes his teeth.

"Now!" Nate shouts.

And suddenly all of them—Nate and Victoria and Kip and Dean and all of Fall's former followers—rush at the creature, overpowering him, beating at the thing with their hands until there is nothing left to beat.

"Nooooooo!" Fall screams. "It mustn't end this way! Not again! Not again!"

His followers pulverize him with their hands.

Just as they had 305 years ago, in this very church, putting an end to his evil and to his control over their lives.

"No!" Fall rasps. "Not again! Noooooooooooooo!"

His voice fades away.

They look down.

John Fall is no more.

All that remains are black, stinking rags.

Just then, the floor above them bursts into flame.

"Come on," Nate shouts to Dean. "Help me get these people out of here. The wounded first!"

Saturday, December 7, 6:33 A.M.

In front of the burning church, the people of the town tend to their own.

"Hang on, Chief," Nate says. "They're clearing the roads. We're going to get you to the hospital as soon as we can."

The older man manages to grab his arm. "You're going to have to give Dean a promotion," he says, stretched out in the back of a police cruiser, covered with a blanket.

Nate gives him a smile. "You bet. Didn't he arrive just like the cavalry?"

Just beyond the cruiser, Dean stands with his arm around Carolyn. Nate looks over as the movie star gives his deputy a kiss. He approaches them.

"Everything okay?" Nate asks.

"From now on, it will be," Carolyn says.

"So long as you stick with Dean here," Nate tells her, smiling.

She looks over at him. "I intend to," she says.

Even in the glare of the blaze, Nate can see Dean blush.

Flames lick their way up the newly rebuilt steeple. Several in the crowd applaud. Firefighters stand idly around the scene, their hoses at the ready—but only to keep the flames from spreading. "Let the thing burn!" Chipper Robin had declared to the cheers of the crowd.

The sun is beginning to edge over the horizon. Long shadows

spread across the town, the colors of dawn reflecting against the snow. In the back of her van, Catherine Santos wraps a blanket around Job Emerson. "Your head feel any better?" she asks.

"Yes." He looks around. "Did you bring Jamal?"

"He's right here," Catherine tells him.

The boy climbs up into the van to embrace his father. "Mom is very happy right now," Jamal says. "She told me so. I see her when I close my eyes."

Job runs a hand over his son's hair. "Thank God you see Mom now, and nothing else."

Kip Hobart approaches Nate. "Is Chief doing okay?"

Nate sighs. "I think it's mostly shock. But we need to get him to Cape Cod Hospital as soon as we can. And Edmond Tyler, too. And Cliff Claussen, and quite a few others."

Kip shakes his head as he watches the church burn. "You know, Nate, once morning is here and Falls Church is opened back up to the rest of the world, there's going to be an awful lot of questions asked."

Nate nods. "But I'm not worried about that now. I'm just glad it's over."

The steeple finally collapses. The roof of the church falls in.

"Okay, boys!" Chipper Robin calls. "Now you can turn your hoses on!"

Six powerful jets of water suddenly attack the burning structure.

"Nate," Catherine says, suddenly coming up behind him and touching his arm. "It's the chief."

Nate hurries back over. The chief's face has turned a terrible shade of gray.

"Chief," Nate pleads, "hang on! We're going to get you help."

"Nate, Ellen's here," the chief rasps. "Can you see her?"

Nate's throat tightens. "No, Chief. Don't go with her. Please—"

"Don't *go* with her?" The chief's eyes are closed. "Oh, but she's calling for me. She's telling me she's proud of me, Nate, and that now I can join her. Now we can finally see the fjords of Norway . . ."

"But we need you *here*, Chief—"

"I leave everything in your good hands, Nate. You're a good man. The son I never had."

"Chief—"

The old man lifts his hand weakly. Maybe it's a reflection from the burning church, but Nate sees a spark of light touch the chief—*it looked like another hand—Ellen's hand*—and then Chief Philip Hutchins is gone.

Tears fall silently down Nate's face.

From the churchyard Victoria watches by herself as the flames are extinguished by the firefighters' hoses. The church smolders, sending thick black smoke into the morning air, smelling of old wood and dead flesh, and leaving a foul, acrid taste in her mouth.

It's the same smell, the same taste, as I watched my house burn.

Mom, Dad, Wendy, Petey—you're all avenged. You can rest in peace now.

She smiles.

And I was indeed stronger than what haunted me.

Stronger than the thing that has haunted this town for centuries, returning time and time again to wreak havoc and destruction—

Victoria makes a little sound.

There.

Over there. Something standing in the snow, behind an ancient brownstone grave marker.

No, it can't be.

The ghost.

The thing with the sheet draped over its head.

"Dear God," Victoria says, and suddenly she understands.

Saturday, December 7, 7:30 P.M.

"What do you *mean*," Nate asks, "we have to go *back into the church?*"

Victoria has waited until the smoke has cleared and the ruins have ceased their smoldering. The wounded have been taken to the hospital, the dead to the morgue, and already the media have swarmed into town, taking pictures of the carnage and badgering police and townsfolk for answers to their questions. It's quite the news story: town officials charged with murder, a night of arson and multiple deaths, Mark Miller's church destroyed by fire. Nate's been doing his best to deal with it all. Victoria understands the pressure he's suddenly found himself under as the acting chief of police, but what she has to tell him can't wait any longer.

"We have to go back in," she says again, "back to the basement of the original church, and we have to find John Fall's bones."

Nate quickly closes the door to his office. "Sweetheart, what are you talking about?"

"He's not gone, Nate. Oh, sure, maybe for now. But he'll be back. Just as he's returned every generation for the past three hundred years."

Nate runs his hands over his face. "Victoria, we have been through enough—"

"I'm asking you to *believe*, Nate."

He lets out a long sigh. "That's just it. I *do* believe you. Kip said something similar earlier today, wondering if what we did has ended Fall's power forever or just temporarily."

"Fall showed himself to me," Victoria tells him. "In the churchyard, as the ghost from my childhood."

Nate looks at her. "He was taunting you."

"Partly," she says. "But there's something else, Nate. I think on one level he was also pleading with me to put an end to all of this—for *his* sake."

Nate makes a confused face. "For *his* sake?"

"Do you remember what he said once? About the *unholiness* he was forced to endure? He was talking about his lack of burial, Nate. At Will McDaniel's funeral, Kip told me that Miller spoke of the importance of a proper Christian burial. You see, when the church burned three hundred five years ago, his body was left to rot, unburied among the ruins. That was unthinkable to a man like John Fall."

"He wanted that 'ashes-to-ashes, dust-to-dust' ceremony."

"Yes. Because—as we know—John Fall's bones never *did* undergo the whole dust-to-dust routine. They've remained there shamefully unburied, only to rise every generation."

Nate's at a loss. "But we can't, Victoria. We can't go back in there."

"We have to. Remember Sargent Crawford's message from Constance Ward? She wanted us to know he was in the basement of the church. We thought we knew what that message meant— but she was talking about John Fall, not Mark Miller. His *bones*. She was telling us we needed to deal with John Fall's bones if we ever wanted to end his power over this town."

"So what are you saying, Victoria?"

She looks at Nate firmly. "I believe the only way to end John Fall's power forever is to go back into the church and find his bones." She pauses. "And then we must bury them."

Already many of the specific memories of Fall's evil are receding from people's minds. They remember the horrors, of course—the arsons, Rusty's tragedy, the murders of Claudio Sousa and Mary Silva and Richie Rostocki and Laura Millay, among others—but all of the little intricacies leading up to them have become fuzzy in people's minds. They know Reverend Miller had something to do with it, and those who were his church members recall the tone of some blistering sermons, even if the actual words are rapidly fading away. Eventually even these things will be pushed far to the back corners of their minds, just as happened with memories of Tommy Keegan and Grace West. To survive, the people of Falls Church have already begun the process of forgetting the Devil. They have more pressing business to think about: rebuilding their town.

"I understand the surviving selectmen have asked Marcella Stein to come back and serve as acting town manager," Chipper Robin tells Nate and Victoria as he surveys the ruins of the church.

"It's a good choice," Nate agrees.

"And plans are already under way to have Martha Sturm come back as principal. The selectmen are offering a formal apology. It's only right, if you ask me."

They all nod in silent agreement.

A few firefighters still stand watch over the wreckage. It's been roped off from public access with bright yellow police tape. The husk of the blackened church stands against the violet night sky as a twisted hulk. The stench of the conflagration still hangs heavy in the air.

"Chipper," Nate says. "I need your cooperation. We need access into the church."

The fire chief looks at him as if he's crazy. "Nate, it's too dangerous still. Nothing's secure. The whole thing could come crashing down on top of you."

"Then could you guide us into the basement? We could enter through the side door. There's not as much damage there."

Chipper shakes his head. "No way, Nate. I'm telling you, it's too dangerous to do."

"And I'm telling you, it's too dangerous *not* to."

The two men look at each other. Chipper understands: Nate can see that much in his eyes. He's been ensnared twice by Fall's power. Whether he can remember all the precise details with absolute clarity—an ability even Nate is finding increasingly difficult—Chipper can understand the policeman's determination.

"All right," he says. "We've already put in place some

supports in the church hall; I can take you in, but I can't guarantee how far you'll be able to go."

"We know exactly where we need to go," Victoria tells him.

Chipper hesitates. "Look, if anything happens, we could just end up bringing more problems for the town. You know that, don't you? *Police and fire chief allow woman into fire scene.* I can just see the headlines."

"We have no choice," Victoria says.

Chipper understands. He doesn't like it, but he understands.

They bring shovels with them. They slip masks over their faces, enabling them to breathe through the smoke that still rises from the interior of the church. Between the floor of the church hall and the nave above, iron beams have been inserted for some measure of support.

Chipper steps aside so that Nate and Victoria can peer through the darkness with their flashlights.

"There it is," Victoria says, resting the light on the trapdoor that leads down to the original basement.

Chipper remains anxious. "Are you sure you're going to find whatever it is you're looking for?"

"Not really," Nate admits.

But Victoria *is* sure. In her vision she had seen *exactly* where Fall died. She's convinced Alexis showed her that scene out of the past for a reason.

So I could find his bones now. Just as she had found Petey's. Just as she'd finally given Petey a proper burial. She was *meant* to find Fall's bones, even if they had been undiscovered for decades.

This is it, she tells herself. *My whole life—my whole life lived in terror—has been leading up to this moment. This is my destiny. This is why I came back to Falls Church.*

To end the evil forever.

"I'll go down first," Nate tells her.

Thankfully, the fire never reached this part of the floor. The ladder leading down into the cold earthen darkness remains intact.

Nate takes the first step down.

From somewhere in the ruins comes a shrill scream. Chipper reacts, looking about.

"Pay no attention," Nate says as he disappears into the darkness below. "It's not a scream of the living."

The coldness overwhelms them. Victoria searches the ground with her flashlight. "Somewhere here," she says. "He will be somewhere here."

Chipper remains above at the trapdoor, offering his own flashlight to help their search. Nate follows behind Victoria, increasingly agitated.

"How can we be sure we'll find anything? We should wait until morning, when there's more light."

"I'm telling you, Nate. We have to do this *now*. It may be the only window of opportunity we have. Fall showed himself to me now for a reason." She looks at him. "I'm trusting my instincts, Nate."

He holds up his hands and gives her a small smile. "Okay, Victoria. I *believe*."

She smiles, too, through the glare of her flashlight. "That's good, Detective Tuck. That's what I want to hear."

"Please," Chipper calls from above. "Hurry."

"We're doing our best. I know it's got to be right over—"

Nate sees it first. "Victoria!" he shouts out in warning.

An arm suddenly breaks through the soil. It grabs Victoria around the ankle. She screams.

"He's still alive!" Chipper screams from above, a witness to the horrible event.

The thing sits up. The soil that has covered it for three centuries breaks away, falling off its bones like plaster. Victoria pulls free, rushing toward Nate, but keeping her trembling flashlight trained on the corpse's movements.

"It's not just bones," Victoria says, watching it come to life.

No, not just bones, as one would expect after all these years, but rather putrefying flesh. Victoria moves her flashlight to reveal the face.

"Dear God," she says, covering her mouth.

The face of John Fall grins at them. His eyes are open,

bulging and pulpy. His lips are rotted away, revealing sharp skeletal teeth.

And moving in and out of his teeth: *worms*.

It tries to stand but seems unable to move any more. It struggles a bit, its jaw opening and closing, but no words are uttered. Finally it stops all attempts to rise and just sits there, staring hideously at them.

"We've come to bury you, John Fall," Victoria says, her voice revealing only the tiniest tremor. "At last, you will be properly buried."

Whether the thing has any reason left in its body, any understanding, they do not know. It simply sits there, not moving. Victoria takes a step toward it.

"No," Nate cautions.

"Dig a hole, Nate," she tells him. "Dig a grave for John Fall."

Nate is about to protest again but thinks better of it. "Throw down the shovels," he calls to Chipper, who obeys without saying a word.

Victoria keeps her eyes trained on the body sitting up in the earth in front of her.

Nate tries to stab the earth with his shovel but meets resistance from the frozen ground. "We'll never be able to pick through this," he complains. "It's like solid stone."

Victoria responds without taking her gaze away from the thing. "I can tell you're not originally from the Cape," she says. "What you see is just a thin crust of soil. Underneath, everything on the Cape is *sand*."

Indeed, after some effort, Nate finally breaks the ground and does discover sand. Though tightly packed and heavier than the sand on the beach, it gives way under his shovel. Victoria picks up the second shovel and helps dig, but she always keeps her eyes on the waiting corpse.

They dig a hole about four feet deep. "All right," Victoria says. "Now to get him over here."

Nate recoils. "We have to touch that thing?"

"I don't think so," Victoria says.

It takes only a matter of seconds for her to be proven right. The thing that was John Fall stands on its own, the soil around

its legs breaking free. It stands to its full height of some six
feet, trembling. Then it begins to walk.

"Holy Jesus," Chipper Robin moans from above.

The corpse walks the few feet to its grave. It stands on the
edge, looking down.

"Your power over this place is ended, John Fall," Victoria
says. "Go back to our Maker and beg forgiveness for your
sins."

The corpse breaks apart. Its arms fall from its shoulders. Its
legs buckle; its torso crumbles. It dematerializes as it falls.
What was decaying flesh only moments ago has become dust.
It settles into a heap in the center of the grave.

Nate quickly begins to shovel sand and soil to cover it.

"Wait," Victoria tells him. "We need a *proper* burial. We
must say a prayer."

"A *prayer?* Over the body of this monster?"

She looks at him. "He was a man once. A man taught evil
in the name of religion. A man ruined by the hatred he learned
and the desire for power he came to crave. But a man, still."

Nate is silent.

Victoria makes the sign of the cross. *"Ashes to ashes,"* she
says, *"dust to dust . . ."*

Sunday, December 8, 11:33 A.M.

"I'm going to recommend they level this and then pave over the whole site with concrete," Nate says. "Maybe build a memorial to those who were lost. Starting with Constance Ward."

They've all come down to stare up at the still-smoking ruins of the old church. It's a brilliant day. The sun shines warm and high. Much of the snow has already melted away.

Catherine Santos smiles over at Danny Correia. Kip Hobart puts his arm around Agnes Doolittle, who cries a little, remembering Father Roche. Job holds Jamal's hand as they study the harbor.

They all head over to Clem's Diner for a Sunday breakfast of greasy bacon and eggs. Clem stands outside, dressed in a Santa suit and hat, greeting customers. In the face of tragedy the people of Falls Church have decided to reclaim their spirits. Across the street Isabella Sousa Cook and Hickey Hix string Christmas lights in front of Town Hall. They all share a hearty wave.

" 'Tis the season," Kip says, and they all laugh, heading inside the diner.

But Nate and Victoria fall back first. Nate takes her hand.

"So what's next for you?" he asks.

She sighs. "Well, I have a semester to plan. January will be here before you know it."

He looks down at her. "So you're leaving, then? Going back to Boston?"

"I'm a teacher, Nate. It's what I do."

He smiles. "Yeah. Teaching the rest of us how to *believe*."

She touches his face. "But Falls Church has become home again to me," she tells him. "Largely because of you."

His look turns serious. "I'm going to see to it that this place recovers," he promises. "This town helped me once. Now it's my turn to do the same for the town."

Victoria smiles. "Well, I wouldn't want to miss that."

"So you'll be back," Nate says. "I'll still be able to see you."

She kisses him. "You can be sure of that, Officer Tuck."

Overhead, a gull makes a soaring arc in the sky, over the town, over the beach, over the remains of the old church. The foghorn wails. The sea crashes against the sand—the steady, unending tide.

ABOUT THE AUTHOR

Robert Ross lives in Massachusetts and is currently working on his next novel. He loves to hear from readers; you may write to him c/o Pinnacle Books. Please include a self-addressed stamped envelope if you wish to receive a response. You may also e-mail him at RobertRossAuthor@aol.com.

A World of Eerie Suspense
Awaits in Novels by Noel Hynd

__Cemetery of Angels   0-7860-0261-1 $5.99US/$6.99CAN
Starting a new life in Southern California, Bill and Rebecca Moore
believe they've found a modern paradise. The bizarre old tale about
their house doesn't bother them, nor does their proximity to a graveyard
filled with Hollywood legends. Life is idyllic…until their beloved son
and daughter vanish without a trace.

__Rage of Spirits   0-7860-0470-3 $5.99US/$7.50CAN
A mind-bending terrorist has the power to change the course of world
history. With the President in a coma, it's fallen to hardboiled White
House press aide William Cochrane to unearth the old secrets that can
prevent catastrophe. After an encounter with a New England psychic
he finds himself descending deeper into the shadowy world between
this life and the next…

__A Room for the Dead   0-7860-0089-9 $5.99US/$6.99CAN
With only a few months to go before his retirement, Detective Sgt. Frank
O'Hara faces the most impossible challenge of his career: tracking
down a killer who can't possibly exist—not in this world, anyway. Could
it be the murderous psychopath he sent to the chair years before? But
how? A hair-raising journey into the darkest recesses of the soul.

Call toll free **1-888-345-BOOK** to order by phone or use this
coupon to order by mail.
Name _____
Address _____
City _____ State _____ Zip _____
Please send me the books I have checked above.
I am enclosing $_____
Plus postage and handling* $_____
Sales tax (in New York and Tennessee only) $_____
Total amount enclosed $_____
*Add $2.50 for the first book and $.50 for each additional book.
Send check or money order (no cash or CODs) to:
Kensington Publishing Corp., 850 Third Avenue, New York, NY 1002
Prices and Numbers subject to change without notice.
All orders subject to availability.
Check out our website at **www.kensingtonbooks.com**